D0198026

Praise for #1 *New*
Lin

"Miller's masterful ability to create living, breathing characters never flags....Miller's romance won't disappoint."
—*Publishers Weekly,* starred review, on *McKettrick's Pride*

"Miller's attention to small details makes her stories a delight to read."
—*RT Book Reviews* on *Creed's Honor*

"Miller's down-home, easy-to-read style keeps the plot moving, and she includes...likable characters, picturesque descriptions and some very sweet pets."
—*Publishers Weekly* on *Big Sky Country*

Praise for Carla Cassidy

"Cassidy crafts sympathetic characters...along with a strong, well-developed plot. A charmingly sweet and ruggedly strong hero is the icing on the cake for this romantic treat."
—*RT Book Reviews* on *Cowboy With a Cause*

"Cassidy writes sensitively about the difficult subject of rape in *Snowbound With the Bodyguard.* Janette is a strong heroine, and sexy Dalton stands out as a hero very much her equal."
—*RT Book Reviews*

LINDA LAEL MILLER

Raised in Northport, Washington, as the daughter of a town marshal, Linda Lael Miller is a #1 *New York Times* and *USA TODAY* bestselling author of more than one hundred historical and contemporary novels, most of which reflect her love of the West.

Linda has come a long way since leaving Washington to experience the world. "But growing up in that time and place has served me well," she allows. "And I'm happy to be back home." Dedicated to helping others, Linda personally finances her Linda Lael Miller Scholarships for Women, which she awards to those seeking to improve their lot in life through education. More information about Linda and her novels is available at www.lindalaelmiller.com. She also loves to hear from readers by mail at P.O. Box 19461, Spokane, WA 99219.

CARLA CASSIDY

is an award-winning author who has written more than one hundred books for Harlequin, and currently writes for the Harlequin Intrigue and Harlequin Romantic Suspense lines. In 1995 she won Best Silhouette Romance from *RT Book Reviews* for *Anything for Danny.* In 1998 she also won a Career Achievement Award for Best Innovative Series from *RT Book Reviews.*

Carla believes the only thing better than curling up with a good book to read is sitting down at the computer with a good story to write. She's looking forward to writing many more books and bringing hours of pleasure to readers.

#1 *New York Times* Bestselling Author

LINDA LAEL MILLER

Glory, Glory

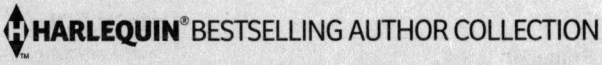

If you purchased this book without a cover you should be aware that this book is stolen property. It was reported as "unsold and destroyed" to the publisher, and neither the author nor the publisher has received any payment for this "stripped book."

Recycling programs for this product may not exist in your area.

ISBN-13: 978-0-373-18072-1

GLORY, GLORY
Copyright © 2013 by Harlequin Books S.A.

The publisher acknowledges the copyright holders of the individual works as follows:

GLORY, GLORY
Copyright © 1990 by Linda Lael Miller

SNOWBOUND WITH THE BODYGUARD
Copyright © 2008 by Carla Bracale

All rights reserved. Except for use in any review, the reproduction or utilization of this work in whole or in part in any form by any electronic, mechanical or other means, now known or hereafter invented, including xerography, photocopying and recording, or in any information storage or retrieval system, is forbidden without the written permission of the publisher, Harlequin Enterprises Limited, 225 Duncan Mill Road, Don Mills, Ontario M3B 3K9, Canada.

This is a work of fiction. Names, characters, places and incidents are either the product of the author's imagination or are used fictitiously, and any resemblance to actual persons, living or dead, business establishments, events or locales is entirely coincidental.

This edition published by arrangement with Harlequin Books S.A.

For questions and comments about the quality of this book, please contact us at CustomerService@Harlequin.com.

® and TM are trademarks of Harlequin Enterprises Limited or its corporate affiliates. Trademarks indicated with ® are registered in the United States Patent and Trademark Office, the Canadian Trade Marks Office and in other countries.

www.Harlequin.com

Printed in U.S.A.

CONTENTS

GLORY, GLORY 7
Linda Lael Miller

SNOWBOUND WITH THE BODYGUARD 203
Carla Cassidy

Dear Reader,

I'm so happy to bring you the story of Glory Parsons!

We've all experienced lost love—and the heartbreak that follows. For Glory, losing Jesse Bainbridge, and the child she never told him about, was devastating. Now she's home for the holidays and dreading every minute of it. She's not sure she can face her family, Jesse or the mistakes of her past.

For Jesse, having Glory back in town is beyond confusing. She's the woman he pledged to love for the rest of his days, but also the one who left him without warning. Being the guardian of his young niece means he can't take those same risks again, but he's not so sure he can resist the woman he's never been able to forget.

Can Glory and Jesse ever believe in trust…and love again?

I truly hope you enjoy this story! Meanwhile, stop on by www.lindalaelmiller.com for my (almost) daily blog, excerpts from my books, and fun contests, along with a few surprises now and then.

With love,

Linda Lael Miller

GLORY, GLORY

#1 *New York Times* Bestselling Author

Linda Lael Miller

For Betty Wojcik, a friend indeed.

Thanks for everything.

Chapter 1

Glory Parsons's gloved hands tightened on the steering wheel when the familiar green-and-white sign came into view. Pearl River, Oregon. Population: 6710.

All it would take was one U-turn, and she could be headed back toward Portland. She'd find another job, and she still had her apartment. Maybe she and Alan could work things out....

She swallowed hard. She would be in Pearl River three weeks at the outside, then she could join her friend Sally in San Francisco, get a new job and start her life all over again. As for Alan, she hoped his teeth would fall out.

The feed store was festooned in lights and sparkling green garlands for Christmas, like the five-and-dime and the bookstore and the newspaper office. The street was thick with muddy slush, but fat puffs of new snow were falling.

Glory passed the diner and smiled to see the cheap

plastic Santa and reindeer perched on the tar-paper roof. She touched her horn once, in a preliminary greeting to her mother, and drove on.

The cemetery was on the other side of town, overlooking the river. Glory parked outside the gates, behind a green police car, and made her way up the curving driveway. She left her purse in the car, carrying a bouquet of holly she'd picked along the roadside earlier in the day.

A crisp breeze riffled the drifting snowflakes and Glory's chin-length silver-gold hair. She pulled up the collar of her long woolen coat, royal blue to match her eyes, and made her way carefully along a slippery walk.

Dylan's grave lay beneath a white blanket of snow, and Glory's throat thickened when she came to stand beside it. "Hi, handsome," she said hoarsely, stooping to put the holly into the metal vase at the base of his headstone. Her eyes filled with tears, and she wedged both hands deep into her coat pockets and sniffled. "You had your nerve, dying at twenty-two. Don't you know a girl needs her big brother?"

She dusted snow from the face of the stone, uncovering Dylan's name and the dates of his birth and death. He'd perished in an explosion soon after joining the air force, and Glory didn't want anyone to forget he'd lived, even for the space of an afternoon snowfall.

She drew a deep breath and dried her eyes with the back of one hand. "I swore I'd never come back here," she went on miserably, "even to see you. But Mama's getting married, so I had to come to her wedding." She took a tissue from her pocket and dabbed at her nose. "I got myself hooked up with a real jerk back in Portland, Dylan. If you'd been around, you probably would have punched him in the mouth. He pretended to love me, and then he stole my promotion right out from under me."

She paused to look up at the cloudy sky. The bare limbs of maple and elm trees seemed to splinter it.

"I quit my job and had my furniture put in storage," Glory confided to her brother, gazing at the marble headstone again. "And after Christmas and Mama's wedding, I'm going to San Francisco to make a life for myself. I don't know when I'll be back to see you again."

A swishing sound in the slush alerted Glory to someone's approach. She looked up, and her blue eyes went wide.

"Jesse."

He was standing on the other side of Dylan's grave, dressed in the standard green-and-brown uniform of the sheriff's department. He wore no hat, and his badge, pinned to his jacket, gleamed in the thin winter light. Like Glory, he was twenty-eight years old.

His caramel eyes moved over her frame then swept back to her face. "What are you doing here?" he asked, as though he'd caught her in a bank vault after-hours.

Glory had known she couldn't come back to Pearl River without encountering Jesse—she just hadn't expected it to happen this soon. Her temper flared, along with an old ache in a corner of her heart she'd long since closed off, and she gestured toward Dylan's headstone. "What do you think I'm doing here?" she retorted. "I came to see my brother."

Jesse hooked his thumbs through the loops on his trousers, and his brazen brown eyes narrowed slightly. "It's been eight years since the funeral. You were really anxious to get back."

Eight years since the funeral, eight years since Glory had laid eyes on Jesse Bainbridge.

Pride forced Glory to retaliate. She took in his uniform and then said, "I see you've been promoted to sheriff. Did your grandfather buy the election?"

His jawline tightened for a moment, but then he grinned in that wicked way that had broken so many hearts in high school. "Why not? He bought you, didn't he?" Like everyone else in Pearl River, Jesse probably believed old Seth Bainbridge had paid her to leave town; Glory was fairly certain he'd never learned about the baby.

Without waiting for a reply, Jesse settled his hat on his head and walked away.

Glory barely resisted the urge to scoop up a handful of snow and hurl it at his back. Only the awareness of where she was kept her from doing just that.

When Jesse was out of earshot, Glory put her hands on her hips and told Dylan, "He really burns me up. I don't know why you liked him so much."

You liked him, too, she heard Dylan's voice say, way down deep in her heart. *You had his baby, Glory.*

"Don't remind me!" Glory snapped, folding her arms. "I was barely eighteen, and my hormones were out of control!"

She thought she heard Dylan's laughter in the chilly winter breeze, and in spite of the unpleasant encounter with Jesse Bainbridge a few minutes before, she smiled.

"I love you, Dylan," she said, touching the headstone again. Then, with her hands in her pockets, she turned and made her way down the walk to the driveway and the towering wrought-iron gates.

It was time to face Pearl River, something she hadn't done since Dylan's funeral, and she was reluctant for more than one reason.

Glory's sports car, the one great extravagance in her life,

started with a comforting roar, and she drove slowly back into town, telling herself to take things one moment at a time. Before she knew it, Christmas and the New Year's wedding would be over, and she could get on with her life.

She parked in front of Delphine's Diner just before an orange snowplow came past, flinging a picturesque fan of slush at the sidewalk. Glancing up at the life-size plastic Santa and reindeer, Glory remembered Dylan sliding around on the roof to put them in place for Christmases past, deliberately clowning because he knew his mother and sister were afraid he'd fall.

The little bell over the door jingled when Glory went inside. Her mother, as slender and active as ever, lit up brighter than the Santa over their heads when she saw her daughter.

"Glory," she whispered with a choked sob of pleasure. And then she was hurrying across the brown-and-white linoleum floor, with its swirls of fresh wax, to embrace her.

The hug brought a lump to Glory's throat and quick tears to her eyes. "Hello, Mama."

"It's about time you got here," boomed a male voice from one of the stools at the counter. Harold Seemer, the good-natured plumbing contractor who had finally persuaded Delphine to marry him after a five-year courtship, beamed at his future stepdaughter. "We were about to send the sheriff's patrol out after you."

Glory tried not to react visibly to the indirect mention of Jesse. She didn't want thoughts of him interfering with her visit. "Hi, Harold," she said, giving the well-fed balding man a hug. He and Delphine had visited her in Portland on several occasions, and she'd become very fond of him.

"You look skinny," Delphine commented, narrowing her green eyes as Glory took off her coat and hung it on one of the chrome hooks beside the door.

Glory laughed. "Thanks, Mama. I've been dieting for two months to make up for all the food you're going to force me to eat."

Harold finished his coffee and replaced the beige china cup in its saucer, with a clink. "Well, I've got to get back to work. I'll leave you two to catch up on everything."

When he was gone, Glory took a stool at the counter, sighed, and pushed back her hair. "No customers," she commented, looking around at the six Formica-topped tables. The chrome legs of the chairs glistened, and so did the red vinyl seats.

Delphine shrugged and, stepping behind the counter, poured a cup of coffee to set in front of her daughter. "The lunch crowd's been and gone. Things'll be quiet until dinnertime."

Glory reached for her cup and saucer and pulled them toward her, feeling the steam caress her face and taking comfort in the familiar aroma, but she didn't drink. "I saw Jesse," she said, and her voice was shaky.

"Did you, now?" Delphine's voice was light as the feathery snow falling past the window with its neon We Serve Pepsi-Cola sign. "How did that happen?"

"I stopped by the cemetery to leave some holly for Dylan, and he was there." Glory raised her eyes, watched her mother's face pale slightly at the mention of her lost son. But Delphine recovered her composure rapidly, like always. She was nothing if not a survivor.

"Jesse's brother, Gresham, is buried there, along with his sister-in-law, Sandy, and his folks. Must be some special day to him, or something."

Glory recalled the plane crash that had taken the lives of Gresham Bainbridge, promising young state senator, and his pretty wife, Sandy. The tragedy had been big news in Oregon. "They left a child behind, didn't they?" Glory asked, because thinking about the Bainbridges' misfortune was better than remembering her own and Delphine's.

Delphine busied herself rinsing out a glass pot and starting a new batch of decaffeinated coffee brewing. "A little girl," she said quietly. After a few more moments, she turned to face her daughter, leaning against the spotless counter, her shrewd eyes inviting—even demanding—confidences. "Tell me about this Alan man. What did he do that made you uproot yourself like that?"

Glory ran her tongue over her lips and fiddled with a paper napkin. She still hadn't touched her coffee. "He was a rat, Mama," she answered after a long time. "He cozied up to all my clients while I was away taking a training course in Chicago, and when I came home, the board had given him the promotion they promised me."

"So you just threw your resignation in their faces, cleared out your desk and left?" Delphine put the question in a nonchallenging way, but it still made Glory's cheeks flame.

And she definitely felt defensive. "What should I have done, Mama? Stayed and brought Alan pencils and files in my teeth? I worked night and day for *four years* to earn that job!"

Delphine shrugged, leaning on the counter again. "I think maybe you just wanted out of the relationship and that was the best excuse that occurred to you. In fact, I wouldn't be surprised to learn that you've never gotten over Jesse Bainbridge."

Glory's hands shook as she picked up the coffee and took an angry gulp. It burned her tongue and the roof of her mouth. "Well, I have!" she sputtered moments later. It still hurt that Jesse hadn't come for her at the unwed-mothers' home in Portland and brought her home to have their baby, even though she knew the scenario was woven of pure fantasy. Jesse couldn't have come for her because he hadn't known she was pregnant. "It was nothing but a childish high-school infatuation in the first place."

Delphine's eyes took on a sad look. "It was more than that," she insisted softly, resting one well-manicured hand on Glory's arm.

Glory pulled away, went to the jukebox and busied herself studying the titles of the songs imprisoned inside. They were all old tunes she couldn't bear to hear when her feelings were so raw.

She turned to the window instead.

Mr. Kribner came out of the drugstore across the street and hung an evergreen wreath on his front door.

"Merry Christmas," Glory muttered, wishing she'd never left Portland. She could have made some excuse for the holidays, then dashed into town for the wedding and out again after the reception.

Her mother's hands gripped her elbows firmly. "You're tired, sweetheart, and I'll bet you didn't have any lunch. Let me fix you something, and then you can go upstairs and rest a while."

Glory nodded, even though she had no appetite and hadn't really rested for days. She didn't want Delphine to worry about her, especially during this happy time, with the wedding and the holidays coming up.

"Harvey Baker was just in the other day," Delphine called sunnily from the kitchen, as Glory stood hugging herself and watching the snow swirl lazily past the diner windows. When it got dark, the Pepsi sign would make a pink glow on the white ground. "He's looking for an assistant over at the bank, you know. Allie Cordman left to take a job in Seattle."

"Smart girl," Glory murmured. Pearl River was a nowhere town, with nothing to offer. Anybody who deliberately made his home here ought to have his head examined.

Delphine hummed in the kitchen, happy with her world, and for one difficult moment Glory envied her profoundly. She wondered what it was like to be in love with a man she could trust and depend on, and to be loved by him in return.

Presently, Glory's favorite lunch—a clubhouse sandwich with potato salad—appeared on the counter, along with a tall diet cola with extra ice.

Glory would have sworn she wasn't hungry, but her stomach grumbled as she got back onto the stool and pulled a fresh napkin from the holder. "Thanks, Mama," she said.

Delphine was busy wiping the already immaculate counter. "There's an old-movie festival at the Rialto tonight," she told Glory cheerfully. "Jimmy Stewart in *It's a Wonderful Life* and Cary Grant in *The Bishop's Wife*."

A poignant sensation of nostalgia came over Glory. "Jimmy Stewart and Cary Grant." She sighed. "They don't make men like that anymore."

Delphine's green eyes twinkled, and she flashed her diamond engagement ring. "Don't be too sure," she said coyly, and Glory laughed.

"Mama, you're hopeless!" But she couldn't help thinking, as she ate her sandwich and tangy potato salad, that it would be nice to have a handsome angel turn up in her life, the way Cary Grant had appeared in Loretta Young's.

Two teenage boys came in, raising a great ruckus lest they go unnoticed, and plunked quarters into the jukebox. A lively old Christmas rock tune filled the diner, and they piled into chairs at one of the tables.

Suddenly wanting to relive her after-school waitress days in that very diner, Glory abandoned her sandwich and reached for a pencil and an order pad.

"What'll it be, guys?" she asked.

The young men ran appreciative eyes over her trim blue jeans and gray cashmere sweater.

"Will you marry me?" asked the one with braces.

Glory laughed. "Sure. Just bring a note from your mother."

The other boy hooted at that, and the first one blushed. The name on the sleeve of his letterman's jacket was Tony.

"I want a cheeseburger, a vanilla shake and an order of curly fries," he said, but the look in his eyes told Glory he had bigger things in mind than food.

Glory was writing the order down when the bell over the door jingled. She looked up to see Jesse dusting snow off his shoulders onto Delphine's clean floor.

His gaze skirting Glory as though she'd suddenly turned invisible, he greeted the boys by name and took a place at the counter. "Hi, Delphine," he said, as the woman poured his coffee. "How's my best girl?"

Glory concentrated fiercely on the second boy's order, and when she'd gotten it, she marched into the kitchen and started cooking. She had to keep herself busy—and distracted—until Jesse finished his coffee and left the diner.

"What's he doing here?" she whispered to her mother, when Delphine joined her to lift the basket out of the deep fryer and shake the golden fries free of grease.

Delphine smiled. "He's drinking coffee."

Glory glowered at her. "I'm going upstairs!" she hissed.

"That'll fix him," Delphine said.

In a huff, Glory took the cheeseburgers off the grill and the shakes off the milk-shake machine. She made two trips to the boys' table and set everything down with a distinctive *clunk.* All the while, she studiously ignored Jesse Bainbridge.

He'd just come in to harass her, she was sure of that. He probably bullied everybody in Pearl River, just like his grandfather always had.

The jukebox took a break, then launched into a plaintive love song. Glory's face was hot as she went back to the kitchen, hoping Jesse didn't remember how that tune had been playing on the radio the first time they'd made love, up at the lake.

She couldn't help glancing back over one shoulder to see his face, and she instantly regretted the indulgence. Jesse's bold brown eyes glowed with the memory, and his lips quirked as he struggled to hold back a smile.

Glory flushed to recall how she'd carried on that long-ago night, the pleasure catching her by surprise and sending her spiraling out of her small world.

"That does it," she muttered. And she stormed out to her car, collected her suitcase and overnighter, and marched up the outside stairs to her mother's apartment.

The moment she stepped through the door, Glory was awash in memories.

The living room was small and plain, the furniture cheap, the floor covered in black-and-beige linoleum tiles. A portable TV sat on top of the old-fashioned console stereo.

Glory put down her luggage, hearing the echoes of that day long, long before, when Delphine had taken a job managing the diner downstairs. Dylan had been fourteen then, Glory twelve, and they'd all been jubilant at the idea of a home of their own. They'd lived out of Delphine's old rattletrap of a car all summer, over at the state park next to the river, but the fall days were getting crisp and the nights were downright cold.

Besides, Delphine's money had long since run out, and they'd been eating all their meals in the church basement, with the old people and the families thrown out of work because of layoffs at the sawmill.

Dylan and Glory had slept in bunk beds provided by the Salvation Army, while Delphine had made her bed on the couch.

Pushing the door shut behind her, Glory wrenched herself back to the present. It was still too painful to think about Dylan twice in one day, even after all the time that had passed.

Glory put her baggage in the tiny bedroom that was Delphine's now, thinking that she really should have rented a motel room. When she'd suggested it on the telephone, though, her mother had been adamant: Glory would stay at the apartment, and it would be like old times.

She paced, too restless to unpack or take a nap, but too tired to do anything really demanding. After peeking out the front window, past the dime-store wreath with the plastic candle in it, to make sure Jesse's car was gone, she went back downstairs for her coat.

The cook who took Delphine's place at two-thirty

had arrived, along with a teenage waitress and a crowd of noisy kids from the high school.

Delphine handed Glory her coat, then shrugged into her own. "Come on," she said, pushing her feet into transparent plastic boots. "I'll show you the house Harold and I are going to live in."

The snow fell faster as the two women walked along the familiar sidewalk. Now and then, Delphine paused to wave at a store clerk or a passing motorist.

They rounded a corner and entered an attractive development. The houses had turrets and gable windows, though they were modern, and the yards were nicely landscaped.

Glory remembered playing in this part of town as a child. There had been no development then, just cracked sidewalks that meandered off into the deep grass. The place had fascinated her, and she'd imagined ghost houses lining the walks, until Dylan had spoiled everything by telling her there had been Quonset huts there during World War II to accommodate workers at the town smelter.

Delphine stopped to gaze fondly at a charming little mock colonial with a snow-dusted rhododendron bush growing in the yard. The house itself was white, the shutters dark blue. There were flower boxes under all the windows.

Glory's eyes widened with pleasure. This was the kind of house her mother had always dreamed of having. "This is it?" she asked, quite unnecessarily.

Proudly Delphine nodded. "Harold and I signed the papers on Friday. It's all ours."

Impulsively, Glory hugged her mother. "You've come

a long way, baby!" she said, her eyes brimming with happy tears.

Both of them stood still in the falling snow, remembering other days, when even in their wildest dreams neither of them would have dared to fantasize about owning a house such as this one.

"Are you going to keep the diner?" Glory asked, linking her arm with Delphine's as they walked back toward the center of town.

Delphine's answer came as no surprise. After all, she'd worked and scrimped and sacrificed to buy the place from her former employers. "Of course I am. I wouldn't know what to do if I couldn't go down there and make coffee for my customers."

With a chuckle, Glory wrapped her arm around her mother's straight little shoulders. "I imagine they'd all gather in your kitchen at home, they're so used to telling you their troubles over a steaming cup."

Back at the apartment, Delphine immediately excused herself, saying she had to "gussy up" for the Stewart-Grant festival at the Rialto.

"Sure you don't want to come along?" she queried, peering around the bathroom door, her red hair falling around her face in curls. "Harold and I would be glad to have you."

Glory shook her head, pausing in her unpacking. "I feel as though parts of me have been scattered in every direction, Mama. I need time to gather myself back together. I'll get something light for supper, then read or watch TV."

Delphine raised titian eyebrows. "You're getting boring in your old age, kid," she said. "Just see that you don't eat over at Maggie's. Last week one of the telephone linemen told me he got a piece of cream pie there that had dust on top of it."

"I wouldn't think of patronizing your archrival, Mama," Glory replied, grinning. "Even though I do think serving pie with dust on it requires a certain admirable panache."

Delphine dismissed her daughter with a wave and disappeared behind the bathroom door.

As it happened, Glory bought spaghetti salad in the deli at the supermarket and ate it while watching the evening news on the little portable TV. Downstairs in the diner, the dinner hour was in full swing, and the floor vibrated with the blare of the jukebox.

Glory smiled and settled back on the couch that would be her bed for the next several weeks, content.

She was home.

After the news was over, however, the reruns of defunct sitcoms started. Glory flipped off the TV and got out her mother's photo albums. As always, they were tucked carefully away in the record compartment of the console stereo, along with recordings by Roy Orbison, Buddy Holly, Ricky Nelson and Elvis Presley.

Delphine probably hadn't looked at the family pictures in years, but Glory loved to pore over them.

Still, she had to brace herself to open the first album—she was sitting cross-legged on the couch, the huge, cheaply bound book in her lap—because she knew there would be pictures of Dylan.

He smiled back at her from beside a tall man wearing a slouch hat. Glory knew the man's name had been Tom, and that he'd been mean when he drank. He'd also been her father, but she didn't remember him.

The little boy leaning against his leg, with tousled

brown hair and gaps in his grin, was another matter. Gently, with just the tip of one finger, Glory touched her brother's young face.

"When am I going to get over missing you, Bozo?" she asked, in a choked voice, using the nickname that had never failed to bug him.

Glory stared at Dylan for a few more moments, then turned the page. There she made her first photographic appearance—she was two months old, being bathed in a roasting pan on a cheap tabletop, and her grin was downright drunken.

She smiled and sighed. "The body of a future cheerleader. Remarkable."

Her journey through the past continued until she'd viewed all the Christmases and Halloweens, all the birthdays and first days of school. In a way, it eased the Dylan-shaped ache in her heart.

When she came to the prom pictures of herself and Jesse, taken in this very living room, she smiled again.

Jesse was handsome in his well-fitting suit, while she stood proudly beside him in the froth of pink chiffon Delphine had sewn for her. The dress had a white sash belt, and she could still feel the gossamer touch of it against her body. Perched prominently above her right breast was Jesse's corsage, an orchid in the palest rose.

She touched the flat, trim stomach of the beaming blond girl in the picture. Inside, although Glory hadn't known it yet, Jesse's baby was already growing.

Glory closed the album gently and set it aside before she could start wondering who had adopted that beautiful little baby girl, and whether or not she was happy.

The next collection of pictures was older. It showed Delphine growing up in Albuquerque, New Mexico, and there were photographs of a collage of aunts, uncles and cousins, too.

Glory reflected as she turned the pages that it must have been hard for Delphine after she left another abusive husband. Her family had understood the first time, but they couldn't forgive a second mistake. And after Delphine fled to Oregon with her two children, she was virtually disowned.

Saddened, Glory turned a page. The proud, aristocratic young face of her Irish great-grandmother gazed out of the portrait, chin at an obstinate angle. Of all the photographs Delphine had kept, this image of Bridget McVerdy was her favorite.

More than a hundred years ago, Bridget had come to America to look for work and a husband. She'd been employed as a lowly housemaid, but she'd had enough pride in her identity to pose for this picture and pay for it out of nominal wages, and eventually she'd married and had children.

The adversities Bridget overcame over the years were legion, but Delphine was fond of saying that her grandmother hadn't stopped living until the day she died, unlike a lot of people.

Glory gazed at the hair, which was probably red, and the eyes, rumored to be green, and the proud way Bridget McVerdy, immigrant housemaid, held her head. And it was as though their two souls reached across the years to touch.

Glory felt stronger in that moment, and her problems weren't so insurmountable. For the first time in weeks, giving up didn't seem to be the only choice she had.

Chapter 2

The next morning, after a breakfast of grapefruit, toast and coffee, Glory drove along the snow-packed streets of Pearl River, remembering. She went to the old covered bridge, which looked as though it might tumble into the river at any moment, and found the place where Jesse had carved their initials in the weathered wood.

A wistful smile curved Glory's lips as she used one finger to trace the outline of the heart Jesse had shaped around the letters. Underneath, he'd added the word *Forever.*

"Forever's a long time, Jesse," she said out loud, her breath making a white plume in the frosty air. The sun was shining brightly that day, though the temperature wasn't high enough to melt the snow and ice, and the weatherman was predicting that another storm would hit before midnight.

A sheriff's-department patrol car pulled up just as Glory was about to slip behind the wheel of her own vehicle and go back to town. She was relieved to see that the driver wasn't Jesse.

The deputy bent over to roll down the window on the passenger side, and Glory thought she remembered him as one of the boys who used to orchestrate food fights in the cafeteria at Pearl River High. "Glory?" His pleasant if distinctly ordinary face beamed. "I heard you were back in town. That's great about your mom getting married and everything."

Glory nodded. She couldn't quite make out the letters on his identification pin. She rubbed her mittened hands together and stomped her feet against the biting cold. "Thanks."

"You weren't planning to drive across the bridge or anything, were you?" the deputy asked. "It's been condemned for a long time. Somebody keeps taking down the sign."

"I just came to look," Glory answered, hoping he wouldn't put two and two together. This had always been the place where young lovers etched their initials for posterity, and she and Jesse had been quite an item back in high school.

The lawman climbed out of his car and began searching around in the deep snow for the "condemned" sign. Glory got into her sports car, started the engine, tooted the horn in a companionable farewell and drove away.

She stopped in at the library after that, and then the five-and-dime, where she and Dylan used to buy Christmas and birthday presents for Delphine. She smiled to recall how graciously their mother had accepted bottles of cheap cologne and gauzy handkerchiefs with stylized *D*'s embroidered on them.

At lunchtime, she returned to the apartment, where she ate a simple green salad and half a tuna sandwich. The phone rang while she was watching a game show.

Eager to talk to anyone besides Alan or Jesse, Glory snatched up the receiver. "Hello?"

The answering voice, much to her relief, was female. "Glory? Hi, it's Jill Wilson—your former confidante and cheerleading buddy."

Jill hadn't actually been Glory's best friend—that place had belonged to Jesse—but the two had been close in school, and Glory was delighted at the prospect of a reunion. "Jill! It's wonderful to hear your voice. How are you?"

In the years since Dylan's funeral, Glory and Jill had exchanged Christmas cards and occasional phone calls, and once they'd gotten together in Portland for lunch. Time and distance seemed to drop away as they talked. "I'm fine—still teaching at Pearl River Elementary. Listen, is there any chance we could get together at my place for dinner tonight? I've got a rehearsal at the church at six, and I was hoping you could meet me there afterward. Say seven?"

"Sounds great," Glory agreed, looking forward to the evening. "What shall I bring?"

"Just yourself," Jill answered promptly. "I'll see you at First Lutheran tonight, then?"

"Definitely," Glory promised.

She took a nap that afternoon, since she and Jill would probably be up late talking, then indulged in a long, leisurely bubble bath. She was wearing tailored wool slacks in winter white, along with a matching sweater, when Delphine looked her up and down from the bedroom doorway and whistled in exclamation.

"So Jesse finally broke down and asked for a date, huh?"

Glory, who had been putting the finishing touches on her makeup in front of the mirror over Delphine's dresser, grimaced. "No. And even if he did, I'd refuse."

Delphine, clad in jeans and a flannel shirt for a visit to a Christmas-tree farm with Harold, folded her arms and assembled her features into an indulgent expression. "Save it," she said. "When Jesse came into the diner yesterday, there was so much electricity I thought the wiring was going to short out."

Glory fiddled with a gold earring and frowned. "Really? I didn't notice," she said, but she was hearing that song playing on the jukebox, and remembering the way her skin had heated as she relived every touch of Jesse's hands and lips.

"Of course you didn't," agreed Delphine, sounding sly. She'd raised one eyebrow now.

"Mother." Glory sighed. "I know you've been watching Christmas movies from the forties and you're in the mood for a good old-fashioned miracle, but it isn't going to happen with Jesse and me. The most we can hope for, from him, is that he won't have me arrested on some trumped-up charge and run out of town."

Delphine shook her head. "Pitiful," she said.

Glory grinned at her. "This from the woman who kept a man dangling for five years before she agreed to a wedding."

Delphine sighed and studied her flawlessly manicured fingernails. "With my romantic history," she said, "I can't be too careful."

The two women exchanged a brief hug. "You've found the right guy this time, Mama," Glory said softly. "It's your turn to be happy."

"When does *your* turn come, honey?" Delphine asked, her brow puckered with a frown. "How long is it going to be before I look into your eyes and see something besides grief for your brother and that baby you had to give up?"

Glory's throat felt tight, and she turned her head. "I don't know, Mama," she answered, thinking of the word Jesse had carved in the wall of the covered bridge. *Forever.* "I just don't know."

Five minutes later, Glory left the apartment, her hands stuffed into the pockets of her long cloth coat. Since the First Lutheran Church was only four blocks away, she decided to walk the distance.

Even taking the long way, through the park, and lingering a while next to the big gazebo where the fire fighter's band gave concerts on summer nights, Glory was early. She stood on the sidewalk outside the church as a light snow began to waft toward earth, the sound of children's voices greeting her as warmly as the golden light in the windows.

Silent night, holy night
All is calm, all is bright…

Glory drew a breath cold enough to make her lungs ache and climbed the church steps. Inside, the music was louder, sweeter.

Holy Infant, so tender and mild…

Without taking off her coat, Glory slipped into the sanctuary and settled into a rear pew. On the stage,

Mary and Joseph knelt, incognito in their modern clothes, surrounded by undercover shepherds, wise men and angels.

Jill, wearing a pretty plaid skirt in blues and grays, along with a blouse and sweater in complementary shades, stood in front of the cast, her long brown hair wound into a single, glistening braid.

"That was fabulous!" she exclaimed, clapping her hands together. "But let's try it once more. Angels, you need to sing a little louder this time."

Glory smiled, brushing snow off her coat as Jill hurried to the piano and struck up an encore of "Silent Night."

The children, ranging in age from five or so to around twelve, fascinated Glory. Sometimes she regretted studying finance instead of education; as a teacher, she might have been able to make up, at least in a small way, for one of the two major losses in her life—she would have gotten to spend time around little ones. As it was, she didn't even *know* any kids—they just didn't apply for fixed-rate mortgages or car loans.

Joseph and Mary looked enough alike to be brother and sister, with their copper-bright hair and enormous brown eyes. Two of the wise men were sporting braces, and the third had a cast on his right arm.

Glory was trying to decide who was an angel and who was a shepherd when her gaze came to rest on a particular little girl. Suddenly she scooted forward in her seat and gripped the back of the next pew in both hands.

Looking back at her from beneath flyaway auburn bangs was the pretty, pragmatic face of Bridget McVerdy, Glory's great-grandmother.

For a moment the pews seemed to undulate wildly, like images in a fun-house mirror, and Glory rested her forehead against her hands. Almost a minute passed before she could be certain she wasn't going to faint.

"Glory?" A hand came to rest with gentle firmness on her shoulder. "Glory, are you all right?"

She looked up and saw Jill standing over her, green eyes filled with concern. Her gaze darted back to the child, and the interior of the church started to sway again. Unless Dylan had fathered a baby without ever knowing, or telling his mother and sister...

"Glory," Jill repeated, sounding really worried now.

"I—I'm fine," Glory stammered. She tried to smile, but her face trembled with the effort. "I just need some water—"

"You sit right there," Jill said in a tone of authority. "I'll get you a drink."

By the time she returned with a paper cup filled with cold water, Glory had managed to get back in sync with the earth's orbit, and the feeling of queasy shock in her stomach had subsided.

Talk about your forties movies and Christmas miracles, she thought, her eyes following the child that had to be her own.

Jill excused herself and looked at her watch as she walked up the aisle. Parents were starting to arrive, peering through the sanctuary doors and congregating in the back pews.

"All right, showstoppers," Jill said, "it's a wrap, for tonight, at least. Angels, practice your songs. You were a little rusty on 'It came Upon a Midnight Clear.'"

Glory wondered if she'd be able to stand without her knees buckling. She fumbled through her purse for aspirin and took two tablets with what remained of her water.

Just then, the little girl on the stage broke away from the other angels and shepherds and came running down the aisle, grinning.

Glory's eyes widened as her daughter drew nearer and nearer, turned slightly in her seat to see her fling her arms around a man clad in blue jeans, boots and a sheepskin coat.

Jesse.

"Hi'ya, munchkin," he said, bending to kiss the child where her rich, red-brown hair was parted.

Glory's mouth dropped open. He knew, she thought frantically. Then she shook her head.

He *couldn't* know; fate couldn't be that cruel. His grandfather wouldn't have told him, Dylan hadn't known the truth, though he might have guessed, and Delphine had been sworn to secrecy.

At that moment Jesse's maple-colored eyes found Glory's face. They immediately narrowed.

Glory felt no more welcome in the First Lutheran Church than she had in the cemetery the day before. She sat up a little straighter, despite the fact that she was in a state of shock, and maintained her dignity. Jesse might be sheriff, but that didn't give him the right to intimidate people.

He opened his mouth, then closed it again. After raising the collar of his macho coat, he turned his attention back to the child, ignoring Glory completely.

"Come on, Liza," he said, his voice sounding husky and faraway to Glory even though she could have reached out and touched both of them. "Let's go."

Liza. Glory savored the name. Unable to speak,

she watched Jesse and the child go out with the others. When she turned around again, Jill was kneeling backward in the pew in front of Glory's, looking down into her face.

"Feeling better?"

Glory nodded. Now that the initial shock had passed, a sort of euphoria had overtaken her. "I'll be fine."

Jill stood, shrugged into her plaid coat and reached for her purse. "Jesse's looking good, isn't he?"

"I didn't notice," Glory replied as the two women made their way out of the church. Jill turned out the lights and locked the front doors.

Her expression was wry when she looked into Glory's eyes again. "You were always a lousy liar, my friend. Some things never change."

Glory started to protest, then stopped herself. "Okay," she conceded, spreading her hands wide, as Jill led the way to a later-model compact car parked at the curb. She was too shaken to offer an argument, friendly or otherwise. "He looks terrific."

"They say he's never gotten over you."

Glory got into the car and snapped her seat belt in place. Strange, she'd spent the past eight years thinking about Jesse, but now a gangly child with auburn hair and green eyes was upstaging him in her mind. "The little girl—Liza. Where did she come from?"

Jill started the engine and smiled sadly before pulling out into traffic. "You remember Jesse's big brother, Gresham, don't you? He married Sandy Piper, from down at Fawn Creek. They couldn't have children, I guess, so they adopted Liza."

Glory let her head fall back against the headrest, feeling dizzy again. The car and Jill and even the snowy night all fell away like pages torn from a book, and suddenly Glory was eighteen years old again, standing in Judge Seth Bainbridge's imposing study....

She was pregnant, and she was scared sick.

The judge didn't invite her to take a chair. He didn't even look at her. He sat at his desk and cleaned out his pipe with a scraping motion of his penknife, speaking thoughtfully. "I guess you thought you and your mama and that brother of yours could live pretty high on the hog if you could just trap Jesse, didn't you?"

Glory clenched her fists at her sides. She hadn't even told Jesse about the baby yet, and she figured the judge only knew because he and Dr. Cupples were poker buddies. "I love Jesse," she said.

"So does every other girl between here and Mexico." At last, Jesse's grandfather raised sharp, sky-blue eyes to her face. "Jesse's eighteen years old. His whole life is ahead of him, and I won't see him saddled to some social-climbing little chippie with a bastard growing in her belly. Is that clear?"

The words burned Glory, distorted her soul like some intangible acid. She retreated a step, stunned by the pain. She couldn't speak, because her throat wouldn't open.

The judge sighed and began filling his pipe with fresh tobacco. The fire danced on the hearth, its blaze reflected in the supple leather of the furniture. "I believe I asked you if I'd made myself clear, young lady."

Glory swallowed hard. "Clear enough" she got out.

The defiance he'd heard in her tone brought the judge's gaze slicing to Glory's face again. He and Jesse had a tempestuous relationship, but he obviously regarded himself as his grandson's protector. "You'll go away to Portland and have that baby," he said. He waved one hand. "For all I know, it could belong to any man in the county, but I'm taking you at your word that Jesse's the father. I'll meet all your expenses, of course, but you've got to do something in return for that. You've got to swear you'll never come back here to Pearl River and bother my grandson again."

She was trembling from head to foot, though the room was suffocatingly warm. "When I tell Jesse about the baby," she dared to say, "he'll want our child. And he'll want me, too."

Judge Bainbridge sighed with all the pathos of Job. "He's young and foolish, so you're probably right," the bitter old man concluded. He shook his head mournfully. "You leave me no choice but to drive a hard bargain, Missy. A very hard bargain, indeed."

Glory felt afraid, and she wished she hadn't been scared to tell Dylan about her pregnancy. He would have gotten mad all right, but then he'd probably have come with her to answer Judge Bainbridge's imperious summons. "What are you talking about?"

The most powerful man in all of Pearl River County smiled up at Glory from his soft leather chair. "Your brother—Dylan, isn't it? He's had a couple of minor scrapes with the law in recent months."

Glory's heart pounded to a stop, then banged into motion again. "It wasn't anything serious," she said, wetting her lips with a nervous tongue. "Just speeding. And he did tip over that outhouse on Halloween night, but there were others..."

Since Jesse had been one of those others, she left the sentence unfinished.

The judge lit his pipe and drew on the rich, aromatic

smoke. He looked like the devil sitting there, presiding over hell, with the fire outlining his harsh features. "Dylan's about to go off to the air force and make something of himself," he reflected, as though speaking to himself. "But I guess they wouldn't want him if he were to be caught trying to break into a store or a house."

Glory felt the color drain from her face. Everybody knew Judge Bainbridge owned the sheriff and the mayor and the whole town council. If he wanted to, he could frame Dylan for anything short of murder and make it stick. "You wouldn't—Judge Bainbridge, sir, my brother doesn't have anything to do with—"

He chuckled and clamped down on the pipe stem with sharks' teeth. "So now I'm 'sir,' am I? That's interesting."

Glory closed her eyes and counted methodically, not trusting herself to speak. She was afraid she'd either become hysterical or drop to her knees and beg Jesse's grandfather not to ruin Dylan's chance to be somebody.

"You will leave town tomorrow morning on the ten o'clock bus," the judge went on, taking his wallet from the inside pocket of his coat and removing some bills. "If you stay, or tell Jesse about this baby, your brother will be in jail, charged with a felony, before the week is out."

Glory could only shake her head.

Seth Bainbridge took up a pen, fumbled through a small metal file box for a card, and copied words and numbers onto the back of an envelope. "When you arrive in Portland, I want you to take a taxi to this address. My attorneys will take care of everything from there."

She was going to have to leave Jesse with no explanation, and the knowledge beat through the universe like a giant heartbeat. Just that day, out by the lake, they'd talked about getting married in late summer. They'd made plans to get a little apartment in Portland in the fall and start college together. Jesse had said his grandfather wouldn't like the idea, but he expected the old man to come around eventually.

All that had been before Glory's appointment with Dr. Cupples and the summons to Judge Bainbridge's study in the fancy house on Bayberry Road.

"I won't get rid of my baby," she said, lifting her chin. Tears were burning behind her eyes, but she would have died before shedding them while this monster of a man could see her.

Bainbridge's gaze ran over her once, from the top of her head to the toes of her sandals. "My lawyers will see that he or she is adopted by suitable people," he said. And with that he dismissed her.

"Glory?"

She was jerked back to the here and now as the car came to a lurching stop in Jill's slippery driveway. She peered through the windshield at a row of Georgian condominiums she'd seen that morning while driving around and reacquainting herself with the town. There had been lots of changes in Pearl River over the past eight years; the sawmill was going at full tilt and the place was prosperous.

Jill strained to get her briefcase from the backseat and then opened the car door to climb out. "I know what you're thinking," she said. "You're wondering how I could afford a condo on a teacher's salary, aren't you?"

Actually Glory hadn't been wondering anything of the sort, but before she could say so, Jill went rushing on.

"Carl and I bought the place when we were married," she said, slamming her door as Glory got out to follow her inside. "When we got divorced, I kept the condo in lieu of alimony."

The evergreen wreath on Jill's front door jiggled as she turned the key in the lock and pushed.

"I guess that's fair—" Glory ventured uncertainly.

"Fair!" Jill hooted, slamming the door and kicking off her snow boots in the foyer. "I should hope so. After all, Carl makes five times as much money as I do."

Glory laughed and raised her hands in surrender. "I'm on your side, Jill. Remember?"

Jill smiled sheepishly, and after hanging up her coat and Glory's, led the way through the darkened living room and dining room to the kitchen. "I thought I'd make chicken stir-fry," she said, washing her hands at the sink.

"Sounds good," Glory replied. "Anything I can do to help?" She felt like a mannequin with a voice box inside. She said whatever was proper whenever a comment was called for. But her mind was on Liza, the little girl she'd been forced to surrender to a pack of expensive lawyers nine years before.

Jill shook her head and gestured toward the breakfast bar. "Have a seat on one of those stools and relax. I'll put water in the microwave for tea—or would you rather have wine?"

"Wine," Glory said, too quickly.

Although she didn't make a comment, Jill had definitely noticed Glory's strange behavior.

Nevertheless the two women enjoyed a light, interesting dinner. After a couple of hours of reminiscing, Glory asked Jill to take her back to the diner.

Glory didn't even pretend an interest in going upstairs to her mother's apartment. She plundered her purse for her keys and went from Jill's car straight to her own.

The sports car wasn't used to sitting outside on snowy nights, instead of in the warm garage underneath Glory's apartment complex, but it started after a few grinding coughs. Glory smiled and waved at Jill before pulling onto the highway and heading straight for the sheriff's office.

The same deputy Glory had encountered earlier that day—she saw now that his name tag said Paul Johnson—was on duty at the desk when she hurried in out of the cold.

It took all her moxy to make herself say, "I'd like to see Sheriff Bainbridge, please."

Deputy Johnson smiled, though not in an obnoxious way, and glanced at the clock. "He's gone home now, Glory."

Of course. Glory remembered that Jesse had been dressed in ordinary clothes when he'd come to the church to pick up Liza, instead of his uniform. "He still lives out on Bayberry Road, with his grandfather?" she asked, hoping she didn't sound like a crazy woman with some kind of fatal attraction.

The deputy plucked a tissue from a box on the corner of the desk and polished his badge with it. "The judge has been in a nursing home for five years now. His mind's all right, but he's had a couple of strokes, and he can't get around very well on his own."

Glory skimmed over that information. She couldn't think about Seth Bainbridge now, and she didn't want to take too close a look at her feelings about his situation. "But Jesse lives in the Bainbridge house?"

Officer Johnson nodded. "Yep." He braced his chubby hands on the edge of the desk, leaned forward, and said confidentially, "Adara Simms will be living out there with him soon enough, unless the missus and I miss our guess. Jesse's been dating her since she moved to town last year. 'Bout time they tied the knot."

Glory did her best to ignore the unaccountable pain this announcement caused her. She nodded and smiled and hurried back out to the parking lot.

The snow was coming down harder than before, and the wind blew it at a slant. The cold stung Glory's face and went right through her coat and mittens to wrap itself around her bones.

The downstairs windows of the big colonial house that had been in the Bainbridge family ever since Jesse's great-great-great-grandfather had founded the town of Pearl River glowed in the storm. Glory parked her car beside Jesse's late-model pickup truck and ran for the front porch.

She pounded the brass knocker against its base, then leaned on the doorbell for good measure.

"What the—" Jesse demanded, pulling a flannel shirt on over his bare chest even as he wrenched open the door. He was already wearing jeans and boots. "Glory," he breathed.

She resisted the temptation to peer around his shoulder, trying to see if the woman Deputy Johnson expected him to marry was around. "Is Liza here?" she asked evenly.

Grimacing against the icy wind, Jesse clasped Glory by one arm and wrenched her inside the house. "No," he said, on a long breath, after pushing the door closed. "I have legal custody of Liza, but she spends most of the time in town, with my cousin Ilene. I'm always getting called out in the middle of the night, and I don't want to leave her alone." He buttoned his shirt and shoved one hand self-consciously through his hair.

Jesse Bainbridge looked for all the world like a guilty husband caught in the wrong place at the wrong time.

Glory didn't care if she'd interrupted something. "Did you know?" she demanded, taking off her coat.

"Did I know what?" Jesse frowned, looking agitated again.

It was possible, of course, that he really hadn't learned who Liza was, or even that Glory had borne him a child, at all; but it seemed unlikely now. She wouldn't have been surprised to learn that Jesse and his grandfather had been in this together from the beginning.

"I guess the joke was on me, wasn't it, Jesse?" she said. Glory was amazed by her calm manner; inside, she was a raging tigress, ready to claw the man to quivering shreds.

He stood so close that she could feel the heat of his body. "Damn it, Glory, what the hell are you talking about?"

It was then that her control snapped, when she thought of all the Christmases and birthdays she'd missed, all the important occasions, like the appearance of the first tooth and the first faltering step. "God in heaven, Jesse," she spat, all pain and fury, "I hate you for keeping her from me like that!"

His hands came to rest on her shoulders, and their weight and strength had a steadying effect. So did the look of honest confusion in his dark eyes. "I get the feeling you're talking about Liza," he said evenly. "What I *don't* get is why she's any of your concern."

Glory's tears brimmed and shimmered along her lashes, blurring Jesse's features. "Liza's my daughter, damn you," she sobbed. "Mine and yours! I had her nine years ago in Portland, and your grandfather made me give her up!"

Jesse let her go and turned away, and she couldn't see into his eyes or read the expression on his face. "That's a lie," he said, his tone so low she could barely hear him.

Chapter 3

Jesse walked into the mansion's massive living room, moving like a man lost in a fog, and sank into a leather chair. Glory followed, though he hadn't invited her, and took a seat on the bench in front of the grand piano, her arms folded.

She reminded herself that Jesse was a good actor. He'd been actively involved in the drama club in high school and probably college, too. Surely police work required an ability to disguise his emotions.

It would be no trick at all for him to pretend Liza's identity came as a surprise to him.

"Why didn't you tell me?" he asked, and his voice sounded hollow, raw.

Glory felt as though she'd been wound into a tight little coil. One slip, one wrong word, and she'd come undone in a spinning spiral. "Spare me the theatrics,

Jesse," she said, wrapping her arms around her middle to hold herself in. "I know your grandfather let you in on his little secret a long time ago."

Jesse pushed aside a tray on the coffee table containing the remains of a solitary frozen dinner, and swung his feet up onto the gleaming wood. He closed his eyes and rested his head against the back of the couch. "This is crazy. Liza was Gresh and Sandy's child—they adopted her through some agency in California."

Glory stood, shaking her head in angry wonder. "You're incredible," she breathed, bolting from the piano bench and storming back out into the entry hall. Her coat had fallen off the brass tree, and she retrieved it from the floor.

She had one arm in the sleeve when Jesse gripped her by the shoulders and whirled her around.

"Just a minute, Glory," he told her, his brown eyes hot with golden sparks. "You're not going to walk in here and announce that you had my baby and then waltz right out again. Furthermore, you'd better face the fact that Liza isn't that child."

In that moment, Glory made up her mind to stay in Pearl River, even if she had to support herself by working at the diner, and become a part of Liza's life. She'd been forced to give her daughter up once, but she was a big girl now, and it was time she stopped letting people push her around.

Including Jesse.

"You can't get rid of me so easily this time, Jesse. I want to get to know Liza."

A myriad of emotions flickered in Jesse's eyes before he spoke again. "I didn't 'get rid' of you before," he said, his voice husky. "You left me, remember? Without even taking the trouble to say goodbye. My God, Glory, I looked *everywhere* for you. I begged your mother to tell me where you were, and Dylan and I got into three or four fights about it."

Glory didn't try to defend herself. She didn't have the strength. "Dylan couldn't have told you, Jesse, because he didn't know." She paused and sighed. "I guess you and I just didn't have whatever it takes."

She would have turned and walked out of the house then, but without an instant's warning, Jesse dragged her close and brought his mouth down on hers in a crushing kiss.

At first Glory was outraged, but as Jesse held her in place, his hands cupping her face, all the tumblers inside her fell into place and her heart swung open like the door of a safe. The old feelings rushed in like a tidal wave, washing away all the careful forgetting she'd done over the biggest part of a decade.

"Didn't we?" he countered harshly, when he finally let her go.

Glory was devastated to realize that Jesse still wielded the same treacherous power over her he had when they were younger. She'd been so certain that things had changed, that she was stronger and wiser now, but he had just proven that at least part of her independence was pure sham.

For all of it, she was still Jesse's girl.

She said a stiff goodbye and opened the door.

The snowstorm was raging and the wind caught Glory by surprise, pushing her back against the hard wall of Jesse's chest. She launched herself toward her car, and Jesse was right behind her.

"That glorified roller skate isn't going to get you

back to town in this weather!" he bellowed. "Get into the truck!"

Glory considered ignoring his command until she got a glimpse of his face. The look in his eyes, coupled with the rising ferocity of the storm, effectively quashed her plans for a dramatic exit.

She let Jesse hoist her into his pickup truck and sat there shivering and hating herself while he ran back into the house for keys and a coat.

"Don't get the idea that this thing is settled," she warned, when he was behind the wheel, starting the engine and pushing buttons to make the heater come on. The motor roared reassuringly, and Glory had to raise her voice. "Liza is my daughter, and I'm not going to turn my back on her a second time."

Jesse shifted the truck into Reverse and clamped his teeth together for a moment before answering, "I think it would be better if we talked about this tomorrow, when we're both feeling a little more rational."

Glory folded her hands in her lap. She was overwrought, on the verge of screaming and crying. She desperately needed a night of sound sleep and some time to think. "You're right," she said, hating to admit it.

"Well, glory be," Jesse marveled in a furious undertone, jamming the gearshift from First to Second, and Glory ached inside. Once, he'd used that phrase in a very different way.

She bit down hard on her lower lip to keep from shouting at him for stealing all those minutes, hours, weeks and months when she could have been with Liza. And she wept as she thought of the things she'd missed.

When they finally reached the diner, Jesse got out of the truck and came around to help Glory down from the high running board. She pushed his hand aside, and suddenly she couldn't contain her anger any longer.

She stood staring up at him, her hands knotted in the pockets of her coat. "You cheated me out of so many things," she said coldly. "First-grade pictures, Jesse. Dentist appointments and Halloween costumes and bedtime stories. You had no right!"

His hand crushed the lapels of her coat together, and his strength raised her onto her tiptoes. "I loved you," he seethed. "I would have done anything for you, including break my back at the sawmill for the rest of my life to support you and our baby. I've been cheated out of a few things, too, Glory. I figure we're even."

With that, he released her and climbed back into the truck.

Glory grimaced as he sped away from the curb, his tires flinging slush in every direction and then screeching loudly on a patch of bare pavement.

Delphine was waiting up when Glory let herself into the apartment. A symmetrical five-foot Christmas tree stood in a corner of the living room, fragrant and undecorated.

"Was that Jesse?" Delphine asked without preamble.

Glory sighed. "Yes," she answered despondently, peeling off her gloves and coat and putting them away in a tiny closet.

"He sure had his shorts in a wad about something," Delphine commented, obviously fishing for more information.

"Sit down, Mama," Glory said wearily.

Delphine was sipping herb tea from a pretty china cup as she settled herself at one end of the sofa. "If you're going to tell me that Jesse was the father of your baby, Glory, save it. It's no flash."

Glory had a pounding headache, and she sat opposite her mother in a cheap vinyl chair, resting her elbows on her knees and rubbing both temples with her fingertips. "There's a lot more to it than that," she said wearily, wondering how to start. "Mama, you've lived here in Pearl River all this time. You must know about the child Jesse's brother and his wife adopted."

The teacup rattled against its saucer as Delphine set it on the coffee table. It was plain that she was making some calculations. "Yes," she said in an uncertain tone. "It was tragic when they died. Everybody said that plane crash brought on the judge's first stroke."

Glory nodded glumly. "Mama, the baby they adopted was mine." The tears she had been battling all evening welled up and trickled down her cheeks. "Jesse knew—that's the worst part. He sided with his grandfather."

"Are you sure about that?" Delphine frowned thoughtfully. "I'd have thought it would be more Jesse's style to hunt you down in Portland and confront you with the facts. He was shattered when you left, Glory—it was all I could do to keep myself from giving him the address of that home for unwed mothers you were staying in. He definitely wasn't buying my standard story that you were back East, living with my sister and attending a private school, but I think everybody else did."

Sniffling, Glory thrust herself out of her chair and went into the kitchenette for a paper towel. Her reflection showed in the window over the sink, and she could see that her mascara was smeared all over her face and her hair looked as if she'd just stuck one hand into a toaster.

She mopped her cheeks with the towel, not caring what she looked like, and went back to the living room. Seated in her chair again, she blew her nose vengefully. "You had a lot on your mind that summer, with me pregnant right out of high school and Dylan going off to the air force."

Delphine leaned forward slightly, her voice gentle. "Why didn't you want Dylan to know about the baby, Glory? We were a family—we shared everything."

Glory sighed. There was no point in keeping the secret any longer; Dylan couldn't be hurt by anything Judge Bainbridge or anyone else might do. "Because Jesse's grandfather said he'd have Dylan arrested for something serious, so the air force wouldn't take him. I was left with only one choice."

The color drained from Delphine's cheeks. "My God. Glory, why didn't you tell me all this *then?*"

"Because you would have told Dylan, and he'd have done something really stupid and gotten himself into even worse trouble."

Delphine reached across to clasp Glory's hand. "All of this is in the past," she said with a sigh and a resigned shrug. "What will you do now?"

Glory took a deep breath before answering, "I'm going to stay right here in Pearl River, so I can be near Liza."

"That might not be wise, dear," Delphine pointed out gently. "Liza's life will be turned upside down. She'll be terribly confused."

Shoving a hand through her rumpled hair, Glory

sighed again. "I'm not going to tell her who I am, Mama," she said sadly. "I just want to be her friend."

Delphine rose off the old-fashioned couch and folded it down flat. "It's late, sweetheart," she said, disappearing into her bedroom for a few moments and returning with blankets, sheets and a pillow. "And you don't have to make any decisions tonight. Why don't you get some sleep?"

Together the two made up the bed, and Glory went into the bathroom to change into her nightgown, wash away her makeup and brush her teeth. When she returned, Delphine was waiting, perched on the arm of a chair.

"Glory, I know you've had a shock," she said quietly, "and I understand that your mind is in an uproar. But please don't forget how hard you worked to put yourself through school and build a fine career. Pearl River isn't going to be able to offer you what a big city could."

There was nothing Glory wanted more than to be close to her child. She would have lived in a metropolis or a remote Alaskan fishing village and given up any job. She kissed her mother's cheek without speaking, and Delphine went off to her room.

Glory got out the photo album and flipped to the page where Bridget McVerdy's picture was displayed. Sitting cross-legged in the middle of her couch bed, she touched the eternally youthful face and marveled. If she hadn't been one to pore over old family portraits, she'd never have suspected the truth about Gresham and Sandy Bainbridge's adopted daughter, even though it all seemed so obvious now.

After a long time, Glory set the album back in its

place in the cabinet of her mother's old-fashioned stereo, switched off the lamp and crawled into bed.

Beyond the living-room windows, in the glow of the street lamps, transparent, silvery snow edged in gold drifted and swirled hypnotically.

Glory settled deeper into her pillow and yawned. Tomorrow she would pay a visit to Ilene Bainbridge, who ran a bookstore at the other end of Main Street. Glory had never met Ilene before, since, according to Delphine, the woman hadn't come to Pearl River to live until after the judge's first stroke.

Her mind drifted from the future to the past, back and back, to the night Liza was probably conceived. She and Jesse had gone to the lake for a moonlight picnic after the spring dance, and spread a blanket under a shimmering cottonwood tree....

The leaves above them caught the light of the moon and quivered like thousands of coins, and Jesse's dark eyes burned as he watched Glory take sparkling water, delicate sandwiches and fruit from the picnic basket. The surface of the lake was dappled with starlight, and soft music flowed from the radio of Jesse's flashy convertible.

He caught her wrist in one hand and pulled her to her feet to stand facing him on the blanket. "Dance with me," he said.

She'd already kicked off her high-heeled shoes. Laughing, Glory cuddled close to Jesse and raised her head for his kiss. He took her into his arms at the same time he was lowering his mouth to hers.

As always, Jesse's kiss electrified Glory. She didn't protest when he smoothed her white eyelet dress off her shoulders, his hands lightly stroking her skin as he bared it. She and Jesse meant to get married.

Glory's naked breasts glowed like the finest white opal when he uncovered them. The nipples hardened and reached for him, because they knew the pleasure Jesse could give.

"Glory be," he whispered in a strangled voice. "You're so beautiful it hurts to look at you."

She reached up with both hands to unpin her hair, and while her arms were raised, Jesse leaned forward and caught a coral-colored morsel between his lips.

Glory moaned and tried to lower her arms, but Jesse wouldn't let her. He closed one hand over both her wrists and held them firmly in place, and he gave as much pleasure as he took.

In the next few minutes, their clothes seemed to dissolve. Jesse lowered Glory gently to the blanket and stretched out beside her. While they kissed, his hand moved restlessly over her breasts and her taut stomach.

"Forever," he said breathlessly, his lips moving against the flesh of her neck. "I'll love you forever."

Jesse had long since taught Glory to desire him—their first encounter had taken place on that very spot just a few months before, and she didn't want to talk, not even about forever. Her young body was hungry, and she couldn't think beyond the moment.

"Make love to me, Jesse," she whispered, teasing him by nibbling at his lower lip, and he poised himself above her with a moan. She tasted his earlobe and kissed his neck, and when he entered her with a sudden, desperate thrust, she received him eagerly.

"Tell me you love me," he pleaded raggedly. His back was moist under Glory's hands, and she could see a fine sheen of perspiration glistening on his forehead and along his upper lip.

Her own body was catching fire, and she was moving faster and faster to meet his thrusts and increase the friction. "Jesse—you know—I do—"

"Say it!"

"I love you," she gasped as her body arched suddenly, like a bowstring drawn taut, and pleasure splintered through her. "Oh, God, Jesse, *I love you!*"

Now, lying on a made-down couch in her mother's living room a full decade later, Glory wept. Those two trusting, innocent children were gone for all eternity, replaced by angry and embittered adults who could barely exchange a civil word.

In the morning, just as she'd expected, Glory looked terrible. Her eyes were puffy and red-rimmed, and there were shadows underneath them, purple as bruises. She showered, put on jeans and a navy blue turtleneck sweater, and pulled her hair back into a French braid. Knowing there would be no hiding the ravages of the night before, she wore very little makeup—just some blusher and lip gloss.

Delphine presented her with a steaming cup of coffee and a bowl of hot oatmeal when she arrived in the bustling diner. The short-order cook was busy in the kitchen, frying up traditional breakfasts for a hungry crowd.

Glory tried to fade into the wall at the end of the counter, but there was no such luck. People knew she was back in town, and they were anxious to talk with her.

No sooner had the telephone lineman gotten off his

stool to go out and battle the weather than someone else replaced him. By the time she'd finished her breakfast, Glory had explained to three people that she'd be staying on in Pearl River for a while and agreed just as often that, yes, it was about time her mother finally remarried.

She was just about to make an escape when the little bells over the diner's door jingled and a stream of cold air swept into the warm, brightly lit interior.

"Good heavens, Jesse," Delphine fussed as she set four breakfast specials down in front of as many customers, "shut the door. The furnace in this place burns five-dollar bills!"

Glory felt her throat go tight, as she watched Jesse push the door closed and grin at Delphine. It seemed to Glory that everyone in the place was either looking at him or at her.

"Sorry," he said, taking off his snow-dusted hat with an exaggerated politeness.

At the same time he was zeroing in on the empty stool next to Glory. Reaching it, he turned and looked at her with eyes as cold as the slush outside in the gutter and said, "I brought your car to town."

She would have stood, but he reached out and caught hold of her forearm, effectively pressing her back down.

"Thank you, Jesse," he coached, and though he sounded as though he was teasing, his dark eyes snapped.

"Go to hell," Glory replied in a normal tone. She wasn't about to forget what this man had stolen from her.

Delphine had always said Jesse's grin ought to be registered as a lethal weapon, and he obviously had no compunctions about using it. He smiled at Glory and, for just a moment, she was a teenager again, willing to share her body and soul with this man.

"There's something on the seat of your car that you might be interested in," he said. Then he pushed away from the counter and strolled toward the door, stopping to joke with some of his constituents as he went.

Glory waited until he'd driven away with the waiting Deputy Johnson before hurrying out to her car. She found a plastic bag lying on the seat, filled with snapshots and school photos of Liza. Glory held the package close to her heart as she sped up the outside stairs to the privacy of Delphine's apartment.

While this unexpected gift might have surprised other people, Glory knew it was typical of Jesse. Even when he was angry with someone, he was still more inclined toward kindness than anything else.

She poured coffee in the tiny kitchenette and sat down at her mother's table to go over the pictures, one by one, noting even the smallest changes as Liza progressed from a plump infant to a shy fourth-grader.

"Don't worry, kid," Glory whispered, smiling through her tears. "You'll get past this gangly stage, I promise. And you'll be the prettiest girl in Pearl River."

After putting the pictures carefully back into their plastic bag, she grabbed her purse and coat and went downstairs once more. The breakfast rush was slowing down, but Delphine and her helper were still pretty busy.

"I'm driving back to Portland today, after I stop by Ilene Bainbridge's bookstore," Glory told her mother.

Delphine looked as though she'd drop the tray of dirty dishes she'd gathered up. "What?"

"I just want to pick up a few things I left in storage,

Mama. My résumé, some job-hunting clothes. I'll be back tonight."

"Those roads are icy," Delphine warned. "You be careful, and call when you arrive."

Glory kissed her mother's cheek. "I will. See you."

Five minutes later, Glory's car nosed to a stop in the hard, dry snow in front of Ilene's Book Store. Parallel parking had never caught on in Pearl River; people still left their cars at right angles to the sidewalk, the way they'd left horses and wagons years before.

There were Christmas lights in the window of the bookstore, along with a display of crystals catching the cold winter light.

Glory pushed open the door and walked in.

The place had a friendly ambience; there was a rocking chair, complete with a gray tabby cat curled up on the cushion, and a cheerful fire burned in a small Franklin stove. The selection of books, Glory saw at a glance, was eclectic.

"Hello?" Glory called, when no one appeared to wait on her.

A plump woman dressed in a caftan of gold-and-mauve paisley came out of a back room, smiling. Her brown hair was braided and wound into a coronet at her nape, with a bright yellow feather for accent.

"Jesse's friend, Glory," she said with a smile.

Given the new-age flavor of the place, Glory wondered for a moment if the woman was psychic. "Just Glory," she corrected quietly.

"Ilene Bainbridge," the bookshop owner said, extending a bejeweled hand. "I've been hearing about you for years, and just lately the news has gotten even more interesting. It's good to finally make your acquaintance." She shooed away the tabby cat and gestured for Glory to sit down in the rocking chair. "Would you like a cup of licorice tea?"

Before Glory could respond, Ilene disappeared again. Her voice came clearly from the back room.

"Shall I add sugar?"

Glory was looking out the window, watching as fat snowflakes began tumbling from the sky. "Just a teaspoon, please."

Ilene returned with two steaming cups. Handing one to Glory, she pulled up a plain folding chair and sat down. Her kind eyes were eager and warm. "It's nice to sit by a fire on a day like this," she commented.

Sipping her tea, Glory nodded. "Jesse tells me that Liza spends most of her time here with you."

Since Ilene didn't look at all surprised at the sudden shift in conversation, Glory assumed Jesse had told her about their relationship and her claim that Liza was her child. The other woman, who was probably in her late thirties, smiled. "Liza and I have a little apartment upstairs."

Glory sensed that Ilene was a gentle, even-tempered woman. She was probably very good to Liza. "I take it she's had a difficult life so far," she said, feeling guilty. In those moments, Glory sorely regretted not standing up to Judge Bainbridge and going straight to Jesse with the news of her pregnancy. In trying to protect Dylan, she had caused her daughter a lot of pain and upheaval.

Ilene's smile was gentle. "It's been eventful, that's for certain. But we love Liza, Jesse and I, and she knows it. That goes a long way toward making a child feel secure. Lately, though, she has developed a tendency to speculate almost incessantly about her birth parents."

Glory thought of the house her mother and Harold had bought, and suddenly she wanted with all her heart to live in a place like that with Liza and Jesse. Of course she knew it was impossible—just a Christmas fantasy. She would never trust Jesse again, and he'd never trust her.

"I want Liza to be happy," Glory said, near tears herself.

Ilene reached out and patted her hand. "Jesse told me you were planning to stick around, and I think that's a good idea. You never know what might happen."

Glory set her teacup aside and smiled at the tabby cat, who was curled up a few feet away on the hooked rug in front of the stove, waiting for the human intruder to get out of the rocking chair. "Thank you," she said to Ilene, standing.

The other woman rose and took Glory's teacup. "You'd be welcome to stop by anytime," she said. "Even if you weren't shopping for books."

Glory got the message. When she wanted to see Liza, she would be a welcome guest at the bookstore. That was certainly more than she could say for any reception she might get at Jesse's place. "I'll remember," she replied.

She left the store and got back into her car, cranking up the heat and turning on some music. It was a three-hour drive to Portland, and if she wanted to be back before nightfall, she would have to hurry.

Accordingly, five minutes later, Glory was speeding down the open road. The highway had been sanded, and although there were lots of cars in the ditch from the night before, driving conditions were good. The snow had stopped and patches of blue sky were visible in the distance, along with clouds that looked like well-used cotton balls.

She drove straight through, except for a brief stop at the drive-in window of a fast-food restaurant for lunch, and when she reached the storage place, it took a long time to locate the particular boxes she wanted. She found an expensive gold bracelet Alan had given her in the pocket of a tweed blazer.

On impulse she drove to his apartment building, meaning to leave the piece with one of his neighbors, but his car was parked in the lot, so she knocked on the door. Something inside made her want Alan to know she was all right; that she had hopes and plans, that he hadn't destroyed her.

"Come in, it's open!" he called out, and when Glory stepped inside, she saw that he was packing up his books.

Glory felt only a slight ache in her heart at the sight of him. He was a good-looking man, with his dark hair and blue eyes, but she knew she didn't love him. Maybe she never had.

"Hi," she said, closing the door. "I thought you'd be working." She held up the bracelet. "I just wanted to leave this."

Alan nodded, a sad grin lifting one corner of his mouth. "The bank is sending me to work in one of its outlying branches. You can probably appreciate the irony of that."

Glory was taken aback. If what Alan said was true, she could probably return to her old job right there in Portland. She'd been decisive when she gave notice, but not rude.

Just a few days ago, that position had meant everything to her, but now she could hardly wait to be in Pearl River again. "I'm moving back to my hometown," she said. It seemed strange that she'd once thought she loved this man desperately. Now he seemed insipid, even a little on the wimpy side.

Alan paused in the packing of books to rest his hands on his hips. "Ah, yes—Pearl River. The heartbeat of the American financial community."

Glory ignored his sarcasm, drew a deep breath and took a step backward, reaching for the doorknob. "Well, Alan—goodbye, and good luck in your new job."

He stretched out a hand toward her. "Glory, stay. At least have dinner with me—we can part friends."

"We can never be friends," Glory responded, and then she opened the door and went out. The moist, chilly wind felt good on her face.

Alan followed her all the way to her car. "I suppose you arrived in the old hometown and found out none of the local women had managed to sink their claws into Jesse Bainbridge," he said, his arms folded across his chest.

She swallowed. "This has nothing to do with Jesse," she said. It wasn't the complete truth, but none of this was any of Alan's business, anyway. "Besides, I think I'm a small-town girl. The cutthroat ways of big-city banking are not for me."

Alan jammed the fingers of one hand through his hair. "Damn it, Glory, I only wanted that promotion so you and I could finally get married and start a family. I knew that wouldn't happen if you were up to your eyeballs in loan applications and appraisals—"

"You *knew,*" Glory corrected, "that I'd studied and

slaved for that job for years. And when my back was turned, you elbowed your way in."

"Glory, I'm sorry," he said.

She opened the car door. "Gee," she replied cuttingly, batting her eyelashes at him. "You're *sorry.* Well, why didn't you say so before, Alan? That just changes everything."

With that, she got behind the wheel and slammed the door.

Alan slammed his hands down on the hood of her car in pure frustration, and although Glory had never known him to be violent before, she was angered and frightened by the action. She shoved the engine into Reverse and sped away.

Reaching the edge of the city, she stopped at a busy restaurant for a cup of coffee and a sandwich. While she was waiting for her order, she got out her cell and phoned Delphine at the diner.

"Hello, Mama," she said, when her mother answered. "I arrived safely, and now I'm ready to leave again. I'll see you in a few hours."

Delphine's quicksilver sense of humor came through just at the moment when Glory needed it most. "Who is this?" she asked.

Chapter 4

Glory arrived back in Pearl River, as promised, before nightfall. She and Delphine and Harold had dinner out in nearby Fawn Creek and went Christmas shopping at the mall, another new addition since Glory had first left home.

The next morning she put on a suit in a pale shade of rose, accented with a cream-colored silk blouse and gold jewelry, and went down the street to the bank to pay a call on Harvey Baker. Glory hadn't forgotten her mother's remarking, that first day, that Mr. Baker needed an assistant, since the old one had taken a job in Seattle.

Mr. Baker was a substantial man with a full head of white hair and exceptional manners. And he'd already heard that Glory was looking for a job. He took her into his modest office, looked over the résumé she presented, and hired her on the spot.

Glory left the bank feeling almost euphoric. Now all she needed was a place of her own, so she could get out of her mother's way. She called the town's only motel, but it was full. Then she telephoned the real-estate agency and learned there was a one-bedroom place available in an old Victorian house down by the river.

By the time she went into the diner for a very late lunch, Glory not only had a job but a place to live. She would make arrangements for her furniture and personal belongings to be moved as soon as possible.

"Don't you think you're being a little hasty, here?" Delphine asked, when they were alone in the diner after the lunch rush. The fry cook was outside in the alley, arguing with the man who delivered fresh produce. "Glory, maybe it would be better if you just went on with your life and tried to forget about Liza."

"Forget her?" Glory's spoon rattled in her coffee cup as she stirred unnecessarily. The two women were sitting at a table close to the counter. "Mama, could you have ever forgotten Dylan and me?"

"Of course not, but it wasn't the same. I didn't just give birth to you, I raised you." For a moment she averted her eyes, displaying great interest in the rusted metal thermometer affixed to the outside window casing. The snow was coating it, hiding its imperfections. Finally Delphine looked back at her daughter again. "Glory, Jesse's involved with somebody. Her name's Adara Simms and she owns the beauty shop."

Although she wouldn't have shown it, the reminder made Glory feel as though she'd just been slammed in the stomach with a board. She *had* been fostering a fantasy that included Jesse and Liza, whether she wanted to or not, neatly ignoring Adara's existence, and she realized now what dangerous emotional ground she'd been on. "Why didn't you tell me this the other night," she asked moderately, "when you were so sure I had a date with Jesse?"

Delphine sighed. "That was before Mavis Springbeiger came in and told me Jesse planned to give Adara an engagement ring for Christmas."

Glory closed her eyes tightly for a moment. Lord, but it hurt, the idea of Jesse slipping a ring onto someone else's finger. She didn't dare imagine the wedding itself. "I see," she said woodenly.

Her mother reached out and closed her hand over Glory's fingers, to still their trembling with a squeeze. "Honey, you're young, you're beautiful—you're smart and educated. You don't need Jesse, or even Liza, to make your life complete. There are other men to love you, and you can still have all the babies you want. *Please,* don't limit yourself by staying here and living for the occasional glimpse of your daughter!"

Glory understood what her mother was saying, and it all made sense to her intellect. But her heart, never very amenable to logic, was balking. She sniffled. "If I didn't know better, Mama, I'd swear you were trying to get rid of me."

There were tears in Delphine's eyes, even though she was smiling. "Heaven help me, Glory Parsons, if my conscience would allow it I'd beg you to stay. But I love you very much, and I want you to have the best possible life."

The bell tinkled over the door, and long habit made

Delphine stand up and smooth her crisp apron. When she saw that the visitor was Jesse, however, she didn't offer any of her standard greetings. She tossed her daughter a meaningful look and disappeared into the kitchen.

Without being invited, Jesse dragged back Delphine's chair and sat. The expression in his caramel eyes was guarded, and there was a stubborn set to his jaw. Glory sensed that he was full of questions, that beneath his calm exterior was an urge to grab her and shake her until she told him everything about her past.

"You sure know how to clear a room," Glory said, because somebody had to say something and it was clear Jesse wasn't going to extend the courtesy first.

He managed a rigid smile, and Glory noticed that there were snowflakes melting in his glossy brown hair. Jesse had never liked hats. "Ilene told me you visited her yesterday."

Glory drew a deep breath and let it out slowly. "Guilty," she confessed, raising one hand as if to give an oath.

He sat back in his chair for a long moment, regarding Glory as though he expected her to do or say something outlandish. Then he muttered, "I'm prepared to concede that Liza is our child."

"That's big of you," Glory replied smoothly, getting up from her chair and going behind the counter for a cup and a pot of coffee. She poured a cupful for Jesse, refilled her own, and returned the pot to its place before going on. "I assumed you'd come to terms with the idea, when you gave me those pictures of Liza. Thank you for that, by the way."

Now Jesse leaned forward, ignoring the steaming

coffee before him. "What I'm *not* willing to concede," he went on, as though she hadn't spoken, "is that you have any right to interfere with Liza's life now. She's been through enough, as it is. I don't want her upset."

Glory's hands trembled as she lifted her cup to her mouth and took a sip. Delphine's coffee was legendary, since she added a secret ingredient before brewing it, but the stuff passed over Glory's tongue untasted. "I've never said I would tell Liza who I am," she said evenly, once she'd swallowed. "I just want to spend time with her. And I will, Jesse, whether you like it or not."

Again, Jesse's jawline tightened. He took a packet of sugar from the container and turned it end over end on the tabletop. "You gave her up," he said. "You handed her over to the authorities and walked away. As far as I'm concerned you made your decision then, and you can't go back on it now."

Glory's instincts warned her to drop the subject for the moment. Jesse wasn't feeling real receptive just then, and pushing would only make him more stubborn. "I hear you're getting married." She said the words as cheerfully as she could.

He averted his wonderful brown eyes, gazing out at the drifting snow, and for a moment he looked so desolate that Glory wanted to put her arms around him and offer him whatever comfort she could. "You hear a lot of things in small towns," he murmured. Then he pushed back his chair and stood. "You're not going to give ground on this, are you? You're going to insist on hanging around."

Glory felt color pool in her cheeks, and she knew her eyes were shooting blue sparks. She'd tried to be civil, but Jesse evidently wasn't going to allow that. "Yes,

Jesse," she said quietly. "I'll be staying in Pearl River. I have a job and an apartment."

"Great," he rasped, shoving a hand through his snow-dampened hair.

"There's an old adage, Jesse, about accepting the things you can't change. This is one of those things."

He bit out a curse word. "I suppose you're planning to drag some big-city lawyer into this."

Glory straightened her shoulders. She was glad she was still wearing her suit, because it gave her an added air of dignity. "If necessary, I will. But it doesn't have to be that way."

Jesse turned and walked away without another word. The little bell over the door jangled angrily as he wrenched open the door and left.

Delphine came out of the kitchen. "I have to hand it to you, Glory—you were diplomatic."

"I tried," Glory answered. She wanted to go upstairs, throw herself down on the sofa and sob, but she couldn't face the emotional hangover that would come afterward. She glanced at the clock on the wall behind the counter and sighed. "Do you need any help?"

"Roxy will be coming in at the regular time," Delphine replied sympathetically. "You've had a big day. Why don't you get some lunch and then go upstairs and take a nice nap?"

Glory chuckled, but there wasn't even a hint of humor in the sound. "Do I look like such a wreck that I should be in bed convalescing?"

"Yes," Delphine retorted. But she was smiling.

"Well, I'm not going to lie around with a rose in my teeth," her daughter said firmly. "I have things to do. The first of which is to call the moving company and ask them to bring my furniture. Then I'd better do a little emergency shopping. I'm going to need some stuff to tide me over, in the meantime."

Delphine's expressive eyes went wide. "Nonsense. You can just stay with me until your things arrive. I don't want you camping out in some apartment, sleeping on the floor and eating your meals out of aluminum trays."

Glory took her coat from a hook by the door and put it on. Slinging her purse strap over her shoulder, she smiled and replied, "Mama, I called the Stay Awhile Motel, but there's no room at the inn. You're madly in love and about to be married. What you don't need right now is a woebegone daughter sleeping on your sofa."

With that, Glory went out into the biting wind again and up the stairs to her mother's apartment. After making the necessary arrangements for her belongings to be brought to Pearl River, she came back downstairs and climbed behind the wheel of her car. Praying her snow tires were as good as the people in the TV commercials maintained, she set out for the mall in the next town.

There, she bought a sleeping bag and an air mattress, a card table and two cheap folding chairs, towels and other necessary household items. Then she returned to Pearl River, driving cautiously in the ever-wilder flurries of snow to the supermarket at the north end of town.

She couldn't help noticing that people were pointing to her and whispering. Glory was sure none of them knew about the baby she'd borne nine years before, but there was no question that the inevitable small-town speculation was going on. The general population was obviously wondering why she'd left town so suddenly all those years before, deserting "poor Jesse

Bainbridge" without so much as a fare-thee-well, and whether or not she'd prove to be a problem where his new relationship was concerned.

After she'd taken everything to her empty, chilly apartment and put it away, Glory went on impulse to Ilene's bookstore. Heaven knew, the woman was nothing if not unconventional, but there was a quiet warmth about her that drew the troubled spirit. Glory had no doubt that the local bookseller was a trusted confidante to many people.

Ilene was busy with a customer when Glory entered, but she still greeted her with a wide and welcoming smile and a "come-in" gesture of one beringed hand.

Glory went to the shelves and busied herself selecting mystery novels. She had a passion for the books, especially if they boasted some unusual element, such as a vampire or a werewolf.

"I take it you've talked to Jesse recently," Ilene said softly, startling her newest customer. Glory hadn't heard her approach.

"You must be psychic," Glory replied with a sigh.

Ilene smiled and glanced at the books in Glory's hands. "You don't have to buy things for an excuse to talk to me," she said. "I consider you a friend, and you're welcome here anytime."

Glory felt quick, illogical tears burn behind her eyes, but she managed to hold them back. She held the books a little tighter. "I read a lot," she said in a small voice.

Ilene took her arm and gently ushered her toward the rocker and the warm stove. She shooed away the tabby cat and bid her guest to sit down. "What did Jesse say to you?" she asked, taking the other chair.

After a pause, Glory replied with a despondent

shrug, and said, "He thinks I ought to leave town." Although neither woman had ever mentioned the fact, Glory knew Ilene was aware Glory had borne Jesse's child, and that the child was Liza.

Ilene sat forward in her chair, her hands calmly folded. "Will you?"

Glory shook her head, arranging and rearranging the paperback books on her lap. "No. I must admit my mother suggested the same thing—that I just go on with my life somewhere else—but I can't. Something inside insists on staying right here where I can be close to my child."

"Then that's probably what you should do," Ilene commented. "Do you plan to tell Liza who you are?"

"No," Glory replied quickly. "That would only confuse her. I just want to be her friend, and I don't know why Jesse can't understand that."

Ilene smiled. "He's not trying, at least not at the moment. But I'm sure this has all been a terrific shock to him. After all, it isn't every day a man finds out that his niece is really his daughter. Jesse must feel as though he's wandered onto the set of a soap opera."

"I know," Glory agreed with a nod. "Believe me, I didn't expect to come home for Christmas and my mother's wedding and find out that the baby I'd given away was right here in Pearl River, being raised as a part of the Bainbridge family."

With a chuckle and a responding nod, Ilene got up to brew tea. She returned minutes later with two steaming cups.

"This time it's chamomile," she said. "That's really soothing, you know."

Glory was all for anything that would calm her jangling nerves.

"I'll talk to Jesse myself," Ilene said decisively, while her guest sipped herbal tea. "Perhaps I can get him to see reason."

"I'd be very grateful," Glory said. "I don't really want to approach Liza until Jesse gives me some kind of go-ahead, but I can't wait forever."

"Of course you can't," Ilene agreed as an older man bustled eagerly in from the cold.

Glory recognized him as Mr. Pellis, the principal at Pearl River High back when she and Jesse were in school.

"Got any more of that tea, Ilene?" he demanded jovially, in that booming voice that had called a halt to so many food fights and hallway spit-wad barrages. "This weather is enough to chill a man to the marrow!"

Ilene bustled back to brew another cupful, and Mr. Pellis turned his kindly gaze to Glory.

"Aren't you the Parsons girl?" he asked. "The one who took up two pages in your class's senior yearbook?"

Glory smiled, nodded, and started to stand, but Mr. Pellis gestured for her to remain seated. He took off his hat, revealing a perfectly bald head, and then his scarf and overcoat, and hung all the items up.

"I'm retired now," Mr. Pellis went on, taking Ilene's chair. He tapped his temple with one finger. "But I remember things. You dated the Bainbridge boy, didn't you?"

Glory swallowed and nodded again. She supposed she shouldn't be surprised that Jesse found his way into virtually every conversation. After all, this was Pearl River, his hometown, and he was sheriff.

Mr. Pellis chuckled and slapped his thighs with both hands. "Always thought you'd end up in the movies or something, you were so pretty. What do you do for a living?"

"I'm a loan officer," Glory replied, rising from her chair. It was getting late, and Delphine would be watching for her. "As of Monday morning, I'll be working right down the street at the First National."

Mr. Pellis beamed as though she'd just been elected president and he was personally responsible. "Well, good," he said. "I'll stop by and say hello the next time I'm in the bank."

Glory's smile was warm. "I'll be expecting you," she said. Then she paid Ilene for her books and went back to the diner.

She was curled up on the couch, dressed in jeans, sneakers and a red turtleneck sweater, reading one of the mysteries she'd bought, when the telephone jangled.

Startled, Glory jumped before reaching out to snatch up the receiver. "Hello?" she said a little uncharitably.

"Hello," responded a voice she immediately recognized. "This is Jesse." He sounded weary and more than a little annoyed, and Glory guessed without being told that Ilene had talked with him. She held her breath, waiting for him to go on.

After a long, electric silence, he did.

"They still have that community Christmas Party every year, with the sleigh riding and everything," he announced, each word dragged out of him by an invisible mule team. "It's tomorrow night, and I was wondering if you'd like to go. I mean, it won't be a date or anything, because Adara will be along, but you've been wanting to spend time with Liza…."

Glory was well aware that, as a beggar, she couldn't be a chooser. "Thanks," she said softly. Sincerely. "I appreciate it."

"I don't want you telling her anything."

Who, Glory wanted to ask, *Liza or Adara?* But she controlled herself because she was in no position to be making smart remarks. "I've already told you, Jesse—I won't say anything to Liza that would upset her. You can trust me."

"I thought I could, once," he responded in a distracted voice, and Glory closed her eyes against the pain of the jibe. "Listen, just meet us at the hill tomorrow night when the sun goes down. We'll be somewhere around the bonfire."

Glory was nodding, and it was a moment before she realized Jesse couldn't see her and said quickly, "I'll be there. Thanks, Jesse."

"Right," he answered in the clipped tone she'd come to expect from him. And then he hung up.

Glory bounded off the couch, upsetting her book and the crocheted afghan she'd spread over herself earlier. "Yippee!" she yelled.

The cry brought Delphine out of the bedroom, where she'd been dressing for a bowling date with Harold. "You won the lottery?" she inquired with a wry grin.

"Better," Glory crowed. "Jesse's going to let me see Liza."

Although Delphine shook her head, her eyes revealed a mother's happiness in her daughter's joy. She came and took both Glory's hands in hers. "Promise me you'll be careful, baby," she whispered. "This situation has a very high heartache potential—especially for you."

Glory was deflated for a moment, but she immediately perked up. "Jesse did make a point of telling me he was bringing Adara, but I'm not going to let that ruin things. He can marry King Kong, for all I care, just as long as I get to see Liza."

Delphine patted her daughter's cheeks. "Like I said, be careful. Here be dragons, fair maiden. Big ones, with fire in their noses."

Glory chuckled and kissed Delphine's forehead. "I'll get through this without so much as a singed eyelash," she promised.

But Delphine didn't look convinced.

Glory spent the night at her new apartment, staying up late to finish the first of the mystery novels she'd bought because she was too excited to sleep. The place was freezing cold when she awakened, and she shivered while trying to crank on the ancient steam radiators that stood under each window.

Outside, the world was a wonderland of white velvet strewn with tiny diamonds. Snow mounded on top of the row of mailboxes across the street and the cars parked on the road.

After taking a shower and dressing warmly, with long underwear under her jeans and flannel shirt and two pairs of socks inside her hiking boots, Glory donned a jacket and walked to the diner. Her breath made white plumes in the air, and the cold turned her cheeks and nose red.

By the time she reached her destination, she figured she probably looked a lot like Rudolph.

Delphine greeted her as though she'd spent the night in an igloo in the Arctic, shuffling her to a table, pouring coffee for her, insisting that she have a hot breakfast.

"You're not used to this, after Portland's milder climate," Delphine fretted.

Glory just smiled. She'd been on her own a long time, and Alan had never been much for making a fuss. It was sort of nice to have somebody taking care of her, at least for a few minutes.

After breakfast, Glory insisted on staying to help with dishes and then the noon rush. She was living for that evening when she would see Liza, and if she didn't keep busy in the meantime she'd go absolutely crazy.

Once the lunch clientele had eaten and gone, however, things slowed down considerably. Glory called Jill, and the two of them went to a matinee showing of *Gone with the Wind* at the Rialto.

"I've always said curtains make the best dresses," Jill commented as she and Glory left the theater about two hours later.

Glory chuckled. "Are you going to the snow party tonight?" she asked.

Jill shook her head. "Normally I would. But I've got a hot date with a guy over in Fawn Creek. Wish me luck." They crossed the street to where Jill's car was parked—behind a four-foot pile of snow. "The mad plower has struck again."

A teenage boy came out of the hardware store wearing a heavy coat and blushing, either from the cold or from the presence of two women, to shovel a path for Jill. Soon Glory's friend was driving away, tooting her horn and waving.

Glory looked at her watch and groaned. It was still hours until it was time for the community party.

Finally, however, the time came. She rode to McCalley's Hill, which overlooked the town, with Harold and

Delphine, who were bundled up and equipped with hot cocoa in a big thermos bottle. An enormous bonfire was blazing in the big clearing at the bottom of the slope, and already kids and adults alike were racing down the long incline on their sleds.

When Glory spotted Jesse standing with Liza and a slender woman dressed in a stylish ski outfit, she was struck by a sudden attack of shyness. Now that the moment she'd been looking forward to for twenty-four hours had finally come, she wasn't sure how to approach the trio, and she had no idea what to say.

Delphine solved the problem by gripping Glory by one arm and fairly propelling her into the cozy little circle. "Hello, Jesse," Glory's mother said with a bright smile. "Liza, Adara, I'd like you to meet my daughter, Glory."

Adara had dark hair and beautiful brown eyes, Glory noticed, but her attention immediately shifted to Liza.

The child looked up at her with an unhesitating, friendly smile. "Hi," she said. "I've seen you in Uncle Jesse's yearbook. It says, 'Glory, Glory, Hallelujah' over your picture."

Adara's gaze came quickly to Glory's face, and there was something sad in it.

"It's just a play on my name," Glory told Liza. "Listen, I'm new in town…" She carefully avoided Jesse's gaze, though she could feel it burning against her face, just like the bonfire. "Well, okay, I'm not new, but I've been away for a long time, and I could use a friend to go sledding with."

Liza, who was apparently a naturally gregarious child, looked delighted and pointed to her nifty Red Flier. "I'll share with you. Come on!"

Glory was intent on following Liza up the hill, when Jesse reached out and took a tight hold on her arm.

"Remember," he said cryptically.

Glory understood him all too well. "Your orders are burned into my gray cells, Sheriff Bainbridge," she replied with a cocky grin and a salute, and then she hurried after the eager little girl pulling a sled behind her.

She and Liza raced down the hill on the sled among a horde of other sledders, and then, laughing, ran up again. They repeated the process until their cheeks, feet and mittened hands were numb.

"I think we'd better stand by the fire for a while and have something warm to drink, don't you?" Glory suggested breathlessly to the sturdy child standing beside her, surveying the hillside with an attitude of conquest.

Liza sighed, her green eyes rising to Glory's face. She smiled, and her freckles showed like specks of gold in the firelight. "Okay," she said. Her gaze was full of generous curiosity. "You said you were new in town. Where do you live? Do you have a job?"

Glory explained about her new position at the bank and her apartment in the blue-and-gray Victorian house near the bend in the river.

Liza was familiar with both places.

Adara was standing next to the fire, sipping cider, when Glory and Liza approached with cups of their own. There was no sign of Jesse, and his girlfriend looked politely uncomfortable.

While Liza was occupied talking to a friend a few feet away, Adara smiled shakily and asked, "Will you be staying in Pearl River long?"

Glory sensed the woman's fears and felt a strange

need to reassure her. "Yes, as a matter of fact, I plan to settle here. I'll be working at the bank."

Adara seemed composed, although her hand trembled a little, causing some of her cider to spill over into the snow. "Isn't that nice," she said, and though she didn't speak unkindly, there was no conviction in the words.

Before Glory could reply, Adara spotted some people she knew, trilled out a hello, and hurried off toward them.

Glory was relieved. Adara was probably a relatively new arrival in Pearl River, but she had to know that Jesse and Glory had been high-school sweethearts. Like every small town, this little burg had its busybody contingent.

"Ready to go again?" Liza asked eagerly, just as Glory was finishing her cider.

"Sure!" Glory responded. She was exhausted and cold, but she would have sledded forever if it meant she could be close to her daughter. She would be grateful until the day she died for the child's ready acceptance.

Each of them took hold of the rope and pulled the Flier up the hill, careful to stay out of the way of the sleds zooming down from the top. Once they reached the summit, however, Jesse appeared out of nowhere.

The look he gave Glory was one of annoyance, as though he'd been dragged to the crest of that hill, kicking and screaming. "Once for old time's sake?" he asked, and the words were, of course, unwillingly spoken.

Glory remembered the winters she and Jesse had sledded down this very slope together, and her heart rate quickened by a beat or two. She looked at Liza and tried to speak in a normal tone of voice. "Would that be okay with you?"

Liza looked pleased, and the pom-pom on the top of her blue stocking cap bobbed as she nodded her head.

Glory settled on the front of the sled, instead of the back as she would have with Liza, and shivered a little when she felt the warmth of Jesse's breath against her nape. He wrapped his legs around her and hooked his heels into the front of the sled, then his arms embraced her, his hands gripping the rope.

They went careening down the hillside, the wind rushing in their faces, cold enough to sting. At the bottom the sled suddenly overturned and sent them both tumbling over the snow.

When they finally came to a stop, Jesse was lying on top of Glory. He swore and rolled away, but not before she felt the hard evidence of his desire pressing against her thigh.

Chapter 5

Jesse dropped Liza off at Ilene's first, then drove to Adara's condo overlooking the river.

She stood waiting for his kiss there on her doorstep, and for the life of him Jesse couldn't give it.

"You might as well tell me about Glory," she said quietly, holding her chin at a proud angle. "I run a beauty shop, remember, and by Monday afternoon I'll know every sordid detail."

He jammed splayed fingers through his hair and swallowed a curse. "We dated in high school, all right?" he finally bit out a few seconds later.

Adara pretended to recoil slightly. "Aren't we defensive?" she inquired sweetly. "I'm not a fool, Jesse. I've already guessed that you loved her."

Loved her? He'd been so crazy about Glory that he couldn't put one sensible thought in front of another.

And after she'd left without one damn word of explanation, he'd honestly thought he was going to die of the pain. He'd hounded her family and friends for weeks, trying to find out where she'd gone.

"What do kids that age know about love?" he countered irritably.

"Sometimes a lot," Adara replied.

"I don't want to talk about it."

"That's obvious, Jesse. But I can't let things go at that. I won't stumble along, thinking you and I have a future together, only to find out that you're still hung up on your high-school sweetheart."

Jesse thought of the diamond engagement ring he'd bought. Until just a few days ago, he'd been sure he'd finally reached the point where he could put Glory out of his mind, get married and start the family he wanted more than anything else. Now he felt as though he'd just collided with a linebacker at a dead run; not only did he hurt everywhere, he no longer knew down from up, or in from out.

"Jesse?" Adara prompted.

He hated himself for the heartache he saw in her eyes. She was a nice person, and she didn't deserve to be hurt. "Maybe we'd better cool it for a little while," he said with extreme effort. "Just until the holidays are over and I can think things through."

Adara kissed his cheek, and her hand shook as she turned the key in the lock. So did her voice. "Call me when you've worked it out," she said. And then she opened the door and went inside.

Jesse stifled a roar of outraged frustration and flung himself down the sidewalk toward his truck, which was parked at the curb and still running.

He guessed that said a lot, right there. He hadn't even bothered to shut the engine off, when even a few days before, he would have stayed until just before the sun came up.

Reaching the truck, Jesse jerked off his gloves and flung them into the cab, one after the other, not giving a damn where they landed. Then he got behind the wheel and sped away.

At home, he brought the truck to a lurching stop in the driveway and stormed toward the front door.

Not only had he wounded Adara, he'd stirred up a whole lot of old sensations he didn't want to deal with. Ever since he and Glory had gone flying off that sled—hell, ever since he'd gotten *on* the damn thing with her—he'd ached in every muscle between his eyebrows and his shins.

He opened the door, went inside and slammed it again. Instead of hanging up his bulky coat, he hurled it in the general direction of the coat tree. Then he marched into the living room, to the liquor cabinet, and poured himself a double shot of brandy.

A few sips settled him down a little, and he ventured into his grandfather's study and squinted at the shelves until he found the Pearl River yearbook from when he and Glory were seniors.

After tossing back a little more brandy, he carried the annual to the heavy rolltop desk, with all its cubbyholes and drawers, and sat down in the swivel chair. His fingers flipped the pages unerringly to the layout honoring Glory.

She'd been homecoming queen that year, and head cheerleader, and there were shots of her wearing a cropped top and cutoff jeans at the senior picnic, making a speech on graduation day, sitting on Santa's lap at the Christmas dance.

Jesse couldn't help smiling at the banner headline spread across the top of the adjoining pages. *Glory, Glory, Hallelujah.*

"Amen," Jesse said aloud, his gaze going back to the snapshot of Glory at the class picnic. He'd taken her to his room that sultry afternoon and made slow, hot love to her, and she'd responded without holding anything back.

Just the memory made him harden painfully. He slammed the yearbook closed and tossed it onto the desk.

Whatever he did, he had to remember that Glory was Glory. She'd proven beyond a doubt that she cared only about her own interests and she'd betray people who trusted her, to attain her objectives. As delectable as she looked, all grown-up, it was unlikely that she'd changed in any fundamental way.

She wanted Liza, and that meant he had to be on his guard. Despite Glory's protests that she wasn't going to upset the child, Jesse had no illusions about her conscience.

She probably didn't have one.

Still he needed to see her, talk to her, hold her. He phoned the office to let them know he'd be on the road, put his coat back on, and went out to his truck again.

He knew Glory had taken an apartment, he even knew where it was. But some instinct took him by the diner instead, and he saw her through the snow-trimmed window, sitting there all alone, her head bent over a book or something.

Almost as furious with himself as he was with Glory, he parked the truck and strode over to the door.

The closed sign was in place and the door was locked, but Glory came and admitted him right away. Her blue eyes were wide and wary, and standing there, Jesse forgot everything he'd meant to say.

"What have I done now?" Glory asked with a sad smile as she relocked the door and went back to the table where she'd been sitting, going over Delphine's quarterly taxes. Earlier, it had seemed like a good, practical way to pass what remained of the evening, as well as an excuse to get out of her lonely apartment.

Jesse helped himself to coffee behind the counter, then crossed the room to join her. After taking off his jacket and hanging it over the back of his chair, he sat down. "I just wanted to tell you that Liza had a really good time with you tonight."

Glory could tell he hadn't meant to say that, and the bewildered expression in his eyes made her feel strangely jubilant. "She's a wonderful, outgoing child," she replied. "You and Ilene must be doing a very good job with her."

He relaxed at that, and took a sip of his coffee. "Ilene strikes most people as a little weird, at first, but she'd walk through fire for Liza, and the kid knows it. That makes for a lot of security."

It was so nice to be talking civilly with Jesse for once that Glory felt her throat tighten. "We had that, Dylan and I, whatever else we were lacking. We both knew Mama was committed to us with her whole heart."

Jesse shifted in his chair, looking slightly uncomfortable again. "I don't remember my parents very well.

Gresh was a lot older than I was, of course, and Gramps had his own fish to fry. As you know, he and I never got along very well."

Glory found it impossible to picture that vicious old man in such a homey context as "Gramps." "I've heard your grandfather suffered a couple of strokes and had to be confined to a nursing home. I'm sorry." And she was, though she felt no remorse for hating Seth Bainbridge for so long, just a certain weariness.

"They take good care of him at the convalescent center," Jesse said. He was avoiding her eyes.

Glory glanced down at her mother's receipts and tax forms, at a temporary loss for something to say, and Jesse's chair legs scraped against the linoleum floor as he stood.

The idea of his leaving alarmed Glory, and she was further upset to find herself wanting him to stay.

But he only went to the jukebox and leaned against it, studying the selections. Delphine believed in moldy oldies, as she called them, and many of the songs dated from the fifties and sixties. The latest offerings were from the early seventies.

After a few moments Glory heard a coin drop into the slot, and she braced herself. Sure enough, Jesse chose the ballad that had been playing on the radio when they'd made love for the first time up at the lake.

She squeezed her eyes shut as an avalanche of emotional pain cascaded down on her.

Then Jesse took her hand, pulled her to her feet and into his arms and they danced. Glory was overwhelmed not only by memories but by the presence and the substance and the scent of Jesse. She wanted to melt against him, become a part of him.

He held her close, and the contact was so excruciatingly sweet that it brought tears to Glory's eyes.

"Don't do this," she pleaded in a bare whisper, certain that he understood his power over her and meant to use it. "Please."

He curved a finger under her chin and lifted. The words he said then were the first gentle ones he'd spared her since her return to Pearl River. "All I want is to hold you, Glory."

It wasn't all he wanted, and Glory knew it. She'd felt his need earlier, when they'd fallen off the sled, and she could feel it now. She fought to reason with him, and with herself. "This isn't right. You're engaged."

He maneuvered them over to the switch beside the door and turned off the lights, so that nothing illuminated the diner except for the multicolored glow of the jukebox. Their song finished and started again, and Jesse bent his head to nuzzle at Glory's neck.

"I'm not engaged," he finally countered, his voice a sleepy rumble, his breath making Glory's flesh tingle under its warmth. "I haven't asked Adara to marry me, and I told her tonight that I needed some time."

Glory swallowed and wondered if he felt the tremor of elation that went through her at this announcement. She was quick to remind herself, however, that it didn't really mean anything. For all that he was holding her so tenderly now, a part of Jesse hated her and he wouldn't hesitate to wreak any kind of vengeance he could manage.

"Jesse, go home," she said thickly. "You shouldn't be here."

He spread his hands over her trim bottom and pressed her close against him and, God help her, she couldn't even take a step back in the interest of self-preservation. Her nipples were throbbing beneath her flannel shirt and winter underwear, and there was a soft, expansive ache where Jesse would enter her.

He found her lips with his own and kissed her treacherously, encircling her mouth with the tip of his tongue and then invading her with it. Instead of fighting, she bid him welcome with her own, sliding her arms up his chest and plunging her fingers into his hair.

The kiss ended, but Jesse didn't withdraw. He bit Glory's lower lip lightly and lifted one of his hands to her breast, cupping it in his fingers, teasing the nipple with his thumb.

"Come home with me," he pleaded in a ragged whisper, "or God help me, I'm going to take you right here."

The words brought Glory abruptly to her senses, and she pushed back out of his arms, gasping for breath as though she'd just surfaced after long minutes underwater. "Damn you, Jesse," she sputtered, "we're not eighteen anymore. And you're not going to get back at me for my supposed wrongs by dragging me off to your bed!"

He hooked his fingers into the waistband of her jeans and hauled her forward, so that she collided with his thighs and the hard heat of his shaft. "Remember how it felt when I was lying on top of you in the snow tonight?" he breathed, and Glory was awash in yearning. "I'm surprised we didn't turn the whole hill to slush."

Jesse was right; there was something hot burning between them, even after all that time and heartbreak. He could take her there in the dark diner if he chose to, and she despised him for that power.

"Get out," she ordered with the very last of her strength.

Miraculously he retreated a step, allowing her to put things somewhat back into perspective again. "I want to take you to dinner Monday night," he said. "We need to talk."

Glory still couldn't manage to speak normally. "J-just about Liza," she stammered. "N-no more dancing."

He reached out and touched the tip of her nose in a gesture that was achingly familiar. "No promises," he said hoarsely. And then he opened the door and went out, just as their song began to play for the third time on the jukebox.

Glory spent Sunday working at the diner and then helping Delphine and Harold put away early wedding presents and various personal belongings in their brand-new house. The next day she started her job at the bank.

She had a small office and plenty of people wanted to borrow money, since Pearl River seemed to be in some kind of development boom, so the morning went by rapidly. She had lunch in the coffee room with some of the tellers and assistants, then returned to the pile of work left behind by Mr. Baker's previous assistant.

It was a surprise when, at quarter after three, Glory's office door squeaked open and Liza's bright green eyes peered at her around the edge.

"Am I bothering you?"

Glory couldn't think of anyone she'd rather have seen, though her mind *had* been straying to Jesse with disturbing frequency. Thanks to him, she'd been in misery most of the weekend.

"Of course you're not bothering me," she said quickly. "Come in."

Liza took in the office in a series of thorough glances. "Nice place," she said.

Glory gestured toward a chair. "Sit down, if you'd like."

The child wriggled into the seat facing Glory's desk, unbuttoning her coat at the same time. Although she was the spitting image of Glory's great-grandmother, there were things about Liza that reminded her of Jesse, too, and of herself.

The steady gaze was Jesse's, the tremulous voice her own.

"I'm adopted," Liza announced without preamble.

Glory was grateful for the chair that supported her, because she knew her legs wouldn't have managed it at the moment. "I see," she finally replied after a long time. She remembered then that Ilene had told her Liza thought a lot about her birth parents.

"Susie Harbrecker says my mom and dad didn't want me, so they gave me away."

A momentary desire to find Susie Harbrecker and shake her until her teeth rattled possessed Glory, then she regained her equilibrium. "I'm sure that isn't true," she said as evenly as she could. "There are lots and lots of good reasons why people put babies up for adoption, Liza. Sometimes they're too poor to care for them properly, and sometimes they're too young and immature." *And scared,* Glory added in her mind.

Liza gave a philosophical sigh, apparently willing to accept Glory's words at face value. She seemed naturally drawn to Glory, just as Glory was to her. "I'm going to be in the Christmas program at church."

Glory smiled, relaxing a bit. "I know. I watched you practice one night."

That seemed to please Liza, but then she frowned. "Of course, I'll probably have trouble coming up with an angel costume. Aunt Ilene sewed in one of her past lives, but she doesn't know how anymore."

Before Glory could comment on that startling statement, there was a brisk rap at the door and then Jesse came in. His expression was stormy, as though he'd just caught Glory plotting the downfall of the free-enterprise system.

If Liza picked up any of the difficult undercurrents in the room, she gave no sign of it. "Hi, Uncle Jesse," she chirped, jumping up and throwing her arms around him.

He gave her an easy hug, but his dark eyes were fixed on Glory, and they were full of wariness and suspicion. "Why don't you wait outside in the car?" he asked politely, his hand resting on Liza's shoulder. "I want to talk with Ms. Parsons for a moment."

Somewhat reluctantly, Liza said goodbye to Glory and left.

"That was some pretty fancy detective work," Glory said, when they were alone. "How did you know she was here?"

He braced his hands against the edge of her desk and leaned forward, glowering ominously into her face. "I know everything that goes on in this town, so don't try to pull anything."

Glory snapped the pencil she was holding into two pieces, though her manner was otherwise pleasant. Or at least courteous. "Why are you acting like I was about to kidnap her and head for South America? We were only talking."

"You have a nasty habit of skipping out at the most

inopportune moments," Jesse said. "I wouldn't put anything past you."

"Then there would seem to be no point in our going out to dinner tonight and talking this thing over like adults. You've already drawn the battle lines."

Jesse sighed raggedly and turned away to stand at the office's one window. Once again, snow was coming down. "Maybe I did overreact," he conceded in a barely audible voice. He looked back at her over one sturdy shoulder. "I don't know if I can talk this out with you, Glory, when I haven't even managed to work it through for myself yet."

"Have you told Liza that you're her father?"

He rested his back against the sill and folded his arms. "No," he replied. "She's a sharp kid. If I told her, it wouldn't be long before she guessed who her mother is."

"What would be so terrible about that?"

Jesse thrust himself away from the window, crossed the small room, and opened the door. "It would give you a kind of power I don't want you to have," he answered flatly. "I'll pick you up at six and we'll have dinner in Fawn Creek, if that's all right with you. They've got a pretty classy Mexican place."

Glory couldn't imagine why she wasn't refusing to go out with him, why she wasn't telling Jesse Bainbridge what to do with his Mexican dinner. "Okay," she said. "You know where I live?"

He raised one eyebrow. "I know where you live," he responded. And then, to Glory's enormous relief, he was gone.

At five she left the office, bundled up in her coat, laughing and talking with the other employees who were on their way out, too. In just a few minutes she arrived at her apartment.

There, Glory stripped off the blue-and-gray striped suit she'd worn to work that morning, took a shower, blew her hair dry, and put on a black knee-length pleated skirt and a sweater of the same color, threaded through with silver. She had just finished applying her makeup when the doorbell rang.

Glory crossed her empty living room and opened the door to admit Jesse, who looked handsome in charcoal slacks and a cream-colored fisherman's sweater. He wore a tweed overcoat, too, and his brash brown eyes moved over Glory's figure with undisguised appreciation.

She longed for an excuse to touch him, but there was none. "You look very nice," she said.

There was something wry about his grin. "So do you," he answered.

At first, it was like old times. Jesse helped Glory into her coat and held her elbow protectively as he escorted her to the classic old luxury car parked outside.

"No truck?" Glory teased, as she sank into the cushiony leather seat.

Jesse shut the car door and came around to get behind the wheel before answering. "Nothing but the best for you," he said, and each word was stretched taut, like a violin string.

Heat flowed out of the vehicle's heater, ruffling Glory's thin skirt, and soft music streamed from its impressive stereo system. "Your grandfather's car," she reflected, just to break the silence. "We went to the prom in this car, didn't we?"

She regretted the question instantly.

Jesse's eyes smoldered as he looked at her for a long moment before nodding and pulling away from the curb. They'd made love that night after the dance, and they'd been so excited that they hadn't even taken off all their clothes. Jesse had set Glory astraddle his lap and, gripping her hips, lowered her onto his shaft…

She was desperate, so she tried again. Reaching out to switch off the heat, she asked, "Do you think it's going to keep snowing like this?"

Jesse was no help, at all. "Until February or March, probably. I guess you're not used to it anymore, since you've been living in the western part of the state."

Glory gave a strangled cry of frustration. "Jesse, don't just leave me dangling. I need some assistance here."

He gave her a teasing glance that did as much to ignite her senses as her memories had. His eyes said assistance wasn't what she needed, though his lips moved only to curve into a half grin.

"So, did you win the election by a wide margin, or what?" she threw out, in another wild attempt at normal conversation.

"Were you in love with that guy you left behind in Portland?" he countered out of the blue.

Glory was instantly defensive, and she was grateful for it. "How did you know about Alan?"

"I asked you if you loved him."

"No—yes—I don't know!" How could she say, straight out, that she'd never loved another man besides Jesse himself? "Damn it, this isn't fair. You said we were going to talk about Liza!"

Jesse was shaking his head, and though his tone was polite, his words were downright inflammatory. "At least I know I'm not the only guy you ever ran out on. How many others were there?"

Glory wanted to slug him, but the roads were slick and she couldn't be sure he wouldn't lose control of the car, so she knotted her fists in her lap and savored the fantasy. "Take me home."

"I'll be glad to—at the end of the evening, when we've settled something. Anything."

They were leaving the city limits and climbing along the well-plowed tree-lined highway that led to Fawn Creek. Glory was startled when Jesse pulled the car off the road into a secluded rest area that was familiar for all the wrong reasons.

He shut off the engine and the lights and, after Glory's eyes adjusted, she could see him fairly clearly in the muted glow from the dashboard. "You're driving me crazy," he said, as though that explained everything.

"Start this car this instant," Glory sputtered, on the verge of panic. She was a strong woman, certainly not promiscuous, but Jesse Bainbridge had always been her downfall. "I want to go home."

"I know damn well what you want, and so do you. And maybe we're not going to get anywhere with the rest of our lives until we've taken care of it."

Glory grabbed ineptly at the door handle, but she never made contact. "Jesse, if you force me—"

"I won't have to force you," he pointed out, his fingers resting lightly on the back of her neck. "And we both know it."

He pushed a button somewhere, and the seat back eased slowly downward until she was lying prone. Before she could cope with that development, Jesse was kissing her, and one of his strong hands was resting on her thigh.

He snapped open her seat belt and laid it aside, then went right on kissing her, while his hand moved her skirt slowly upward.

She managed to free her mouth from his, though it didn't like its liberty and wanted to surrender. "Jesse—"

Jesse eased her soft, glistening sweater up and over her head, and deftly unfastened the front catch on her bra. He was watching, waiting, when her plump breasts spilled out, their tips already seeking him.

With a husky chuckle, he took one nipple into his mouth, and the sensation made Glory moan aloud and stretch out on the seat in involuntary abandon. His hand found the top of her panty hose and began rolling them slowly and surely downward.

Everything was happening as fast as a sleigh ride down McCalley's Hill, but Glory couldn't put on the brakes. She'd been without Jesse's touch for too long, craved it too desperately.

He found the aching center of her femininity and delved under its mat of silk to the quavering nubbin beneath. Glory groaned again as he rolled her between his fingers.

"Oh, Jesse—" she pleaded.

He bent until his head was lying in her lap, and then his lips and tongue replaced his fingers, and Glory gave a lusty shout and thrust her hips high.

Jesse chuckled against her, but he showed no mercy of any kind. His hands clasped her bottom, and he held her to his tender vengeance, taking everything she had to give. He laid her back on the seat, only to ignite the blazes all over again by sucking at her breasts and stroking them.

When she was twisting beneath his hands and mouth, feverish for the union she knew she should deny herself, he shifted her, so that he was lying on the seat and she was kneeling over him. He opened his slacks and lowered Glory onto him.

Her body surged into reflexive action, but Jesse gripped her hips and measured the pace, whispering ragged, senseless words as he sheathed and unsheathed himself in her.

"Jesse—*Jesse*—" She sought his mouth with hers, and he gave her a brief, fiery kiss. But he was caught up in a tender agony of his own, and he finally thrust his head back and uttered an exclamation.

In the next moment, their bodies made a pact independent of their minds, fusing together in a hot, searing thrust. Glory cried out and arched her back when Jesse intensified every sensation by pulling her forward and catching one of her nipples in his mouth.

When she collapsed against him, she was crying. "Damn you, Jesse," she sobbed brokenly. "Are you satisfied now?"

His chuckle was more tender than amused. "A strangely appropriate question," he gasped. And then he wrapped his arms around Glory and he held her for a long time, until they'd both recovered a little.

Only then did Glory realize that Jesse had shed not only his overcoat but his sweater, too. And her coat was jumbled into a corner with them. It scared her that she didn't remember the process of that.

"Oh, God," she sniffled, as Jesse dislodged himself to pull on his sweater and raise the seat back.

"Glory, it's all right," he rasped, as she dried her eyes with some tissue from the glove compartment and did her best to straighten her clothes.

Glory slammed the glove compartment and snapped her seat belt back into place. "Well, now you've proved it," she said, in a furious, singsong voice riddled with tears. "For a good time, a guy just has to call Glory Parsons!"

He silenced her by taking her chin in his hand. His grasp was hard but not painful. "Don't ever say that again," he bit out. "I made love to you because I wanted to, not because I was trying to make a point!" He paused to drag in a deep, ragged breath. "Now, maybe we can concentrate long enough to figure out what the hell we're going to do about our daughter."

Chapter 6

Because Jesse insisted, they went on to the restaurant in Fawn Creek, and Glory headed straight for the women's room to make repairs on her hair and makeup. When she came out, Jesse was waiting for her, and his brash brown eyes smiled even though his lips were still.

"Don't worry," he whispered a few moments later, as they followed a waitress to their table. "Nobody would ever guess that half an hour ago you were having your way with me."

Glory's cheeks burned and she glared up at Jesse, her lips drawn tight across her teeth, as he pulled back her chair for her.

"You did all the seducing," she pointed out, once they were alone with their menus and a flickering candle.

Jesse leaned forward in his chair. "Maybe so." He grinned. "But when you got warmed up, you were plenty willing to play the game."

"We came here," Glory reminded him stiffly, snapping her menu open, "to discuss Liza."

"By the way," Jesse began, drawing his eyebrows together briefly in a frown. "Are you doing anything for birth control, or did we just make the same mistake twice?"

Glory gave a hissing sigh and slapped her menu down on the table. "It's so typical of you to ask after the fact. Yes, I've got an IUD. And furthermore, I don't consider Liza a mistake."

"I can see we're going to get a lot settled tonight," Jesse replied through his teeth.

The waitress returned, and they both ordered chicken enchiladas with beans and rice. Glory wondered why they couldn't agree on anything besides food and sex.

Neither of them spoke again until their dinner salads had been delivered.

"I guess things must have been pretty serious between you and that Alan character, if you have an IUD," Jesse commented.

Glory took aim and fired back. "I guess things must be pretty serious between you and Adara, too, since everybody in town knows you bought her an engagement ring for Christmas."

"Adara and I are finished," he said, stabbing at his salad with his fork.

Glory smiled acidly. "What a coincidence. So are Alan and I. So why would we want to talk about them?"

Jesse shrugged and tried to look nonchalant, but Glory wasn't fooled. It troubled his male ego to know she'd had a long-term relationship with another man; Jesse had always been a very proprietary animal.

"I think you should tell Liza you're her father," Glory

ventured to say, long minutes later, when their dinners had arrived. "I mean, it must have been hard on her, losing Gresham and Sandy."

Jesse sighed, and the look in his eyes was, for a moment, grievously sad. "It was," he said gravely. "I don't mind admitting I had some trouble with it myself. Gresh was busy with politics, even when I was a kid, but he always had time for me."

A knot formed in Glory's throat. She knew how close a person could be to his brother, and how much it hurt to lose him. A part of her was still standing beside Dylan's grave, watching in numb disbelief as they lowered his coffin into the ground, aching because a stupid mistake on another airman's part had robbed him of his life. She nodded, because that was all she could manage.

Accurately reading the expression on her face, Jesse reached out and closed his hand over hers. "If Gresh and Dylan were here," he said quietly, "they'd tell us to stop worrying over the dead and think about the living."

Glory nodded again. "I know."

Over coffee, Jesse was the one to bring up the subject of their daughter. "Why is it so important to you that I tell Liza I'm her father?"

It was a question Glory had thoroughly examined in her own mind. "Kids tend to find out things like that. And when they do, they're devastated because nobody told them the truth."

He arched one eyebrow. "No ulterior motives? Like wanting her to put two and two together and decide that if I'm her father, you must be her mother?"

Glory met his gaze steadily. "I'd love for Liza to know who I am, under the right circumstances. But I care more about her happiness and welfare."

At that, Jesse looked skeptical, and their brief, tenuous truce was over. "Either that, or you have a rich relative somewhere, and the only way you can inherit is by proving you've produced offspring."

Even though his expression had forewarned her, Jesse's words still came as a slap in the face. "Did I hurt you that much?" she asked, when she'd gotten her breath back.

"Yes," he answered coldly. "I was eighteen, Glory, and gullible as hell. You'd told me with words and with your body that you loved me. When you ran off without telling me why it was over, the pain was so bad that I couldn't stand still. When I tried, it consumed me like fire.

"I did everything I knew to find you, but nobody wanted to help me, including Dylan and your mother." He paused, and his eyes, averted from Glory's face, were haunted. "I'll never forget the day I finally had to give up. Gresh had taken me fishing, trying to snap me out of it. He said if I didn't tell somebody about my feelings, they'd never go away, they'd just get worse. I threw my fishing pole down and yelled, it hurt so much. When Gresh put his arms around me, I cried like a two-year-old."

Glory had seen the images vividly in her mind as Jesse was talking, and she ached. Driven to distraction by her own pain, she'd inflicted agony on a person she loved with her whole heart. "I don't suppose it would help to say that I'm sorry, that I was hurting, too?"

Jesse threw two bills down onto the table to cover the cost of their meal and shoved back his chair. His eyes were hot with remembered frustration, as Glory stood with him. "Maybe someday it will," he responded in a low voice. "Right now, I feel like it all happened last Tuesday."

At the coatrack beside the restaurant's front door, he settled Glory's coat on her shoulders, then shrugged into his own. Although he was unfailingly polite, linking her arm with his so she wouldn't fall in the icy parking lot, opening the car door for her, something in his manner chilled Glory through and through.

Shame all but crushed her as she realized that, whatever he'd said to the contrary, Jesse had made love to her that night to avenge himself. He didn't care for her, and probably hadn't even especially wanted her. God knew, Jesse could have had just about any single woman in Pearl River County for the asking.

"We should have left well enough alone, Jesse, and stayed away from each other," she said miserably, when he brought the elegant old car to a stop in front of her building.

He was staring straight over the wheel instead of looking at her, and his profile was rigid. "I tried to tell you that," he answered gruffly after a long, difficult interval. His brown eyes were full of accusations when he turned to her. "For your own sake, Glory, and for Liza's and mine, please let this thing alone. Go back to Portland and your boyfriend and forget we made a baby ten years ago."

Glory's eyes filled with tears. In a way, she thought Jesse was right, she should go, but she knew even then that she wouldn't be able to make herself do it. The knowledge of Liza's existence would haunt her for the rest of her life.

"If you and I never exchange another civil word," she said, unfastening her seat belt and pushing open the car door, "it'll be all right. But I can't leave my daughter. I won't."

She was halfway up the walk when Jesse caught up with her and forcefully took her arm. The irony of it would have made her laugh out loud, if she hadn't been in so much emotional pain. The sheriff of Pearl River County didn't mind ripping out her heart and stomping on it, but he'd be damned if he'd let a lady walk to her door unescorted!

She shoved the key into the lock and would have gone inside without another word, if Jesse hadn't grasped her shoulders and forced her to face him.

"Damn it, Glory," he breathed, his jaw set so tightly it was a wonder he could speak at all, "leave Liza alone! I don't want her in pieces, when you decide you're bored with Pearl River and need to move on!"

Glory longed to slap him, but her fury was too great. It practically paralyzed her. "Sorry, Sheriff," she told him, "but I'm going to be a part of the landscape around here, and you'd damn well better get used to it!" With that, she shoved open the door.

Jesse yelled a swear word, heedless of the neighbors, shoved his hands into the pockets of his expensive overcoat and stalked back to his car.

All night long, Jesse tossed and turned, alternately burning to feel Glory beneath him, receiving him, and wanting to strangle her. She was like a fever beginning in his brain and spreading into his body, destroying his reason, changing him from a modern man to a cave dweller.

After a shower and a haphazard shave, Jesse put on his uniform and called the office to let them know where to find him. And then he got into his truck, backed it out of the driveway, and practically floor-boarded the gas pedal.

The vehicle fishtailed on the blindingly white packed snow as he drove toward the main road.

A left turn would have taken him into Pearl River, but Jesse turned right. He stopped once to use the winch on his truck to pull a young couple's car out of the ditch.

No one was hurt, but they had a baby with them, and the weather was colder than a witch's nipple. Jesse made sure the old heap they were driving would run before going on.

In a way, he envied those two kids their youth and innocence, as well as the unique young life they'd created together. He hoped they knew they were rich, even if they couldn't afford a decent rig, and that they would fight to hold on to what they had when they hit the inevitable white water.

He set his teeth. At that age, he would have fought any force in the universe to keep Glory and their child at his side—if he'd been given the option.

He was grateful when Twin Poplars Convalescent Home loomed up in the distance; he'd spent the night thinking about Glory, and he needed a distraction.

Vicky Walters, a nurse Jesse had dated briefly before he and Adara had started seeing each other, greeted him with a smile. Only then did it strike him that she bore a faint resemblance, with her blond hair and blue eyes, to Glory.

"Hi, Jesse. Nasty morning out, isn't it?"

He grinned and shivered in reply. "Speaking of nasty, is my grandfather up?"

Vicky laughed. "He's already had his breakfast, and he happens to be in a pretty good mood. He was in his room last time I saw him."

Jesse's grin faded as soon as he got past Vicky. Even on his best days, Seth Bainbridge wasn't an easy man to deal with. And this sure as hell wasn't going to be one of his best days.

Seth sat at the window, slumped in his wheelchair, dressed in his robe and slippers and gazing out from beneath bushy eyebrows at the dazzlingly white world. He still had his hair, though it was mostly gray now, and his eyes were as sharp as ever, like his mind. But the rest of his body had betrayed him by turning feeble.

"Gramps?" Jesse paused in the doorway, his hands braced on either side of the jamb.

The old man wheeled around and scowled at him. "Hello, Jesse."

"Can I come in, or do I have to get a warrant?" Jesse asked, trying to smile. It was tough to keep up a front sometimes, because the old cuss could be so hard and cold. And this was one of his *good* days.

"Come in," the judge grumbled, waving one hand in a desultory gesture. "Come in."

Even after he'd crossed the threshold, Jesse couldn't make himself sit. "How have you been feeling?"

"Like hell," the old man answered gruffly.

Jesse drew in a deep breath, let it out slowly. He had to go carefully here; he didn't want to cause the judge to have another stroke. And yet there were things he needed to know. "Glory Parsons is back in town." He said the words with the same caution he would have used to make sure the ice over Culley's Creek was thick enough to hold his weight.

He'd expected a reaction, and he got one. Seth's gaze snapped to his face and narrowed there, and his gnarled hands clenched on the arms of his chair. "That cheap, lying, little—"

Jesse had a lot of unresolved issues where Glory was concerned himself, but he wasn't about to let the judge insult her. "Hold it," he said firmly, raising both hands, palms out. "I don't want a dose of your venom, Gramps, and I swear to God I'll walk out of here and never come back if you don't watch your mouth."

Seth had few enough visitors, Jesse suspected, because when it came right down to it, he didn't have any friends, at all, except for old Doc Cupples. As for family, Gresham and Sandy were dead, of course, and he'd long since alienated Ilene with his black moods. She refused to subject Liza to the old man's unpredictable temperament, and Jesse backed her up on the decision.

Which left himself and the aging doctor as the only people who ever paid a call of any kind.

"All right," Seth muttered. He was silent for a long time, then he went on. "She shouldn't have come back. She promised she wouldn't."

Jesse's fist knotted; he wanted to slam it down on the dresser top, hard enough to make lamps and ashtrays jump, but he restrained himself. "So you did send her away," he ground out.

"Sit down," fussed the old man. "It hurts my neck to look up at you like that."

Jesse dragged a chair over and sank into it. "All right, you old reprobate, start talking."

"She would have ruined your life," his grandfather insisted. And had Seth been able to close his hands into fists, Jesse figured he would have. As it was, agitation was clearly written in every line of his body. "You wouldn't have gone to college. By God, you wouldn't be sheriff today, with every prospect of entering the state legislature in a few years!"

Jesse rubbed his eyes with a thumb and forefinger and sighed. "Glory was pregnant with my baby, wasn't she? And you ran her off because of your damn family pride."

"The baby was yours," Seth agreed bitterly. "I knew that the moment I saw Liza. But she *could* have belonged to anybody in the county!"

"Watch it," Jesse warned, his voice as rough as two rusty nails being rubbed together. In that moment, Jesse realized that he'd suspected Glory's pregnancy all along; he'd just never been able to get anybody to confirm it.

Seth trembled with frustration and rage and the relative inability to express those emotions. "Glory Parsons wasn't like Gresham's Sandy—she didn't come from a good family. That brother of hers was practically a criminal, and as for her mother—"

"Glory was as good as anybody, Gramps," Jesse interrupted in an angry undertone, "and *better* than you and I put together. Dylan was no worse than any of the rest of us, and let's not mince words here—you didn't like Delphine because you wanted to sleep with her and she told you to go to hell."

For a long time, Seth just sat there, gripping the arms of his chair and swallowing repeatedly. Finally he ground out, "I did the right thing, Jesse. Gresham and Sandy wanted a baby, and I made sure they got one. And I saved you from the mistake of a lifetime, you ungrateful young whelp!"

Jesse rose from the chair, went into the bathroom, and drew a glass of cold water for his grandfather. Seth was still red in the face when he got back. "Take it easy," Jesse said, holding out the glass.

Seth obviously would have liked to knock the cup out of Jesse's hand, but he didn't because he needed the water to steady himself. He drank it down thirstily. "I paid her to leave," he muttered, and the words were ugly to Jesse, even though he'd long since guessed that Glory had sold him out for money.

Hearing the words from his grandfather lifted them out of the realm of theory and planted them squarely in reality. And they were wounding. He averted his eyes to a naked tree beyond the window, but the old man was ruthless. He knew he'd cornered his prey, and he couldn't resist closing in for the kill.

"She could have come to you, Jesse, and told you about the baby. You would have married her. But we both know why she didn't, don't we? Because I told her I'd cut you off without a nickel the day you put a ring on her finger, and she didn't want you *or* the baby if she couldn't have the Bainbridge money, too."

Jesse thrust himself out of the chair and turned his back. He felt broken inside, just the way he had that long-ago summer day when Dylan had told him Glory had gone away and wasn't ever coming back. Only now he didn't have Gresh to help him get his balance back. He didn't have anybody.

"You ought to be thanking me on your knees!" the old man went on, tearing at Jesse's spirit like a frenzied shark. "*I saved you* from that calculating little tease!"

Not trusting himself to speak, Jesse strode out of the room, his grandfather's bitter words ringing in his ears.

* * *

On her lunch hour, Glory left the bank and drove cautiously along the icy roads until she reached the Pearl River cemetery. Then, parking her car outside the gates, she made her way on foot to Dylan's grave.

The headstone was mounded with snow, but the letters of his name were clearly visible. Glory sniffled and shoved her hands into the pockets of her coat. Then, after looking around to make sure she was alone, she started talking.

"Last night Jesse and I went out to dinner," she said, pulling one mittened hand out to wipe her eyes. "We took that fancy old car that belongs to his grandfather and—well—we ended up making love on the seat like a couple of teenagers." Glory paused to sniffle again. "Actually, it wouldn't classify as lovemaking, given the fact that Jesse was just trying to get back at me for hurting him. The Anglo-Saxon term would fit better, but you know me—I can't say that because I think it's so ugly."

An icy breeze swept in among the naked trees, ruffling Glory's hair and stinging her ears. She tried to imagine what Dylan would say if he were there, and it wasn't difficult. He'd have vowed to find Jesse Bainbridge and loosen a few of his teeth.

"Violence won't solve anything, Dylan," she said firmly.

She guessed that then he would have put an arm around her shoulders and told her not to be so hard on herself, that everybody makes mistakes.

"Thanks," she snuffled. Then she took one of the small candy canes the bank was giving away from her purse, stuck it like a little flag in the snow on top of Dylan's headstone, and carefully returned to her car.

She got back to the bank just in time for a staff meeting, and the rest of the afternoon was so busy that quitting time came long before she expected it.

Not wanting to go home to her apartment and sit in a folding chair, staring at a blank wall, Glory went to the diner instead. Delphine was off duty, and her daughter found her upstairs, curled up on the couch with a romance novel.

"Hi," Glory said brightly. And then she promptly burst into tears.

"I'd ask what's bothering you," Delphine said with gentle wryness, patting her daughter on the back, "but I already know it's Jesse. Sit down, and I'll get you a nice hot cup of tea to settle your nerves."

Glory collapsed into a chair without even bothering to take off her coat, and let her purse tumble to the floor. "He hates me," she said, resting one elbow on the arm of the chair and propping her forehead in her palm.

"Nonsense," replied Delphine from the kitchenette. "He just wants your body, and it's making him crazy."

Glory let out a despairing wail. "He's already had my body!" she sobbed.

Diplomatically, Delphine waited a few beats before responding to that. "I take it we're not talking about ten years ago, when you were young, foolish and hormonal."

"We're talking about *last night!*" Glory ranted.

"Good grief," Delphine muttered, materializing at her side with a glass of water and two aspirin tablets. "Get a grip before you give yourself a headache."

Glory swallowed the aspirin and felt a little better just for having been fussed over. "This would all be so much easier if it weren't for Jesse."

"None of this would have *happened* if it weren't for Jesse." She patted Glory's shoulder distractedly.

"Honey, please don't tell me you've come up with some crazy plan to replace Liza by getting pregnant with Jesse's baby all over again."

"Of course I haven't!" Glory cried, getting awkwardly out of her coat and leaving it all bunched up in the chair behind her.

Delphine returned to the stove as the tea kettle began to whistle. "Well, then, how did it happen?"

"I've never been like this with any other man," she marveled furiously. "But for some reason all Jesse has to do is kiss me and I go absolutely wild."

The older woman arched one auburn eyebrow as she handed Glory her cup of tea and then sat down to face her. "You know," she said, her eyes twinkling with mischief as she tapped the cover of her romance novel, "Storm Ravenbrook is having the same problem with her man, if it's any comfort to you."

"It isn't," Glory assured her huffily.

Delphine sighed. "Sweetheart, I warned you about staying here in Pearl River. To quote those old Western movies on TV, this town just ain't big enough for the two of you. And since Jesse owns a mansion, the sawmill, and half the real estate in the county, he isn't very likely to move on. That means—"

"I know, I know," Glory interrupted wearily, taking a somewhat unladylike sip of her tea. "I've either got to leave or learn to deal with our illustrious sheriff."

"That's about the size of it," Delphine agreed. Having listened to people's problems at the diner for so long, she'd probably heard more sad stories than the average psychotherapist. Her basic philosophy was that 97 percent of life was just a matter of showing up, and the other three consisted of rolling with the punches.

"Thanks, Mama," Glory said.

"What for?"

"For not judging me. Until they start a group called Jesse Anonymous, I'm afraid I'm going to have to play this thing by ear."

Delphine laughed. "In your case, I think the affliction may be incurable. Has it ever occurred to you, my darling daughter, that you might still be in love with the man?"

Glory's eyes went wide with alarm at the suggestion. As much as she thought about Jesse, as wantonly as she'd behaved in his arms the night before, the possibility had never crossed her mind.

"No," she said. *"No!"*

Delphine just shrugged and asked Glory if she wanted to stay for dinner. Harold, who was working on a plumbing job in Fawn Creek, was going to stop off on the way home and pick up a big pepperoni pizza.

Glory shook her head and gathered her crumpled coat around her. "I'd just be a drag," she said. Then she stood, bending to kiss Delphine's forehead. "Thanks for everything, Mama. I love you."

Delphine squeezed her hand. "If you decide you want to talk some more or just hang around, I'll be right here until about eight o'clock. Then Harold and I are going over to the new house to put shelf paper in the cupboards."

Glory promised to seek her mother out if she hit another crisis, and left. She was walking back to the bank parking lot, where her car was waiting, when Ilene came out of the bookstore and waved.

"You look half-frozen," the woman called. "Come on over, and Liza and I will thaw you out."

After the past twenty-four hours, the offer of time with Liza was irresistible. Glory looked both ways and then hurried across the icy street and into the bookstore.

A lush-looking artificial tree had been set up in one corner of the shop, which was now closed for the day. Lights were strung among the branches, and Liza was decorating the boughs with old-fashioned glass ornaments.

"Hi, Glory," she chimed with a smile that pulled at Glory's insides and almost brought tears to her eyes.

Glory hid her reaction by taking off her coat and hanging it up. "Hi, there," she finally answered, when she was a little more composed. "That's a pretty tree."

"Thank you," Liza replied. "Aunt Ilene says cutting down a live one is senseless slaughter. Uncle Jesse always gets a big spruce for the big house, though."

Amusement at Liza's vernacular saved Glory from flinching, at least inwardly, at the mention of Jesse. The twinkling colored lights on the tree cheered her a little, and she carefully picked up an ornament and handed it to the child.

Liza hung the piece from a branch and looked up at Glory with Christmas reflected on her earnest little face. "Will you stay for supper, Glory? Aunt Ilene said it was all right to invite you, and we're having Chinese."

Glory glanced at Ilene, who smiled and nodded. "I'd like that very much," she said softly, reaching out one hand to touch her child and then drawing it back at the last moment. Embarrassed, she turned to Ilene again. "Is there anything I can do to help?"

Ilene's expression was one of tender understanding.

"Just keep this young lady company," she said, gesturing toward Liza, "while I deep-fry the wontons." With that, she turned and left the shop for the apartment upstairs.

"Aunt Ilene's a good cook," Liza confided. "She thinks trying foods from other countries will promote peace, so we eat lots of strange stuff."

Glory smiled and began decorating the top portion of the tree, where Liza couldn't reach. The activity was so ordinary—parents and children did this everywhere, every year—but to Glory it was precious. "What are you asking Santa for?" she inquired casually, not sure whether her daughter believed or not.

"Santa's really Uncle Jesse," Liza confided, leaning close to whisper the words gently, lest they come as a terrible shock. "And I already got what I want."

"What was that?" Glory asked, her voice hoarse because of the lump in her throat.

"For Uncle Jesse not to get married to Adara."

"Don't you like her?"

"I like her all right. I just don't think she's Uncle Jesse's type."

Glory smiled. "I see."

"I want somebody who'll bring cookies to school and come in my room and hug me if I have a bad dream—like Mommy used to do."

Glory's heart twisted, and before she thought, she leaned down and kissed Liza on the crown of her head, just where her bright-penny hair was parted. When she straightened, she saw Jesse standing on the other side of the store's front window, glaring at her.

Chapter 7

The bell over the bookshop door didn't jingle merrily as Jesse came in; it jangled in warning.

"Uncle Jesse!" Liza whooped, flinging herself at the man, apparently never noticing his taciturn expression.

Looking on in silence, Glory envied Jesse the child's wild affection.

"Hi, button," Jesse answered distractedly, hugging the nine-year-old and then giving one of her braids a little tug. His eyes never left Glory's face the whole time, and their expression wasn't friendly.

She was saved from having to speak to him, at least temporarily, when Ilene appeared, pushing up the sleeves of her bright purple sweater and smiling.

"Hello, Jesse. Want to join us for supper? We're having Chinese."

He rubbed his chin, which was showing a stubble

of beard, and at last he turned from Glory. He smiled at his cousin. "No, thanks," he answered. "I'm still on duty." He looked down at Liza's face then, and now it was as though Glory was invisible to him. "I'm going out looking for a Christmas tree this Saturday, and I'd like you to come along if you want to."

"Yes!" Liza cried, and her eagerness made Glory's heart constrict. "I want to! Could Glory come with us, please? And Aunt Ilene?"

"Saturday's my busiest day, what with Christmas coming on," Ilene interceded with a gentle shake of her head.

Glory stood awkwardly by, embarrassed, not knowing what to say. It was obvious Jesse hadn't intended to include her in the invitation, and she could have gotten off the hook by saying she had to do her holiday shopping that day. But the painful truth was that she wanted, just once, to go on a Christmas-tree-hunting expedition with her daughter and the man who had fathered her.

Jesse narrowed his eyes at Glory, as though he suspected her of making Liza ask to bring her along by ventriloquism, but then he said grudgingly, "I guess it would be all right."

Liza cheered and hugged Jesse again, then scrambled upstairs to get something she wanted to show him. Diplomatically, Ilene went along.

"What are you doing here?" Jesse immediately demanded, placing his hands on his hips.

Glory stepped away from the artificial Christmas tree, realizing only then that she'd unconsciously been trying to hide among its branches. She sighed. "What does it look like I'm doing here, Jesse? I'm spending time with Liza."

He lifted one finger and shook it at her, starting to speak, but Liza reappeared before he got a word out.

"Here it is, Uncle Jesse," she burst out, waving a sheet of paper. "It's my math assignment. I got an *A*."

Jesse grinned. "That's great," he said, taking the child's eager offering. "Can I keep it? I'd like to pin it up on the bulletin board at my office, so all the deputies will know what a smart kid I've—you are."

Liza was beaming. "Okay," she said. And then she turned her bright green eyes to Glory. "Supper's ready. Aunt Ilene said to lock the door after Uncle Jesse and come up."

With a chuckle, Jesse bent to kiss Liza's forehead. "See you tomorrow, kid," he said. After that, he exchanged a brief look with Glory, silently warning her not to overstep her bounds.

She responded with a grudging nod, and he went out.

That night when dinner was over Glory helped Liza with the dishes and her homework, then read her a chapter of *Little House in the Big Woods* before tucking her into bed. When she'd kissed the child good-night and closed the door of her small room, she sought out Ilene, who was at the kitchen table, tallying the day's receipts for the bookshop.

"Thank you," Glory said.

Ilene gestured toward the colorful teapot in the center of the table with a smile. "Help yourself," she said. "It's herbal, so it won't keep you awake."

Since Ilene had also set out a cup, Glory poured some tea and took a sip. "Why are you so kind to me?" she asked, in a voice carefully modulated not to carry as far as Liza's room. "I mean, I'm a stranger as far as you're concerned."

"I have good instincts about people," Ilene said. "Besides, I believe in families."

Glory swallowed. She simply wasn't up to the topic of families, not after an evening of emotional ups and downs that had left her slightly disoriented and tired to the center of her heart.

Ilene patted her hand. "You've got good instincts, too, Glory," she said softly. "And you loved Jesse once. If you'll just give him time, he'll come to terms with all of this and start behaving like a human being again."

That brought a wan smile from Glory. "I hope you're right," she said as she sighed, "because it will be very hard to have a relationship with Liza, if Jesse and I can't get along."

After that, the two women drank tea and talked about other Christmases, in other places. Glory was tired and pleasantly relaxed when she left to fetch her car from the bank's parking lot and drive the rest of the way home.

"I guess you've done all the thinking you need to do," Adara said, accurately guessing the reason for Jesse's unscheduled visit. He wanted to leave it at that, to get back into his patrol car and drive away, but his sense of honor wouldn't permit such an easy out.

He entered Adara's apartment when she stepped back to admit him. "I'm sorry," he said, standing there in the middle of her living room, shoving his hands into the pockets of his jacket.

The tears shimmering in her eyes filled him with guilt, because he knew she would have done anything to hold them back.

"It's Glory?" she asked with a despairing lilt in her voice.

Jesse raised his shoulders in a shrug. "I'm not sure. The situation is pretty complicated."

Adara nodded. "I imagine so. Five people must have come into the shop today just to tell me that you took her to dinner last night."

"I'm sorry," Jesse said again. The reminder of the night before, when he and Glory had made love, would be sweet torment for some time to come. He supposed he deserved it.

He went to the door, and Adara followed, speaking quickly. "If you're not happy with her—"

Jesse touched her lips with the tips of his fingers. "Don't say it," he replied quietly. And then he left Adara's apartment for the last time.

On Wednesday, the movers stopped at the bank to inform Glory that her furniture and other belongings had arrived, and Mr. Baker gave her the rest of the day off to get things squared away. The moment the movers were gone, she unearthed her espresso maker and brewed herself a latte.

She was sipping the mixture of espresso and steamed milk and trying to decide which carton to unpack first, when her doorbell chimed. Expecting Delphine, or perhaps Jill, Glory was surprised to find Liza standing in the hallway, looking slightly ill-at-ease.

Glory never laid eyes on the child without a painful tug at her heart, but she was ready with a smile. "Hi," she said warmly, stepping back so that Liza could come in.

"Hi," Liza answered, stepping over the threshold and then just standing there in her little coat and boots, shifting back and forth from one foot to the other.

"Does your Aunt Ilene know where you are?" Glory asked, reaching out gently to unbutton Liza's coat.

Liza nodded. "I told her. She has a migraine headache and had to go upstairs and lie down."

Glory was concerned. "Is there anything I can do for her?"

Liza shook her head and tugged off her mittens and stocking cap, all of which Glory laid aside with the coat. "Nothing works but peace and quiet. I'm supposed to wait at the sheriff's office and have supper with Uncle Jesse tonight."

"Did you call him from school?" Glory inquired, wending her way through the stacks of boxes to the kitchen, where she planned to make hot cocoa for Liza.

"No," Liza replied nervously. "He's probably out chasing criminals, anyway. I'll go straight to the office after I leave here."

"I think we'd better call him," Glory said.

Liza stopped her by grasping her hand. "First I have to ask you something."

A chill went through Glory, followed by a wild hope that this bright, perceptive child had already figured out the secret she and Jesse were keeping from her. "Yes?"

"Do you sew in this lifetime?"

Glory chuckled, at once relieved and disappointed. "Yes, a little. Why?"

"Because I'm going to be the only angel in the pageant without a costume if I don't get somebody to help me," Liza blurted out. "Uncle Jesse's got something on his mind—he doesn't even hear half the questions I ask him—and Aunt Ilene used to be a seamstress in France, during a war. It was an unhappy life, and she swears she'll never pick up another needle and thread—"

Glory resisted an impulse to hug the child and laughed softly. "Sure I'll help you. Do you have the directions?"

Liza nodded and threw her arms around Glory. "Oh, thank you!" she cried. While Glory was recovering from that, the little girl hurried to her coat and extracted a folded, much-worried-over piece of paper containing basic instructions and a list of materials for an angel costume.

"The first thing we have to do," Glory reflected, reading over the paper, "is call your Uncle Jesse and let him know exactly where you are. Then we'll drive to Fawn Creek and get the materials we need."

Liza's green eyes were alight at the prospect. "The mall will be all decorated for Christmas!"

Glory nodded, smiling, and went to the telephone affixed to her kitchen wall. She called the sheriff's department, identified herself and politely asked for Jesse.

Another voice came on the line. "Glory? This is Deputy Johnson. Jesse's out on a call right now. Can I help you?"

Twisting the cord around her finger, Glory frowned. She would have preferred to relay the message directly to Jesse, so there could be no mistake, but she couldn't wait. She'd gotten Liza all excited about the project. She asked Liza if Jesse had a cell phone, but the little girl couldn't remember the number. "Just tell him, please, that Liza is with me. We'll be out of town for a while, picking up some things in Fawn Creek."

"I'll make sure he knows," Deputy Johnson promised earnestly.

Glory thanked him and hung up. In the process of preparing Liza and then herself for the cold, she forgot Jesse even existed. She couldn't remember the last time she'd looked forward to anything as much as she did those few stolen hours with her child.

The two of them had just passed the city limits in Glory's sports car, happily singing Christmas carols, when a siren sounded behind them and blue-and-red lights flashed ominously in the rearview mirror.

Knowing she hadn't been speeding, Glory frowned as she pulled over to the side of the road.

It shouldn't have surprised her, she guessed, that the officer who strode up beside her car was Jesse.

She rolled down her window and opened her mouth, but he didn't give her a chance to speak.

"Get out of the car," he ordered in an undertone that, for all its even meter, was girded in steel.

Glory glanced at Liza and smiled to reassure the child, who looked surprised and worried. "It's okay, honey," she said. "Your Uncle Jesse obviously didn't get the message that we left, so he and I have to talk."

Liza looked relieved. "Hi, Uncle Jesse," she sang out, wiggling her fingers.

He managed a semblance of a smile, and even though his eyes were hidden behind mirrored sunglasses, Glory knew they were snapping with controlled fury. "Hi," he replied.

Glory opened the door and stepped out onto the snowy roadside, and Jesse immediately gripped her by the elbow and hustled her around to the back of the car.

"Where the hell were you taking her?" he demanded in a hiss, as Glory wrenched free of his grasp.

Outraged, Glory folded her arms and rolled her eyes. "To China, Jesse," she answered. "We were making a break for it!" She flung her hands out at her sides and then slapped them against her thighs. "Too bad you had to catch us."

"Do you know how scared I was, when I couldn't find her?" Jesse rasped.

Glory found it only too easy to put herself into Jesse's shoes, and she relented a little. "I'm sorry," she said grudgingly. "Liza came by my apartment and asked me if I'd help with her angel costume. I called your office—I swear it—and left a message with Deputy Johnson that Liza and I were going to the mall in Fawn Creek to buy materials."

He turned away for a moment, his hands resting on his hips, seemingly taking a great interest in the snow-draped pine trees along the road. Glory knew he was composing himself.

Finally he looked at her again. "I thought you were leaving town on the spur of the moment, like before," he confessed. "And taking Liza with you."

It was a marvel that she'd been so angry with Jesse only a moment ago, when now all she wanted to do was comfort him. She wedged her hands into the pockets of her black corduroy pants so she wouldn't lay them on his broad shoulders. "Jesse, I'm not a scared eighteen-year-old girl, anymore. I'm not going to vanish, and I'd never, *never* put you or anyone else through the kind of anguish stealing a child would cause."

He faced her with a heavy sigh and shoved one hand through his hair. "Have her back in time for supper," he said. "And be careful. The roads are slick."

Glory smiled. Ilene had expressed the hope that Jesse would turn back into a human being, and it did seem that he was making noticeable progress toward that end. "You'd better go and tell Liza it's all right," she said, gesturing toward the passenger side of the car, "or she'll worry the whole time we're gone. Pleasing you is important to her, Jesse."

He gave her a look that might have contained a modicum of amused chagrin, shoved his hands into his jacket pockets, and proceeded to Liza's window.

"Have a good time, kid," Glory heard him say, as she rounded the car to get behind the wheel again. The lights on top of Jesse's patrol car were still splashing patches of blue and red over the snow.

"Were we going too fast?" Liza asked, with innocent concern, as she and Glory pulled back onto the highway. In the rearview mirror, Glory could see Jesse standing there at the side of the road, watching them go from behind those damnable sunglasses of his.

Glory shook her head. "He didn't get the message we left for him, so he was worried. Sometimes when parents—*people*—are scared, they act the same way they would if they were angry."

Liza nodded thoughtfully. "Then Gramps must be scared all the time," she reflected. "He's always mad."

"Gramps?" Glory asked, before it came to her that Liza was talking about old Seth Bainbridge, Jesse's grandfather. The hatred she'd always felt for the man seemed to ebb away, leaving sadness and pity in its wake.

"His son was Daddy and Uncle Jesse's father," Liza explained in that amusingly adult manner she sometimes assumed.

The reference to Jesse's brother as "Daddy," indirect as it was, reminded Glory that her gain was Gresham and Sandy's loss, and she wished there was a way to promise them that she'd keep their memories alive in

Liza's mind if she could. After all, for six of the little girl's nine years, they'd loved and taken care of her.

"I miss my mommy and daddy a lot at this time of the year," Liza said with a little sigh.

Glory's eyes burned, and she reached out to touch Liza's knee briefly. "I knew your daddy, though not very well." She thought of how Gresham had comforted Jesse after Seth had driven her out of town all those years before. "He was a nice man. Strong, with a ready smile."

Liza giggled. "He used to chase me around the house trying to tickle me," she said.

From then until they reached the mall at Fawn Creek, Glory kept the conversation turning around Gresham and Sandy, and talking about them seemed to be a great relief to Liza. The words and memories, mostly happy, bubbled out of her.

At the mall, Glory bought cups of cocoa for them both, and they sat at a table on the concourse, planning their strategy.

The stores were decorated, and Christmas music was being piped in over a sound system. Although she'd been something of a Scrooge for the past few years, embittered by her breakup with Jesse, the loss of her child and Dylan's subsequent death, Glory found herself getting into the spirit as she and Liza went from shop to shop.

Mindful of Jesse's edict that she have Liza back in Pearl River in time for supper, Glory didn't linger as long as she would have liked. Snowflakes were falling like big feathers shaken from a goose-down pillow, when the two shoppers left the mall with the makings of an angel costume.

It wasn't hard to find Jesse when they got back to town; his patrol car was parked in front of Delphine's diner, and he was standing at the jukebox when Glory and Liza came in.

"I'm going to be the best angel there ever was!" Liza crowed, hurrying to his side and waving the bagful of supplies.

Glory lingered just inside the doorway, very much aware of being outside the circle again. "If Liza could stop by tomorrow sometime, after I get home from work, I'll be able to get started on the costume."

Jesse was holding Liza close against his side, as though he feared to let go, and he didn't look at Glory. "You'll have to talk with Ilene about that," he answered.

After coming close enough to reclaim the shopping bag, Glory turned on one heel, her vision blurred, and hurried out of the diner into the cold and snowy night.

"How come you don't like Glory?" Liza asked, an hour later, when she and Jesse were seated at the table in the mansion's immense dining room, eating her favorite meal of chicken from a bucket.

It occurred to Jesse to hedge, of course, but then he had a strange feeling, as though Gresh were standing in the room with them, urging him to say the right things. He rubbed the back of his neck with one hand. "It isn't that I don't like her, button."

"You used to be her boyfriend," Liza announced, reaching for a drumstick. "I've seen pictures in your yearbook, and you and Glory were *kissing.*"

Jesse chuckled, though he felt sad to the very core of his being. "Yeah. We used to *kiss,*" he retorted good-naturedly. "So what?"

"Did you love her?"

He tried hard, but he found that he couldn't lie. "Yes, Captain Quiz, I loved her. Is there anything else you'd like to know?"

Liza caught him off guard by nodding and saying seriously, "Yes. I'd like to know who had me before I got adopted by Mommy and Daddy."

Jesse looked away. So, she was back on that again. He'd hoped the phase was over. "Does it matter? Your mom and dad loved you a whole lot, and they did all the important stuff."

Liza's tone was solemn. "It matters. Someday, I'm going to find my real mom."

"Sandy Bainbridge was your real mom," Jesse said, and though he didn't mean for it to be, his tone was on the sharp side.

His daughter's large green eyes were filled with lingering grief. Maybe it was worse for her at Christmas, knowing Gresh and Sandy were gone forever, like it was for him.

"I just want to ask my mom why she gave me up," she said with gentle defiance, and her lower lip quivered.

Jesse sighed and shoved his paper plate away, then braced his folded arms against the edge of the table. "She was a kid, Liza. She gave you up because she didn't know how to take care of you."

"Gramps told me once that she was eighteen," Liza argued. "Women get married and have babies at that age all the time."

Tonight, of all nights, she had to go into her forty-year-old-posing-as-a-kid routine. "Trust me." Jesse sighed, before slurping up a drink of soda through his straw. "Your mom wasn't mature enough to take care of a baby."

"Did she have a husband?"

"No. I mean, probably not."

Liza narrowed her eyes. "You know what I think, Uncle Jesse? I think you know who my mom is."

How the hell was he supposed to look the kid in the face and deny that? He stood and started gathering up the debris of their dinner, carefully avoiding Liza's gaze. "How would I know that?" he snapped, turning and striding off into the kitchen.

He could feel Liza's suspicious stare following him.

Jesse didn't come back until he'd stood gripping the edge of a counter for nearly five minutes, trying to compose himself. The fact that none of this would be happening if Glory had just stayed in Portland where she belonged did nothing to improve his mood.

When he returned to the dining room, Liza had her school books and a bunch of papers spread out on the table. Jesse was infinitely grateful that the topic of parenthood had been set aside, at least for the moment.

The telephone rang just as they were working on the last fraction problem, and Jesse went to the sideboard for the extension. "Bainbridge," he answered, expecting the caller to be someone at the office.

"Jesse, it's Ilene," his cousin said. "The headache isn't improving. Could you please keep Liza tonight?"

Despite his discomfort over the secret he was keeping from Liza, he liked the idea of their being like a real family, at least for one night. "Sure. But maybe I should call Doc Cupples and send him over to have a look at you."

"That old quack?" Ilene retorted. "I wouldn't let him

clip my toenails. Besides, I know I'll be better by morning."

"Call if you need anything," Jesse instructed. Then he said goodbye to his cousin and hung up. "Ilene wants you to sleep here tonight," he told Liza. "She's still not feeling well."

Liza relaxed visibly, and Jesse realized she'd been expecting bad news. It broke his heart that the kid was only nine years old and already trained in the adult art of bracing herself against tragedy. "Maybe she needs to go to the hospital."

Jesse kissed the top of his daughter's head. "She'll be fine, spud," he promised. "Did you work out that last problem?"

The child nodded, closing her books and putting her papers in a neat stack. It was a trait she'd probably gotten from Glory, Jesse reflected, since he tended to leave things scattered about.

"So what do you want to do?"

Liza's face brightened. "Let's get the Christmas stuff down from the attic. That way, we'll be all ready to decorate when we get the tree."

Jesse sighed dramatically, but he liked the idea as well as Liza did. He was looking forward to Christmas this year, though he'd spent the past ten dreading it. "Okay," he said, shaking his finger. "But it's a school night and you're not staying up till all hours."

She grinned. "Don't worry, Uncle Jesse. I'll mind real good."

They brought the nativity scene down first; it had been one of Jesse's mother's most valued possessions, and he carried it carefully. The porcelain figures had been handcrafted in Italy before he was born, but he and

Gresham had built the stable out in the carriage house one year, as a surprise.

After the crèche had been set in its place of honor, on the raised hearth of the living-room fireplace, the figures arranged just so, Jesse and Liza went back to the attic for the boxes and boxes of delicate ornaments and lights that always graced the tree.

Jesse was actually humming a Christmas carol as he sat in the middle of the living-room floor, a fire blazing on the hearth, untangling strings of lights. Liza had hooked them all together and plugged them in, and he suddenly found himself surrounded by bright knobs of color.

He laughed. "You're no help, at all."

Liza came and sat beside him, amid the twinkling tangle, and laid her head against his shoulder. Her statement caught him unaware, even though he should have been on the alert after that conversation they'd had earlier. "I think my real dad and mom might live around here."

We got trouble, Jesse thought, *right here in Pearl River. And it starts with a capital G.* "Why do you say that?" he asked, still working with the twisted strings of rubber-coated wire.

"It's just a feeling," Liza answered. But then she pinioned him with those eyes of hers and asked him straight out, "Do you know who my dad is, Uncle Jesse?"

He answered hoarsely, without knowing why he did it. He was sure of only one thing: that lying to this kid was impossible. "Yes, button. I know."

"Who is he?"

Jesse drew a deep breath, exhaled, and set the lights

aside to draw Liza gently onto his lap. She gazed into his face with total trust.

"He's me," he said raggedly, holding her tighter.

She didn't seem shocked. In fact, she didn't even seem surprised. "How come you gave me to Daddy and Mommy?"

"I didn't, exactly." Jesse tucked her head under his chin. "But it worked out okay, didn't it? I mean, your daddy and mommy really loved you, and they took good care of you."

Liza twisted in his lap, so she could look him directly in the eye again. "But they're gone," she reasoned. "If you're my dad, you know who my mother is. Tell me, Uncle Jesse—please."

Jesse shook his head. He'd had all the emotional strain he could handle for right then, and besides, he needed time to think before he gave Glory a permanent place in Liza's life. She swore she'd changed, but Glory had a habit of disappearing just when somebody started loving her with everything they had. "I can't do that, sweetheart. At least not tonight. For right now, I'm going to ask you to trust me and to believe that I'll tell you when the time is right."

She reached up to kiss his cheek, then settled her head under his chin again. "I love you, Jesse," she said, and for a moment the scattered tree lights blended before Jesse's eyes, making a collage of Christmas colors.

"I love you, too, kid," he answered gruffly.

Chapter 8

Liza arrived at the bank about five minutes before closing time and waited quietly in one of the chairs in Glory's office. The child seemed distracted, and Glory was troubled by that.

"Is something wrong?" she asked, as she put on her coat and reached for her purse.

Liza's small shoulders moved in a shrug. "Sometimes I wish I could be Nancy Drew and go around solving mysteries."

Glory put a hand on Liza's back and ushered her through the office door. "What mysteries would you solve?"

The little girl looked up with an expression of despairing resignation. "I'd find out who my real mom is, and ask her why she didn't want me."

A painful lump formed in Glory's throat, but she

made herself smile in spite of it. "I'll bet she wanted you very, very much," she said.

Liza shrugged again, and the two of them hurried out to Glory's car. Glory turned on the engine and shivered as she waited for the heater to kick in.

At home, Glory made cocoa for Liza and a latte for herself. The apartment was warm; evidently the temperamental radiators were having a good day. Since Glory had spent the evening before putting things away, the place looked relatively tidy.

"You should put your Christmas tree right here," Liza announced, standing by the bay windows that overlooked the street. She turned in a circle, with her arms stretched wide, as though clearing a space in the cosmos.

"I thought I would," Glory agreed, setting the cocoa and latte down on the coffee table in front of her pale rose couch.

"When are you going to put it up?" Liza inquired.

"This weekend, I hope. I'll probably get one while we're out tree hunting on Saturday."

Liza's smile was a little forlorn as she came to sit in Glory's wing chair and reached for her cocoa. It was plain she was trying to work up her courage to say something, and when she did, the words practically stopped Glory's heart. "If a person loses one daddy, and then they get another one, can the second one die, too?"

She set her latte on the coffee table so it wouldn't spill over onto the rug. Obviously, Jesse had told Liza who he was, but what had he said about her biological mother? Damn it, he might have warned her! She drew a deep breath and forcibly controlled herself. "Honey, anybody can die, and most of the time we don't know when it's going to happen." She paused, praying silently for the right words. "The thing is, you can't plan your life to avoid pain. You can't say, 'I'm not going to love this person, because if I do, I might get hurt somewhere down the road.'"

Unexpectedly, Liza began to cry. She put her cocoa down, crossed the distance between their chairs and scrambled into Glory's lap, sobbing.

Glory held her child, her own eyes blurred with tears. "It's okay, darling. You go right ahead and cry."

"Uncle Jesse is a cop!" wailed the little girl. "He could get shot by a bad guy, or his car might go off the road when he's chasing somebody—"

Glory kissed Liza's temple. "He could also live to be a very old man, honey, like his grandfather."

After a while, Liza began to settle down. "I g-guess you'd better measure me for my costume," she said, sniffling. "I have to go and practice for the pageant tonight, and Aunt Ilene will be here to pick me up after she closes the store."

With a nod, Glory set her daughter on her feet and went to get her sewing basket. She measured Liza according to the photocopied directions.

It was Jesse who came by to pick the child up a few minutes later, not Ilene. He sent Liza to wait in the car and lingered outside Glory's door, his hands in his coat pockets, his expression guarded and remote.

"You told her," Glory said, standing there in the doorway. She knew he wouldn't come in even if she invited him.

Jesse sighed. "Yeah. I told her part of it." He paused for a moment before dropping the bomb that blew Glory's tentative dreams to bits. "Liza's been through more at nine than most people endure in a lifetime," he said. "I want you to stay away from her until everybody gets their emotional balance back."

For a moment, Glory held on to the hope that she hadn't heard him right. "Stay away?" she echoed in a small voice.

"I don't want her to get attached to you, Glory, only to be hurt later when you decide small towns and kids aren't 'you' and move on."

There was, unfortunately, no doubting what he'd meant that time. "I won't let you do this, Jesse—I love that child as much as you do."

His response was a quietly furious, "You can talk about love, but it takes a hell of a lot more than that to raise a kid. You've got to be able to stick out the tough times, and I don't think you know how to do that."

He turned then, and started to walk away. Glory started to call him back, then stopped herself. Jesse had obviously made up his mind and, for now, there would be no reasoning with him.

She closed the door quietly behind him, spread the white synthetic taffeta for Liza's costume out on the kitchen table and tried to focus her tear-filled eyes on the printed instructions. She worked straight through dinner and by ten o'clock she had the outfit finished, right down to the tinsel halo and gauze wings trimmed with silver garland.

The next morning Glory dressed and went to work as usual, dropping off Liza's costume at Ilene's bookstore without saying more than a muttered, "Good morning." Reaching the bank, she got out Pearl River's thin phone book and looked under "attorneys" for the name of a lawyer.

There were only two in town, and the first one, Glory recalled, had been one of Jesse's closest friends since kindergarten. She called the second, a man named Brock Haywood, and made an appointment.

He agreed to see her during her lunch hour.

On Saturday morning, Glory bought a tree from the straggly group displayed in front of the supermarket. One of the bag boys tied it to the roof of her car, and she headed straight home.

Whatever Christmas spirit she'd mustered was gone—she was only putting up the tree for appearance's sake. Delphine and Harold would be worried if she didn't do something to observe the holiday.

She was putting lights on the tree, having set it in its stand in front of the bay windows in her living room, when Jill pulled up. Glory was relieved to see her friend, but she also felt a desire to hide.

Of course she couldn't since Jill had seen her.

"I thought you were going tree-hunting with Jesse and Liza," Glory's friend commented as she divested herself of her coat, hat and gloves. "I wouldn't have stopped, if I hadn't caught a glimpse of you through the window as I was driving by."

Glory repeated a silent litany of reasons why she must not burst into tears and then said, in an awkward attempt to change the subject, "Weren't you supposed to be skiing this weekend with that new boyfriend of yours?"

Jill rolled her eyes. "He turned out to be another creep." She plopped herself down in one of Glory's chairs. "I swear, if I ever do find a man I like they'll probably feature him on 'Unsolved Mysteries' as an ax murderer."

Glory laughed, despite the pain of her own situation. "How about some hot cider, or a latte?"

"A latte? You sophisticated creature! I'll have one of those."

The process of brewing two of the concoctions gave Glory time to pull herself together. It was inevitable, after all, that Jill would ask again why she wasn't spending the day with Jesse and Liza as planned.

She sprang the question as soon as Glory returned with the two steaming cups and sat down on the sofa. "What happened between you and Jesse?"

Glory sighed. She'd never told Jill the whole truth, but it spilled out of her now, all of it. She related how the judge had forced her to leave town, how she'd come back and discovered that the daughter she'd given up had been adopted by Gresham and Sandy, how Jesse had ordered her to stay away from Liza for the time being.

"And you're letting him get away with it?" Jill demanded, her face a study in disbelief.

"No," Glory answered, shaking her head. "I've filed a suit for visitation rights." She glanced at her watch and sighed again. "Jesse should be getting the papers soon."

Jill put down her cup and covered her ears with both hands, as if expecting an explosion. After a moment, she grinned shakily and dropped them to her lap. "This ought to give tonight's Christmas pageant a high degree of dramatic tension. You are coming, aren't you?"

Glory nodded. "Nothing could keep me away."

"Good for you," Jill answered resolutely. That was easy for her to say, Glory thought. She wasn't playing with emotional dynamite.

"Jesse Bainbridge?"

Jesse stopped in the hallway of Pearl River's tiny

courthouse, frowning at the old man who stood before him. "You know who I am, Harry," he said. "I used to deliver your newspapers."

Harry flushed. "I'm sorry, Jesse," he said. And then he held out a folded document.

Jesse muttered a curse and accepted the papers without asking for a further explanation. He knew a summons when he saw one, and nobody needed to tell him who was behind it.

Delphine and Harold arrived at Glory's apartment at six o'clock sharp, bringing a potted red poinsettia. While Delphine set the plant on the coffee table, Harold sniffed the air and smiled appreciatively.

"Something sure smells good," he boomed in his big voice. "I'll bet you're as good a cook as your mother." He put an arm around Delphine's slender shoulders and squeezed.

Glory made an effort at a smile. "It's my specialty, Spanish rice," she replied.

Harold said he was looking forward to supper and sat down in one of the living-room chairs to watch the news on TV. Delphine joined Glory in the kitchen.

"You look like hell warmed over," she told her daughter bluntly. "What's happened?"

Glory made a major enterprise of taking the casserole dish from the oven and getting the salad out of the fridge. "Thanks for the poinsettia, Mama," she said, hoping to deflect the conversation. "It's lovely."

"Glory."

She sighed and faced her mother squarely, setting the Spanish rice on a trivet on the counter. "Jesse declared war a few days ago, and I fired back."

"What do you mean, Jesse declared war?"

"He told Liza that he's her father. Then he told *me* to stay away from her until further notice. So I saw a lawyer and filed for visitation rights."

Delphine's normally pink cheeks went white for a moment. "Uh-oh. What was Jesse's response to that?"

"I don't know yet," Glory said. "He probably didn't get the papers until this afternoon."

Delphine gave a deep sigh, then put her arms around Glory and hugged her tightly. "Well, what's done is done. Harold and I will stick by you, of course."

Glory returned her mother's embrace before stepping back. "I'm sorry this had to happen now, Mama, right before your wedding and everything."

Delphine and Harold were to be married on New Year's Eve, in a candlelight service at the First Lutheran Church. "You have enough to worry about without fretting over that," the older woman said. "We'll all just have to take this one step at a time."

"You're on my side?" Glory asked, surprised, as, still wearing oven mitts, she picked up the casserole dish to carry it to the table in the dining area. Delphine followed with the salad.

"Good heavens, sweetheart, did you expect me to take Jesse's part? I'm *your* mother."

"I know you like Jesse."

Delphine kissed Glory's cheek. "Maybe so, but I *love* you."

After that, she and Delphine and Harold had a quiet dinner amid the twinkling sparkles cast by the tree. As soon as they'd cleared away the dishes, it was time to leave for the Christmas pageant.

"When you get home tonight, after seeing Liza

again," Glory said to her mother, when she was settled in the backseat of Harold's car, "I want you to take a good look at that old picture of your grandmother Bridget."

Delphine nodded, but her smile was tempered with sadness, and she was quiet as they all drove to the church.

The requisite snow was falling as they left the car and followed the crowd up the steps and into the building. In the sanctuary, fragrant garlands of evergreen decorated the altar railings, and someone had constructed a remarkably authentic stable on the dais, complete with straw. There were candles waiting on the pews, and each person took one before sitting down.

Glory quickly scanned the crowd for Jesse and was relieved not to see him. Maybe, she thought in a spate of wild optimism, he was somewhere battling crime and wouldn't be able to attend the pageant, at all.

He came in about one second after she'd formulated the idea and took a place in the pew directly in front of hers, turning to give her a challenging stare.

Harold, who suspected nothing, thrust out his hand and said, "Hello, Jesse. How's the lawman business these days?"

Jesse's face thawed visibly as he shook Harold's hand. "Unfortunately, it's thriving." He looked at Delphine and gave her a roguish wink. "By the way, Harold, congratulations on marrying the prettiest girl in town."

His friendliness to Harold and Delphine, which clearly shut her out, was almost as difficult for Glory to cope with as the cold anger he bore toward her. It was a tremendous relief to her when the organist started the prelude and everyone sat down.

Candles were lit, and the lights turned down, and the pastor delivered a short sermon on the significance of the season. Glory tried to concentrate on the real meaning of Christmas, but all she could do was stare at the back of Jesse's head and ache because even after all these years they couldn't be civil to each other.

Presently the pastor finished speaking, and the pageant began. Mary and Joseph came up the center aisle to a cardboard door set up at one side of the dais, and Joseph knocked, causing it to waver dangerously.

The innkeeper opened it and, with audible prompting from Jill, who was sitting in the front pew, informed the weary couple that there was no room at the inn. They could, however, sleep in the stable if they wanted to.

Mary and Joseph trekked wearily over to the makeshift barn. They knelt in the straw, as if to pray, and there was a moment of dramatic import before Jill rushed up and put a baby doll in the manger.

Meanwhile, shepherds came up the aisle in burlap robes, with bath towels on their heads and sandals on their feet, and angels fluttered in through the doorway to the pastor's study. Glory's heart surged into her throat as she watched Liza take her place with the others, resplendent in her costume.

There were songs and Bible verses, but Glory had eyes and ears only for her daughter. Like Mary, she pondered the miracle of birth in her heart.

All too quickly, the evening ended. As the players filed down the aisle to collect their reward of cookies and hot cider in the church fellowship hall, Liza's eyes linked with Glory's, and Glory felt a stab at the sorrow she saw in her child's gaze.

Obviously Jesse had announced his decision to keep

Glory and Liza apart. An anger entirely unsuited to her surroundings welled up inside Glory, and she rushed out of the sanctuary, through the narthex, and outside into the biting cold. There she stood gripping the stair railing, her eyes burning with furious tears.

She sensed Jesse's presence a moment before he came to stand on the step beside her.

"Glory—"

She crammed her hands into her coat pockets so she wouldn't start pounding at his chest in a hysterical rage. "Did you think I wouldn't fight back, Jesse?" she whispered. "Did you think I'd let you take Liza away from me, like your grandfather did?"

"Glory, listen to me."

"No, I won't listen to you!" Glory blurted out, moving the rest of the way down the steps. "I've heard it all, Jesse. You say you're afraid I'll make Liza love me and then desert her, but the real truth is you want to punish me for hurting *you!* You're not thinking about her, you're thinking about yourself!"

Although most people had gone downstairs to share in the celebration and the refreshments, there were a few souls trailing out to go home. Both Glory and Jesse lapsed into a stiff silence until they were alone again.

Then he took her arm and hustled her a little way down the street. "Maybe I am thinking about myself—after all, I'm the one who's had the most experience with your methods—but you're not operating out of pure altruism yourself, lady. You want to soothe your conscience, and you're not going to use Liza to do it!"

"She'll guess, Jesse," Glory said evenly, having made a great effort at keeping her temper. "It doesn't take a rocket scientist to count backward ten years and look at the pictures in a high-school yearbook!"

"I'll handle that when it happens. Right now, I want you to leave her alone."

Before Glory could reply, she saw an angel with pigtails standing on the church steps and gazing wistfully in their direction. Glory ached with everything in her to gather the child into her arms and tell her that she loved her, that giving her up was the single greatest regret of her life. "Let's call a cease-fire for now, Jesse," she said with a sigh. "An angel has just stepped into range."

Jesse turned and saw Liza there and instantly he was in motion. "You were fantastic!" he told his daughter, scooping her into his arms and starting up the church steps. "Let's go get some of that cider before it's all gone."

Over Jesse's shoulder, Liza stared forlornly back at Glory and wiggled her fingers in farewell.

Struggling to regain her equilibrium, Glory waited on the steps until Delphine and Harold came out a few minutes later. Maybe Jesse was right, she thought miserably, as her mother and future stepfather drove her home. Maybe she was just thinking of herself, and it would be better if she moved on and started a new life somewhere else.

After saying good-night to Delphine and Harold, Glory went into her apartment and flipped on the Christmas-tree lights, leaving the rest of the living room dark. Then she sank down onto the couch, still wearing her coat and gloves, and murmured, "Oh, Dylan, what should I do—stay or go?"

She supposed talking to her dead brother—a foible that seemed excusable when she was standing beside his grave—meant she'd finally gone around the bend in the river and would never be able to paddle back, but she didn't care.

The radiators clanged, but Glory knew that wasn't a message from the other side. It just meant the landlord was too cheap to put in a modern heating system. With a sigh she took off her coat and gloves, kicked away her boots and flipped on the television set.

Glory watched one program and then another and then another, and if her life had depended on it she couldn't have said what any of the shows were about. Awakening to find herself hunched up on the couch, cold and achy, she rose, switched off the TV and the tree lights and went to bed.

Tomorrow was another day, and the war between her and Jesse would undoubtedly continue. She'd need her strength.

In the morning, Glory went through her usual routine of showering, eating breakfast, putting on her makeup, blow-drying her hair and getting dressed. She felt like a wooden mannequin, caused by some unseen magician to move and function but not quite brought to life.

Since the bank didn't open until ten, and Glory reported to work at nine, she used her key to let herself in. The two tellers smiled and said, "Good morning" in chorus, and Glory, still the mannequin, responded as if she'd been programmed.

She'd no more than put away her purse and gotten out her appointment book for the day when Shelby, one of the secretaries, came in with coffee. She was a pretty dark-eyed girl with long chocolate-brown hair.

"Someone evidently came by to see you either last night or this morning," Shelby said with a smile, producing an envelope and setting it on Glory's desk, along with the coffee. "I found this in the night depository."

A feeling of dread clenched Glory's heart and stomach as she picked up the envelope. Her name was written across the front in teetering cursive letters. "Thank you," she said distractedly, wanting to be alone.

Shelby left, and Glory opened the envelope and took out the folded page of notebook paper inside.

Dear Glory, the same childish hand had written, and Glory groped blindly for the telephone receiver as she read on.

Liza stood uncertainly beside the railroad track, holding her Uncle Jesse's high-school yearbook under one arm and her piggy bank under the other. When the train stopped—as yet, there was no sign of it—Liza meant to climb into one of the freight cars just like she'd seen a girl do in the movies once.

Her feet were cold, even though she had two pairs of socks inside her boots. She'd worn jeans and a flannel shirt and thermal underwear so she wouldn't get sick and die, like Beth in *Little Women.*

She sniffled. She probably shouldn't have climbed up on the concrete edge that protected the flower bed at the bank and dropped that stupid note into the night-deposit box, because Glory would most likely call Uncle Jesse as soon as she read it.

Glory. Awkwardly, Liza set the piggy bank and the yearbook down in the snow and hugged herself. If Glory didn't want to be her mommy, it was all right. Liza didn't want to be Glory's daughter, either.

Much.

In the distance the train whistle hooted, and Liza

drew in her breath. She was afraid the tears would freeze in her eyelashes if she cried, and she *really* wanted to cry.

She supposed she'd known Glory was somebody special from the first time she'd met her. Last night, lying in bed, all wide-awake from the excitement of the Christmas pageant, the whole thing had come to Liza in a shattering flash. The words she'd heard Glory say on the sidewalk in front of the church had come back to her, their meaning crystal-clear.

She'll guess, Jesse. It doesn't take a rocket scientist to count backward ten years and look at the pictures in a high-school yearbook!

Uncle Jesse was her father, he'd admitted it himself. And he and Glory had been in love ten years before, and Liza was nine years old. It took nine months for a baby to grow inside a woman's stomach, according to a special she and Aunt Ilene had watched on PBS. Besides that, Aunt Ilene had told her just the other day that Uncle Jesse was always mad at Glory because he'd loved her very much once upon a time and she'd gone away.

Liza wiped her nose with a mittened hand. If she could have had any woman in the world for a mommy, besides the one she'd lost in the plane crash, of course, she would have picked Glory Parsons. That made the thought that Glory hadn't wanted her, that she'd gone off and left her all alone in some hospital right after she was *born,* for pity's sake, impossible for Liza to accept.

She'd decided to go away somewhere and raise herself. Even the fact that it was almost Christmas and she probably would have gotten a video game from Uncle Jesse couldn't make her stay.

The train chugged around a corner, coming out of the snowy trees, making a great clatter as it approached. Liza had seen it stop in just this place about ten million times, so she stooped and picked up the yearbook and the piggy bank and prepared to jump on board.

The whistle shrieked a greeting, and Liza waited patiently, hoping that raising herself wouldn't cost more than $15.87.

"Jesse!" Glory gasped the moment the sheriff of Pearl River County came on the line. "Liza's run away! She left a note in the night depository— Oh, God, Jesse, *do something!*"

His voice was surprisingly calm. "Glory, take a deep breath and get a grip on yourself. Did she say where she was going?"

"No," Glory burst out, half sick with panic.

"Read me the note," Jesse said evenly.

Glory began, the lined notebook paper crackling in her hand because she was trembling so hard.

Dear Glory,
If you don't want me, that's okay, because I don't want you, either. You left me at the hospital. The reason I can't stay is, I don't want you and Uncle Jesse to fight about me anymore. And I don't want to see you in the bank and know you didn't like me enough to keep me. I know Uncle Jesse and Aunt Ilene will miss me a whole lot, and I would have got a bunch of presents at Christmas. I guess they can take back whatever stuff they bought and get a refund.

Love, Liza

"Listen to me," Jesse said, his voice stern. "We're going to find her. I'll send a deputy to the bus station and we'll cover all the highways leading out of town. *Liza will be all right,* Glory."

"Like Dylan was all right?" Glory cried. "Like Sandy and Gresham—"

"Stop it, Glory. I don't have time for this."

"Come and get me, Jesse. I want to go with you."

Jesse gave in, but reluctantly. "I'll be there in five minutes. If you're not waiting on the sidewalk, I won't even slow down, let alone stop and twiddle my thumbs until you come out of the bank. Is that clear?"

Glory was already out of her chair and groping for her purse. "It's clear, Jesse. I promise it's clear."

He hung up with a crash, and Glory ran to tell Mr. Baker there was an emergency in the family, but she didn't explain the details. He very kindly excused her to go and take care of it, calling after her that he hoped everything would work out all right.

Jesse's patrol car appeared an instant after she stepped out of the bank and, as good as his word, he just barely stopped at all. The tires were spinning again before Glory had managed to close her door or fasten the seat belt.

"I hope you're satisfied," Jesse rasped, just before he reached for the microphone to radio the men he'd dispatched to different parts of town.

Glory bit her lower lip and said nothing. If anything had happened to Liza, she was never going to forgive herself.

Chapter 9

"This is all my fault," Glory fretted as she and Jesse began the search for their runaway daughter. "If I hadn't come back here—"

Jesse's jawline hardened for a moment, but then he reached out and touched Glory's knee. "Take it easy," he told her. "Liza's nine years old—she couldn't have gotten far."

Glory didn't find it at all comforting to realize that Jesse was taking the road that led to the small park down by the river. The water would be frigid at this time of year, even frozen over in places, and Glory's whole being seemed to clench in terror as she prayed Liza hadn't gone there.

"Wh-why the river?" she managed to ask, when Jesse brought the patrol car to a stop in the small, freshly plowed parking area that overlooked an array of snow-mounded picnic tables and barbecue pits.

"We've had some happy times here," Jesse said in a hoarse, distant voice. "Watch out that you don't break your neck in those damn high heels."

Only then did Glory realize that she wasn't suitably dressed for a search in her gray suit, ruffly blouse and charcoal eel-skin heels. She was out of the car as fast as Jesse was, but keeping pace with him immediately proved impossible.

He started down the pristine slope toward the picnic area, his strides long, his plain boots perfectly suited to the task. Cupping his hands to his mouth, he yelled, "Liza!"

Glory picked her way along behind him, moving as fast as she could, her eyes scanning the river, with its shards of sun-glittered ice. *Please God,* she prayed, *don't let her be in that water.*

Jesse gave the landscape around them what Glory perceived to be a cursory examination, then announced, his breath white in the crisp air, "She isn't here."

"How do you know?" Glory demanded. Even though she'd just prayed that Liza hadn't come near the river, she wanted to leave no stone unturned.

With a sweeping gesture of one arm, Jesse took in the whole park. "No tracks in the snow. Nobody's been down here in the last few days except us." His brown eyes ran over Glory's inadequate clothing with a sort of tolerant contempt. Then, without a word of warning, he strode over to her, lifted her up into his arms, and started carrying her toward the parking lot. "You're heavier than you look," he commented.

Glory tried to ignore what being held so close to Jesse did to her, even under such uncertain circumstances. If she'd known Liza was safe and warm somewhere, Glory would have wanted him to make love to her. "Thanks," she retorted.

Reaching the parking lot, Jesse set Glory back on her feet with an exaggerated sigh of relief. Moments later, he was in the front seat of his car, the microphone to his radio in one hand.

Glory heard the blunt, static-ridden answers to his questions as she snapped her seat belt in place, but she couldn't make sense of what was being said.

"They didn't find her at the bus station," he said, staring out at the river as he put the microphone back in place, "and there's no sign of her along any of the roads leading out of town."

Panic rose around Glory like invisible floodwaters, threatening to drown her, but Jesse offered her hope as he started the car and shifted into Reverse.

"That probably means she's still somewhere in Pearl River," he said.

Shivering with cold and fear, Glory hugged herself. "Maybe she went to your house, Jesse. There are a lot of outbuildings there, if I remember correctly, and she probably has happy memories of the place."

"It's worth checking out," Jesse agreed. And then he headed back to the main highway.

It took a full forty-five minutes to search every nook and cranny in the Bainbridge mansion, and there was no sign of Liza anywhere between the wine cellar and the attic. The stables, carriage house, storage sheds and the guesthouse were all empty, too.

In the mansion's huge kitchen, Jesse made instant coffee for Glory, lacing it generously with brandy, and then grabbed for his cell phone as it rang. Glory knew without being told that it was his office, and she hoped against hope that there would be some word.

She thought she'd faint with relief when, after barking a greeting, Jesse grinned. "Liza's been found," he said to Glory. "She went to the diner after she missed her train, and she's okay."

Glory swayed against the counter and took a restorative sip of her coffee. *Thank you, God,* she thought, closing her eyes. *Thank you, thank you, thank you!*

After a few more words, none of which Glory was able to grasp, Jesse hung up the receiver with a triumphant crash.

Glory started to set her coffee aside, but Jesse stopped her with a crisp, "Drink it down. You're white as hell." Then he took her arm and led her to the bench beside the big trestle table.

Knowing Jesse wouldn't take her to her daughter until she'd done what he said, Glory sat down on the bench and drank her spiked coffee as fast as she could swallow it. Then they returned to Jesse's squad car and started toward town.

Instead of heading toward the diner, Jesse took the first right turn after they crossed the city limits and brought the squad car to a stop in front of Dr. Cupples's humble office. It was a small blue house with white shutters, and the doctor's shingle hung from the scrollwork above the porch.

Glory hadn't been near the place since that day a decade before, when she'd learned she was pregnant with Jesse's baby. Despite the unhappy memories, she was right behind Jesse as he strode up the walk.

"I thought you said Liza is all right!" she cried

breathlessly, when he reached the porch and wrenched open the front door.

"Johnson brought her here, just to make sure," Jesse answered shortly. And then he was looming over the receptionist's desk, demanding, "Where's my daughter?"

"Right in there," the middle-aged woman replied, pointing toward a doorway, not in the least intimidated by the sheriff's manner.

As quickly as Glory moved, Jesse was through the doorway first.

Liza sat on the end of an examining table, wrapped in an oversize, old-fashioned felt bathrobe with Native American designs on it, sipping hot cocoa. Her eyes went wide when she saw Jesse.

He shook his finger at her. "You're just lucky I'm too glad to see you to tan your hide!" he told the child furiously.

Liza looked from Jesse's face to Glory's, then sighed like a ninety-year-old woman. "I'm sorry," she said, her little shoulders stooped.

Glory spoke far more gently than Jesse had. "Why did you do it?" she asked. Even though she was sure she knew, she still hoped she'd been wrong. "Why did you run away?"

Liza's gaze was level. "Because you didn't want me. I would probably be halfway to California by now, if that darned train had just stopped."

Just then Dr. Cupples appeared in another doorway. He was an old man now, with white hair and kindly blue eyes. "Hello, Jesse," he said. Then hesitantly he added a greeting for Glory. "Ms. Parsons. I wonder if I could speak with the two of you in my office."

Jesse nodded shortly, and his brown eyes were hot

as they swung back to his daughter. "I still haven't decided against spanking you," he warned, "so don't you dare move!"

Glory, for her part, was swamped with memories as she preceded Jesse into the doctor's small office. Here, the physician had given her happy news that was to have tragic, far-reaching results. She felt weak as she sank into one of the chairs facing Dr. Cupples's desk.

Jesse took the other, lifting one booted foot to rest on the opposite knee.

The doctor carefully closed the office door, then went behind his desk to sink into his swivel chair with a weary sigh. He pressed a button on his telephone and said, "Doris, will you please hold my calls for a few minutes?"

Jesse shifted uncomfortably in his chair, then leaned forward, his brows drawn together in a frown. "What's this all about?"

The old man sat back, making a steeple of his fingers beneath his double chin. "I have a confession to make, and it's not an easy thing to do, Jesse Bainbridge, so I'll thank you to keep your pants on until I get it said!"

Still glowering, Jesse subsided a little, settling back in his chair. Glory, meanwhile was perched on the edge of hers, sensing that Dr. Cupples was about to make an important announcement.

"After you came to see me that day ten years ago, Glory," he said with resignation, "I betrayed your trust—and my own vows as a physician—to call my friend Seth Bainbridge and tell him you were expecting a baby, and that Jesse was the father."

Glory wasn't surprised; she'd deduced that long ago.

But Jesse straightened in his chair, poised like a rocket about to shoot off the launchpad.

"What?" he rasped.

"I thought I was doing a friend a favor. Now, of course, I wish I'd just stayed out of the whole thing. That little girl out there might have been a whole lot happier if I had." Dr. Cupples sighed and leaned forward, bracing his forearms against his cluttered desk. "The judge thought it was important for you to go to college and marry well, Jesse, so he paid Ms. Parsons to leave town."

Jesse shot a lethal look in Glory's direction. "Don't blame yourself too much, Doc," he rasped. "The plan wouldn't have worked if Glory hadn't been so damn willing to be bought off!"

Glory would have liked to think Jesse didn't mean what he was saying, that he was just reacting to the unavoidable stress of losing a child and finding her again, but she knew he meant every word. And she was too crippled with hurt and regret to defend herself.

"Glory was eighteen," Doc Cupples pointed out kindly. "A fatherless girl, with nobody to take her side." His blue eyes shifted to Glory's face. "You have no idea how sorry I am for my interference, my dear, or how much I wish I'd done something to help you."

Jesse thrust himself out of his chair and stormed out of the office, and Glory followed him, after one apologetic look at the doctor.

In the examination room, Jesse scooped Liza up in his arms, borrowed bathrobe and all, and held her tightly against his chest. His gaze punctured Glory's spirit like a lance. "You and your lawyer wanted a fight," he breathed. "Well, lady, you've got one!"

Before Glory could work through the wall of pain that surrounded her and respond, Jesse strode out, carrying Liza with him.

Dr. Cupples laid one hand on Glory's shoulder. "Jesse's a good man," he said quietly, "even if he is hot-tempered. He'll come to his senses if you just give him a day or two."

Glory felt broken and bruised inside. She nodded distractedly and went out.

Walking to her mother's diner, she heard Liza's words over and over in her mind… *You didn't want me….*

When Delphine saw her daughter, she was visibly horrified. Stepping back to admit Glory to the little apartment over the diner, she said, "Glory, sweetheart, what's happened? I thought you'd be happy, finding Liza safe—"

Glory sank into a chair and kicked off her eel-skin shoes. They were completely ruined, but she didn't give a damn. "You were right," she said brokenly. "You were right."

Delphine bent to unbutton Glory's coat, as she might have done when her daughter was a child, and pushed it back off her shoulders. Then she took the crocheted afghan from the sofa and draped it tenderly around Glory's legs. "There, now," she whispered soothingly. "What was I so right about?"

"I shouldn't have come here," Glory fretted in utter despair. "All I did was mix Liza up. She ran away because she thought I didn't want her. And, Mama, she could have been hurt or even killed. Someone awful might have picked her up—"

"Hush!" Delphine interrupted with affectionate

harshness. "The child is safe and sound, Glory—that's all that matters." She moved toward the kitchen to brew the inevitable cup of tea, always part of her solution to any heartbreak. "You were right about one thing," she said cheerfully. "That little girl is the spitting image of Bridget McVerdy!"

Glory began to cry softly. Liza might have been saved all this trauma if Glory had just kept her promise to the judge and stayed away from Pearl River. But no, she'd had to come here and blow the lid off everything. Now Liza would not only grieve for Sandy and Gresham, she would suffer with the knowledge that her birth parents had failed her.

When Delphine returned with tea, a little plate of colorful Christmas cookies and a packet of tissue, Glory was slightly calmer. She dried her eyes, no doubt smearing her makeup all over her face, and then blew her nose. When that process was completed, she accepted one cookie and the strong, fragrant tea.

"There is one obvious solution to all this, you know," Delphine said gently, sitting down on the sofa facing Glory and folding her hands.

"What?" Glory sniffled, taking a disconsolate bite out of an angel's wing.

"You and Jesse could get married. Then the two of you could go about making a life for yourselves and your daughter."

Glory shook her head. "I'll admit it, Mama—I'm just crazy enough that I'm as much in love with Jesse as I ever was. I g-guess I'm one of those women who loves pain. But there's no hope for us. Jesse's furious with me—he can't see past the fact that I took money from the judge when I left Pearl River. I hurt him far more deeply than I ever dreamed I could, and he's never going to forgive me."

"Why don't you decide that after you've gone to him and told him the truth, Glory—that you love him desperately?"

Glory imagined the scenario and shrank from the accusations she knew she would see burning in Jesse's eyes. "I can't."

"It would seem you're not all that crazy about pain, after all," Delphine observed with a wry twist to her mouth. She reached for a reindeer cookie and bit off its antlers.

Glory sighed. "You know, Mama, I wish I were more like you. You've had lots of heartache in your life, but it never broke you. You were brave. You just kept putting one foot in front of the other and, lo and behold, here you are with a business of your own and a man who adores you."

"Do you think I never ran away from a problem?" Delphine asked, raising her eyebrows. "If you do, you don't have a very good memory. When we came here to Pearl River, you and Dylan and I, we were on the run from a very bad situation."

"But you started over. You made the best of things. What would you do if you were me?"

"Knowing what I know now? I'd stand toe-to-toe with Jesse Bainbridge and tell him I loved him. Then I'd work at my job and I'd find a way to build some kind of relationship with Liza."

Glory set her teacup aside. She wasn't as courageous as her mother; she couldn't endure Jesse's hatred, or the knowledge that she'd done her own child more harm than good. No, the best thing to do would be to go away.

Eventually Liza's wounds would heal over and so, hopefully, would her own.

She set the afghan aside and rose shakily to her feet. "I'd better go home," she said. "I have things to do."

"I'll drive you there," Delphine told her, standing and going to the closet for her own coat.

"That won't be necessary, Mama," Glory protested woodenly. "My car's at the bank."

"You're in no shape to walk even that far," Delphine insisted. "And you've ruined your shoes. I doubt they'll even stay on your feet."

Sure enough, the high heels were destined for the rubbish bin. Glory accepted a pair of her mother's slippers, since any of her shoes would have been too small, and obediently followed her downstairs to Delphine's little silver car.

Delphine didn't take Glory to the bank parking lot, she took her directly to her apartment. There, she undressed her like a child, put her into a warm flannel nightgown, turned up the heat, and tucked her into bed. Then Delphine brought her a cup of hot lemon juice mixed with water and honey and two aspirin tablets.

Glory dutifully took the aspirin and sipped the lemon concoction. "I'm not sick," she protested.

"You will be, if someone doesn't take care of you," Delphine responded firmly. And then she left the room, and Glory heard her talking on the telephone, telling Harold she was spending the night at her daughter's apartment.

When Glory had finished her drink, she settled down into the covers and closed her eyes. She'd just rest for a few minutes, then she'd get up and telephone her attorney, and Mr. Baker at the bank.

When she awakened, she was instantly aware that hours had passed. Delphine was humming along with Christmas carols on the radio, and something smelled heavenly.

Glory got out of bed and, after a short visit to the bathroom, ventured into the kitchen. The tree was lit, belying the fact that suffering existed anywhere in the world.

Pulling back a chair at the table, Glory sat down. "Hi," she said.

Delphine kissed her forehead, and once again Glory thought how much she'd missed having someone to fuss over her when things were going wrong. "Hi, sweetie. I cooked your favorite for supper—spaghetti and meatballs."

Glory sighed. "That was a good trick, since I didn't have anything in the cupboards or the fridge—I was planning on going shopping tonight after work."

Back at the stove, Delphine was stirring the savory sauce she and she alone could make. Her slender shoulders moved in a pretty shrug. "Harold stopped by the supermarket for me."

"You should have invited him to stay for supper," Glory said, feeling guilty. Here she was, a grown woman, getting in the way of her mother's romance.

"I did," Delphine answered. "He said we needed this time together without him hanging around, getting in the way. Those were his words, by the way, not mine."

Glory propped her chin in one hand. "He's a great guy," she said. "I think if I didn't love you so much, I'd be jealous."

Delphine smiled. "You might find that Jesse is a

'great guy,' if you'd just wade through all that hostility until you reached the real man."

"That calls for a braver soul than mine," Glory answered softly. "And what makes you think Jesse is so wonderful, anyway? Some mothers would resent him, you know, for making their teenage daughter pregnant."

After dishing up two plates of spaghetti and meatballs and bringing them to the table, Delphine went back for salad, wine and garlic bread. Not until everything was ready and she'd taken her seat at the table did she respond. "Jesse had more privileges than you and Dylan did," she said in a thoughtful voice as she and Glory began to eat. "But he's had just as much unhappiness, if not more. First his parents died, then he lost the girl he loved, then Gresham and Sandy perished in that plane crash. I'll wager that on some level Jesse's afraid to let you know how much he still cares for you, thinking you'll either die or disappear again if he does."

Glory bit her lower lip for a moment to keep from crying. She'd done enough of that. "What makes you think Jesse still loves me?"

Delphine chuckled softly. "I *should* have realized it that first morning you were home. He watched you every single minute, except when you were looking at him, of course. And his rage tells me a lot, too. Fury isn't the opposite of love, Glory—indifference is. And Jesse Bainbridge is *anything* but apathetic, where you're concerned."

Swallowing, Glory remembered the night she and Jesse had gone to dinner and ended up making love in his grandfather's car. His passion had been partly anger, but he'd taken the utmost care to please her. Still, when it was over, things hadn't been any different between them. "Face it, Mama. You were right in the first place—I should have stayed away from Jesse and Liza, even after I discovered the truth. Once your wedding was over, I could have gone on to San Francisco, and nobody would have been any the wiser where Liza's parenthood was concerned. I really blew it."

"I'm not so sure of that, darling. A little girl needs a mother, and there's no doubt that that child's been lonely, even though Jesse and Ilene have done their best by her."

Glory's throat thickened. "Big girls need their mothers, too, sometimes," she said, grateful that Delphine had come through when she needed her. Glory had wanted to be there for Liza, but she'd botched everything, and the damage seemed irreparable.

Delphine made a bed on Glory's sofa that night, and Glory slept better, knowing she wasn't alone. In the morning, though, her resolve was as firm as ever. She would make the necessary arrangements and leave Pearl River before she did anything else to hurt her child.

Since it would take time to orchestrate everything, Glory didn't give notice when she reported to work at the bank that morning. She just threw herself into her job and avoided every attempt anyone made at conversation. Everyone from Mr. Baker down to the lowliest file clerk, of course, was wondering exactly what had happened the day before, although most of them had probably gotten the general details by means of the grapevine.

After work she drove to the mall in Fawn Creek, where she bought Christmas presents for Liza, Jill, Ilene, and her mother and Harold. The bright decorations and happy music that had pleased her so much before, when she'd shopped with Liza, were a mockery now. She could hardly wait for the holiday to be over.

Later, at home, she wrapped each present with great care and placed them under the tree as she went. When the doorbell rang, her heart fluttered, but she knew better than to expect Jesse. He'd made his feelings perfectly clear the day Liza ran away.

When Glory pulled back the door, however, there he was.

"Delphine told me you're planning to leave," he said, and he might have been wearing his mirrored sunglasses, his eyes were so devoid of any emotion.

Glory nodded, knowing she should say something but unable to think of anything. And even if she'd managed that, it would have been hard to force words past the twisted knot in her throat.

"Could I come in?" She heard in Jesse's voice what she hadn't seen in his eyes; the effort he was making at self-control.

Still unable to speak, Glory stepped back, and he crossed the threshold warily, moving without his usual confidence and purpose to stand beside the Christmas tree.

Glory had just put a package underneath with Liza's name written on it in big gold letters, and she waited for him to say *his* daughter didn't need any presents from her. If he did, she knew she'd go at him like a wildcat, kicking and screaming and scratching.

But he only said, "Nice tree."

Reluctantly, Glory closed the door. "Thanks," she managed to croak.

He turned to face her. "Liza's doing okay," he said hoarsely.

Glory folded her arms, shielding her heart. "Good," she replied.

Jesse sighed. "I suppose it's for the best. Your leaving Pearl River, I mean."

Glory prayed she wouldn't cry. She had so little pride left as it was. "I suppose," she said.

He took a step toward her, and there was something tender in his eyes, behind the cautious expression she realized now had always been there, even when they were kids. "Glory," he murmured, and the name was a sentence in itself. It was a plea, a reprimand, a shout of fury, a kiss.

His hands rested on the sides of her waist, and Glory gave a despairing whimper, knowing that even now, with her world lying in pieces around her, her need for Jesse was as great as it had ever been.

He pulled her into his kiss and she went willingly, wrapping her arms around his neck. He cupped his powerful hands under her bottom and pressed her to him, while his tongue conquered hers.

"Jesse," she gasped, when he finally broke the kiss, but he didn't hear her. He lifted her T-shirt off over her head, and she let him—she let him because she knew this time was going to be the last, that it would have to sustain her for the rest of her life.

He pushed her bra down, without bothering to unsnap it, so that it rested around her waist in a gossamer pink circle, then lifted her high, so that her plump breasts were level with his face. Glory wrapped her legs around his lean hips and thrust her head back with a cry of relief and welcome when she felt his warm mouth close over a nipple.

Jesse was greedy at her breasts—it was as though

he couldn't get enough of them. He went from one to the other, suckling, nibbling, nipping lightly with his teeth. But after a time, he carried Glory into her room and laid her on her unmade bed with her hips on the edge of the mattress.

She tossed her head from side to side and clutched at the sheets and blankets as he lowered her jeans and panties and then tossed them away, along with her shoes and stockings. Then he parted her legs and slid his hands under her bottom to raise her to his mouth.

When he captured her, she arched her back and clawed frantically at the bedclothes. The last bit of her pride was gone, shriveled to cinders in the heat of his passion. "Jesse—oh, yes—please—*Jesse*—"

He brought her swiftly to a scorching release, stroking her quivering bottom as she flailed under his tongue, stripping off his own clothes while she lay trembling in the aftermath of her satisfaction.

Jesse entered her in one powerful thrust, and she raised her hips to take him to her very depths. He buried his face in her neck as they moved together, now nibbling at the skin there, now raising his lips to her earlobe.

Glory threw herself against him with all the strength she had, desperate for the sweet union that would not be complete until she and Jesse collided in that final, explosive contact, their cries mingling in the velvety darkness of the night.

Jesse burst out with a ragged oath when passion finally overtook him, making him drive deep into Glory's body and remain there, trembling violently as she forced him to give up his seed. Beneath him, she sobbed his name, clasped her hands behind his head and dragged him into a kiss.

"We'll always have that to remember," he said a long time later, sitting up and reaching for his clothes, "if nothing else."

Glory pulled the covers up to her chin and stared at the darkened ceiling. It took all her remaining strength to say the words.

"Goodbye, Jesse."

Chapter 10

Ilene Bainbridge's usually serene eyes flashed with annoyance and frustration. "*Grow up,* Jesse!" she snapped, making no effort to keep her voice down because the bookstore was empty of customers and Liza was still at school. "Here's a bulletin for you, Sheriff—you're not the first guy who's ever been hurt. And if you don't change some of your attitudes, you're going to end up a bitter, vindictive old man, just like Seth!"

Jesse stared at his cousin in amazement. He'd never seen her so angry. "Next you're going to tell me I should expect three ghosts to drop by tonight and point out the error of my ways," he said, trying to lighten the mood.

Ilene went back to unpacking a new shipment of books then, and her movements were still angry and abrupt. "Just go away, Jesse. I don't want to talk to you right now, because I'm going to end up saying a lot of things I'll regret."

He remained where he was, standing beside the counter with his arms folded. "What do you think I should do?" he asked quietly. Jesse wasn't one to let others dictate his opinions, but he had a lot of respect for Ilene. Ever since Gresham and Sandy's death, when custody of Liza had fallen to him, Ilene had been there to provide the female companionship the child needed.

She sighed heavily. "That's not for me to say, Jesse. But if I were you, I'd examine my feelings very closely before I let Glory leave my life again. And I'd try to understand what it is to be eighteen and intimidated by a powerful man like Seth, and I'd be a little forgiving. After all, 'tis the season."

Jesse's phone rang just then and, frowning, he reached for it. "Bainbridge," he said, and his admin answered.

A car accident had been reported, five minutes north of town, the woman told him, and the State Patrol was shorthanded because of all the holiday travelers and the uncommonly heavy snow. They wondered if Jesse's department would take care of this one.

"Tell them I'm on my way," he said. "Are there ambulances on the scene?"

"They're en route," she replied. Jesse thanked her and hung up.

"Merry Christmas," he said to Ilene in a distracted tone of voice, as he wrenched open the door of the bookshop and headed out into the cold. Once he was inside the patrol car, he switched on the lights and siren and made a wide U-turn.

All during the drive, he braced himself for what he might find when he reached the scene of the accident.

"Just don't let there be any kids," he muttered, in case some guardian angel was listening.

Liza came slowly toward Glory, who stood by the little Christmas tree they'd decorated together a few nights before, there in one corner of Ilene's cozy little bookshop. Glory was holding the presents she'd bought for her daughter in arms that trembled slightly.

"Hello, Glory," Liza said cautiously, as though speaking to a bird that might take flight at any instant. Ilene put the closed sign in place, locked the door, and retreated behind the counter to empty the cash register.

Glory held out the presents, and Liza accepted them shyly, with a murmured, "Thank you. I've got something for you, too, but it's upstairs."

Don't let me cry, Glory prayed desperately. *Please, just get me through this, and give Liza a happy life, and I won't ever ask You for anything else.* She waited, not trusting herself to speak, and the child hesitated, too, as though afraid that Glory would leave if she turned her back for a moment.

"You'll wait?" she asked. The slight quaver in the little girl's voice was almost Glory's undoing.

"I'll be right here," she said softly.

With that promise, Liza set the packages Glory had given her on the seat of the rocking chair and scampered upstairs.

Glory swallowed and turned her gaze toward Ilene, who was watching her. "I guess Liza's going to stay right here with you, even though she knows Jesse's her father," she said.

Ilene shook her head. "Jesse's hiring a nanny and

a housekeeper," she said. "He wants Liza to live with him."

"Won't you miss her?" Glory asked, putting her hands in the pockets of her coat in an effort to keep them still.

Ilene smiled. "Of course I will. But I'll see her often."

Before Glory could say any more, Liza returned, proudly carrying a small box wrapped in red-and-white striped paper and tied with curling ribbons of both colors.

"Would you please open it right now?" the child asked.

Glory's heart caught at the carefully contained eagerness she heard in her daughter's voice. Unable to speak, for the moment at least, she began undoing the ribbon and paper. Inside a plain white box, nestled on a bed of cotton, lay a beautiful silver locket.

Sinking her teeth into her lower lip, Glory opened the locket and found a miniature photograph of Liza inside. Several awkward moments passed before she dropped to her knees and took the little girl into her arms. "Oh, Liza, thank you. It's the finest present I've ever had, and I'll wear it always. Whenever I touch it, I'll remember you."

Liza stepped back in Glory's embrace. "Remember me?" she echoed. "Are you going away?"

Glory felt the tears she'd sworn not to shed stinging her eyes. "Yes, baby."

"Why?" The word was plaintive, despairing, and it practically tore out Glory's heart.

Glory took the time to put the locket around her neck and clasp it, needing those moments to get a new grip on her composure. Then she laid her hands on Liza's small shoulders. "Sweetheart, the things I'm going to say might be hard to understand, but I hope you'll try very hard, because it's so important.

"I love you, and I've thought of you every single day of the nine years since I turned you over to the adoption people. And there will never be a day in the future when I don't hold you in my heart and pray that you're happy and well.

"But I know now that it was a mistake for me to stay here in Pearl River, once I realized who you were. Sweetheart, all I've done is cause you trouble and pain, and I'd rather die than go on doing that. So I've got to go away."

"No!" Liza cried, twisting out of Glory's grasp only to fling frantic little arms around her neck. "No! You're my mommy, and you can't go away and leave me—*Please* don't—"

Glory held the child close. Walking out that door in a few minutes was going to be the hardest thing she'd ever done, more difficult even than leaving Liza the first time. But she and Jesse couldn't go on pulling their daughter back and forth between them. "Darling, I promise I'll write, and when you're older, if it's all right with your dad, you can come and visit me." She pulled back far enough to take Liza's quivering chin in her hand and look straight into her tear-filled eyes. "And I want a promise from you, too, Liza Bainbridge. I want your word that you won't ever, ever run away again."

"Glory, *please*—"

She swallowed and held her chin high. "Liza."

"I promise."

Glory kissed her daughter's forehead. "Good. I love

you," she finished. And then she got slowly to her feet and went toward the door.

"Glory!" Liza wailed brokenly.

"God forgive me," Glory whispered, as she wrestled with the lock and then opened the door to go. The thought of Jesse came to her on the cold wind. "God forgive us both."

Without looking back, she hurried out into the dark, chilly night, half-blinded by tears and grief.

Back home, she packed her suitcases, threw away all the food in the refrigerator, and took all the lights and ornaments off the Christmas tree.

Then, after taking a long, hot bath, she dressed and got into her car. Glory drove by Jill's place, but didn't stop, since she'd left an awkward farewell message on her friend's answering machine. And then she went past the diner.

Through the colorfully festooned windows, she saw Delphine and Harold presiding over a punch bowl full of eggnog, and the place was packed with friends. They were expecting Glory, but she couldn't bring herself to stop and go in. She'd telephone later, from somewhere down the road, and hope Delphine and Harold would understand why she was skipping out before their wedding.

There was just one more place she needed to go before leaving Pearl River forever. With a glance toward the little potted Christmas tree she'd bought at the supermarket earlier, Glory headed for the cemetery.

"Drunk driver," one of the ambulance attendants confided to Jesse when he arrived. The man paused after wrapping the patient in warm blankets and strapping him to the stretcher.

Jesse swore and scanned the scene, seeing a large car that looked relatively unmarked and a little one that appeared hopelessly battered. "How many people were hurt?"

"Just this guy," the attendant answered. "He's had a few too many, and his head's banged up pretty good, but my guess is he'll be out of the hospital in time to have turkey dinner with his family tomorrow."

"If he was driving with more than the legal limit of alcohol in his blood," Jesse said quietly, "he's going to spend Christmas in the county jail. Have you got a reading?"

The attendant gave Jesse a number that made him swear again and handed him the man's driver's license. After checking the identification, he bent over and looked down into the party boy's face. "Hey, buddy," he began jovially, "I want to wish you a Merry Christmas on behalf of the Pearl River County sheriff's department. I'm here to offer you our hospitality, since as soon as they're done with you over at the emergency room, we'll be coming by to pick you up. You have the right to remain silent, Mr. Callahan. Anything you say can and will be used against you in a court of law…"

"You don't understand, Sheriff," Mr. Callahan whined, when Jesse had finished reading him his rights. "I only had a couple of eggnogs. Damn it, it's Christmas!"

"Ho, ho, ho," Jesse replied. And then he turned his attention to the shaken family huddled in the small, dented car on the side of the road.

He walked over, smiled and bent to look through the

window as the driver rolled down the glass and said, "Hello, Officer."

Jesse saw two kids with freckles and pigtails sitting in the backseat, clutching their dolls and looking scared, and silently thanked the benevolent fates for sparing them. "Merry Christmas," he said. "Is everybody sure they're okay?"

The driver, a man about Jesse's age, sighed. "We're fine," he said. "Just a little shaken up, that's all."

"How about the car? Does it run?"

The Christmas traveler shook his head. "The ambulance people radioed for a wrecker," he said. "But there probably won't be room in the cab for all four of us, and it's getting pretty cold in here."

Jesse nodded and thrust his hands into the pockets of his jacket. "I'll drive you into town," he said. "But before we go, I need you to tell me exactly what happened here. Is somebody expecting you in Pearl River?"

The woman leaned forward and smiled wanly, and Jesse watched her for signs of shock. "My grandmother, Alice Northrup. She's probably been watching the road ever since noon."

Jesse didn't remember the woman in the car, but he knew right where to find her grandmother. Miss Alice was a little old blue-haired lady who was always hearing prowlers in her backyard. He grinned and opened the door so the little girls in back could get out. "I'll radio the office and have them get in touch with her," he said.

The children looked up at him with serious faces. "Are we arrested?" one of them asked.

The young parents laughed affectionately, but Jesse squatted down to look straight into the child's eyes. "No, ma'am," he said. "If I were to do a thing like that,

Santa Claus would be real put out. And he's one man I don't like to cross."

"We've got presents in the trunk," said the other little girl.

Jesse settled the woman and the two kids and the presents in the patrol car, with the heater going full blast, then radioed the office. Deputy Johnson promised to let Mrs. Northrup know that her loved ones were safe and would be arriving soon.

While the three females sang Christmas carols, Jesse and the husband went over the accident scene. Soon, Jesse's report was complete, and he drove the family to Grandma's house.

He felt a little envious, watching the old woman run out to greet them. That was what Christmas was all about, he thought to himself, and wondered why he couldn't get things right in his own life.

Stopping by the office, he left the report to be typed by Deputy Johnson, who'd drawn duty that night, took a package from the top drawer of his desk, and went back to his car.

The lights of a huge tree were visible through the big front window of the nursing home when Jesse arrived, and he heard the voices of carolers from one of the churches as he came up the walk. The residents, male and female alike, were gathered around the main room, singing, their faces splashed with color.

Jesse smiled and greeted a few of the patients as he worked his way through the room toward the hallway. He'd known without looking that his grandfather wouldn't be among the merrymakers; Seth had never cared much about Christmas.

Reaching the door of the judge's room, Jesse paused and knocked.

"Come in," grumbled a familiar voice.

Jesse went in grinning. "Well," he said, going to stand beside his grandfather's bed, "if it isn't Scrooge himself. Merry Christmas, Gramps."

"Humph!" said Gramps, but he reached out for the present Jesse had brought. "Probably slippers. Or another box of chocolates."

"Wrong," Jesse replied easily, dropping into a chair. He wanted to be home with Liza and Ilene—how he wished Glory would be there, too—but he loved this old coot, for all his cantankerous ways.

The judge ripped open the paper to reveal a kit for building a ship in a bottle. Despite his effort to appear singularly unimpressed, he opened the instructions with fumbling, awkward fingers and peered at them. "Get me my glasses!" he snapped.

Jesse chuckled and took the familiar leather case out of the drawer beside Seth's bed, handing him the bifocals. "I figure it'll take you till next Christmas to put the thing together," he teased. "Then you can just wrap it up and give it back to me."

Seth laughed, in spite of himself. "The hell I will," he said. "Don't you have anything better to do on Christmas Eve besides pick on an old man?"

Sadness touched Jesse's spirit as he thought of Glory again. "I can hang around for a while," he told his grandfather quietly.

"That woman still in town?"

Jesse felt his hackles rise, but he reminded himself that it was Christmas, that Liza and Ilene were waiting for him at the mansion, and that Alice Northrup's family had made it home, safe and sound, to hang up their stockings. Maybe that was all he could ask of the holiday. "You mean Glory?" he asked.

Seth nodded.

"She's leaving soon," Jesse said, and the words left him feeling raw and hollow inside.

"I paid her off, you know."

"Yes, Gramps." Jesse sighed. "I know."

"Told her I'd send that brother of hers straight to jail if she didn't leave you alone," the judge reflected proudly.

Jesse sat bolt upright in his chair, feeling as though somebody had just goosed him with a cattle prod. *"What?"* he rasped. "You involved Dylan in this?"

The judge chuckled, obviously reveling in his own cleverness. "He was a troublemaker. It would have been easy to have him sent up."

Standing now, Jesse gripped the lapels of the old man's bathrobe. He didn't want to scare him, just get his undivided attention. *"You told Glory if she didn't leave, you were going to frame Dylan?"*

Seth nodded, his beetle eyebrows rising a notch. He looked somewhat less amused. "I wanted to protect you, Jesse. And she wasn't going to take the money. I had to do something—"

"Fool," Jesse rasped, turning away, and he wasn't talking to the judge. He was talking to himself. "You damn fool!"

"Now, Jesse, I—"

It was too late for the old man; he'd probably go to his grave believing he'd done the right thing. But Jesse still had time to undo some of his mistakes, and he didn't want to waste a minute.

"Merry Christmas," he said, excited as a kid, giving Seth a quick, affectionate slap on the back. "I'll come out tomorrow and make sure you eat all your turkey and stuffing. But right now, I've got to go!"

"Hey, wait a—"

Jesse was gone before the sentence was completed, striding down the hall, joining a chorus of "God Rest Ye Merry Gentlemen" as he hurried through the main room and out into that cold, snowy Christmas Eve.

He went to Glory's apartment first, breaking the speed limit all the way, but when he pulled up out front, her windows were dark. She was probably with Delphine, over at the diner.

Making a wide turn, Jesse bumped the tires over the sidewalk on the other side of the street and sped toward Delphine's.

There were people jammed inside the diner—mostly folks who didn't have anywhere to go—and carols were being sung at ear-splitting volume. Jesse waded through the crowd until he found Delphine, gripped her gently by one elbow, and hustled her into the kitchen.

"Where's Glory?" he demanded.

Delphine glanced at her watch and frowned. "I don't know. She should have been here by now. I'd better call."

Jesse's throat felt tight for a moment, then he managed to grind out, "I was just at her place. It was dark as a mole's fruit cellar."

Glory's mother gave him an accusing look. "She's been depressed lately," she said pointedly. Then she marched over to the wall phone and punched out her daughter's number. A long time passed before she hung up, her teeth sunk into her lower lip, her brows drawn together.

Before Jesse could say anything else, Jill appeared in the doorway. "I come bearing sad tidings," she said dismally. "It's bad news, bears."

"What?" Jesse snapped.

Jill glared at him. "Don't you get smart with me, Jesse Bainbridge. As far as I'm concerned, this whole thing is your fault!"

"Jill, please," Delphine pleaded, her voice small, and Jill put an arm around her.

"When I came home from doing some last-minute shopping just a few minutes ago, there was a message from Glory on my answering machine. She said she hoped everybody would understand, but she had to leave Pearl River while she still had some of her soul left." Jill paused to narrow her eyes at Jesse, holding Delphine tightly against her side. "She left for San Francisco tonight."

Delphine looked as if she was going to cry, and Jesse hadn't seen her do that since that night ten years before, when he'd come to her half-drunk and begged her to tell him where Glory was. "Without saying goodbye to Harold and me?" she whispered disbelievingly.

"I'm sure she means to call you later tonight," Jill said comfortingly.

"I guess Glory isn't very good at saying goodbye to anybody," Jesse muttered, and then he left the diner by the back way, unable to face any more holiday cheer.

As he slipped behind the wheel of the patrol car, soft, fat flakes of snow began to fall.

"You're not getting away with it this time, Glory," he whispered, reaching for his radio mike. He contacted the office, and got the long-suffering Deputy Johnson. "Call my place, will you, and ask Ilene if Glory's been by."

"Roger," replied the deputy.

A few minutes later, as Jesse was cruising the main street of town, the answer came. Glory had stopped by the bookstore briefly, just about closing time. She'd said goodbye to Liza and left.

Swearing, Jesse pulled over to the side of the road and pulled out his phone. Three long rings later, Ilene answered his telephone at home.

"Bainbridge residence. This is Ilene."

"How is Liza?" Jesse blurted, rubbing his eyes with the thumb and forefinger of one hand.

Ilene sighed. "She's doing okay for somebody who's lost two mothers and one father."

"What the hell did Glory say to her?"

"She said she loved her," Ilene answered somewhat acidly. "Terrible woman."

"Damn it, Ilene, I don't need this right now. I just found out that Gramps forced her into leaving town ten years ago by threatening to throw her brother in jail. I've got to find her."

"Are you thinking what I hope you're thinking?"

"If—*when* I find Glory, I'm going to admit I'm an idiot and beg her forgiveness. And then I'll propose, and if she says yes, we'll go drag Judge Jordal away from home and hearth to issue us a special license and perform the marriage ceremony."

"That would be one jim-dandy Christmas miracle if you could pull it off," Ilene said eagerly. "Good luck, Jesse."

"Thanks," Jesse said, and even though he was grinning like a fool, his voice came out sounding hoarse.

The cemetery was well-lighted, and Glory wasn't surprised to see other people visiting lost loved ones on Christmas Eve. It was the most difficult time of year for the bereaved.

She dusted the snow off Dylan's headstone and then put the little potted tree in front of it. "Merry Christmas," she said, putting one hand to her throat and sniffling once. She squatted down beside the grave and rested one hand against the cold marble stone.

"I know, I know," she said. "I've got to quit hanging around here this way. But you must remember how I was always tagging after you." Glory took a tissue from her coat pocket, dried her eyes and dabbed at her nose. She sighed, and a smile crept across her face. "Remember that Christmas when we hid flashlights under our mattresses and practically synchronized our watches so we could peek at the presents after Mama put them out? You got a baseball glove, and I got one of those dolls that talked when you pulled the string."

Suddenly Glory began to cry. Hard. She put her hands over her eyes and sobbed.

"There now, miss," said a kindly voice, and strong fingers closed around Glory's shoulders and lifted her to her feet. "I like to think them that went before are having Christmas tonight, too, somewhere."

Stunned, Glory lowered her hands to stare into a gentle, weathered old face. "Who are you?"

"Name's Clyde Ballard," the elderly gentleman said, touching the brim of his snow-dusted fedora. "My wife, Sylvia, is buried out here, and I like to come by of a

Christmas Eve and leave her a poinsettia plant. She always loved those pretty red blossoms, and she could make 'em bloom year after year, too. Used to fill our living room with the things."

Glory dried her eyes with the back of one mitten, since she'd already exhausted her tissue supply, and squinted at the man. He didn't look familiar. "You must miss her very much," she said, a little ashamed of her outburst a few minutes before.

"Oh, I certainly do," agreed Mr. Ballard, bending to read the words and dates on Dylan's stone. "And you miss this young fellow, too. It's a pity he died so early."

Glory nodded. She was beginning to feel better. "He was killed in an explosion a couple of months after he joined the air force."

"That's real sad," said Mr. Ballard sincerely. "But I know he wouldn't want you here in the graveyard, crying your pretty eyes out, on Christmas Eve!"

Glory chuckled. "You're right about that."

"Of course I am," the old man responded. "I'm on my way over to Delphine's Diner for some pecan pie and eggnog. You ought to come along—there's always room for one more when *she* throws a party."

Nodding, Glory smiled. "I know," she answered.

Mr. Ballard started to say something else, but just as he opened his mouth, Glory saw a patrol car pull up down by the gates, lights flashing. Her heart surged into her throat.

"Jesse," she whispered.

Mr. Ballard gave a pleased cackle. "You wanted for some crime, young lady?" he teased.

"I'm an incorrigible jaywalker," Glory confided, and Mr. Ballard laughed.

"I'd better run along before the pie's all gone. You sure you don't want to come along?"

Impulsively Glory kissed his cheek. "Maybe I'll be by later," she said. Her heartbeat was loud and fast now, pounding in her ears. "Merry Christmas, Mr. Ballard."

"Merry Christmas to you, little lady," he responded. He passed Jesse on his way down the hill and touched the brim of his hat in that same courtly manner as before.

Jesse didn't even seem to see Mr. Ballard; he was looking up at Glory. Reaching her, he took her shoulders in his hands.

"I thought you left for the money," he said gruffly. "But tonight Gramps told me he threatened to have Dylan framed for some crime if you stayed."

"Or if I said so much as a word to you," Glory clarified, swallowing. "What are you doing here, Jesse?"

He grasped her hand and led her to a nearby bench. After dusting off some of the snow so she could sit, Jesse pressed her onto the bench and dropped to one knee in front of her. Snow and mud were probably seeping through his pant leg, but he didn't seem to care. "Glory, I was wrong. I was stubborn and prideful, and you were right when you said I was only thinking of myself. Will you forgive me? Please?"

Glory blinked, uncertain that any of this was really happening. Maybe it was all an illusion. "Well—okay."

Jesse gave a jubilant burst of laughter, rising to his feet and hauling Glory with him. He put his arms around her and kissed her thoroughly. "I love you," he said when it was over.

She stared up at him. This was real, all right. No

fantasy kiss had ever felt like that. "Well, I love you, too, but—"

He laid a finger to her lips. "But nothing. Will you marry me, Glory? Now—tonight?"

She kissed the tip of his finger and then reluctantly shook her head. "No, Jesse. We have too many things to work out. But I'll marry you in the summer if you still want me."

Jesse held her close, and it felt impossibly good. His lips moved against her temple. "But you won't leave again—you'll stay right here in Pearl River?"

Glory cupped her hands on either side of his face, feeling a new beard scratch against her palms. "I'll stay, Jesse. I promise," she said, and then she stood on tiptoe to kiss him.

Chapter 11

The lights of the Bainbridge mansion glowed golden through the snowy night, and as the patrol car reached the top of the driveway, the door burst open and a small silhouette appeared in the opening.

"Today Ilene told me to grow up," Jesse confessed hoarsely, as he brought the car to a stop in front of the garage, "and I think I finally have. No matter what happens between us over the next six months, Glory, Liza is your child as much as mine, and I won't ever try to keep you away from her again."

Glory squeezed his hand and pushed open the car door. "Liza!" she called in a happy sob.

The little girl scrambled toward her, her voice shrill with surprise and delight. "Glory, *you came back!*"

Glory enfolded her daughter in her arms and held her close, right there in Jesse's snowy yard. "I'll stay if you want me to," she managed to whisper. "Oh, baby, I'm so sorry for the trouble I've caused—I never meant to hurt you…"

Liza pulled back from Glory's embrace and looked up at her, and for a moment it was as though their roles were reversed, and Glory was the child. "I understand, Mom. Aunt Ilene explained about all the things that happened to make you and Uncle Jesse—Dad—unhappy."

The word *Mom* had brought a sheen of tears to Glory's eyes. "Here you are, outside without a coat," she scolded good-naturedly. "Let's get inside before you catch pneumonia."

The interior of the mansion was decorated with cheerful good taste. The scent of a live tree filled the air, and instrumental Christmas music provided a cozy background.

Ilene came forward to kiss Glory soundly on the forehead, Jesse on the cheek. "It's about time," she said, and then, claiming she had to baste tomorrow's turkey, she disappeared into the kitchen.

Jesse put one hand on Glory's back and one on Liza's and ushered his family into the huge living room, where an enormous tree towered in one corner and a fire snapped on the hearth. He took Glory's coat and laid it aside before removing his own and squatting down to look into Liza's eyes.

She was seated in one of the leather wing chairs, her face shining brightly enough to rival the star of Bethlehem. "You're going to marry Mom," she said with the confidence of a seasoned game show contestant.

Jesse glanced back at Glory over one shoulder and grinned before facing his daughter again. "Yeah, I'm going to marry her. But how did you know? Things have been pretty bad lately."

"I wished it, that's why. And I asked my other mommy and daddy to talk to God about it special. After all, they're angels, and they're right there in heaven with Him."

Glory's throat was tight again. She perched on the arm of Liza's chair and laid a hand on her shoulder. The beautiful man and child before her blurred for a moment.

Jesse reached out and tugged affectionately at one of Liza's braids. "I'm sorry I was so bullheaded, sweetheart," he said, his voice low and a little husky. "Will you forgive me?"

She threw her small arms around his neck. "Sure I will, Dad!" she crowed. "I'm not some immature kid, you know!"

Jesse laughed and held her tightly, but the look in his eyes was strictly for Glory, and so was the saucy wink. "I think you'd better call Delphine," he said after a few moments. "Jill reported you officially missing from the fold, and it didn't exactly make your mother's Christmas."

Glory nodded and pulled her phone out of her pocket. She walked over to one of the towering windows and dialed the number at the diner, fiddling with the silver locket Liza had given her earlier while she waited.

Delphine answered almost immediately, and she sounded breathless. "Hello?"

"Mama, it's me, Glory."

"Mr. Ballard said he saw you at the cemetery!" Delphine cried. "Sweetheart, are you all right?"

Glory lifted her eyes and saw Jesse sitting in the

wing chair, with Liza balanced happily on his knee. "Oh, I'm more than all right, Mama. Jesse and I have agreed to try to work things out, and I'm staying here in Pearl River. With any luck, I'll be a bride this summer."

It was plain that Delphine was crying, and that her tears were happy ones. "Oh, darling, that's wonderful."

"And Jesse has promised not to try to keep me away from Liza even if we don't end up as a family."

"You will," Delphine said with certainty. "I swear, this Christmas is just like in the movies. I wouldn't be at all surprised if there was an angel involved somewhere."

Glory watched her daughter's glowing, animated face. "There's an angel involved, all right. Merry Christmas, Mama. I'll see you sometime tomorrow."

Delphine made a sound she called "kiss-kiss," bid her daughter a magical night, and hung up.

Liza was about to hang up her stocking, when Glory returned from making the call. It was an enormous thing, almost as tall as its owner. Jesse lifted his daughter by the waist so she could reach one of the special hooks set into the underside of the mantel.

The knowledge of those hooks eased a tightness in Glory's heart. Knowing Seth Bainbridge had once been a little boy, eagerly hanging a stocking above this same fireplace, washed away the last of the bitterness she'd held toward the old man. Even better was the relative certainty that other Bainbridge children would celebrate their Christmases here, too. Her children and Jesse's.

"I've got to get back to work," Jesse said with a sigh when he'd set Liza on her feet again.

Liza nodded, evidently used to his erratic schedule. Then her eyes shifted to Glory. "You'll stay, won't you? You'll be here in the morning, when I wake up?"

Under any other circumstances, Glory would have gently refused. She didn't have any compunctions at all about sleeping with Jesse—as far as she was concerned, he was already her mate—but she hadn't planned on sharing his bed with Liza in the same house until after the wedding. Still, Liza had been through a great deal in her young life, and she deserved to have her mother nearby on this special night.

"I'll stay," Glory said with a shy glance at Jesse.

His dark eyes smoldered with teasing passion as he gazed at her, making a blush rise from her breasts to her face. After kissing Liza good-night and sending her off to find a favorite storybook, Jesse took Glory's hand and pulled her close to him. "I'm going to make very thorough love to you tonight," he vowed quietly.

Glory trembled against him, feeling the promises his body was making to hers. "Jesse—"

"I know," he interrupted, his lips almost upon hers. "It's only for tonight, and you're not moving in until after the wedding. Which is not to say I won't have you at *your place* whenever I get the chance." He kissed her, his tongue seeking entrance to her mouth with gentle insistence and then breaking down the barriers to conquer her utterly and give her a foretaste of what awaited her.

When he finally released her, Glory was clinging to the front of his shirt with both hands just so she wouldn't slide to the floor. "D-do you still sleep in the same room?"

Jesse grinned. "No, ma'am. That room is Liza's now. I'm in the big master suite at the other end of the hall."

Glory blushed and swallowed. Where this man was concerned, she had no pride, at all. But then, she'd always known that. "I'll be there waiting when you get home, Jesse," she promised.

He took a teasing nibble at her lower lip before responding, "Don't expect one ride over the moon and the proverbial long winter's nap," he warned, his voice throaty and low. "We've got a lot of time to make up, and I intend to show you what you've missed."

She let her forehead rest against his shoulder for a moment, then looked up at him with a soft smile. "You enjoy the idea that I'll be thinking about all the things we're going to do, and wanting them, don't you?"

"Yes," he answered without hesitation, and then he kissed her again, swatted her once on the bottom and went out.

Moments later, Liza returned, her storybook gripped in both hands. "Will you read this to me, please?" she asked hopefully. "It's *A Visit From St. Nicholas*."

Sitting down in Jesse's chair and pulling the child onto her lap, Glory uttered a silent prayer of thanks and began to read. Ilene crept in, with hot buttered rums for both herself and Glory, and listened to the old favorite with a smile on her face.

When she'd completed the poem, Glory just sat, reveling in the fact that she was holding the daughter she'd once thought she'd never see again. It was pure bliss knowing they wouldn't have to be separated anymore. And then there was the sweet certainty that later, when the presents had been set out and Christmas Day was about to dawn, Jesse would take her to his bed and make love to her.

Presently, Liza laid her head against Glory's shoulder and yawned hugely.

"I think somebody needs to say good-night," Ilene observed gently.

Liza looked up at Glory's face. "But you won't go away, will you, Mom?"

Glory touched the tip of Liza's nose with an index finger. "I won't go away," she promised. "Not only that, but I'll tuck you in and hear your prayers, too."

A few minutes later, mother and daughter climbed the stairs, with their intricately carved banister. Jesse's old room had been so thoroughly changed that Glory wouldn't have recognized it. Pink-and-gold-striped paper covered the walls, and there was a four-poster, billowing with lace and ruffles, where Jesse's bed had been. Teddy bears and dolls lined the window seat, instead of model airplanes and copies of *Sports Illustrated.*

After brushing her teeth and putting on a flannel nightgown in the small adjoining bathroom, Liza knelt down beside the bed, and Glory took a place beside her.

"Thank you, God, for letting me have a mom and dad again. And thank You that it's Christmas. You've been real good to me, so if Santa Claus—" Liza paused here to looking meaningfully at Glory, letting her know she was speaking in the figurative sense "—if Santa Claus doesn't bring me a new video game or a Barbie, I'll be perfectly happy. Good night, God, and Merry Christmas."

Glory rested her forehead against her folded hands for a few moments to hide the tears in her eyes. Although they sprang from joy, not sorrow, she was afraid Liza would misunderstand them and be worried. "Thank You, God," she echoed in a broken voice.

After that, Liza climbed into bed, and Glory tucked

the covers in around her and gave her a sound good-night kiss.

"I'm so glad you came back," the child whispered.

"Me, too," Glory answered, her voice shaking. "I love you, sweetheart."

"I love—you," Liza replied, stopping once to yawn.

Downstairs, Glory found that Ilene had reheated her buttered rum, and she raised it gratefully to her lips. "This has been quite some day," she told her friend.

Ilene smiled. "Yes, it has." She paused to sip from her cup and gaze at the glowing embers in the fire. "Jesse was planning to roust Judge Jordal from his bed and force him to marry the two of you this very night."

Glory laughed as an image of Jesse strong-arming an old man in a flowing nightshirt and matching cap filled her mind. "We've agreed to wait six months before we get married. Not that I have any doubts. I want to show Jesse that I'm in for the duration this time."

Ilene reached out to pat her hand. "You're a wise woman, Glory Parsons. By the time June rolls around, our stubborn Jesse should be in a very flexible frame of mind."

The two women sat and talked for about an hour, and then Ilene excused herself. "Liza will be up early, tearing into the presents," she said. "Therefore, I'm off to get whatever sleep I can."

Glory nodded and, when Ilene had been gone for a few minutes, she went to the fireplace and threw in another chunk of wood.

A little after midnight, Jesse returned, smiling when he saw Glory sitting there, enjoying the quiet, the fire and the lights on the tree.

He approached and pulled her out of the chair just

long enough to sit in it himself. Then he placed her carefully on his lap. "I stopped a fat guy for speeding tonight on my way home," he told her, looking solemn as he traced her jawline with a chilly finger. "He was driving a sleigh, if you can believe it, pulled by eight tiny reindeer."

Glory laughed, thinking if she loved this man any more, she'd burst like an overfilled balloon. "I *don't* believe it, Sheriff. I think you must have been hallucinating."

He shifted and pulled a small velvet box out of the pocket of his coat. "If I was hallucinating," he reasoned, "how come he gave me this?"

Glory stared at the object. "Is that…?"

Jesse attempted to look very exasperated. "Of course it isn't the same ring I bought for Adara. Don't you think I have any class, at all? I persuaded Harvey Milligan to open the jewelry store." He set the box in her palm.

Her fingers trembled slightly as she lifted the lid. Immediately a cluster of diamonds caught the lights of the Christmas tree and the flicker of the fire and held them fast. "Oh, Jesse, it's beautiful."

He took the ring out of its little slot and slid it onto her finger. Only then did he ask, "Will you marry me, Glory?"

She kissed him, treating him to previews of coming attractions. "Yes," she finally answered. "Next June, just like we planned."

Jesse sighed philosophically. "Next June," he agreed. Then he gave Glory a swat and set her on her feet. "Let's get busy, wife-of-Christmas-future. We've got a stocking to fill, and toys to set out. Then I'm going to take you upstairs and do right by you."

He peeled off his jacket and tossed it aside, then removed his gun and holster and locked them carefully away.

Glory had never had so much fun as she did filling Liza's stocking with an orange and a candy cane and a variety of other goodies. She helped Jesse set out the video games and other toys Liza had wanted, including the Barbie doll she'd asked for, a set of delicate little china dishes and a huge stuffed horse.

Jesse and Glory stood holding hands for a while, admiring their handiwork, then Jesse checked the screen on the fireplace and turned out the Christmas-tree lights. Glory was caught by surprise when he swept her into his arms, Rhett Butler–style, and carried her up the stairs and along the hallway.

The master suite was enormous, with its own wood-burning fireplace and room enough for a couch and two chairs, not to mention the bed. There was a table, too, beside bay windows, and Glory dreamed of sitting there, watching the moonlight play on the snow.

"Do you always work nights?" Glory asked.

Jesse set her down and immediately started unbuttoning his uniform shirt. "My hours are crazy." He sighed. "Sometimes it's nights, sometimes it's days, sometimes it's twenty-four or forty-eight hours straight." He bent his head and nipped at one of Glory's nipples, causing it to push against the fabric of her bra. "I guess you're just going to have to figure I'm going to be making love to you at some very weird times. I can promise you one thing, Glory—it'll happen often. Want to share my shower?"

Glory nodded, and her eyes drifted closed as Jesse began unbuttoning her shirt. He stripped her slowly, pausing to kiss and nibble on everything he bared, and Glory was trembling by the time he took her hand and led her into the bathroom.

After making sure both spigots in the double shower were spraying warm water, Jesse stepped into the stall and pulled Glory after him.

She knew if she didn't take the lead right away, Jesse would, so she reached for the soap and a large sponge and began to wash him gently. He gave a low groan and braced himself against the wall of the shower with both hands when she reached his manhood and knelt to rinse him under the spray.

He cried out like some magnificent, wounded beast when she began treating him to some very deliberate attentions. "So long," he moaned after several moments of hard breathing. "Oh, God, Glory, it's been so long…"

"Shh," she soothed, and then she made a circle with her tongue and Jesse's buttocks tensed under her hands.

He pleaded raggedly, and she gave him what he asked for, along with a series of little bites and kisses calculated to drive him crazy. Finally, in a fever, he hauled Glory to her feet and devoured her mouth in a kiss that left no doubt who was in charge.

She was dazed when he'd finished, and nothing could have made her protest when he turned her and set her hands on the steel safety bar affixed to the inside of the shower. He set her legs apart, and she drew in a deep breath because she knew actual intercourse with Jesse was going to be better than anything her fantasies could offer up.

His hands caressed her naked breasts for a few moments, then went to her hips, holding her firmly, setting her in position. "Do you want me, Glory?" he asked, his lips moving against her neck, the warm water streaming over both of them.

"Oh, yes," she answered. "Yes, Jesse." And she felt him at the center of her femininity, seeking entrance.

He gave her an inch of himself, just enough to tease. She was expanding to take him in, and the sensation was urgent and sweet. He continued to taste her neck. "I could make you wait," he reflected sleepily. "I could make you wait for a long time."

"No, Jesse—I want you—I need you *now*—" Because she was not without power herself, Glory gave a little twist of her hips and wrung a long groan from Jesse's throat.

He muttered words of surrender, and love, and then he drove deep into her, and she welcomed him with a gasp of joy.

At first their movements were slow and measured, but as the friction of that most intimate contact increased moment by moment, passion drove them before it, like a giant, swelling tide threatening to swallow them up.

When they were breathless from the chase, Jesse suddenly stiffened and uttered a warrior's low cry, his hands tightening over Glory's breasts. Glory felt his warmth spilling deep inside her and welcomed him, and in the next instant she went soaring over the precipice herself. Hoisted high on his shaft, his fingers working her nipples, Glory quivered repeatedly and then collapsed against the shower wall, exhausted.

But just as he'd promised, Jesse was far from through with her. He vowed to spend fifty years making up for the ten they'd sacrificed to pride and youth, and Glory looked forward to every minute.

After they'd gently washed and dried each other, Jesse took his bride-to-be to his bed and laid her there, watching the firelight play over her skin with solemn, hungry eyes. "You're so beautiful," he rasped, "and I need you so much."

Glory put her hands behind his head and pressed him to her breast, where he drank hungrily, while his fingers trailed over her thighs. Presently, Jesse caught Glory's hands together and held them high above her head, and she whimpered at being made more vulnerable to him.

It was only the beginning of vulnerabilities, and of pleasure. Over the course of that night, Glory surrendered again and again as Jesse put her through her paces, changing their positions and his demands regularly. Sometimes it was Jesse who submitted, but more often it was Glory.

And during those brief moments when her thoughts were at all coherent, she wondered how she had survived ten years without Jesse tuning her body and then causing it to play symphonies.

They slept for an hour, but then Jesse awakened Glory in a most delicious way and had her thoroughly, all over again. She was allowed to shower in peace only when Liza was up and around.

Her suitcase was lying on the bed when she came out wrapped in a towel.

"I stopped by your car and picked this up on the way home last night," Jesse said, watching her with those brazen brown eyes of his. "Can you imagine the speculation that must be going on? I can hear it now—'I tell you, Mavis, she parked her car at the graveyard and disappeared without a trace.'"

Glory laughed and took out clean underwear, a pair

of jeans and a roomy aqua-blue cable-knit sweater. "Give the gossips their due, Jesse," she said, beginning to dress. "They're saying I've been in your bed all night, and they're right."

He stopped her as she would have hooked her bra and gave each nipple a warm suckling before snapping the front catch himself and pulling the straps up onto her shoulders. "I love you, Glory."

Her cheeks heated as she looked up at him because, after all of it, she found herself wanting him to lay her back on the bed and take her again. She didn't know how she was going to wait six months to share this room with him on a regular basis, but she was determined to do it, because she wanted their marriage to be long and unshakably solid. "Oh, Jesse, I'm so wanton."

Jesse laughed. "Patience, Glory. There's always tonight at your place."

She smiled and put her arms around his neck to kiss him, teasing his lips with her tongue. "Since it's my bed, Sheriff," she said, "I'm going to be calling all the shots."

Reluctantly Jesse backed away, but not before Glory lightly touched the front of his jeans and found him reaching for her.

They went downstairs separately, Glory first, and Jesse about five minutes later.

It snowed on New Year's Eve, but that didn't stop Harold and Delphine's guests from attending the wedding. The church was still decorated with poinsettia plants from Christmas, and candlelight flickered romantically.

Glory stood at the front of the church, wearing her royal blue bridesmaid's dress. Happy tears dropped into her bouquet of roses and carnations, and soon the vows had been exchanged and the bride and groom were hurrying down the aisle to strains of joyful music. As Glory turned to follow, she made eye contact with the man who would be her groom when summer came, and six months seemed to be a very long time.

On the other hand, when you compared it to forever, half a year was nothing. Glory and Jesse had arranged for special counseling with the pastor, for themselves and for Liza, and they were already working hard at learning to be a family.

She'd messed up badly once, and Glory didn't intend to make the same mistake again. She knew now that love doesn't just happen, it has to be nurtured and cared for.

Jesse was waiting at the foot of the aisle, his arm out for Glory, and she went into its curve willingly. "I'll drive you over to the reception," he whispered into her ear, managing to trace it once with the tip of his tongue, "but I can't promise to take the most direct route."

Glory was grateful that everyone was looking at Delphine, who made a lovely bride in her pale rose dress and big picture hat, because she herself was blushing. "Jesse Bainbridge," she scolded. But she let him put her into his grandfather's fancy car, and she didn't say a single word when he turned off down a side road and headed for the rest area overlooking the river.

Her protests were cut off with a kiss that made her go damp all over, and when Jesse made the seat go back, she just went with it, already too weak to sit up without support.

"Jesse, they'll miss us—my mother's wedding—"

"We'll be back in plenty of time for the pictures and

the cake," Jesse said, raising her billowy skirt to find her with his hand and caress her.

Instinctively, Glory raised her knees up, then let them fall wide apart. Her hands gripped the tufted seats as Jesse ducked under her skirt to tease her through the thin, tautly drawn panty hose. When he peeled them down, there were no protests from Glory, because he'd already created a need that made it hard for her to lie still.

He parted her, and she heard his muffled chuckle under all those ruffles. She would have sworn he said, "Glory, Glory, Hallelujah!"

* * * * *

Mr. and Mrs. Harold Seemer
request the honor of your presence
at the marriage of their daughter,
Glory Ann Parsons,
to Mr. Jesse Alexander Bainbridge on
Saturday June twenty-second at 2:00 p.m.
First Lutheran Church Pearl River, Oregon

Dear Reader,

A snowstorm, a handsome bodyguard and a woman on the run with her precious baby. What more do you need to create a thrilling romance?

Snowbound with the Bodyguard was originally one of the books in the Wild West Bodyguard miniseries, a series I wrote with great enjoyment.

I love a man who is a natural protector, one who would take on anything and anyone to protect a vulnerable woman and her child. Dalton West is that man. I fell in love with him as he came to the aid of Janette Black, a woman who needed a hero as danger closed in.

I hope you enjoy reading their story as much as I enjoyed writing it.

Happy reading!

Carla Cassidy

SNOWBOUND WITH THE BODYGUARD

Carla Cassidy

Prologue

"Order up." Smiley Smith, owner and short-order cook at Smiley's Café, banged the small bell on the counter to punctuate his words.

Janette Black wiped her hands on her cheerful red-and-white apron, then walked over to retrieve the Thursday special.

She grabbed the plate and served it to the man seated at the long counter. "Here you go, Walter." She smiled at the old man who came in every Thursday afternoon regular as clockwork for Smiley's meatloaf.

"Thank you, honey. Can I bother you for another cup of coffee?" Walter offered her a sweet smile.

"For you, Walter, it's no bother." She turned around and went to get the coffeepot, grateful that the lunch rush was over and she only had two more hours in her shift. Then she could go home and snuggle her little boy and visit with Nana until it was time for her to be back here first thing in the morning.

"How's that grandmother of yours?" Walter asked as she poured his coffee.

Janette's heart warmed at thoughts of her grandmother. "She's okay. We have her heart condition under control. She tires easily, but she's doing just fine."

Walter laughed. "She's a corker, that one. It will take more than a couple of strokes to keep her down."

As Janette began to wipe down the countertop, she smiled. Her grandmother wasn't just a corker, she was the woman who had raised Janette from the time she was three and the woman who was now helping Janette raise her little boy. Nana's last stroke had been nearly a year ago, but she had astounded the doctors with her recovery.

Janette was just giving the shiny surface a final swipe when the tinkle of the bell over the front door indicated another diner arriving.

She looked up and her blood froze. There were three of them, all wearing the khaki uniforms of law enforcement. Sheriff Brandon Sinclair led the way, swaggering in followed by two of his trusted deputies.

There were only two cafés in Sandstone, Oklahoma, and she'd chosen to work at Smiley's because the other place, Lacy's, was where Sinclair and his men usually ate their lunch.

Sheriff Sinclair surveyed the café like a king overseeing his domain, his ice-blue eyes narrowing just a touch as his gaze landed on Janette.

Take a table, she mentally begged. If they sat at the table, then Heidi, Janette's coworker, would wait on them. Janette had spent the past year of her life doing everything possible to avoid contact with the sheriff.

As he and his deputies headed toward the counter, her stomach bucked with a touch of nausea and her heart began to beat the rhythm of panic.

She couldn't lose it. Not here. Not now. She refused to let him know how he affected her, knowing that he would relish her fear.

He's just another customer, she told herself as the three seated themselves at the counter. "Can I take your orders?" she asked, surprised to hear her voice cool and collected despite all the emotions that quivered inside her.

"Coffee," Sinclair said. "What kind of pie is good today?"

"Apple," Janette replied tersely, then added, "the apple is always good."

"Then let's make it coffee and pie for all of us," Sinclair said.

Janette nodded and turned to get the coffeepot. She could do this. As long as she didn't look at him too long, as long as she didn't get close enough to smell his cologne. She had a feeling if she got a whiff of that cheap, cloying smell she might vomit.

She filled their cups, trying to ignore the way Sinclair's eyes lingered on her breasts. Her throat tightened and her heart banged harder against her ribs.

"Never guess what I heard through the grapevine," Sinclair said to his deputies.

"What's that, Sheriff?" Deputy Jed Billet asked.

"I heard that Janette has a little baby boy. What is he, about five months old, Janette?" Sinclair gazed at her knowingly.

She turned to get their pie, her hands trembling as she opened the display case that held the desserts. He knew. Dear God, he knew.

"Gonna be tough, being a single parent," Deputy Westin said.

As she placed the pie in front of Sinclair he reared back on the stool. "A boy. There's something special about a boy, don't you think so, Jed? I mean, I love my three little girls, but I always dreamed about how great it would be to have a son. Unfortunately, all my wife could pop was girls. Still, a boy needs a father, don't you agree?"

A roar went off in Janette's head. She had to escape. She had to take her son and leave Sandstone because she knew what evil Sheriff Brandon Sinclair was capable of, and as long as she remained in Sandstone he had the power to do whatever he wanted to do.

If he decided he wanted her baby boy, she knew he'd find a way to get him.

Chapter 1

"I'm sorry, ma'am, but I just got word that the bus isn't coming."

Janette blinked and stared up at the man in charge of the Cotter Creek bus station. She straightened in her chair as she realized she must have dozed off. She wrapped her arms around her still-sleeping son and gazed at the man with confusion.

"Excuse me?" she said.

"The bus. It's not coming. It's been held up by weather."

"By weather?" Dulled by sleep, she stared at him as if he were speaking a foreign language.

He nodded. "Ice." He pointed out the window. Janette followed his finger and gasped in surprise as she saw the icy pellets falling from the sky. The ground was already covered with at least an inch.

Where had it come from? When she'd arrived at the bus station two hours ago the skies had been thick with gray clouds, but there hadn't been a hint of snow. Of course the last thing on her mind when she'd left Sandstone had been the weather forecast.

She looked back at the man and tried to swallow against the sense of panic that had been with her since she'd packed her bags and left Sandstone that afternoon. A friend of her grandmother's had driven her the thirty miles to Cotter Creek, where a bus to Kansas City ran every other day. It was supposed to run today.

"Will it be here tomorrow?" she asked.

"Depends if the weathermen are right or wrong. They say we're in for a blizzard, but they're wrong more often than they're right." He shrugged his skinny shoulders and pulled a stocking cap over his head. "You best get settled in someplace for the night. I've got to close down here. Check back in the morning and I'll know more about the schedule." He was obviously in a hurry, tapping his heel as he looked at her expectantly.

"Of course." She stood, grateful that Sammy still slept in his sling against her chest. She didn't want to show how scared she was, didn't want to do anything that might draw unnecessary attention to herself.

She'd find a pay phone, call the nearest motel and get a room for the night. Hopefully she'd still have time to get as far away from Sandstone as possible before Brandon Sinclair even knew she'd left the small town.

She grabbed the handle of her large suitcase and draped the diaper bag over her shoulder, still groggy from the unexpected catnap.

She was barely out the door before the bus station, little more than a shack, was locked up behind her. The ice that fell had coated the sidewalk and created shiny surfaces on everything else in sight. Under different circumstances she might have found it beautiful.

With Sammy safely snuggled beneath her wool coat, she looked up and down the street. She didn't know Cotter Creek well. Perhaps there was a bed-and-breakfast someplace nearby where she could spend the night.

A new disquiet soared through her as she eyed the deserted streets. It was just after six but it was as if the entire town had packed their bags and left. There wasn't a person or a car on the street.

She should have asked to use the phone in the bus station. She should have asked the man where she could get a room for the night. But the nap had dulled her senses, and he'd hurried her out too fast for her to think clearly.

The sight of a phone booth in the distance rallied her spirits. Cotter Creek was near a major highway, and that meant there had to be a motel somewhere nearby.

Pulling the suitcase behind her, she hurried as fast as the slick concrete would allow toward the phone booth, feeling as if luck was on her side as she spied the small phone book hanging on a hook just inside the door.

She stepped into the booth and closed the door behind her, grateful to be out of the cold wind and stinging ice. With cold fingers she thumbed through the book until she found the page with the motel listings. Make that one listing. The Cotter Creek Motel.

Digging change from her purse, she felt Sammy stir as if the rapid beating of her heart disturbed his sleep. She drew a deep breath to steady her nerves.

She'd wanted to get as far away as possible as quickly as possible from Sandstone and Brandon Sinclair. Okay, so she couldn't get on the bus tonight. She'd cool her heels in a motel room and catch the bus the next day. Although she hated to part with a dime of the money that was neatly folded and tucked into a side pocket in her purse, she really didn't have a choice.

She *had* to get out of town tomorrow. Thirty miles was far too close to the devil and his minions. She wouldn't be satisfied until she was a thousand miles away. Once she got settled in a new town, she'd send for Nana and the three of them would build a new life where Brandon Sinclair couldn't bother them.

She dropped the change into the slot and punched in the number for the Cotter Creek Motel. A man answered on the third ring. "No room at the inn," he said.

"Is this the Cotter Creek Motel?" she asked, her hand tightening on the receiver.

"Yeah, but if you're looking for a room, we're full up. They've shut the highway down up north and I've got a houseful of travelers. I've even rented out my sofa in the lobby." He sounded positively gleeful. "Sorry." He hung up.

Janette held the receiver for a long moment, her heart pumping with panic once again. She hung up and frantically thumbed through the skinny phone book, looking for a listing of a bed-and-breakfast, a rental room, anywhere she could get a warm bed for the night. There was nothing.

She wanted to call her grandmother and ask her what to do. Where to go. But she'd only worry Nana, and that was the last thing she wanted to do.

Besides, Janette was an adult. She had to handle this. She was twenty-four years old and a mother, and the most important thing in her life at the moment was little Sammy. She had to get him someplace safe and warm.

She leaned her head against the cold glass of the booth and watched as the ice began to turn to snow and pick up in intensity. What was she going to do? She and Sammy couldn't spend the night out in the elements.

Desperation filled her and she felt a panic attack coming on. The palms of her hands grew slick with sweat as her throat seemed to constrict. She closed her eyes and drew in deep breaths, forcing the attack away. She didn't have time to be weak now. Sammy needed her, and she needed to get him someplace safe for the night.

She opened her eyes once again. The clouds and ice were creating an early twilight. She straightened as she saw a light shining from a window of one of the storefronts in the next block.

Where there was light there might be somebody who could direct her to a place for the night. She checked to make sure her coat was securely fastened to keep Sammy as warm as possible, pulled up her hood and tied it beneath her chin, then stepped out of the phone booth and into the wind that had begun to howl with fierce intensity.

She kept her gaze focused on the light, a beacon of hope. It didn't take long for her gloveless fingers to turn numb and her cheeks to burn with the cold. Ice pellets pinged on the sidewalk and her bare skin.

She walked slowly, carefully, not wanting to fall on the slick walkways. Before she reached the radiating light, she saw the shingle that hung above the doorway. West Protective Services.

She knew that name. She frowned thoughtfully, then

remembered. There had been an article in the paper not too long ago, a human interest story about the family who owned and operated a bodyguard business. The article had described the family as honorable, trustworthy people who put their lives on the line for their clients.

If she remembered the article correctly, they had been instrumental in cleaning up Cotter Creek when a development company had tried to take ranch land and had hired people to kill the ranchers.

You have to trust somebody, a little voice whispered in her head. She had no other choice. Once again she felt her throat closing up, a quickening of her heart and a sense of doom that portended one of her panic attacks.

Not giving herself a chance to second-guess her decision, she started for the door. She reached for the door handle just as a man barreled out and into her.

He bumped her with just enough force to cause her to lose her footing on the slippery sidewalk. She felt herself careening backward, but before she could fall, two big strong hands grabbed hold of her shoulders and steadied her.

"Sorry. Are you all right?" His deep voice was nearly carried away by the wind.

She looked up into the greenest eyes she'd ever seen. In an instant she assessed him. Shockingly good-looking, bold features, tall, with broad shoulders beneath a thigh-length black coat. He looked at her as if she were an apparition blown from the North Pole.

She had no idea if she could trust this man or not. Under any other circumstances she would never ask a stranger, particularly a man, for help. But she was out of options. "Please…I need help."

* * *

All Dalton West wanted was to get home and out of the snow. He'd been absorbed in paperwork and hadn't noticed the weather until he'd gotten up to stretch and had realized the forecasted storm was upon them. He'd hurriedly shut down the computer and turned off the coffeepot, his only goal to get to his nearby apartment. The last thing he wanted was to be snowed in at the office.

But with this woman looking at him with eyes the color of a summer Oklahoma sky, eyes that were filled with both desperation and wariness, he reopened the office door and ushered her inside. She swept past him, pulling a large suitcase behind her as she entered.

As he stepped back inside she turned to face him. "I… You protect people, right?"

He nodded, wondering what she was doing out in the snow. "That's my job."

"I want to hire you for the night…to protect me."

"Protect you from who?" he asked.

She gave a nervous laugh. "Not who…what. I need you to protect me from the weather. I arrived here in Cotter Creek a couple of hours ago to catch the bus, but it seems the bus isn't coming this evening. I need a place to stay for the night, but the motel is all booked up." At that moment the sound of a crying baby came from beneath her coat.

She unfastened the buttons to reveal a tiny boy in a blue coat. Dalton didn't know much about babies, but the little guy looked to be only a couple of months old. As his blue eyes landed on Dalton, he grinned and bounced in his sling.

"This is my son, Sammy, and I'm uh…Jane Craig. I

was hoping you could find us a room or something for the night," she said. "I can pay you for your trouble."

There had been just enough hesitation before she spoke her name that Dalton sensed she was lying. She had a pretty face, heart-shaped with those big blue eyes and pale eyebrows that arched perfectly above them. Her trembling full lips were a faint shade of blue, indicating to him that she had already been outside too long.

Why would she lie about her name? Or had he just imagined that moment of hesitation? Business had been slow enough lately that maybe he was looking for mystery where there was none.

"I'm Dalton West," he replied, then frowned and looked out the window where the blowing snow was creating almost whiteout conditions. He could think of several places he might be able to get her a bed for the night, but none of them were within walking distance, and nobody in their right mind was going to get in a car to come and pick her up.

There was really only one alternative, and it wasn't one that made him a happy man. "Look, I have an apartment two blocks from here. You can stay there for the night and I'll bunk downstairs with my landlord."

It was obvious from the expression on her face that she didn't like the idea. Dalton raked a hand through his hair and tamped down an edge of impatience. He certainly could understand her reticence. She was a young woman alone with a baby and he was a virtual stranger. In her circumstances he wouldn't be thrilled by his suggestion.

"Oh, no…I couldn't," she began.

"Look, Jane. I'm a bodyguard by profession. I make a living protecting people. You'll be safe for the night.

Besides, I don't know what else to tell you. We're out of options." His glance went back out the window, then he looked back at her. "And we need to get going before we can't get out of here."

She hesitated another minute. "I'll hire you for the night to protect me. We'll keep it a business deal."

"Fine. You can write me a check when we get to my place." It was obvious to Dalton that she couldn't afford their usual fee. Her coat was worn and her shoes looked old. This was not a woman rolling in dough.

As she rebuttoned her coat to protect her son from the elements, he grabbed hold of her suitcase.

They stepped back out into the howling wind and stinging snow, and Dalton fought the impulse to take her by the elbow to help her keep her balance on the slick sidewalk. There was something about her posture, something about the look in her eyes that warned him she would not appreciate it.

The howling wind made conversation next to impossible so they trudged side by side in silence, heads bent against the mix of ice and snow falling from the sky.

It was difficult to pull the suitcase on its wheels through the thick snow that blanketed the ground. Instead Dalton picked it up by the handle to increase their pace.

The two-block walk seemed to take an eternity. He breathed a sigh of relief as they turned off Main onto Maple Street. He could barely see just ahead the white two-story house with the wraparound porch he called home.

Normally, Dalton didn't mind being snowed in for a day or two. He was a solitary man who enjoyed being alone, but it looked as if at least for the short-term he'd be spending his snow time with his landlord, George.

When they reached the house he motioned toward the staircase that led up the outside. His apartment was the top floor. She went up the stairs before him as he hefted the heavy suitcase up stair by stair.

At the top he unlocked the door, then opened it and gestured her inside. He followed just after her, flipping on the interior light and welcoming the warmth the place offered.

He turned to look at her. Her lips were now completely blue and she trembled almost uncontrollably. "Let's get out of these wet coats and shoes," he said.

The whole scene felt a little surreal. The snow outside, a mysterious woman and baby…it was like the setup of some ridiculous movie.

He unbuttoned his coat and watched her do the same. Her gaze didn't meet his but rather swept around the room like a rabbit hunting for a safe burrow.

He followed her gaze, taking in the place he'd called home for the past two years. When George's wife had died five years ago, the old man had renovated the house with this apartment upstairs. It was a way for him to keep his house and not feel so alone.

The apartment was roomy, with a nice-sized living room, a small but fully functioning kitchen, a half bath off the laundry room and a large bedroom with a full bathroom. Dalton had furnished it in a minimalist, functional style. But as he saw it through another's eyes he realized it was a cold space, with little personality.

He frowned and took her coat from her to hang in the small utility room off the kitchen. "Make yourself comfortable," he said and gestured to the sofa. "I'm just going to put these wet things in the other room."

He left her there, hung the wet coats on hangers to dry, then returned to find her still standing in the center of the room, rubbing the baby's back as he once again slept.

"Where were you headed?" he asked.

She jumped at the sound of his voice, as if she'd momentarily forgotten he was there. "Uh, Kansas City. I was going to visit my sister."

Again he had a gut feeling she wasn't telling him the truth. She refused to hold his gaze and even though the room was warm, her lips trembled slightly. And he realized she wasn't cold. She was afraid.

"Look, why don't we just get you settled in. The kitchen is there." He pointed to the doorway. "If you want anything to eat feel free to help yourself. I'll just go change the sheets on the bed then I'll be out of your hair." He started toward the bedroom but stopped as she called his name.

"If you just tell me where the sheets are, I'll change the bed. And I need to pay you."

"The sheets are on the bottom shelf in the bathroom, and it really isn't necessary for you to give me any money."

"Yes, it is," she countered, and her chin rose with a show of stubbornness. "It's important we keep this a business transaction."

"Fine," he replied. He named a nominal fee and watched as she opened her purse and carefully withdrew the amount in cash. "I'll just get a few things together then I'll head downstairs," he said as he took the money from her. He shoved the bills into his pocket, then grabbed her suitcase and wheeled it into his bedroom. He gathered a small overnight bag, then returned to the living room where she still stood in the center of the room, as if frozen in place.

"You should find everything you need for the night, but if you need anything you can't find, I'll write down my cell phone number and leave it on the kitchen table."

She gave an imperceptible nod of her head. "I… Thank you for this. I wasn't sure what I was going to do."

"You'll be fine here for the night and we'll sort things out in the morning."

"Thank you again," she said, then disappeared into the bedroom and closed the door behind her. He heard the click of the lock being turned.

Dalton stared at the closed door for a long moment. His family would probably tell him he was crazy for allowing a stranger to take up residence in his place even for one night. But they hadn't seen the vulnerability, the sheer desperation that clung to her closer than her coat.

Besides, what was she going to do? Tuck his television under one arm, her son under the other and run out into a blizzard? There was nothing here for her to steal that wasn't insured. He didn't know if he believed that she'd told him her real name or her destination, but he knew for sure that she'd needed someplace warm and safe and she'd found it here.

He went into the kitchen and wrote his cell phone number on a sheet of paper and left it on the small oak table. Then he wrote his own home phone number down and returned to the bedroom door and knocked. She opened the door, her eyes wide and wary.

"I just wanted to let you know there's leftover roast

beef in the refrigerator if you get hungry and there's extra blankets on the shelf in the closet if you need them. If you need to call your sister to let her know where you are, here's the phone number." He held out the slip of paper.

"Thank you, I'm sure we'll be fine." One hand snaked out to take the piece of paper from him. "I guess I'll see you in the morning." She closed the door again but not before Dalton saw something flash in her other hand, something silver like a blade.

A knife?

Every instinct he owned shot to high alert. He'd been trained to look for trouble, and he had a horrible feeling he'd just invited trouble into his home.

Well, he couldn't do anything about it now. He headed for the interior staircase that led downstairs to George's living quarters.

He would have to face it—her—in the morning.

Chapter 2

She saw the red lights flashing in her rearview mirror and glanced down at her speedometer. Damn. It looked like she was going to get a speeding ticket.

She supposed she was lucky that she hadn't gotten one before now. Two nights a week she'd been making the twenty-five mile drive from Sandstone to a local community college, taking classes to eventually take the GED test. She always drove too fast on this particular stretch of deserted highway.

Pulling over to the side of the road, she wondered how many extra hours she'd have to work to pay for this particular mistake. As if money wasn't already tight enough.

Glancing in her rearview mirror once again she saw the patrol car pull to a stop just behind her. The flashing red light went off, as did the headlights. As the driver's door opened she recognized Sheriff Brandon Sinclair getting out of the car.

She fumbled in her schoolbag for her license as he approached the side of her car. She rolled down her window and offered him a small smile. "Sheriff Sinclair," she said.

"Turn off your lights and get out of the car," he told her.

She frowned, but didn't think about not doing as he asked. As she got out of the car Sheriff Sinclair smiled. "Well, well, don't we look all sexy in that little skirt," he said, and there was something in his eyes that made her suddenly afraid.

Janette awoke with a gasp, heart pounding as she sat up and stared wildly around the unfamiliar room. The large mahogany dresser and the navy overstuffed chair weren't hers. She wasn't in her room. Where was she?

Then she remembered. She was in Cotter Creek, in Dalton West's bedroom. Sammy slept peacefully next to her on the king-size bed. She lay back down and shoved the last memories of her nightmare away.

The large bed had been a luxury after years of sleeping on a twin in her tiny bedroom in the trailer where she lived with Nana. Despite the luxury, sleep had been a long time coming. She'd jumped and tensed at each moan and groan of the unfamiliar house. Even when she had finally fallen asleep, it had been a night of unrelenting nightmares.

Surely by noon or so the streets would be cleared of whatever snow had fallen overnight and the bus would finally arrive. It had to come today. She needed to get as far away from here as possible.

When the streets are cleared, he'll come looking for you, the little voice whispered in her head. She felt like a fish in the bottom of a barrel, far too close, far too easily caught.

She'd left the bedroom only once during the night, to make a bottle for Sammy. Knowing that he would probably sleep for another hour or so, she got out of bed and headed for the adjoining bathroom. She wanted to be dressed and ready to leave as soon as possible.

It wasn't until she stood beneath a hot spray of water that she thought of the man who had allowed her into his home. In another lifetime, under different circumstances, she might find herself attracted to him. He was certainly easy to look at, with that thick dark hair and those gorgeous green eyes.

He reminded her of another man—a man who had not been quite as handsome but had devastated her, bitterly disappointed her at the time she'd needed him most.

She didn't need a man in her life. She and Sammy and Nana would be fine. All she had to do was get out of this town and decide where they would all begin a new life, far away from the reaches of Sheriff Brandon Sinclair.

After showering she wrapped herself in one of the large fluffy towels and walked over to the window for her first look outside.

She gasped as she saw that the storm hadn't passed by but instead seemed to be sitting right on top of the little town of Cotter Creek. It was impossible to discern street from sidewalk. Snow had transformed the earth into an alien landscape where nothing looked as it was supposed to.

There weren't just a couple of inches on the ground, there was at least a foot and a half and it was still falling from the gray, heavy sky.

Janette knew someplace in the back of her mind that it was beautiful, that the world looked like a winter wonderland, but all she could think was that the snow was a disaster, big fat fluffy flakes of doom falling from the sky.

Trapped. She was trapped there, and the only faint comfort was that if she were trapped by the weather, then so was Sheriff Brandon Sinclair.

She turned away from the window and crouched on the plush rug to open her big suitcase. The first thing she saw inside was the bright red book bag she'd thrown in at the last minute. Inside were the books she'd bought to study for her GED and the tape recorder she'd used in class.

It had been more than a year since she'd opened the bag that now represented not only the dream she'd once had for herself of getting more education, but also the worst night of her life.

She hadn't opened the bag since the night she'd been pulled over for a speeding ticket, and she didn't open it now. She set it on the floor and dug out a pair of jeans and her favorite blue sweater. She didn't have a lot of choices as she'd packed only a minimum of clothes for herself. Most of the suitcase contents were cans of powdered formula, cereal and diapers and clothing for Sammy.

Once she was dressed and had brushed out her long, wet hair, she eyed the phone on the nightstand. She should call Nana and let her know what was going on. The old woman would worry if she didn't hear from

Janette. Thank goodness the call wasn't long distance, Janette thought as she punched in her grandmother's number.

Nana answered on the second ring and Janette pressed the phone to her ear as if to get closer to her grandmother. "Nana, it's me."

"Janette, honey, where are you?" Nana asked. "Did you get off before this storm?"

"No, I'm still in Cotter Creek."

"At the motel?" Nana asked.

"The motel was already full by the time I found out the bus wasn't coming. The snow was coming down and I didn't know what to do, but then I saw a light on in the West Protective Services office." Janette twisted the phone cord around her little finger. "I hired Dalton West to be my bodyguard and he brought me to his apartment for the night."

"Are you safe there?" Nana asked, her voice filled with concern.

Janette considered the question. "Yes, I think I'm safe," she finally replied. It was odd, but having survived the night she did feel safe.

"I've heard about those Wests," Nana said. "Supposed to be good solid men. I'm just grateful that you and that precious little boy are away from here and not out in this storm someplace."

Janette glanced toward the window and frowned. "It looks like I'm going to be stuck here for a while." She twisted the phone cord more tightly around her finger. "Has anyone been by to ask about me?"

"Nobody, honey. The storm moved in and nobody is going anywhere at the moment. Don't you worry none. He'll never know from me where you went and by the time he makes his way here to ask questions you'll be far out of his reach."

"Let me give you the phone number here, just in case you need to reach me." Janette read the number off the piece of paper Dalton had given her the night before. "I'll call you when I'm about to board the bus. Maybe they'll get the streets cleared by tomorrow."

"You just take care of yourself and Sammy. Don't worry about things here. I got my friends at the trailer park to take care of me and I'll be fine as long as I know you're fine."

Janette unraveled the cord from her finger. How she wished she could crawl through the phone line and feel her grandmother's loving arms around her, to go back to a time when she didn't know about fear, about evil.

Afraid that she might cry if she remained on the phone much longer, she quickly said goodbye then hung up. Checking to make sure that Sammy was still sleeping soundly, she arranged the bed pillows on either side of him then walked to the bedroom door.

She hesitated before turning the knob to step out of the room. She'd told Nana she was safe, and at the moment she *felt* fairly safe, but she'd also been unaware of any danger on the night Sheriff Sinclair had pulled her over on the side of the road.

As much as she'd love to stay holed up in the bedroom until the bus pulled in, that was impossible. She hadn't eaten since lunch the day before and her stomach was protesting its neglect in loud angry growls.

The scent of freshly brewed coffee greeted her as she opened the bedroom door, letting her know she was no longer alone in the apartment.

Energy surged through her as all her senses went on

high alert. Her feet whispered against the living-room rug as she moved toward the kitchen.

She hesitated in the doorway. Dalton stood at the stove with his back to her. A white, long-sleeved jersey clung across his broad shoulders and worn jeans hugged the length of his legs. He was barefoot and his hair was rumpled like he'd just crawled out of bed.

A sizzling noise was quickly followed by a whiff of bacon and Janette felt the nerves in her stomach calm. It was hard to be frightened of a barefoot man frying bacon.

She must have made some sort of sound for he whirled around to look at her. "Good morning," he said. "There's coffee in the pot if you're interested."

"I'm interested," she replied.

He gestured to the coffeemaker on the counter. "Cups are in the cabinet above."

She walked over to the cabinet, retrieved a cup, then poured herself some coffee. She carried it to the table and sat, unsure what else to do.

Dalton turned back around to flip the bacon. Janette was aware of a tension in the air, the tension of two strangers sharing space.

"It looks like you're going to be stuck here for at least another day or two," he said.

"Maybe I could find another place to go to," she offered.

Once again he turned around to face her. "It would take me half the day to shovel enough snow just to open the outside door. Trust me, nobody is going anywhere today." A muscle in his jaw tensed, letting her know that he wasn't particularly happy about the unforeseen circumstances.

"I'm sorry about all this," she said. He'd never know just how sorry she was that she was stuck here in Cotter Creek.

"We'll just have to deal with it," he replied, then turned his back on her once again.

Taking a sip of her coffee, she had a vision of Brandon Sinclair tunneling his way through the snow to find her. She mentally shook the thought out of her head.

Once again she stared at Dalton's back. He was a fine-looking man and so far he'd been nothing but honorable. He made a living protecting people. Maybe she could tell him. Maybe she could tell him the truth. The thought of telling somebody and having them believe her was wonderful.

"How about an omelet?" he asked. "I'm making myself one and can split it with you."

She felt bad, that this man was not only having to share his personal space but also his food. Still, she was starving and it seemed silly to refuse. "That sounds good," she agreed.

Once again she sipped her coffee, watching as he prepared the ingredients for the omelet. "Is there anything I can do to help?" she asked.

"No, thanks, I'm used to doing things my way," he replied.

"Tell me about this business of yours. I read an article not too long ago about West Protective Services. If I remember correctly it's a family business, right?"

He nodded. His tousled hair made him appear less daunting than he had the night before. "It was started by my father, Red West. Eventually all of us started working for the business."

"All of you?"

"I've got four brothers and a sister. Joshua is the youngest and he just got married to Savannah, who owns the local newspaper. Then there's Clay, who met his wife when he was on assignment in California. They have a little girl, Gracie. There's Tanner, the oldest. He and his wife, Anna, just had a baby."

Janette felt herself relaxing as he talked. Not only did he have a nice, deep voice that was soothing, but it was obvious from the affection in his voice as he spoke that the West family was a close one. It was easier to trust a man who loved his family.

"Then there's Meredith. She recently moved to Kansas City with her fiancé, Chase. She and Chase are planning on coming back here in March to get married. Finally there's Zack. He doesn't work for the family business anymore. He married Katie, the woman who lived next door to our family, and he's the sheriff of Cotter Creek."

Any hope she might have entertained of being truthful with Dalton West crashed and burned. *He's the sheriff of Cotter Creek.* The words echoed inside her head.

There were only thirty miles between Cotter Creek and Sandstone. There was no reason for her not to believe that Brandon Sinclair and Zack West were not only acquaintances but also perhaps friends. She had no idea how far-reaching the good-old-boy network was in the state of Oklahoma.

One thing was clear. For as long as she was stuck in this apartment, she couldn't tell Dalton the truth. Her very life and the life of her son might depend on her keeping her secrets.

At that moment, as if he'd awakened and sensed his mother's despair, Sammy began to cry from the bedroom.

Dalton drew a deep breath as "Jane" hurriedly left the kitchen to get her son. He was exhausted, having spent the night on George's tiny sofa after hours of listening to George talk. And the old man could definitely talk.

He'd already been feeling a little irritable when he'd climbed the inside staircase back to his apartment. As if spending an evening with George hadn't been enough, he was now stuck in his apartment with a stranger, a woman whom, he had to admit, stirred something inside him just by being there. A woman who'd had a knife in her hand the night before.

Could he really blame her for wielding a knife? After all, as much as she was a stranger to him, he was a stranger to her. She'd had no idea what kind of a man he was, what she'd been walking into when she'd entered his apartment.

He cut the omelet in half and placed it on two plates, then added the bacon and put the plates on the table.

She couldn't know that he was a solitary man who didn't particularly enjoy sharing his space, his world, with anyone. Even though he found her amazingly attractive, all he wanted was for her and her son to move on.

She returned to the kitchen, her son and a bottle in one arm and a box of powdered cereal in the other. "I need to make some cereal for Sammy. Do you have a small bowl I can use?"

Dalton got out the bowl, then watched as she tried to maneuver with the wiggly baby in her arms. "You want me to hold him while you get that ready?" he asked reluctantly. He didn't particularly like kids, had only thought about having a couple once, a long time ago, but it had been nothing more than a foolish dream.

"Thanks." She smiled at him for the first time, a real, open genuine smile that unexpectedly shot a flash of heat through his stomach.

As she offered the baby to him, Sammy seemed to vibrate with excitement and offered Dalton a wide, drooling grin. As soon as Dalton had him in his arms, Sammy reached up and grabbed hold of his nose, then laughed as if finding the West nose vastly amusing.

"He likes you," Jane observed as she measured out the rice cereal and added warm formula.

"You sound surprised," Dalton replied.

"I am. He's usually not good with strangers, especially men."

"What about his father?" Dalton asked as she stirred the cereal, then set the bowl on the table.

Her eyes darkened. "His father isn't in our lives." To his relief she took the baby back and sat at the table.

For the next few minutes they sat in silence. She alternately fed Sammy and herself while Dalton ate his breakfast.

Sammy laughed and smiled at Dalton every time Dalton looked at him. He had to admit, the kid was cute with his tuft of dark hair and blue eyes. Dalton finished eating before Jane, or whatever her real name was. "Do you need to call your sister in St. Louis to tell her you've been delayed?"

"I already did," she replied.

Dalton stared at her. She'd told him the night before that she was on her way to visit her sister in Kansas City. Women interested him, but a woman with secrets definitely intrigued him.

He didn't call her on her slip, but instead leaned back in his chair and watched as she finished feeding Sammy. He didn't want to be intrigued by her. He wanted the snow to melt quickly and her and her cute baby to move along on their way to wherever. However, the weather report that morning hadn't been exactly favorable for her to make a quick escape out of his house.

Taking a sip of his coffee, he gazed out the window where the snow still fell in buckets. At least she didn't seem to be a chatterer. She didn't expect him to entertain her with lively conversation.

Silence had always been Dalton's friend. Growing up in a household with a rambunctious bunch of siblings had made him appreciate his solitary life now. Odd that he suddenly found the silence strangely stifling.

"We're lucky we still have power," he finally said to break that uncomfortable silence. "The news report this morning said that half the town is without power and phone service."

"That's terrible," she exclaimed.

"Most folks around this area are prepared for situations like this. They have wood-burning fireplaces or generators that will be cranked up. We Oklahoma people are solid stock and know how to deal with an emergency."

She frowned. "I certainly wasn't prepared for this particular emergency."

"According to the weather report I heard the snow is supposed to end by nightfall. If that happens, then first thing in the morning the locals will get out and clear the streets."

"It can't happen fast enough for me," she replied. She looked up from Sammy, her blue eyes dark and troubled. "I'm sorry I can't get out of your hair right now. I know when you offered me a place to stay last night you had no idea that I'd still be here today."

Dalton shrugged. "We'll just have to make the best of it."

"I just hope if they get the streets cleared in the morning then the bus comes tomorrow afternoon." There was a thrum of desperation in her voice.

"Surely your sister will understand the delay."

"Of course." She averted her gaze from his and focused on her son in her arms. "I'm just anxious to get gone."

"Is this a vacation trip?"

She kept her gaze firmly on her son. "Yes. It's been a long time since I've seen my sister and she hasn't met Sammy, so I thought it would be nice to take a trip to visit her. I suppose it was foolish to plan a trip in late January. But babies are only babies a short time."

She was rambling, and it was Dalton's experience that people who rambled were usually hiding something. She seemed to realize what she was doing for she suddenly clamped her lips closed and frowned.

Getting up from the table she started to grab for her plate. "I'll take care of that," he said.

She gave him a grateful nod, then once again disappeared from the kitchen. Dalton remained seated at the table. He sipped his coffee and looked out the window. Although he stared at the snow, his mind was filled with those blue eyes of hers.

At thirty-three years old, Dalton had worked the family business for twelve years. He'd spent that time studying people, and the assessments he made of those people sometimes made the difference between life and death.

Jane Craig was lying. He'd seen it in those impossibly blue eyes of hers. Secrets and lies. There had been something in her eyes that had looked not only like quiet desperation, but also screaming fear.

His mind whirled with all kinds of possibilities. Who in their right mind planned a bus trip in the Midwest in January? Especially with an infant? He could write off the appearance of the knife the night before as a wary woman in the home of a stranger. But what was she doing with a wicked-looking knife like that in the first place?

Secrets and lies. What he was suddenly eager to find out was whether her secrets and lies could be the difference between life and death, and whether the snowy conditions had suddenly made him a player in a drama he wasn't prepared to face.

Sheriff Brandon Sinclair stared out the window and silently cursed the snow. He'd been in a foul mood since the day before, when he'd gone back to the diner to have a little chat with Janette and discovered she'd up and quit her job, just like that.

He'd been on his way to the little rattrap trailer where she lived with her grandmother when a six-car accident just outside town had required his immediate attention. By the time he'd finished up, the ice had begun to fall in earnest.

He tried to ignore the sound of his three daughters

playing in the middle of their living-room floor. He hadn't thought about Janette Black since the night they'd had sex over a year ago.

Then yesterday morning he'd heard the rumor that she had a little baby boy, a rumor that had been confirmed when he'd spoken with her at lunch.

Since that moment, he couldn't get her—or more precisely the boy—out of his mind. *His son.* He knew in his gut that the kid was his.

"Brandon, honey, your breakfast is waiting," Brandon's wife, Sherrilyn, spoke from someplace behind him.

He grunted but didn't turn around. Sherrilyn was a good woman. She'd come into the marriage not only crazy about him, but with the kind of respectability and a trust fund that Brandon had desired. She kept the large house neat and tidy, tried to anticipate his needs before he knew them and was an adequate if boring bedmate.

She loved being the sheriff's wife, and while Brandon was feared and respected by the community, Sherrilyn was loved for her charity work and big heart.

But, when it came to giving Brandon what he'd wanted most in life, she'd failed miserably, pumping out three girl babies instead of the boy he desperately wanted.

"Mommy, Susan won't share," Elena, his youngest, whined from the living room. She was always whining about something. Girls whined. Girls cried, and he had three of the whiniest, weepiest girls in the county.

He narrowed his gaze as he turned away from the window and headed for the kitchen. As soon as the snow stopped, he'd get that boy. He didn't much care what he had to do, but eventually that little boy would be living with him, being raised by him. Boys needed their daddies, and if the only way to get that kid was over Janette Black's dead body, well then that could be arranged, too.

Chapter 3

Janette stayed in the bedroom with Sammy for most of the morning. She played peekaboo with him, laughing as he grinned and squealed at her antics. When he started to get sleepy, she picked him up in her arms and sat in the chair near the window, rocking and singing softly to him until he fell asleep.

She placed her lips against Sammy's downy hair, drawing in the sweet baby scent of him. He was her heart, this little boy. Before his birth she had loved him, but nothing had prepared her for the depth of her love for him now.

Her heart squeezed as she thought of the threat that felt ominously close, a threat to this baby and their future together. She would do whatever it took to keep him safe and away from the man who was his biological father. She shoved aside thoughts of Sinclair, unwilling to allow the chill that thoughts of him always produced to consume her.

She was conscious of the sounds of Dalton in the next room. It was a good thing he'd told her about his family before she'd confessed what was really going on.

She should have known it wouldn't be safe to tell him the truth. Bodyguards probably had to work closely with law enforcement officials. For all she knew, Brandon Sinclair could be a drinking buddy of the entire West clan.

When Sammy was sleeping soundly, she gently laid him in the middle of the big bed and tucked the pillows around him to stop him from rolling anywhere. She stood for a long moment staring down at the baby who owned all of her heart.

She would do whatever it took to keep Brandon Sinclair away from Sammy. She would run to the ends of the earth, hide for the rest of her life if that's what it took.

You're nothing but trailer trash, Janette. Nobody is going to believe you if you ever tell. Those were the last words she'd heard from Sinclair that night on the highway. He hadn't spoken to her again or even looked at her until yesterday in the café when he'd told her he knew she had a son.

She'd tried to be so careful during her pregnancy. Thankfully she'd gained little weight and had been able to hide her condition until her eighth month. It was only then that she'd told the people who'd noticed that she was pregnant that she'd had a fling with a man passing through town. Because she believed Sinclair—nobody would ever believe her if she told the truth.

Tired of being cooped up, she finally left the bedroom and entered the living room where Dalton sat in a chair reading a book as a saxophone wailed the blues from the stereo. She wasn't concerned about the noise waking Sammy. From the time he'd been born he had slept like the dead, undisturbed by loud noises.

Dalton looked up and nodded at her. "Are you ready for lunch?" he asked and closed his book.

"No, thanks. I'm fine." She gestured to the book on his lap. "Please, don't let me interrupt you."

"You aren't. It isn't a very good book, anyway."

She glanced to the overflowing bookcase against one wall. "You must read a lot."

"I enjoy reading," he agreed. His piercing green eyes seemed to peer directly inside her. "What about you? Are you a reader?"

She sat on the edge of the sofa. "I'd like to be, but there never seems to be enough time. Between taking care of Sammy and my job there aren't many hours left in the day."

"What kind of job do you have?"

"Right now I'm a waitress, but that's not what I want to do for the rest of my life." She hesitated a moment, then continued, "I had to drop out of high school my junior year because my nana…my grandma got sick, so the first thing I need to do is get my GED."

She wasn't sure why she'd told him that. It was more information than he'd asked for and she was certain he didn't care what her future plans might be.

Those direct green eyes of his held her gaze. "Your grandmother is important in your life?"

"Definitely. She raised me. It was just me and her, and of course my sister," she hurriedly added. She'd never been a liar, and the lies she now found herself spouting bothered her more than a little bit.

"What about your parents? Where are they?"

"Who knows? I never knew my father and when I was three my mother dropped me off at Nana's house and we never heard from her again. Nana told me she was a troubled woman with drug problems. I think she's probably dead by now."

Janette had long ago made peace with the fact that her mother had been unable to parent her. At least she'd been unselfish enough to put her in Nana's care, where she'd been loved and looked after.

"I'm sorry to hear that," he said, and she was surprised by the touch of empathy she heard in his deep voice. "My mother was murdered when I was just a boy."

"That's horrible," she exclaimed.

He shrugged. "You deal with the bumps life throws you." He stood suddenly, as if to end the conversation of that particular topic. "Are you sure you aren't ready for some lunch? I'm going to make a sandwich."

"I guess I could eat a sandwich," she agreed and got up to follow him into the kitchen. Once again she found herself sitting at the table while he fixed the meal. "I need to give you more money," she said. "You're feeding me and everything. I feel terrible about all this."

He smiled then, and the power of his smile shot a wave of heat through her. It was the heat of a woman intensely aware of an attractive man. It shocked her, but she embraced it, for it was something she hadn't felt for a very long time, something she'd thought Brandon Sinclair had killed.

"I think I can manage to feed one slender woman for a couple of days without declaring bankruptcy," he said.

She returned his smile. "I just want you to know that I appreciate it." She glanced toward the window where the snow appeared to be slowing down. Surely by tomorrow she could leave.

She gazed back at Dalton. "So, I guess your dad raised you, then? It must have been quite a challenge, considering how many of you there were."

Once again he grinned, transfusing his rather stern features with an unexpected warmth. "Ah, Dad had a secret weapon. He hired a cantankerous old cowhand as a housekeeper. Smokey Johnson not only threatened to beat our butts if we got out of line, he followed through on his threats often enough to make us take him seriously."

Despite his words it was obvious he held a lot of affection for the cowhand turned parental figure in his life. For the first time since she'd stepped out of the bus station yesterday evening, some of the tension that had coiled inside her eased.

"Ham and cheese okay?" he asked.

"Perfect. Is there anything I can do to help?"

"Nah, sit tight. I can handle it. Besides, if you work as a waitress I doubt you get too many people offering to wait on you."

She laughed. "That's the truth." He smelled nice, like minty soap and a touch of sandalwood, and she felt herself relax just a little bit more.

"Is your sister older or younger than you?"

The question came out of left field but reminded her that she couldn't let her guard down for a minute. "Older," she said. "Why?"

"Just curious." He walked over to the table with their lunch plates. "What would you like to drink? I can offer you milk, water or a soda."

"Milk would be nice."

He rejoined her at the table a moment later with two tall glasses of milk. For the next few minutes they ate in silence. "From what you told me earlier it sounds like all of your brothers and your sister are married and having kids. Why aren't you married?" she asked to break the uncomfortable quiet.

A flash of darkness momentarily chased across his green eyes. "I guess after growing up with a houseful of people I've discovered in my adult years that I enjoy my solitude," he replied. "I like living alone and not having to answer to anyone, and have no plans to ever get married."

He took a drink of his milk, then continued, "What about you? I'm assuming things didn't work out with you and the baby's father?"

She looked down at her sandwich and pulled off part of the crust. "No, we tried to make it work. He's a great guy and everything, but we just weren't good together." She looked at Dalton once again and forced a small smile to her lips. "But thankfully we have managed to remain good friends."

How she wished this were true. How she wished that Sammy's father was a good man who could help her instill the right qualities in their son instead of a monster who would taint the innocence of the little boy.

Dalton leaned back in his chair and studied her. "You're a pretty woman. I'm sure you won't have any problems finding some special guy to share your life."

There was nothing in his voice to indicate he was

flirting with her in any way, but she touched a strand of her hair self-consciously. She hadn't felt pretty in a very long time and she was surprised to discover that his comment soothed a wound she hadn't realized she possessed.

"I'm in no hurry at the moment to make any commitment to anyone," she replied. "I just want to be able to take care of my son and myself."

At that moment the phone rang, jolting every nerve in Janette's body. What if it was Dalton's brother, the sheriff? What if Dalton mentioned that he had a young woman and a baby staying with him?

What if Sinclair had already begun the search for her and had contacted Dalton's brother? Horrible scenarios went off in her head, mini-movies of doom.

As Dalton started to rise to answer, she grabbed him by the forearm and held tight. Her heart beat so hard, so fast she wondered if he could hear it. "Please, please don't tell anyone I'm here."

His eyes pierced her with a sharpness that was almost painful. He didn't answer but instead pulled his arm out of her grasp and walked over to the phone.

"Hello?" he said, his gaze never leaving Janette. "Yeah, hi, Dad. I was just eating lunch."

As Dalton continued his conversation, he never broke eye contact with Janette. The tension that had dissipated earlier crashed back through her, twisting in her gut like a deadly Oklahoma tornado.

His voice remained pleasant as he carried on his conversation with his father. When he finally hung up he returned to the table and reached out to grab her forearm as she had done his.

"Now, Jane," he said, his voice deceptively calm. "You want to tell me just what the hell is going on?"

Dalton stared at the woman and tried to ignore how fragile, how warm, her slender arm felt beneath his grasp. Her stunning blue eyes were wide and darted around the room as if seeking somewhere to run, to escape. She tried to pull her arm free from his grip but he held tight, just as she had a moment earlier.

"Talk to me," he said. "Tell me why you don't want me to mention to anyone that you're here."

This close he could smell the scent of her, clean with a touch of honeysuckle fragrance. She closed her eyes and he couldn't help but notice the length of her eyelashes. She tried to pull away from him again and this time he let her go.

She wrapped her arms around herself as if she were cold and looked at him. "I'm sorry. I lied to you before." She looked down at the table.

He frowned. "Lied about what?"

She got up as if she wanted as much distance from him as possible, but he had a feeling that what she was really doing was giving herself time to think. He wasn't at all sure he was going to believe anything that fell out of her mouth at this point.

Moving to stand next to the window, she turned to face him. "I lied about Sammy's father. He isn't a nice man. He…he used to beat me. He was abusive and I needed to get away."

There was a tremble in her voice, a timbre of fear that made him want to believe her. "You think he's looking for you?"

Again she wrapped her arms around her middle.

"You can bet on it. And if he finds me he'll hurt me. He might hurt Sammy."

"That's not going to happen here," Dalton said firmly. He offered her a smile. "After all, you've hired me as your personal bodyguard and I promise you I'm damned good at what I do."

She didn't return his smile and that, along with the darkness in her eyes, made him believe her. "Is that why you carry a knife?" he asked.

She raised a pale eyebrow. "How do you know about that?"

"I saw it last night when you opened the bedroom door."

She returned to the table and sat, her gaze going out the window. "I won't let him hurt me again." She looked back at Dalton and there was a hard glint in her eyes. "I just want to get out of here. Once I get to my sister's I'll be just fine."

"What's this guy's name?" Dalton asked.

"What difference does it make?"

He shrugged. "Just curious. I know most of the families in this area. Just thought I might know him."

She blinked once…twice. "His name is Billy Johnson. I doubt if you know him. He's not from around here. His family is from someplace back East."

Once again he had the feeling she wasn't being completely honest with him. Did he care? If he were smart he would stop asking questions now. In the next day or two she wouldn't be his problem.

"I'd better go check on Sammy," she said and rose from the table.

He watched her hurry away, unable to stop himself from noticing how the worn jeans fit snugly across her shapely butt. He was acutely aware of the fact that physically he was attracted to her, but that didn't mean he wanted to be pulled into her life drama.

He got up from the table, carried their lunch dishes to the sink and began to rinse them. As he worked, his thoughts drifted to his last assignment.

It had been over a year since Dalton had worked a case as a bodyguard. Her name had been Mary Mason, she'd lived in Tulsa and she, too, had been the victim of domestic violence. He'd worked for her for almost four months, guarding her between the time she'd filed for divorce and the divorce proceeding itself, which had been expedited by a judge sympathetic to her situation.

Mary had known the statistics, that in these kinds of cases the most dangerous time for an abused wife was in the weeks prior to the divorce.

In those four months, he'd fallen head over heels in love with her and she had appeared to feel the same way about him. They had forged a bond that he thought would last the rest of their lives. They'd made plans for a wedding after her divorce, laughing as they created a fantasy event fit for a king and a queen.

It wasn't until the day after the divorce proceedings that the fantasy exploded. Mary told him she needed some time to regroup, that he should return to his home in Cotter Creek and give her a little time alone.

He'd understood the request, had encouraged it, so certain was he that they would be together. He'd called her often, they'd emailed, but after only a month he'd received a Dear John letter. She'd fallen in love with another man. They were getting married. Dalton had made a wonderful temporary hero, but that's all he had been.

He scowled as he put the dishes in the dishwasher.

The whole thing had left a bad taste in his mouth, a heartache that had been long in healing. Since that time he'd worked the office, answering the phones and keeping the books. He preferred dealing with paperwork instead of people.

Footsteps sounded on the inside staircase that led from George's place upstairs to Dalton's. A moment later, a knock sounded on the back kitchen door.

Jane might not want anyone to know she was here, but it was already too late to keep that piece of information from his landlord.

George would have thought it damned odd that Dalton wanted to sleep on his sofa if Dalton hadn't told the old man that he'd given harbor from the storm to a young woman and her baby.

He opened the door to see George wearing hot pads on his hands and carrying a fresh pie. "Had some canned apples and thought it was a good day for some pie and coffee." He swept past Dalton and into the kitchen, where he deposited the pie on the table. "So, how about making us some coffee to go with this work of art." He pulled out a chair and sat.

Dalton grinned. "Feeling a little cabin fever, George?" He got a pot of coffee ready to brew.

"I hate being cooped up. You know me, Dalton, I'm a social kind of man. Sitting and listening to my own thoughts bores me to death. Where's your houseguest?"

At that moment Jane appeared in the doorway with Sammy in her arms. She froze at the sight of George. "Jane, this is my landlord, George, from downstairs," Dalton said.

George popped up from the chair and walked over

to where she stood. "Jane, nice to meet you. And who is this little fellow?"

Sammy took one look at George's big, silly grin and screwed up his face. He wailed as if George were the devil himself and burrowed closer to Jane's chest.

"Oh, my." George quickly stepped back.

"I'm sorry," Jane said. "He's hungry. I was just going to fix him a bottle."

Dalton realized she not only held the boy in her arms, but also juggled a bottle and a can of powdered formula mix, as well. Short of putting Sammy on the floor, it was going to be next to impossible for her to hold him and make the bottle.

"Want me to take him?" he asked and gestured to the crying child.

She shot him a grateful look. "If you don't mind. It will just take me a minute to get this ready."

He nodded and took Sammy from her. Almost immediately Sammy not only stopped crying but grinned at Dalton as if the two were best buds.

"Would you look at that?" George exclaimed. "That boy is plum crazy about you."

"He'll be a lot crazier about that bottle," Dalton replied, grateful a moment later when Jane took her son back. She sat at the table, Sammy in her arms sucking on his bottle with obvious contentment.

"George brought up a freshly baked apple pie," Dalton said as he got out coffee mugs from the cabinet.

"Hmm, that sounds good. Apple is my favorite." She offered George a tentative smile.

"My missus, God rest her soul, loved my apple pies. Always told me if God served pie in heaven, then he'd be serving mine," George replied. "Guess this snowstorm took you by surprise."

"Definitely," she agreed.

George could talk, and that's what he did for the next hour. Sammy finished his bottle and fell asleep. Dalton sat and sipped his coffee as George entertained Jane with colorful descriptions of people in town, humorous stories of his misspent youth and his fifty-year marriage to the woman who had owned his heart since he was sixteen.

Dalton had heard the stories before. What he found far more interesting than George's conversation was watching Jane interact with the old man.

As she listened to George, she looked relaxed. Her long blond hair was so soft-looking, so shiny, it made a man want to reach out and touch it, coil it around his fingers, feel it dance across his chest. The first time she laughed aloud, Dalton was shocked by the pleasure that swept through him. She had a great laugh, one that would easily evoke smiles in others.

Although she visited with George in general terms, he noticed that she gave nothing of herself. She didn't mention family or friends, didn't speak of her hometown or her job.

Irritated with these kinds of thoughts, he got up to pour himself another cup of coffee, then returned to the table. He didn't want to think about how sweet she smelled or how her lips were just full enough to tempt a man.

She'd given no indication that she might be up for a short, reckless affair to pass the time until she got on the bus out of town. And the last thing he wanted was any kind of an emotional entanglement with any woman. She'd be gone soon, and that was that.

It was just after three when George finally got up from the table. "It's been a real pleasure," he said and smiled at Jane. "There's nothing nicer than spending a snowy afternoon in the company of a beautiful woman. Unfortunately, at my age, a good nap is also a pleasant way to spend the afternoon, and I'm past due mine."

She offered him a sunny smile. "Thank you for the pie, George. Your wife was right. It was the best I've ever eaten," she replied.

George beamed as if kissed by an angel.

"George, have you mentioned to anyone that I'm here?" Jane asked.

"Can't say I have." George scratched the top of his head. "Haven't talked to anyone except Dalton since this storm moved in."

"I would appreciate it if you wouldn't mention it to anyone." She flashed him a bright smile. "I'm kind of hiding out from somebody."

George's eyes lit up. "Ah, a woman of mystery. Your secret is safe with me." He started to turn to head out the way he had come, but paused and pointed to the window. "Would you look at that?"

Both Dalton and Jane looked through the window where the snow had finally stopped and the sun peeked out from behind the last lingering gray clouds.

Chapter 4

"You think the bus will run tomorrow?" Janette asked Dalton. The three of them were in the living room, having just eaten supper. He was seated in the chair and she was on the sofa. Sammy was gurgling happily from a blanket on the floor.

"Doubtful," he replied.

For the past hour they'd heard the sounds of plows starting the storm cleanup and each grind of gears had been like music to her ears. She just hoped and prayed she got out of there before Sheriff Brandon Sinclair somehow discovered where she was.

"Although most of the locals who have plows will be out and have our streets cleaned, it will probably be at least another day or so before the highways are completely cleared and the bus can show up." He gazed at her curiously. "Surely you can't be afraid that your boyfriend will find you here. You didn't know you were going to be here, so how could he know?"

"Logically, I know that, but emotionally, I just have this terrible need to get out of town, to get as far away as possible," she replied. "I just want to stay safe."

"I told you that you'd be safe here," he said. "When that bus comes, I'll personally see you safely aboard and in the meantime nobody is going to harm you while you're in my home."

A new burst of gratitude filled her. She'd taken a terrible chance coming into the home of a stranger, but Dalton had proved himself to be nothing other than a good, honorable man. She leaned back on the sofa. "So, what do you do when you aren't bodyguarding?" she asked. She'd been in his home for twenty-four hours but didn't really know anything about him.

"I mentioned before I like to read, and when the weather's nice I do a little work at the family ranch."

"Family ranch?" She could easily imagine him, long legs astride a powerful horse, a cowboy hat pulled down low over his brow.

"My dad has a huge ranch north of town. It's become something of a family compound. My brother Tanner has a house on the property, and Clay and his wife, Libby, have been talking about building there."

"Hmm, that sounds nice. It must be wonderful to have such a close, loving family unit. I used to wonder what it would be like to have a whole mess of siblings."

He laughed, a deep low sound that warmed her. "Believe me, it's not as wonderful as it sounds. You wait in line for the bathroom, you wait to be served at the table, you share everything you're given and there's incessant noise."

She searched his features. "But there must have been something wonderful in it."

He frowned, the gesture doing nothing to detract from his handsomeness. His gaze drifted to the window and he stared out for a long moment before answering. When he looked back at her the deep lines in his face had softened.

"I suppose there was something wonderful about it," he said as if conceding a huge point. "I definitely never felt lonely and I knew my family always had my back when I got into trouble."

"And did you do that often?" she asked. "Get into trouble?"

His eyes gleamed with a hint of mischief. "Probably more than my share, although nothing serious. What about you? Were you a wild child or one of those Goody Two-shoes who always played by the rules?"

It was the first conversation they'd had where she didn't feel on edge, wasn't afraid of screwing up the lies she'd already told with new lies. Maybe she was feeling more relaxed because the snowplows sounded like imminent escape.

"I was in-between," she said. "I'm sure my grandmother would tell you that I had some wild moments, and like your Smokey, she didn't hesitate to burn my butt if I needed it. But I never broke any laws or anything like that."

"That's a relief. I wouldn't want to be harboring a criminal in my house," he said, his green eyes teasing.

She returned his smile. In different circumstances she had a feeling it would have been easy to like Dalton…really like him. Although he seemed reserved, when he smiled at her she wanted to break through that reserve and get to the heart of the man.

But she couldn't afford to be attracted to him. As soon as the streets were cleared she'd be out of his apartment and as far away from Cotter Creek as she could get.

This was nothing more than a temporary respite from the drama that her life had become on the afternoon that Sheriff Brandon Sinclair had walked into the café.

"I'll bet you spend a lot of time with your family," she said.

"Not really. Oh, we get together for the usual holidays, but most of the time I'm perfectly satisfied alone."

"Still, I imagine it's a good feeling to know that they're there if you need them," she replied.

Sammy cooed like a dove as he found his own fingers, his legs kicking with happiness. She watched Dalton as his gaze went to her son. Dalton looked back at her. "You've got a tough road ahead of you."

"What do you mean?"

"A single mother, no father in the picture and you mentioned that you don't have your GED yet. You've got an uphill battle ahead of you."

"I know," she agreed, suddenly sober as she gazed down at Sammy. "I might have grown up poor in a trailer park, but I'm going to make something of myself so that Sammy has everything he needs." She heard the angry resolve in her own voice, a resolve that had strengthened when Sinclair had told her that she was nothing but trailer trash and nobody would believe her if she told what he'd done.

"There's nothing wrong with being poor, or growing up in a trailer park," Dalton said softly.

She smiled. "Spoken like a man who has never known what it's like to be poor."

"You're right," he conceded. "I was lucky never to have to worry about finances. The bodyguard business pays well and we all share in the profits of both the business and the ranch."

"Did you always want to be a bodyguard?"

"When I was ten I wanted to be a rodeo clown," he said. "When I was twelve I wanted to be an astronaut, then a treasure hunter and a gold miner."

She laughed. "For me it was a movie star, a ballerina then a princess." She sobered. "It never entered my mind that in reality I'd be an abused woman on the run with a small baby."

"Your sister will take you in?"

"Of course," she replied around the lump of fear that swelled in her throat. She had no idea where she was going, no idea what she'd find when she arrived. Her only support system was a sixty-eight-year-old woman with a bad heart.

Dalton ran a hand through his thick dark hair, not breaking eye contact with her. "Why do I get the feeling that you aren't telling me everything?"

"I don't know what you're talking about," she said and looked down at Sammy, who had begun to fuss. "I'd better get him a bottle," she said as she got up from the sofa.

It was a relief to escape those piercing, intelligent eyes of his. She didn't know what he saw that made him think she was keeping secrets, but there was no way she could tell him the truth. And in any case, it didn't matter. She would be gone soon enough.

She fixed Sammy his bottle, then picked him up off

the floor. "I think I'm going to go ahead and call it a night," she said.

He nodded. "Unless it will freak you out entirely, I'm planning on sleeping here on the sofa tonight. I like George a lot, but his sofa is small and last night he kept me up until long after midnight telling me stories I'd heard a dozen times before."

She was surprised to realize the idea didn't freak her out. She trusted him to remain the perfect gentleman he'd already been. "Would you rather stay in your own bed? Sammy and I could bunk in here," she offered.

"No, I'll be just fine. Good night, Jane," he said.

She wished she could hear her real name on his lips, but fear still ruled her decisions, including the decision to tell him little white lies, as much as she hated it. "Good night, Dalton."

Even though it was relatively early, Janette breathed a sigh of exhaustion as she got ready for bed. It was hard work watching every word that fell from her mouth and being careful not to say too much or too little.

When she was in her nightgown she moved to the window and stared outside. The street in front of Dalton's had been plowed, leaving piles of snow on either side that glistened in the streetlights.

The sooner she got on the bus the better she'd feel, but escaping this part of the country certainly didn't ease the fear that was a constant inside her.

She might escape Sinclair but then she'd have to face settling into a new place, finding work and taking care of Sammy *and* earning enough money to send for Nana. Dalton was right. She had a tough road ahead of her.

Sammy finished his bottle, and she sang softly to him until he fell asleep. It took her longer to sleep and when she finally succumbed, the dream began almost immediately.

"Well, well, don't we look all sexy in that little skirt," Sinclair said, and there was something in his eyes that made her suddenly afraid.

Janette held out her driver's license, but he didn't take it from her. Instead those cold, blue eyes of his swept leisurely down her body. "You were going awfully fast. You doing drugs?"

"I don't do drugs, Sheriff," she exclaimed.

"I'm going to have to frisk you to make sure you have nothing illegal on you." He stepped closer to her and she smelled the scent of him, a stale sweat odor mingling with an overly sweet cologne.

Unconsciously she took a step backward, heart pounding painfully hard. He narrowed his eyes. "Don't you fight me, girl. I'll have you in handcuffs so fast your pretty little head will spin." He grinned. "Or maybe I'll just have to shoot you for resisting." And then he put his hands on her.

Hands. Everywhere on her. And hot breath on her face. And in her dream she did something she hadn't been able to do that night.

She screamed.

The scream pulled Dalton from a dream of a naked Jane in his bed. He shot upright on the sofa, for a moment not knowing what it was that had awakened him. Then it came again, a scream of such terror it raised the hairs on his arms, on the nape of his neck.

Jane!

He stumbled from the sofa and into the bedroom, adrenaline surging and heart pounding. He flipped on the overhead light and instantly realized Jane was in the middle of a nightmare. She thrashed on the bed, flailing her arms and legs as if fighting for her life.

Sammy cried out, too, and his eyes fluttered open, but he settled back to sleep, as if accustomed to his mother having bad dreams. "Jane," Dalton called softly.

She moaned, whipping her head from side to side, but she didn't open her eyes. He approached her, trying not to notice that the sheets had slipped down to her waist and the pale-blue silk nightgown she wore did little to hide her full breasts.

The fight-or-flight adrenaline that had filled him at the sound of her scream now transformed to another kind of energy as a surge of desire struck his midsection.

"Jane," he said again as he moved closer to the edge of the bed. Still she didn't respond. He was going to have to touch that soft-looking pale skin and he knew he was going to find it far too pleasant.

"Jane, wake up. You're having a nightmare." He leaned over and took her by the shoulders.

Her eyelids snapped open and she looked at him, wildness in the depths of her eyes. She stared at him and the wildness left as recognition struck. She released a little gasp and to his surprise launched herself out of the bed and into his embrace.

She trembled in his arms and sobbed silently into the crook of his neck. He tentatively slid a hand down the cool material that covered her back. "Shh, it was just a dream," he said softly.

It would be easier to comfort her if he wasn't bare-chested, if he wasn't so intensely aware of every point where her bare skin made contact with his.

She raised her face to look at him. Her eyes were misty with tears but her full lips parted as if in invitation or some kind of strange desperation.

He didn't think about kissing her ahead of time. He didn't consciously plan to. It just happened. One minute he was gazing at her face and the next minute his mouth covered hers. He didn't just kiss her, she kissed him back, her mouth opening against his as he pulled her closer to him.

The kiss lasted only a second or two, then she pulled away from him, a horrified look on her face. "I'm sorry," she said, her cheeks blossoming with high color.

"No…I'm sorry," he replied stiffly. "You were screaming and obviously having a nightmare and I…I just meant to wake you."

She released a breathless, embarrassed laugh. "I'm definitely awake."

"Then I'll just…uh…let you go back to sleep." Dalton backed out of the room, afraid that if he remained another minute longer he'd want to kiss her again.

What was he doing? he wondered as he threw himself back onto the sofa. Every nerve in his body was electrified, every muscle tense. His response to that kiss stunned him. He knew virtually nothing about Jane Craig except that her skin had been soft as silk and her lips had been hot and willing.

It was possible by tomorrow she'd be gone. It was even more certain that he didn't want to be involved with her. He didn't want to know what she dreamed about, he didn't want to share his life with her in any way, shape or form. It had been wrong to kiss her, because all he could think about now was how much he wanted to kiss her again.

He fell asleep dreaming of the sweet heat of her mouth and awakened the next morning stiff and sore from the night on the sofa. He got up, nearly tripping over Sammy's diaper bag on the floor. He swallowed a curse.

By the time he'd made coffee, some of the stiffness of his muscles had begun to ease, as had his foul mood. He sat at the table, his hands wrapped around a mug of fresh brew. Even though it wasn't quite seven o'clock he could hear the sounds of plows already at work.

Maybe the bus would come this afternoon, he thought. That would be a good thing. He could see Jane and Sammy to the bus stop, wish them well on their way, then return to his solitary life without temptation. And Jane Craig had become a definite temptation.

He still sat at the table with thoughts of Jane when a knock sounded on his door. He jumped up from the table and hurried to answer. He pulled open the door to see his brother Zack standing on his landing, his gloved hands holding a shovel.

"Hey, bro, just thought I'd check in to see if you survived the storm. I just finished clearing off the driveway and your car and thought you might have a hot cup of coffee for me."

Dalton held the door tightly. *Please, please don't tell anyone I'm here.* Jane's words pounded in his head as he stared at his brother. "You didn't have to do that," he said. "And you don't want to come in here, Zack," he finally said. "I've got the flu, been throwing up off and on all night."

Zack frowned and took a step backward as if to avoid any germs floating in the air between them. "You need anything? We've about got all the major roads cleared in town and some of the stores are opening this morning."

"Nah, I'm fine. I just think I might be contagious so it wouldn't be a good idea for you to come inside, but I really appreciate you cleaning off the driveway. I'm sure George appreciates it, too. I'd love for you to come in, but I'm really not feeling well." Dalton couldn't tell if Zack believed him or not but he breathed a sigh of relief as Zack backed down the stairs, promising to check in on him later.

Dalton closed the door, hating the fact that he'd lied to his brother for reasons he didn't quite understand. If Jane's abusive ex-boyfriend had somehow tracked her to Cotter Creek, then why on earth would it matter if the local sheriff knew about it?

He turned to see Jane standing in the bedroom doorway, Sammy in her arms. "Thank you," she said.

"Don't thank me. I'm not happy about lying to my family." He walked back into the kitchen, aware of her following just behind him.

When he saw that she was about to prepare a bottle for Sammy, he held out his hands to take the kid from her arms. As always, Sammy looked delighted to see him. He launched himself into Dalton's arms with a big grin that lit up his entire little face.

"Is this kid ever in a bad mood?" Dalton asked as he sat in a chair. Sammy smelled like baby powder and lotion, a pleasant scent that reminded Dalton of dreams half-forgotten and abandoned.

"Rarely," she replied, moving to the sink. As she stood with her back to him he couldn't help but notice again the tight fit of her worn jeans across her butt. She had a great butt. Besides the jeans she wore a pink sweater that hugged her slender curves and complemented her blond coloring.

She fixed the bottle, then took Sammy from his arms and sat in the chair next to his, her hair falling softly around her shoulders. "If the streets are clear enough maybe it would be best if I found someplace else to go until the bus runs again."

She looked so small, so utterly vulnerable, and at that moment Sammy smiled at him around his bottle's nipple, the gesture sending a stream of formula down the side of his mouth.

"That isn't necessary," he replied. "Zack just told me the streets are practically clear, so I imagine that the bus will run tomorrow."

"Good." She held his gaze. "About last night…"

"You had a nightmare. I comforted you. That's all there was to it." He got up to pour himself another cup of coffee. "You want some breakfast? I was thinking maybe I'd make a stack of pancakes."

"You don't have to go to all that trouble for me," she protested.

He grinned at her. "I'm more than willing to go to that kind of trouble for me."

She returned his smile. "Well, in that case pancakes sound wonderful."

Breakfast was pleasant. Sammy entertained with coos and grins as his mother and Dalton ate pancakes and talked. The conversation was marked with a new easiness that he suspected came from the fact that they both saw the end of their confinement together.

She made him laugh as she shared with him funny stories about her grandmother. He noticed that in none of the stories did she mention the older sister she was supposedly on her way to visit, but he didn't call her on it. Instead he simply enjoyed the way her eyes sparkled as she spoke of the old woman who had raised her.

She might not have graduated high school, but she was smart as a whip. She argued politics with him and spoke easily of current affairs. He had a feeling she would do well no matter what path she chose in life.

The rest of the day passed pleasantly. As Sammy took a late-afternoon nap, Dalton and Jane sat at the table and played poker with toothpicks as chips.

"You're one heck of a bluffer," he said after she'd won her third pot.

She laughed. "If you think I'm good, you should play with Nana. She's the ultimate poker player in the family. In fact, she gets together once a week with some of the other ladies in the trailer park and they tell everyone they're playing bridge, but they really play poker."

He laughed, but his laughter was cut short by a knock on his door. "Sit tight. I'll get rid of whoever it is." She cast him a grateful look as he got up from the table.

It was probably one of his other brothers coming to check in on him. He'd have to play the sick card again. Hopefully he could bluff as well as Jane when it came to fooling his family members.

He pulled open the door to see a burly, dark-haired man he'd never seen before standing there. He wore the khaki pants and coat of law enforcement. "Yes?"

"Dalton West?"

"Yeah, I'm Dalton."

"I'm Sheriff Brandon Sinclair from over in Sandstone. I hate to bother you, but I'm looking for a woman named Janette Black. She's traveling with a baby and I have reason to believe she might have come here." His gaze went over Dalton's shoulder, as if trying to see inside the apartment.

Dalton tensed but offered the man a frown of confusion. "There's no woman or baby here," he said. "What makes you think she'd come to me? I've never heard of this Janette Black before." That part, at least, was true. But it didn't take a rocket scientist to know that Jane was really Janette.

"She stole money from the café where she worked and when we went to find her just before the storm hit we discovered more serious crimes. Her grandmother has been murdered and Janette is a person of interest. Your name and phone number were on a piece of paper next to the old woman's bed, so we thought maybe she'd come here."

"Sorry, I'm afraid I can't help you." Dalton's head whirled with the information Sheriff Sinclair had just given him. What in the hell was going on?

Sinclair studied him for a long moment, then held out a card. "If you see her, or if she tries to make contact with you, give me a call. She's dangerous, Mr. West. She needs to be behind bars."

"I'll keep that in mind," Dalton said. He murmured a goodbye, then closed his door. He waited until he heard the sound of the sheriff's boots going back down the stairs, then he went into the kitchen.

Janette sat at the table, her face devoid of all color. As she stared at him a deep, wrenching sob ripped from the back of her throat. "He killed Nana. First he raped me, and now he's killed Nana," she cried.

She jumped up from the chair. "I'm—I'm going to be sick." She ran for the bathroom as Sammy began to cry.

Chapter 5

Janette stood in the bathroom fighting not only an all-encompassing grief, but wave after wave of nausea, as well. Just hearing his deep voice had made her ill. Knowing he'd been on the other side of the door had sickened her.

He'd found her.

He'd said he found a notepad with Dalton's name and number next to Nana's bed. There was no way Nana would have willingly given him that information. Oh, God, she must have died trying to protect Janette and Sammy.

Blinded by her tears, she leaned weakly against the wall and wondered if it were possible to die of grief. She felt as if she were dying. Her heart felt as if it might explode at any moment.

Nana was dead.

Nana was dead.

Never again would Janette feel Nana's arms around her, never again would she see the old woman's eyes shining with love, her wrinkled face wreathed with laughter.

And Janette was wanted for her murder. That's how he would get Sammy. He'd see her tried for a murder she hadn't committed. She'd spend the rest of her life in prison, and Brandon Sinclair would have her precious boy. And her nana, the woman who had meant the world to her, was dead.

"Janette?" Dalton knocked on the door.

She sucked in air, trying to stanch the deep sobs that ripped through her. She didn't want to face him, was afraid that he might believe all the horrible things that Sinclair had said. And if he did believe Sinclair, there was nothing to stop him from contacting the lawman and letting him know she was here.

"Janette, come on out. We need to talk." His voice held a quiet command.

She grabbed a handful of tissues and wiped at her eyes, at her nose, then tossed the tissues into the trash. But she was reluctant to open the door, afraid to face him. What if she told him the truth and he didn't believe her? She didn't think she could handle it.

"Janette, you can't stay in there all night."

He was right. She couldn't stay in the bathroom. She opened the door. He no longer held Sammy, but as she stepped out of the bathroom Dalton opened his arms to her. She walked into them as tears of rich, raw grief began to flow again.

His strong arms surrounded her, and they felt like shelter from a world that had been terrifying for a very long time. She cried into the front of his shirt, wondering how she was going to survive without Nana's loving support.

After several minutes, Dalton released her and led her to the sofa. Sammy was once again on his blanket on the floor, staring up at the ceiling as if fascinated by the patterns the late-afternoon sunshine made as it drifted through the window.

Dalton sat next to her, his features inscrutable. "The truth, Janette. I need to know the whole truth," he said softly. "You said *he* raped you. Were you talking about your old boyfriend?"

She had two choices. Continue with the lies she'd told him, or tell the truth about everything. Her heart banged against her ribs. "No." The word whispered out of her on a wave of despair. She knew it was time to tell the truth. She had nothing to lose now and she wanted—needed—Dalton to know.

She grabbed a strand of her hair and twisted it around her finger. "There is no ex-boyfriend. The man who raped me, the man who killed my grandmother, is Sheriff Brandon Sinclair."

Dalton's eyes narrowed and he drew in a quick breath of surprise. "I think maybe you need to start at the beginning and tell me everything."

She leaned back against the plump sofa cushion and closed her eyes, fighting the overwhelming grief that still reached out to smother her in its clutches. She opened her eyes and gazed down at Sammy, who in the midst of her heartbreak had fallen asleep.

Looking at Dalton, she fought against the tears and drew a deep, steadying breath. The beginning. "It happened one night when I was driving home from the classes I was taking to study for my GED. They took place at a community college about twenty-five miles from where I lived in Sandstone."

She rose from the sofa, unable to sit as she fought against the panic that remembering that night always brought. It was a panic that constricted her lungs, closed up the back of her throat and quickened her heartbeat. It was the fear of having to remember and the additional stress of wondering if Dalton would believe her.

"Janette." He reached out and took her hand. Holding it firmly he drew her back on the sofa next to him. "It's okay, you're safe for now." He didn't let go of her hand. It was as if he knew she needed support, something to cling to as she went back to that horrible night.

She nodded and swallowed hard. "The highway between the community college and Sandstone is pretty deserted after dark. I was about halfway between the college and home when I saw the lights of a patrol car in my rearview mirror. I knew I was speeding so I pulled over to the side of the road, figuring I was about to get a ticket."

She paused and drew another deep breath, trying to still the frantic beat of her heart. Dalton squeezed her hand, as if to give her strength, and she desperately needed it. She needed all the strength he could give her to get through the rest of it.

"I thought something was odd when he told me to turn off my headlights and get out of the car. He told me I had been speeding and asked if I was doing drugs. I've never touched drugs in my life," she stated emphatically.

Dalton nodded, his expression giving nothing away of his inner thoughts. "Had you had run-ins with him before that night?"

"Never," she replied. "I'd seen him around town, on the streets, but he'd never spoken to me before, never even noticed me that I knew of."

"What happened next?" he asked.

A trembling began deep inside her. It was as if all the warmth of the room had been sucked out and an arctic chill had taken over the world. Tears blurred her vision once again and she blinked them away, angry that after all this time the memory of what happened still had the power to make her cry.

"He told me he needed to frisk me and he warned me that he'd hate to have to shoot me for resisting." She looked down at Dalton's hand around hers, unable to look him in the eyes.

"He raped me there on the side of the road." The words didn't begin to describe the horror, the violation of that night.

Her nose filled with the sweaty, ugly scent of Sinclair. Her skin wanted to crawl off her body as she thought of the way he'd touched her, the sounds he'd made as he pushed himself against her. "I won't bore you with all the ugly details."

She pulled her hand from Dalton's, afraid he could feel the ugliness inside her. She couldn't look at him, was afraid to see disbelief in his eyes. She'd fall completely to pieces if she saw doubt or condemnation there.

"What happened after?" His voice was soft, as if he understood the emotions blackening her soul. Thank God he didn't press her for any of the details of the rape itself, for she'd shoved those particular memories deep inside her in a place where she wouldn't easily retrieve them.

She looked up into those warm green eyes of his.

"Nothing," she said simply. She forced a smile of dark humor. "I guess I should be grateful that at least I didn't get a speeding ticket." The smile faltered and fell away as tears once again burned at her eyes.

He raised a dark eyebrow. "You didn't tell anyone?"

She leaned back and stared at a point just over his shoulder. "Who was I going to tell? I couldn't exactly report the crime to the sheriff." There was more than a touch of bitterness in her voice.

She shook her head. "I didn't tell anyone. I didn't want to tell Nana because I thought it might destroy her. It wasn't until I realized I was pregnant that I finally told Nana and the man I'd been seeing at the time." A shaft of pain stabbed through her. "He asked me what I'd been wearing that night, implying that it was somehow my fault. Needless to say that was the end of that relationship."

"And you're sure Sheriff Sinclair is Sammy's biological father?" There was a faint note of apology in his voice.

She wanted to be offended by the question, but realized Dalton really didn't know anything about her. It was a fair question, she supposed.

"I'm positive. The guy I was seeing at the time…we hadn't…you know, been intimate." Her cheeks burned and she kept her gaze averted from his.

"So, you realized you were pregnant. What happened then?"

She looked at him once again. It was impossible to read him. She had no idea if he believed her or not, couldn't get a sense of anything that might be flowing through his head.

"The last thing I wanted was for Brandon Sinclair to

know that I was pregnant. I managed to hide my condition from everyone until late in the pregnancy, then I told people who noticed that I'd had a fling with a salesman passing through town." She gazed down at Sammy. "As far as I was concerned Brandon Sinclair had no right to know about my condition. From the very beginning Sammy was my baby and nobody else's."

"So, he didn't know anything about Sammy."

"I didn't think he knew until three days ago when he walked into the café where I worked." She told him about Sinclair and his deputies coming in and the sheriff asking her about her son.

"There was something in his eyes, something in the things he was saying that let me know I had to take Sammy and run and so that's what I did. I didn't steal anything from the café, but the moment the sheriff left, I told Smiley, the owner, that I didn't feel well. I also told him I wasn't happy working there and I was quitting, then I went home."

She paused a moment to draw a deep breath then continued, "Nana agreed that I needed to take Sammy and leave town, get as far away as possible from Sheriff Sinclair. One of Nana's friends drove me here to catch the bus. Our plan was that I'd get settled someplace far away from Oklahoma, then I'd send for Nana and we'd start building a new life together." Grief once again rocked through her and new tears burned at her eyes as she thought of her grandmother.

Dalton studied her, a tiny frown furrowing the area in the center of his forehead. "After that night of the rape, did he continue to bother you? To threaten you in any way?"

She shook her head. "No. Of course, I went out of my way to avoid him. I kept my pregnancy pretty well hidden, too. The few times we did run into each other, it was as if nothing had ever happened. He'd look right through me, as if he had no memory of what he'd done."

She wrapped her arms around herself, fighting a new chill. A bitter laugh escaped her. "Who was I going to report it to?" she said more to herself than to him. "Who was I going to tell about the rape? The sheriff? His deputies? Brandon Sinclair owns Sandstone."

Leaning forward she stared at the wall just over Dalton's shoulder. "Everyone is afraid of him. He'll get Smiley, my boss at the café, to agree that I stole money. He'll get anyone in town to say anything whether it's true or not, because nobody wants to get on his bad side. Besides, when he was done with me he reminded me that I was nothing but trailer trash and nobody would ever believe my word over his."

"I believe you."

Those three words, so simply spoken, wove a strand of warmth around her heart. She hadn't realized how badly she'd wanted to hear somebody other than her nana say them. She began to cry again.

Dalton pulled her against his broad chest as her tears flowed once again. He believed her. Dalton, better than anyone, knew that a gold badge of law enforcement could hide a sick, twisted soul.

There was no way she could fake the grief she felt for her grandmother and there was no way she could have manufactured the trauma she'd exhibited as she'd told him about the rape.

He tightened his arms around her. There was a special place in hell for men who raped women, and a place beyond hell for men in authority who abused women.

Janette's tears finally ebbed and she raised her head and looked at him, the blue of her eyes dark with tortured sorrow. "I just can't believe she's gone," she said, her voice hoarse with emotion. "I just talked to her yesterday morning."

"Yesterday morning?" Dalton frowned, the sheriff's words replaying in his mind. "You spoke to your grandmother yesterday morning?"

She nodded and moved out of his embrace. She wiped at her cheeks and tucked a strand of her shiny hair behind her ear. "I called her from here to let her know that I was stuck here because of the storm."

"But according to what Sheriff Sinclair told me, he found her dead before the storm moved in."

Janette blinked in confusion. "But that's impossible." Her tears disappeared as a tenuous hope shone from her eyes. "He lied. And if she wasn't dead when he said she was, maybe she isn't dead at all. Maybe he just said that to get you to turn me over to him." She jumped up from the sofa and headed to the cordless phone on the end table.

Dalton leaned forward and watched her. As she punched in numbers she looked small and fragile, and the thought of a man touching her, taking her with force filled him with a simmering rage.

He watched her face as she gripped the phone receiver tightly against her ear. The hope that had momentarily lit her eyes faded.

"Nobody answered," she said as she hung up. "Even

the answering machine didn't pick up." Her eyes grew shiny with tears once again.

"Is there anyone else you can call to see what's going on?"

"Nana's friend, Nancy." She quickly punched in the number. "She lives next door to Nana at the trailer park. She'll know what's going on. Nancy," she said into the phone. "It's me."

Myriad expressions played across her face as she listened to the voice on the other end of the line. "Oh, God, is she…" Tears once again fell from Janette's eyes but she offered him a tremulous smile.

"Nana, are you all right?"

As she said these words a knot of tension eased in his chest. Either she was a better actress than Meryl Streep or she was now talking to the grandmother she'd thought murdered.

"Does he know where you are now?" Janette asked. "Are you sure you'll be okay?" She paused and listened for several minutes, then continued, "We're fine and hopefully tomorrow we'll be on the bus. Don't worry, Nana, everything is going to be okay. I love you, too. I'll stay in touch."

Janette hung up the phone and stared at Dalton, her eyes once again haunted with fear. "She's alive, thank God." She returned to the sofa. He saw the tremor that went through her body, but when she gazed at him he realized it was anger shining from her eyes, not fear.

"What's happened?" he asked.

"Yesterday morning Nana braved the snow to go to Nancy's and have coffee. She was there for about two hours. When she got home she had the feeling somebody had been in her trailer. She didn't find anything out of place or missing so she chalked it up to her imagination. Then last night she was feeling lonely and unsettled, so she went back to Nancy's to play some cards and spend the night. During the night her trailer was set on fire."

Shock filled Dalton at her words.

"Thank God she wasn't home. He meant to kill her, Dalton." Janette's hands clenched into fists at her sides. "He meant to kill her and blame me so he can see me in prison. Then he'll be free to claim Sammy."

They both looked at the sleeping child on the floor. A weary resignation filled him. He'd offered her safe harbor from a snowstorm but now it appeared that the storm in her life had nothing to do with the weather outside. And he had a feeling whether he wanted it or not, her storm had become his.

"Why don't we get something to eat? It's past dinnertime and I think we both could use something warm in our bellies." He got up from the sofa and she followed him into the kitchen. "Grilled cheese and soup?" he asked and pointed her to the table.

She shrugged, as if it didn't matter what he offered her. He opened a can of tomato soup and poured it into a saucepan, then when he had it warming up he prepared the grilled cheese for the awaiting skillet. As he worked, she stared out the window where darkness had begun to fall.

He had to admit that there was something about her that touched him, that called on protective instincts he'd thought had been lost when he'd lost Mary.

"It must have been a tough decision to have the baby under the circumstances," he said. "A lot of women would have chosen a different option."

"I thought about an abortion," she replied. "But, to be honest, it was just a passing thought. It might be an option for a lot of women, but it wasn't for me. I was easily able to separate the innocent baby from the monster who had raped me."

She smiled then, the first smile he'd seen from her since the appearance of Brandon Sinclair on his doorstep. It was like sunshine breaking through chill wintry clouds. "Sammy is the best of me and there hasn't been a single minute that I've regretted my decision to give him life."

That's mother love, he thought. That fierce, shining emotion he saw in Janette's eyes, that was what he'd lost when his mother had been murdered. Dalton rarely thought about the mother he couldn't remember, but a shaft of unexpected grief stabbed him now.

"It was a sheriff who murdered my mother twenty-five years ago," he said. Her eyes widened as she stared at him. "The sheriff of Cotter Creek, Jim Ramsey. He was arrested a couple of months ago when he stalked my sister."

"Why? Why did he kill your mother?"

Dalton stirred the soup, then placed the first two sandwiches into the skillet. "He said he loved her, but it wasn't love, it was a sick, twisted obsession. He approached her one night on the highway and told her he loved her, that he wanted her to leave my dad, and when she refused he lost it and strangled her."

He didn't miss the parallel in what had happened to his mother and what had happened to Janette. Men they should have been able to trust had accosted both on a lonely stretch of highway. The only difference was, Janette had survived and his mother had not.

"Oh, Dalton, I'm so sorry."

He nodded and swallowed around the unexpected lump of emotion that rose up in his throat. "It was a long time ago. She was a wonderful, loving person."

"And your father never remarried?"

Dalton flipped the sandwiches. "No, never even looked at another woman. He and my mom were true soul mates and when she was gone he never showed any interest in pursuing a relationship with anyone else."

"From what my grandmother told me, my mother wasn't even sure who my father was." Her gaze went back to the window again and when she looked back at Dalton a tiny frown furrowed her forehead. "Why would he tell you that I'd killed Nana?"

Dalton took up the grilled cheese sandwiches and placed them on two separate plates. "If he burned down her trailer last night it's possible he doesn't know she isn't dead. If he puts out the word that you're wanted for questioning in a murder case, then you're going to have trouble hiding out. He can get law enforcement officials in every county keeping an eye out for you."

He set the plates on the table then went back to grab the two bowls of soup. "If you're trying to cheer me up, it isn't working," she said dryly.

She placed her spoon in her bowl, but didn't begin to eat. Instead, she looked back out the window, where night had completely fallen. "Do you think he believed you when you told him you didn't know me, that I wasn't here?"

Dalton followed her gaze to the window and a tight knot of tension formed in his chest. "I have a feeling we'll know before the bus shows up in town."

* * *

Brandon raised his collar against the stiff wind that blew from the north. He stood across the street from Dalton West's place, eyes trained on the upper windows. She was in there. He smelled her, the trailer trash tramp who was trying to keep his son from him.

He'd known that she'd blown town, had taken his son and left Sandstone. A visit to her grandmother's house yesterday had given him his clue. The old lady wasn't home but he'd gotten inside and taken a look around. The minute he'd seen the name and phone number on the nightstand, he knew in his gut that he was on her trail.

It was obvious from the condition of the small bedroom in the trailer that Janette had packed up and left. Clothes were thrown helter-skelter and there wasn't a baby article to be found except for the crib, which was stripped of bedding.

He'd been enraged. He'd gone back to his office, researched to find out what he could about Dalton West, then late last night had returned to the trailer and set it on fire. He considered the death of Janette's grandmother collateral damage. He hadn't yet gotten the official report of the fire from their fire chief, but he knew the man would write up whatever Brandon told him to.

With the old woman dead and Janette wanted as a suspect in an arson-murder case, she'd find it difficult to get out of Cotter Creek. She was a wanted woman, and if he put a reward on her head, she wouldn't be able to show her face anywhere.

He'd known he'd find Janette, and he had. He narrowed his eyes as he watched the windows. Even though

Dalton West had told him he'd never heard of Janette Black, that there was no woman with a baby inside his place, Brandon knew he'd lied.

The sheriff had done his homework. He knew Dalton West was a bachelor who lived alone. But he'd watched the silhouettes move back and forth in front of those windows and knew the professional bodyguard wasn't alone. And if that wasn't enough, when Dalton had opened the door and Brandon had gotten a glimpse inside, he'd seen a diaper bag on the living-room floor, a diaper bag with the same blue teddy bear print that had decorated one area of one of the small bedrooms in the trailer.

She was in there, and there was no way she was going to escape him. One Oklahoma bodyguard wasn't going to stand in the way of Brandon Sinclair getting exactly what he wanted.

Chapter 6

The cough woke Dalton. An irritating cough that pulled him groggily from his sleep. His eyes burned as he sat up on the sofa and realized the air was filled with the acrid scent of smoke.

Fear shoved aside the last of his sleepiness as he grabbed his gun off the coffee table where he'd placed it before going to sleep the night before.

He turned on the lamp next to the sofa and gasped as he saw the dark smoke that swirled in the room. Fire! They had to get out.

Maybe George had forgotten to turn off a stove burner and something had caught flame. Dalton didn't give much thought to what caused the smoke, he just knew he needed to get Janette and Sammy out, for the smoke appeared to be thickening by the second. Fire could be dangerous, but smoke was just as deadly.

He pulled on his boots, then grabbed a coat, his cell phone and car keys and hurried into the bedroom where Sammy and Janette were asleep. He turned on the overhead light and Janette stirred, but didn't awaken.

"Janette." He walked over to the bed and shook her shoulder with a sense of urgency. A spasm of coughing overtook him as she opened her eyes. "We need to get out of here," he finally managed to gasp.

She didn't ask questions, obviously aware of the imminent danger that whirled and darkened the room despite the overhead light. "I'll get your coat," he said. "Just grab what you need."

As Dalton raced back through the kitchen into the small utility room where he'd hung her coat the night she'd arrived, he felt no heat beneath his feet, heard no ominous crackle of flames. But that didn't mean they weren't in danger.

She met him at the bedroom door, pulling her suitcase behind her and Sammy in her arms with a blanket over his head. He thought about telling her to forget the suitcase, but realized the case contained all the possessions she and Sammy had left in the world.

He grabbed the suitcase from her and motioned her toward the door that led to the interior staircase. He needed to make sure George got out, as well.

Before he opened the stairwell door he felt the wood, wanting to make sure it wasn't hot, that deadly flames weren't already attempting to burn through. The door radiated no heat so he opened it and motioned for her to precede him down the stairs.

The smoke wasn't as intense in the staircase, and still he could feel no heat radiating from any of the walls. But where there was smoke, there had to be a fire.

They hit the landing to the first floor and Dalton entered George's area of the house. "Wait here," he said to Janette as he raced through George's living room and down the hallway to the bedroom where the old man slept.

It took him only minutes to rouse George from sleep and get his coat and shoes on him, then together they all made their way to the front door.

It wasn't until they opened the front door to get out that Dalton's brain fully kicked into high gear. "Wait," he said urgently before Janette ran outside.

His mind whirled with suppositions. Brandon Sinclair had burned down Janette's grandmother's place. This evening he'd come to ask if Janette was here. Was it possible Sinclair hadn't believed Dalton when he'd said he didn't know Janette? Was it out of the question that he'd set a fire to try to smoke her out?

"Janette, my truck is in the driveway. I'm going out first and when I get outside you run for the truck. George, you come out after Janette." He released the lock on his gun, knowing he might have to provide cover for her if Sinclair was outside.

He knew by the look in Janette's eyes that she perceived his thoughts, realized the potential for danger. She gripped Sammy more tightly against her as George took the suitcase from her hand.

"Problems?" George asked.

"Possibly," Dalton replied. George nodded and straightened his thin, sloped shoulders.

Dalton went out the door, gun drawn, and with every sense he possessed on high alert. The night held the eerie silence that snow-cover produced, a preternatural calm that could be deceptive.

Snow crunched beneath his boots as he stepped onto the front porch. The cold air stabbed his lungs as he drew deep, even breaths. He looked both directions, seeing nothing amiss but unwilling to trust that the night shadows held nothing dangerous.

He took several more steps, then turned back to the house, noting dark smoke rolling out of a partially opened basement window. Had George left it open? The old man had a workshop downstairs where he did some woodworking. Had he left his wood-burning tool on, and somehow it had caught fire?

His heart pounded as adrenaline continued to pump through him. He had no idea how big a fire might be burning there, but it was apparent he needed to get the others out of the house as soon as possible.

Looking around once again he saw nothing that indicated any danger. He walked back up to the door and motioned for Janette to follow him as he tried to watch every direction around them.

The gunshot came from the left, the bullet whizzing by Janette's head as she screamed in terror. Dalton's body slammed her to the ground, and he hoped that in the process Sammy wasn't hurt.

"Get down, George," he yelled at the old man, who had just stepped off the porch. George dove into a snowbank with the agility of a man one-fourth his age.

Another gunshot exploded in the quiet of the night and the snow next to where Dalton and Janette lay kicked up. The shots had come from the direction of a large oak tree in the distance. Janette screamed again and Sammy's cries added to the melee.

Dalton's heart crashed against his ribs and he thought he could feel Janette's heartbeat through their coats.

"I'm going to roll off you and start firing. When I do, run like hell to the truck and get inside. Stay down." He fumbled in his pocket for his keys and gave them to her. "And if anything happens to me, drive away and don't look back."

He didn't give her time to protest or accept, he rolled off her and began firing at the tree. At the same time he heard the sound of a siren in the distance and knew that somebody had heard the shots and called for help.

When he saw that Janette was safely in the truck, he stopped firing and waited to see if there would be an answering volley.

Nothing.

For a long moment he remained where he was, not moving, but listening…waiting…wondering if the threat still existed or not.

He got up into a crouch as the siren grew louder. Still no answering shots. He had a feeling the shooter had run at the first sound of the siren. He hurried to the driver's side of the truck and was surprised to see George come burrowing up from the snowdrift and running to throw the suitcase in the back of the truck bed.

Dalton had just backed out of the driveway when Zack's patrol car came screaming to a halt. "Get down," he ordered Janette. She bent so she wasn't visible and Dalton was grateful that at the moment Sammy wasn't wailing. He rolled down his window as Zack rolled down his.

"Call the fire department, and see to George," Dalton said. "I'll be in touch." As Zack yelled a protest, Dalton pulled out onto the street and sped away from his brother, the house and the quiet, solitary life he'd led.

Thankfully, Janette remained silent as he headed out

of town and kept a watchful eye on the street behind him for anyone that might be following.

He needed to think.

Zack was a newly elected sheriff and aware of everyone's eyes on him. After the disgrace of Jim Ramsey, the last sheriff of Cotter Creek, Zack was proving himself to be a strictly by-the-book kind of lawman.

Dalton believed in rules, but sometimes rules had to be bent, even broken, and he wasn't convinced that Zack would see things his way.

If Brandon Sinclair had an arrest warrant for Janette, then Dalton feared his brother would feel it necessary to turn her over to him. He wouldn't want to put himself in the middle of a problem that wasn't his, especially in bucking the authority of a fellow sheriff.

"Where are we going?" Janette asked, finally breaking the tense silence in the truck as they left the town of Cotter Creek behind.

"A place where you'll be safe until we can figure things out," he replied.

Besides, if he did decide to confide in Zack, what could he tell him? That a strange woman had shown up on his doorstep and had initially lied about everything, but finally had told him a story that he believed?

Zack would ask for cold hard facts and Dalton had none. He couldn't prove that Brandon Sinclair had set the fire tonight or fired the shots. No doubt Sinclair hadn't used his service weapon; ballistics would probably lead to a dead end. He couldn't prove that Janette hadn't stolen money from her employer, although he could attest to the fact that she hadn't been anywhere near that trailer when it had gone up in flames. Unless Sinclair screwed around with the reported date of the fire.

He didn't want to put his brother in the untenable position of having to choose between doing his job or supporting Dalton's decision to break the law by hiding Janette.

He'd talk to Zack, tell him who he thought was responsible for both the fire tonight and the gunfire, but he wouldn't tell Zack where Janette was hidden away. He wouldn't give her over to Zack, who might find himself with no alternative than to turn her over to Sinclair.

He cast a quick glance at the woman in the passenger seat. She bounced Sammy in her arms and asked no more questions about where they were going or what they were going to do.

She trusted him.

After two snowbound days together, she trusted that he was taking her someplace where she'd be safe. It shocked him, awed him, and if he were to admit the truth to himself, it scared him more than just a little bit. She was placing not only her life, but also the life of her little boy directly in his hands.

He clenched the steering wheel tightly. He hadn't signed on for this, had simply offered a woman and her baby shelter from the storm. A tiny spark of anger filled him. He didn't want this responsibility. Since the debacle with Mary he'd consciously backed away from being involved with anyone, even his family. He didn't want anyone depending on him, needing him.

He didn't want the responsibility, but now that he had it, he couldn't turn his back. Janette had been trapped by the storm, and now he was trapped by her circumstances.

* * *

Janette thought she might be in a mild state of shock. She couldn't process the fire, the gunshots and now a drive down narrow, slick roads with darkness all around.

She should be terrified, but she wasn't. She was beyond terror and instead felt only a weary resignation, a stunning knowledge that she was no longer in control of her own life.

She glanced at Dalton. In the faint illumination from the dashboard his handsome features looked grim and more than a little bit dangerous. She could only imagine what was going through his mind right now.

Because of his kindness to a stranger, his home had been set on fire, he'd been shot at and he was now making a dash over the snow-slick roads to a safe place.

"I'm so sorry I got you involved in all this," she said. "All I wanted to do was leave town."

His knuckles turned white on the steering wheel as she felt the back end of the truck slide out. She caught her breath, then relaxed as he skillfully steered into the skid and straightened out the truck.

"I know," he replied. "We'll talk when we get where we're going."

That comment effectively stanched any other conversation she might have wanted to have. She cuddled Sammy closer against her and stared out the passenger window, where no lights from houses broke the darkness of the night.

He seemed to have a plan and she was grateful, because she had none. She couldn't return to his apartment because it was obvious Sinclair knew she was there. She felt terrible that she'd now placed Dalton in a horrible position. If he didn't turn her over to the sheriff, then he was breaking the law and could face even uglier repercussions of his own.

She'd like to be able to tell him just to drop her off somewhere, that she'd figure things out on her own. But that wasn't an option either. She couldn't go back to Sandstone and she couldn't get out of Cotter Creek. She was in a horrible state of limbo, with Brandon Sinclair like a hound dog sniffing her scent.

She sat straighter in the seat as Dalton turned off the main road and through an iron gate. He doused his headlights as they approached a large ranch-style home.

"That's my dad's place," he said as they drove past the sprawling one-story house. "It would be better if nobody knows you're here on the property."

That explained him dousing the truck lights. They entered a pasture area and he threw the gears into four-wheel drive as they hit the thicker snow where no plows had been.

They passed another house where lights shone from several windows. "That's my brother Tanner and his wife's place," Dalton said.

Still they didn't stop. Once they'd passed the second house Dalton turned the truck headlights back on. There were other tracks in the snow. In one area it looked as if several trucks or cars had made figure eights.

An area of thick woods was on their right, mostly evergreen trees, which she assumed provided windbreaks. Eventually Dalton turned through a small break in the trees and pulled to a halt in front of a small cabin. Trees completely surrounded it, tall evergreens that made it impossible to see the place unless you were right on top of it.

"Who lives here?" she asked, nerves jumping in her stomach.

"For now, you do," he said as he shut off the engine. "At one time or another, I think all of my brothers have lived here for short periods, but for the last couple of months it's been empty. You should be safe here."

She *should* have been safe on the road between her home and the community college. She *should* have been safe in Dalton's apartment. She couldn't afford to take her safety for granted anymore.

"Come on, let's get you inside and settled," he said as he opened his truck door.

Janette got out of the truck and stared at the cabin. There was nothing welcoming about it. Illuminated only by the faint cast of the moon filtering through the trees, it looked dark and cold and forbidding.

She tightened her grip on Sammy as she followed Dalton up the stairs to the front door. He used a key to unlock it, then pushed it open, flipped on a switch that lit a small table lamp and ushered her inside.

The sense of welcome that had been absent from the exterior was present inside. Plump throw pillows covered a dark green sofa, and a rocking chair sat next to the fireplace. The wood floor gleamed with richness except where it was covered by braided rugs.

"It's nothing fancy," Dalton said as he wheeled the dial of the thermostat on the wall. "There's a bedroom and bath and a small kitchen." He turned to face her. "We're deep enough in the woods that no one should see the lights, but I won't light a fire. I don't want smoke from the chimney to draw any curious people."

He motioned her to follow him into the small kitchen, where he opened cabinets to show her a stockpile of canned goods. "There's enough here to hold you for a night or two."

"You're not staying?" She tried to keep the fear out of her voice but didn't quite succeed.

"I've got to get back to town and check on George and talk to my brother."

"What are you going to tell him?" She studied his features, wondering if he'd decide to give her up, that this was all trouble he hadn't bargained to take on and he was finished with her and her mess.

He swiped a hand through his thick dark hair and leaned against the wall, his expression unreadable. "I don't know for sure. I'm still sorting out things in my head. But I promise you I won't tell him you're here."

He shoved off from the wall. "Things are pretty dusty in here, but there's fresh bedding in one of the dresser drawers in the bedroom, and it won't take long for the furnace to warm things up."

"I'm sure we'll be fine," she replied, although she wasn't sure of anything. She wanted to tell him not to leave her, that she needed him to hold her, to wrap her in his strong arms and make her feel safe.

She couldn't remember the last time she'd truly felt safe. On second thought, yes, she did remember. It had been the night of her bad dream when he had held her and soothed away her fear.

He walked over to the doorway that led off the kitchen and flipped on the light to illuminate a small bedroom with a double bed and a long dresser. "It's late. You should try to get some sleep. There's a phone in the living room. I'm assuming you don't have a cell phone."

"Where I come from cell phones are a luxury, not a necessity."

He nodded and headed for the front door. "You've got my cell phone number. If you need anything don't hesitate to call."

She followed him to the front door, nerves jangling inside as she watched him go out to the truck then return with her suitcase, which George had thrown into the back at the last minute.

"Will you be back later tonight?" she asked.

His green eyes narrowed intently. "I don't know. I can't make any promises. For sure I'll try to be back here sometime tomorrow. Is there anything you need for Sammy?"

"It depends on how long we're here. If it's for too much longer I'm going to need some more diapers." A sense of urgency swept through her. "Surely the bus will run tomorrow and I can get on it and away from here."

He stared at her for a long moment, and she had a feeling he wanted to say something to her, something she might not want to hear. Instead he turned toward the door. "I'll see you sometime tomorrow."

And with that he was gone.

Sammy slept soundly as she laid him on the sofa with pillows surrounding him while she went into the bedroom to make up the bed.

The last thing on her mind was sleep. Restless energy filled her, coupled with a simmering sense of terror that was unrelenting.

Was Sinclair still in Cotter Creek? Those gunshots tonight were intended to kill her. Had his intention been to kill them all, then pluck Sammy from her dead arms?

She now recognized that Sinclair would do anything to get Sammy. The man was insane. Was it truly about him wanting a son, or was it more than that?

Maybe he was angry that she'd left town and was afraid that once she was out of Sandstone, she'd feel safe enough to talk about what he'd done to her. It was impossible to know the man's mind. A chill washed over her, and it had nothing to do with the coolness of the room.

Once the bed was made she placed Sammy in the middle, then walked back into the living room, knowing that sleep would be a long time coming.

She stood at the living-room window and stared out into the darkness of night, her thoughts going to the man who had just left.

Smelling the scent of his pleasant cologne, which lingered in the air, she wrapped her arms around her middle and tried not to allow herself to wish for a life different than the one she'd been handed.

The memory of that single kiss she'd shared with Dalton warmed the chilled places inside her. What would it be like to kiss him longer, harder? What would it be like to lie naked in his arms, to make love with him?

She hadn't been with any man since the night of her rape, but she knew how good lovemaking could be if it was between two people who cared about each other. When she was twenty-one she'd had a relationship with a man that had lasted almost a year. They had enjoyed a healthy sex life for the last three months of their time together.

Although that relationship had ended, she was grateful now that she'd had it. It would have been terrible to know nothing about sex except those horrid minutes on the side of the road with Sinclair.

She could care for a man like Dalton West, a man

who not only stole a bit of her breath away whenever she looked at him, but also radiated the strength and assurance of a good man.

Turning away from the window she released a deep sigh. The last thing she needed to be thinking of was indulging in an affair with Dalton. She was an uneducated woman with a son who was the product of rape. What made her think a man like Dalton West would ever want anything to do with her?

What she'd better figure out instead was how she was going to stay one step ahead of a demented man who wanted to take the only thing she cared about, a man who would stop at nothing to get what he wanted.

Chapter 7

Zack's patrol car was still in front of George's place when Dalton pulled into the driveway. He'd spent the entire drive back from the cabin trying to figure out exactly what he intended to tell his brother.

His first priority was to protect Janette, but equally as important was his desire to protect his brother. He refused to put Zack in a position where he had to choose between doing the right thing and handing Janette over to Brandon Sinclair, or doing the wrong thing and jeopardizing the job he loved.

He got out of his car, aware that he was about to walk a very fine line. George's front door was open, and when Dalton walked in Zack greeted him with a deep frown of frustration.

"It's about time you showed up. You want to tell me what's going on?" Zack asked. "A fire of suspicious origins and gunshots, and I can't get George here to tell me anything."

George sat on his sofa, his arms folded across his chest and a stubborn glint in his brown eyes. "I can't tell you what I don't know," he exclaimed fervently. "I don't know how those rags started on fire in my basement and I sure as hell don't have a clue who shot at us when we ran out of the house."

"How much damage did the fire do?" Dalton asked, stalling for time.

"Thank God it was more smoke than flame," George replied. "Burned up a couple of boxes I had stored down there, but nothing too serious."

"Good." Dalton turned to his brother. "Why don't you and I go up to my place and let George get some sleep? He's not used to this much excitement in the middle of the night."

"You got that right," George exclaimed.

Zack nodded, his jaw muscle knotted with obvious frustration. Dalton told George good-night, then together he and Zack went upstairs.

Once in Dalton's living room Zack sat on the edge of the sofa and stared at his brother. "Now talk," he demanded. "I need some answers from somebody and as far as I can tell you're the only one around here who might have them."

Dalton remained standing. "Earlier this evening Sheriff Brandon Sinclair from Sandstone knocked on my door and told me he was looking for a woman wanted for theft and questioning in a murder case and had reason to believe she had come to me. I told him I didn't know the woman, but I don't think he believed me."

Zack frowned. "Why would he think this woman would come to you?"

"I don't know. He said something about finding my name and number in the trailer where this woman lives."

Zack watched him intently. "And you don't know this woman. What's her name?"

"According to Sinclair, her name is Janette Black, and, no, I don't know her. I can't imagine why she would have had my name and phone number."

"So, what? What does Sinclair have to do with the fire and the gunplay that took place here tonight?"

Dalton shrugged. "All I can tell you is that he was here asking about a woman named Janette Black. I told him I'd never heard of her and she certainly wasn't here, then he left. Hours later I woke up to smoke filling the house and I ran downstairs and woke up George. We ran out the front door and somebody started shooting at us."

Zack's frown deepened. "Why would Sinclair do something like that?"

"I don't know. All I can tell you is what happened," Dalton replied. The most difficult thing he'd ever done was hold his brother's gaze while he knew he wasn't telling the whole truth.

"Was the shooter targeting both you and George?"

"No, just me," Dalton answered. "I returned fire, jumped into my truck and that's when you got here."

"Handy that you just happened to have your gun with you when you ran out of the house."

"Dad always taught us to be prepared for anything," Dalton replied easily. "And to be honest, something about Sinclair didn't sit quite right with me. Call it instinct."

"Where have you been for the last hour?" Zack asked, watching Dalton intently.

"Driving…making sure nobody was following me." Although the lie fell effortlessly from his lips, he hated the way it felt inside. "I wanted to draw any danger there might be away from this house and George, but I didn't see anyone following me."

Zack frowned again. "This just doesn't make any sense. Why would Brandon Sinclair do something like this? I know Brandon. We've met for beers a couple of times. He's always seemed like a stand-up guy to me."

"If you're investigating the shooting and the fire, I recommend you start the investigation by checking Mr. Stand-up Guy's alibi," Dalton countered lightly.

"Is there some history here that I don't know anything about? Have you and Brandon had run-ins before?"

"Definitely not. I'd never met the man before he showed up on my doorstep earlier this evening."

"You having problems with anyone else? Are you working on something that I don't know about? Something to do with West Protective Services?"

"Nothing."

Zack stood, obviously as frustrated as he had been when Dalton had arrived. "I don't know, bro. I get the feeling you're not telling me everything."

"Believe me, when I figure out what's going on you'll be one of the first to know," Dalton promised.

Zack headed for the door. "You want me to put one of my deputies on the house? Keep an eye on things for the rest of the night?"

Dalton shook his head. "I have a feeling the excitement is over for the night." With Janette out of the apartment there was no reason for Brandon Sinclair to come calling again. And if he did, Dalton would be ready.

"You'll let me know if you think of anything else?"

"Of course," Dalton said. He watched as his brother opened the door and started to step outside, then paused and turned back to look at Dalton.

"Must have been a fast-moving bug," he said.

"Excuse me?" Dalton frowned in confusion.

"The flu. You seem to be feeling much better now." Zack had a knowing glint in his eyes.

"I am. Must have been a twenty-four-hour bug that ran its course." Dalton hoped his cheeks weren't dark with the color of the lie.

Zack held his gaze for a long moment. "Dalton, you'd tell me if you were in trouble, right?" This time there was no frustration on Zack's features, only the deep concern of a brother.

Dalton wanted to tell him everything, but before he could do that he needed to talk to Janette. "I'm fine, really," he said, but he could tell his words did nothing to assure his brother.

Zack disappeared out the door. Dalton breathed a huge sigh of relief and sat on the edge of the sofa where Zack had been only seconds before.

It was obvious that George had stayed true to his word and hadn't breathed a word to Zack about Janette and Sammy being there.

A glance at the clock let Dalton know it was almost four. The last thing on his mind was sleep. He dropped his head into his hands and tried to make sense of everything that had gone down, everything he hadn't told his brother.

If he were smart, he would have told Zack everything. Zack would have probably honored whatever arrest warrant Sinclair had and turned Janette over. Then she would have been out of Dalton's life. He wouldn't feel responsible for her.

Zack would tell him that he was making decisions based on something other than his brain. Was that what he was doing? Was he allowing Janette's beautiful blue eyes and the memory of the hot kiss they'd shared to twist his logic?

Was it possible she and Sinclair had indulged in an affair, one that had gone bad? Was she the kind of woman to take money from her workplace? Make up a story about rape?

No. Even though he'd only known her for a brief time, he knew she wasn't that kind of woman. Granted, he couldn't deny that he felt a strong sense of physical attraction to her, but that didn't mean he didn't believe what she'd told him. That couldn't take away the likelihood that tonight Brandon Sinclair had set a fire, then had tried to kill them both. Those weren't the actions of a man who had nothing to hide.

Dalton had no doubt that the sheriff was behind what had happened. But knowing and proving were two different things and until he had proof, he wasn't going to tell his brother anything. He stretched out on the sofa and listened to the quiet.

He should be thrilled. He finally had his place to himself again. He was blessedly alone, just the way he liked it. No fuzzy baby, no soft female voice singing lullabies. So why did it suddenly seem far too quiet?

She thought she might scream. It was too quiet. Janette sat at the kitchen table in the little cabin sipping a cup of hot tea. It was just after eight, but there was no morning sun shining through the windows. The skies were as gray as her mood.

Sinclair knew she was in Cotter Creek. He'd be looking for her. He also knew she'd been with Dalton, so he'd be watching Dalton's every move, waiting to see if Dalton eventually led him to her. How long would it take before he'd think that she might be holed up on the West property?

She wrapped her hands around the mug, seeking the warmth to banish the chill inside her. The short night had seemed to last forever. Sleep had been impossible even though she'd eventually gotten into bed and tried to rest.

Her mind had whirled, trying to process the events that had brought her to the small cabin, and each thought was tinged with an underlying fear. Would *he* find her there? Would *he* somehow be able to ferret out where Dalton had stashed her? She was all alone, without a weapon except the knife she carried.

She'd finally gotten up and retrieved her knife from her purse, then had slid it beneath her pillow, where it would be in easy reach should she need it. The night had held sounds that made her jump and had kept sleep at bay.

Releasing a deep, weary sigh, she gazed out the window and took another sip of her tea. Would Sinclair be watching the bus stop, ready to pounce if she so much as showed her face?

How was she ever going to get out of town? Out of Dalton's life? Certainly he'd made it clear on more than one occasion that he didn't want to be responsible for anyone, that he preferred a life lived alone.

He probably couldn't wait to get her on her way. How long before he tired of this…of her? And when he got tired of the hassle, of the drama, it was possible he'd turn her in to Sinclair.

He wouldn't do that, the little voice inside her head protested. If he intended to do that he would have done so when the sheriff showed up on his doorstep.

The morning passed with her feeding and playing with Sammy and her thoughts alternating between worst- and best-case scenarios. After lunch, when she put Sammy down for his nap and stretched out on the bed next to him she wondered when Dalton would show up.

What if he never showed up? What if Sinclair murdered him? Her heart began to pound at the very idea. A new grief tore through her as she thought of the possibility.

Stop it, she commanded herself. Dalton had proved the night before that he was more than capable of taking care of himself. He was far too strong, too smart to be taken by surprise.

She must have fallen asleep, for the banging on the front door shot her up to a sitting position as her heart crashed against her ribs.

Who was at the door? It couldn't be Dalton. He had a key. Had Sinclair found her? Was he out there now waiting for her to come to the door? She pulled her knife from beneath her pillow and gripped it tightly in her hand.

She slid out of bed and crept to the doorway, unable to see the front door from her vantage point. Her throat narrowed as her breathing came in half-panicked gasps.

There was a phone in the living room, but she couldn't get to it without the person at the front door seeing her.

Once again the sounds of a fist against the door filled the cabin. "Janette, open the door. Dalton sent me." It was a female voice and some of Janette's panic dissipated.

Still clutching the knife, afraid of a trick, she walked cautiously to the door. Peering out she saw a woman with shoulder-length riotous red hair standing on the porch, a grocery bag in her arms.

Janette unlocked the front door and pulled it open only an inch, just enough to see the friendly brown eyes of the woman. "Who are you?" she asked.

"I'm Savannah—Savannah West—and I have some groceries for you."

Janette opened the door and Savannah flew past her on a burst of cold air and with enough energy to light up the entire cabin. Janette relocked the front door then hurriedly followed Savannah into the kitchen.

"I hope you're planning on peeling an apple," Savannah said dryly and looked pointedly at the knife still clutched in Janette's hand.

A blush warmed Janette's cheeks as she set the knife down on the counter. "So, you're Dalton's sister? I'm sorry, but I can't remember the names of everyone even though he mentioned them."

"Sister-in-law," Savannah said as she began to take items out of the bag. "I'm married to Joshua, the youngest of the bunch."

"Is Dalton not coming?"

"Maybe later. He was worried about being followed so he called me." Savannah's brown eyes radiated sympathy. "He told me what's going on and asked for my help. Don't worry, I won't tell anybody you're here." She pulled a package of disposable diapers from the bag. "Is your baby sleeping?"

Janette nodded. "So what exactly did Dalton tell you?"

"That you were in trouble, that he was keeping you hidden here until you both can figure out the next step. You want to put these in the freezer or refrigerator or wherever you want them?" She pulled out two small packages of hamburger and a wrapper of deli meat.

"How about you make a pot of coffee while I finish unloading these things," Savannah suggested. "Then we can have a nice chat."

Janette readily complied, grateful to have somebody to talk to, somebody to break up the silence that had plagued her since Dalton had left.

Within minutes the groceries were put away and the two women sat at the table with fresh coffee. "I'm so grateful to have somebody to talk to," Janette said. "The silence was really starting to get to me."

Savannah smiled. "Joshua would tell you that silence never bothers me. If I don't have anyone to talk to then I'm perfectly satisfied to talk to myself."

Janette returned her smile, deciding at that moment that she liked Savannah West. "How long have you been married?"

"Only three months. We're practically newlyweds, but at the moment he's off in New York. He flew up last week to do a job for a friend and should be coming home sometime later this week. I can't wait for him to get back to me."

For the next few minutes Savannah told her about leaving Arizona and settling in Cotter Creek. She'd met her husband-to-be when a mutual friend of theirs had been murdered and the two had put their heads together to investigate a land scandal taking place in the small town.

"Are the West men all so…so…"

"Handsome? Strong? Stubborn?" Savannah laughed. "All of the above. They're good people, the whole West clan." She sobered. "You can trust Dalton. He's quiet and reserved, but he's a good man."

Janette nodded. "Are you a stay-at-home wife?"

"Heavens, no. I bought the local newspaper not long ago and most days I'm either writing news stories or editing to get out the daily newspaper."

"I appreciate you taking time off to come here."

"I'd do anything for Dalton, for any of the Wests, but I have to admit I was also curious when he explained everything to me. Consider it my reporter nose for news."

Janette shot up straighter in her chair, heartbeat quickening. "But you can't print anything. I don't want any of this to get out. If you even breathe a word of this to anyone you could put my life, my son's life, in danger."

"Relax," Savannah said. "I'm one of those rare birds, a reporter with ethics. I would never do anything to put you and your son at risk. But I do have a few questions to ask you."

Tension twisted Janette's stomach. "Questions about what?"

"About Brandon Sinclair."

Janette got up from the table to pour herself another cup of coffee. "Why would you want to know anything about him?" She remained standing by the counter, certain that she didn't want to have this conversation.

"Because I intend to do a little investigative reporting on my own and see what I can find out about this creep," Savannah said.

Janette returned to sit at the table. She set her cup to the side and grabbed one of Savannah's hands. "Please, please don't do that. If he finds out you're asking questions about him, he'll hurt you."

Savannah squeezed Janette's hand and offered her a reassuring smile. "Believe me, the last thing I want is for Brandon Sinclair to have me in his sights." She released Janette's hand. "I'm very good at what I do and he'll never know I'm gathering facts about him."

"Why would you even want to get involved in all this?" Janette asked.

Savannah leaned back in her chair, her brown eyes contemplative. "From everything I've ever heard about sexual predators, they don't just indulge their ugly impulses once then never do it again. My guess is that you probably weren't the first victim of Brandon Sinclair and you won't be the last."

"I'm sure you're right," Janette said softly.

Savannah leaned forward. "You know something about another victim? Have you heard rumors? Sandstone is a very small town, surely somebody whispered something about the good sheriff."

Janette shook her head. "I never heard anything specific, but I suspected that one of the waitresses I worked with at the café might have had a run-in with Sheriff Sinclair."

"What made you suspect that?"

Janette reached back in her memory to the painful days just after her rape. She'd spent the days trying to act normal, trying to pretend that the terrible violation hadn't taken place. But she'd been desperate to talk to somebody, to anybody.

"Right after it happened to me, I asked Alicia if she'd ever been pulled over for a speeding ticket by Sheriff Sinclair. She said no, but there was an expression in her eyes that made me think she was lying. When I pressed her about it she told me to back off and the next day she quit the job."

"You said her name was Alicia. Alicia what?"

"Alicia Patterson, but she won't tell you anything. Everyone in Sandstone is afraid of him," Janette exclaimed and her throat tightened up a bit. She felt as if things were spinning out of control.

Savannah offered her a reassuring smile. "Too bad for him I'm not from Sandstone."

"Please, don't do this for me."

"I'm not," she replied easily. "I'm doing it for every young woman who lives in Sandstone and the surrounding areas." She finished her coffee and stood. "Don't worry, I know how to be invisible when I need to be and somebody needs to step up. I want to get the goods on this guy and put him away."

"I just want to *get* away," Janette said, more to herself than to Savannah.

She walked Savannah to the front door and on impulse gave her a hug. "Thank you for the groceries and for the talk."

Savannah pulled her hood up and opened the door. "I'm sure we'll see each other again."

Janette watched from the doorway as Savannah got into her car and pulled away. She closed and locked the door and leaned her head against the wood.

Somebody needs to step up.

Sammy began to cry from the bedroom, having awakened from his nap. She hurried into the room and his tears instantly transformed into a watery grin. She picked him up and cuddled him close.

Somebody needs to step up.

"Not me," she whispered. With the weight of her son in her arms, she fought back tears. "Not me," she said more forcefully.

Chapter 8

It was dusk when Dalton pulled up to the cabin. It had been a long tense day. He'd spent most of the day in his apartment, staring out the window, watching for Sinclair and thinking.

He'd set in motion a quiet investigation into Sinclair, enlisting both Savannah and his brother Tanner's aid. As the eldest of the brood, Tanner was not only the most levelheaded of the bunch, but also a whiz with computers.

By morning Tanner would know everything there was to know about Brandon Sinclair. He'd know where he shopped, where he ate, how much he had in his bank account and if there had ever been a complaint filed against the man.

He hadn't told Tanner anything about Janette and Sammy. He'd only said that he was doing a favor for a friend and needed to keep it quiet, especially from Zack.

What had surprised him more than anything during the day was how he'd noticed Janette and Sammy's absence. The quiet of his apartment had never bothered him before, rather he'd relished it. But, today, the quiet hadn't felt good. It had felt lonely. And that had irritated him.

As he shut off his truck engine, the front door opened and she stepped just outside and greeted him with a beautiful smile. Tension instantly built inside him. She looked gorgeous in a pair of jeans and a lavender sweatshirt, and her bright smile only added to her beauty.

He got out and walked to the back of the truck, picked up an oversize wooden cradle, then carried it toward where she stood.

"I thought Sammy might be able to use this while you're here," he said as she held open the door to allow him inside. He set the cradle on the living-room floor. "I know the bed in the bedroom is pretty small, especially by the time you surround Sammy with pillows. I figured this would be more comfortable for both of you."

She knelt down next to the cradle and looked up at him, those Oklahoma sky–blue eyes of hers shining brightly as she ran her hand over the rich wood. "It's beautiful. Where did you get it?"

"It was packed in a shed. It hasn't been used since Joshua was a baby."

"So it's a family heirloom."

"Yeah, I guess." The cabin smelled of lemon furniture polish and that evocative scent of honeysuckle. "You've been cleaning," he observed, noting that all the furniture gleamed with a new sheen.

She stood. "I got bored and found some furniture polish under the kitchen sink."

"Sammy sleeping?"

"I just put him down." She ran a loving hand over the cradle once again. "I think I'll clean this up and move him into it."

As she disappeared into the kitchen, Dalton sat on the sofa. She was in a good mood now, but he had a feeling she wouldn't be in such a good mood when he told her what was on his mind.

She returned with the bottle of furniture polish and a rag and sat on the floor to begin the cleanup on the cradle. "I like your sister-in-law," she said as she worked.

"I know you didn't want me to tell anyone, but I knew I might need some help since Sinclair might be watching my place."

She looked at him worriedly. "Do you think he was watching when you left tonight?"

Dalton shook his head. "He's back in Sandstone."

"How do you know that?"

"I called his office and he answered the phone." Dalton leaned back against the sofa cushions. "He can't stay in Cotter Creek all day and night. He has a job and a family in Sandstone. He can't spend every waking hour hunting you down."

"Thank God for small favors, right?"

It took her only minutes to finish cleaning off the cradle. She folded several thick bath towels into the bottom of it, making a nice soft mattress for Sammy.

She left to get Sammy and Dalton drew a deep breath. Her scent eddied in the air and evoked memories of that single kiss they had shared, a kiss he wouldn't mind repeating even though he knew he was all kinds of a fool to even think about it.

Sammy didn't stir from his sleep as she gently laid

him in the cradle and covered him with another towel. She stood and smiled down at him, her smile so soft, so loving, Dalton felt it in the center of his chest.

"You want some coffee or something?" she asked.

"No, I'm fine. But I would like to talk to you." He sat on the sofa and patted the space next to him.

She eyed him warily but sat, close enough that he could smell her fragrance, but not close enough to touch in any way. "Talk about what?" Her eyes were darker blue than they had been moments before.

"About bringing Brandon Sinclair to justice." He leaned back against the cushion. "I know the special prosecutor in Oklahoma City. His name is Trent Cummings and it's his job to prosecute elected officials, like sheriffs, who break the law. I intend to contact him about Sinclair."

She nodded slowly, her expression guarded. "Good. Somebody needs to stop him before he hurts more women."

"What we need if we're going to stop him is cold hard evidence, and that's where you come in."

Her eyes narrowed slightly. "I don't have any evidence," she protested. Her entire body tensed and she appeared to shrink back from him, becoming smaller and looking more vulnerable.

"You are the evidence," he said, trying not to be affected by her obvious discomfort. "You and Sammy, especially Sammy. His DNA confirms that Sinclair is his father."

Her eyes flashed darkly. "But that doesn't prove he raped me. That just proves we had sex." Her voice was an octave higher than usual and she jumped up from the sofa as if unable to stand sitting next to him another minute longer. "Don't you see? He'll just tell everyone we had an affair. Nobody will ever take my word over his. He's the 'good and noble' sheriff and I'm 'uneducated trailer trash.' Nobody will believe me."

Her chest heaved and her hands clenched into fists at her sides. "Stop saying you're uneducated trailer trash," he said with more than a touch of irritation. "That might be Brandon Sinclair's definition of you, but it sure isn't mine."

"Have you forgotten that he probably has an arrest warrant for me?"

"No, I haven't forgotten," he said. "But he can't make a murder charge stick without a dead body, and we both know your nana is alive and well."

"He can still arrest me on theft charges, or maybe arson, or whatever he decides to conjure up."

"And he tried to kill us last night. He needs to be stopped."

Her eyes flashed once again. "And we can't prove that it was him who set the fire or shot at us last night. And you can bet he's already got a solid alibi set up for the time of the shooting."

She drew a deep breath and her hands slowly unclenched. "Look, I appreciate what you're trying to do, but I just want to get out of here. I intend to be on the next bus out of town, with or without your help."

"And you intend to spend the rest of your life looking over your shoulder? Wondering if and when he's going to find you? Wouldn't you rather stand and fight and stop him from raping other women?"

Her eyes filled with the sheen of tears. "Please, don't ask me to stay."

"But that's exactly what I'm asking of you," he said

softly. "Stay and fight. Help us put him away." He stood to face her.

"It's so easy for you to ask that of me." For the first time a hint of anger deepened her voice and hardened her eyes. "You've probably never had to face anything alone. You have this great big wonderful family to support you in whatever decisions you make. You've never been poor and powerless and all alone."

Her anger rose with each word that left her mouth. "It's easy for you because if things go badly you lose nothing. You go back to your quiet, solitary life and never think about me or Sammy again."

"That's not true," he protested. He had a feeling no matter what happened here and now, it was going to be a very long time before he could forget Janette and her little boy.

He took two steps toward her. "Janette, you won't be alone in this. I'll be right by your side. I've got my brother Tanner checking into Sinclair's background. Savannah is going to try to touch base with the waitress you said might have been another victim."

She backed away from him, tears once again shining in her eyes, but he pressed on. "Don't you want to stand up and put this man behind bars where he belongs? Wouldn't you sleep better at night if you knew he wasn't someplace out on the streets? Maybe hunting you down?"

"You and your sister-in-law and brother can do whatever you think is right, but I intend to be on the first bus out of here." She flew into the bedroom and closed the door after her.

Dalton released a sigh of frustration. He understood her fear, sympathized with it, but he knew she was their best chance in taking down Brandon Sinclair. And he was determined to do just that.

Janette sat on the edge of the bed, her entire body trembling with emotion. Fear, regret and a burning shame all coursed through her.

Somebody needs to step up.

The words haunted her, playing and replaying in her mind like the refrain from an irritating melody that refused to be forgotten.

Somebody needs to step up.

She closed her eyes as a vision of Alicia Patterson filled her head. She remembered vividly the whisper of horror that had filled her eyes when Janette had asked her if she'd ever been pulled over by Sheriff Sinclair. She'd recognized that horror because she'd lived it and it had become an unwanted part of her.

Rubbing her temple where a headache had begun to pound, she tried to banish the vision of Alicia from her mind but it refused to completely go away. How many others had there been? How many more would there be?

He needed to be stopped.

Somebody needs to step up.

None of the women who had been abused by Sinclair were likely to look for a way to bring him to justice. They would feel the same hopeless helplessness that she'd felt. Stuck in a town where the sheriff was king, it was impossible for a mere vulnerable isolated woman to stand up against him.

But she was no longer in Sandstone. She was one step ahead of those women, for she'd already escaped the evil king's kingdom. And she wasn't all alone. She had Dalton standing beside her.

Do the right thing, that little voice whispered in her head. She'd tried to live her life always choosing to do the right thing. When Nana had gotten sick, the right thing for Janette to do had been to quit school to take care of her. When she'd discovered she was pregnant, for her, making the choice to give Sammy life had been the right thing to do.

And stopping Sheriff Brandon Sinclair from preying on any other women was the right thing to do. She got up from the bed, a bone-weariness weighing down her feet as she walked back to the door.

The idea of what she was about to agree to terrified her, but for the first time since that horrible night on the deserted highway, a rage began to build inside her.

Brandon Sinclair had not only raped her. He'd also tried to kill Nana, and last night had tried to shoot an innocent man. It hadn't been safe before this moment to get angry, because while she'd been a resident in Sandstone, anger had been an emotion she couldn't afford.

As she swung open the door and walked back into the living room, the anger flowed, rich and thick and righteous through her veins. Dalton sat on the sofa, but he stood when she came back into the room.

"All right," she said, her voice trembling with the raw emotion. "I'll stick around. I'll talk to your special prosecutor. I'll do whatever it takes to destroy Sinclair, but I have a few requests of my own."

"Like what?" Dalton sat back down and she joined him on the sofa.

"I want Nana out of Sandstone. Sooner or later he is going to find out that she didn't burn up in that trailer. He'll find her, and we can't let that happen."

Dalton nodded. "We can pick her up and bring her here."

She would have loved to have her nana here in this little cabin with her, but she shook her head. "No, I don't want her here. I want her someplace where she'll be safe if this goes bad."

Dalton frowned thoughtfully. "West Protective Services owns a safe house in Kansas City. We could set her up there for the time being," Dalton said. "I can make arrangements with my sister, Meredith, to meet her plane and get her settled in."

"I have one other thing to ask of you." The pounding in her head intensified and she raised a hand to press her cold fingers against her temple. The anger that had filled her dissipated, usurped by a new well of grief.

"What?" he asked, his voice a soft caress. "What else do you need?"

She closed her eyes for a moment and a picture of Sammy's little face filled her head, his downy dark hair above laughing blue eyes and that grin of his that had the capacity to melt her heart.

She opened her eyes and stared at Dalton with intensity. "If something happens to me, if I end up in jail or worse, you have to promise me that you'll take Sammy. You'll hide him where Sinclair will never get hold of him." She reached out and grabbed hold of Dalton's forearm. "You have to promise me that you'll keep him safe, that you'll never allow that man to get custody of him."

Dalton took her hand between his, surrounding her cold fingers with warmth. "Nothing is going to happen to you. You're going to be fine, and you and Sammy are going to have a wonderful life with your nana."

"But you can't promise that."

His eyes darkened slightly. "No, I can't promise that," he admitted. "We'll do everything we can to make sure that all of you are safe. I know how difficult this decision is for you, and I know it probably doesn't matter to you, but I'm proud of you and admire your courage."

She realized it did matter to her, that she cared about what he thought of her. She cared more than she thought possible, but she wasn't satisfied yet. "You have to promise me that you'll take care of Sammy if something happens to me. That's the only way I can go forward with this."

The gravity of his expression let her know he wouldn't take this vow lightly. "Okay, I promise," he replied.

She was surprised by the depth of relief that flooded through her. At least she wouldn't have to worry about Sammy ending up with Sinclair.

"So, what happens now?" she asked. His hands no longer warmed the chill that resided deep inside her.

"First thing in the morning I'll call Trent and we'll set up a meeting with him, then I'll make arrangements to get your nana out of Sandstone. We'll see what Savannah and Tanner found out about Sinclair and hope that they can get us something to help make a case."

"Are you going to tell Zack about all this?" she asked.

He frowned. "Not until we have some solid evidence to present to him."

"I know how much you don't like keeping secrets from him."

He nodded. "That's true, but in this particular case I think it's necessary."

A new cold wind blew through her. "He'll know.

Somehow Sinclair will find out that we're plotting against him. That's going to make him more dangerous than ever."

"Then we'll just have to be careful." He reached up and tucked a strand of her hair behind her ear.

At the moment she felt his gentle touch, she knew that she wanted to make love with him. She wanted… *needed* to make love with him in order to banish the memory of Sinclair's hands on her, his breath hot and sour on her face.

She knew it was crazy, that Dalton West was only a temporary man in her life. Eventually this would all be over and he'd get back to his uncomplicated private life and hopefully she'd get on with her life.

She wasn't fool enough to think that there might be a future with him. Nature had blown her into his life and danger kept her bound to him. But once the snow was gone and the danger had passed, it would be over.

But there was tonight and she felt the need for his warmth, for his gentleness. She felt the need for him. Even as her desire swelled inside her, she was suffused with doubt.

Would he even want her? Certainly she'd tasted hot desire in the single kiss they'd shared. Had that been a momentary flare of madness, or was it reflective of the fact that he might be attracted to her?

"You've gotten quiet. What are you thinking?" he asked.

She breathed in deeply and looked into his beautiful green eyes. Her mouth suddenly felt dry and a trembling began deep within her. "I think maybe I'd like some coffee after all," she said and jumped up off the sofa.

Don't be a fool, a voice whispered inside her head

as she went into the kitchen. Making love with Dalton wouldn't make things better. It would only make things worse when she had to tell him goodbye.

As she fixed the coffee, he came into the kitchen and sat at the table. She was acutely aware of his presence, as if the very thought of making love with him had fine-tuned every one of her senses.

Once the coffee was dripping into the carafe, she joined him at the table. "I don't want to talk about Brandon Sinclair anymore," she said. "I don't even want to think about him. Tell me more about your family. Fill my head with something good and positive."

And he did. As they drank coffee he talked to her about his brothers and sister, sharing childhood memories that made her laugh, sharing moments that made her more than a little bit envious of the close-knit West clan.

Darkness fell, and as he finished his coffee he stood. Dread swooped through her. She knew he was preparing to leave.

"I should get back to town," he said.

She got up from the table, as well. "You could stay here for the night." She swallowed, her mouth once again too dry. "With Sammy in his new cradle, the bed is big enough for both of us." She held her breath.

His eyes flared wider and filled with a heat that swept over her, through her. "I'm not sure that's a good idea."

Emboldened by the look in his eyes, she stepped closer to him. "Why not?" Her heartbeat raced in her chest, this time not with fear, but with something even more primal.

"Because I don't think I can sleep in the same bed as you." His voice was deeper than usual.

"I don't kick and I don't think I snore." She took another step toward him.

"That wouldn't be the problem," he replied.

"Then what is the problem?" She stood so close to him she could feel his body heat radiate toward her, could see the gold flecks that gave depth to his green eyes.

"The problem is that it's been a long time since I've been with a woman and I find you incredibly attractive."

His words gave her permission to take a final step toward him. She now touched him, her breasts against the hard width of his chest. "And I find you incredibly attractive." She raised her hands to his shoulders and leaned into him, her face raised.

She saw the kiss in his eyes before he lowered his head to deliver it. When his lips took hers a fiery heat flooded through her veins and she welcomed it, welcomed him with an open mouth.

He wrapped his arms around her and pulled her close…closer still. His arms felt like safety, like security, and she reveled in the sensations that coursed through her.

His tongue swirled with hers, creating a fire of want inside her. She knew exactly what to expect, a night of passion satisfied and nothing more. At this moment it was enough.

When he broke the kiss she took his hand and led him into the bedroom. Although she didn't think it possible, her heartbeat raced even faster. She wanted this. She wanted him. But she couldn't ignore a tiny sliver of disquiet that raised its ugly head.

The last time she'd had sex it had been a violent, terror-filled event, and she wanted none of that experience to bleed over into this time with Dalton.

When they reached the bedroom he once again took her into his arms and kissed her. The kiss was long and deep, and as he kissed her his hands caressed her back.

She loved the feel of his hard chest, his firm thighs and his obvious arousal against her. He held her tight, but not so tight that she felt captive…helpless.

This time when the kiss ended, her fingers trembled as she unbuttoned his shirt. He stood motionless, as if holding his breath as she pulled the shirt from his chest.

Only then did he move away from her. He walked to the side of the bed and placed his gun, his cell phone and his wallet on the nightstand, then turned to face her. "Are you sure about this?" His voice vibrated with tension.

Instead of answering him with words, she pulled her sweatshirt off over her head and dropped it to the floor beside her.

His eyes glowed in the semidarkness of the room and her breath caught in her throat as his hands moved to the waist of his jeans and he unfastened the button fly.

As he took off his jeans she did the same. Then, with only the aid of the moonlight filtering through the window, they got into the bed.

Instantly he pulled her back into his arms as his lips found hers once again. His delicious skin warmed hers as his mouth took possession of her lips.

It felt right. It felt good, and it didn't matter what tomorrow would bring. Whatever happened, wherever she ended up building her life, she'd have the memory of this kind and good man to carry with her.

They lay side by side facing each other and his lips left hers and rained nipping kisses down her neck to the hollow of her throat. She tangled her fingers in his thick hair as his hands caressed her breasts through the thin material of her bra.

It didn't take long before she wanted to feel the palm of his hands against her naked breasts. She reached behind her and unfastened her bra, loving the deep moan that escaped him as she tossed it to the floor. Within minutes the last of their clothing was gone and their touches grew more intimate.

It wasn't until he moved on top of her that the first stir of panic closed her throat.

His breath was warm against her neck, his body not surrounding her so much as imprisoning her. Just like before.

Hot breath.

Hard body.

Trapped.

She squeezed her eyes tightly closed, fighting the overwhelming sense of dread, trying to catch her breath as the panic fired higher inside her. This wasn't Sinclair, and they weren't on the side of the road. There was no gun pressed to her throat, no reason for her heart to pound so painfully hard.

Dalton seemed unaware of the torment that had unexpectedly stolen passion and exchanged it for dark flashbacks to the worst night of her life. As he kissed her neck, she fought the scream that worked up from the depths of her.

He was suffocating her, his weight oppressive and scary. She couldn't move, had lost control. She couldn't breathe. Unable to stand it another minute she shoved against his chest. "I'm sorry. I can't do this. Please, get off me. Get off me!"

He instantly rolled to the side of her as she burst into tears.

Chapter 9

"I'm sorry. I'm so sorry," Janette cried into the pillow next to Dalton.

"It's okay," he said even as he fought to get control of himself. "It's all right, Janette. We don't have to do anything you don't want to do." Tentatively he reached out and touched her back, trying to comfort but afraid of frightening her.

It was obvious what had just happened, and his heart clenched with her pain. Brandon Sinclair should be stood before a firing squad for what he'd done to her, for the scars he'd left behind.

She didn't move away from his touch so he continued to rub her back and tell her it was okay. He tried not to notice the sexy curve of her back or the sweet scent that emanated from her warm skin.

Slowly her tears dried, but she still kept her face

buried in the pillow, as if afraid to turn over and look at him.

"Janette, I'm not mad. Come on, turn over and look at me."

"How can you not be mad? Women who do what I just did to you are called a terrible name."

"There's a difference between women who get off on the power of playing a man and a woman who is suffering post-traumatic stress. I promise you I'm not mad."

She finally rolled over, the sheet clutched to her chest as she faced him. He leaned up on one elbow and smiled down at her. "It's okay, really."

She reached a hand up and touched the underside of his jaw. "How did you get to be such a nice man, Dalton West?"

"Trust me, at the moment I'm not feeling like such a nice guy. I'd like to find Brandon Sinclair and torture him slowly for a very long time." He started to roll out of the bed but she caught him by the arm.

"Don't go," she said softly. "Can't we just lie here and talk for a little while?"

She had no idea what she was asking of him. Blood still surged thick and hot through his veins. He was a man, not a saint, but maybe if he didn't touch her again he could stand remaining next to her.

He rolled over just long enough to turn on the lamp on the nightstand, then turned back to face her.

"Would it help to talk about that night?" he asked gently.

"No. I was doing fine until you got on top of me." Her cheeks turned pink and she averted her gaze from his. "It wasn't until then that I had a flashback. With you on top of me I felt trapped…like I was suffocating… like I did that night with Sinclair."

"That will teach me to try to be in control," he said with a forced lightness.

She looked at him. "Maybe if I stay in control it will be okay. I mean, my head and my heart want to make love with you, it was just in that last minute that everything went wrong."

"Maybe we should both just try to get some sleep," he countered. He wasn't sure he could go through the same thing again and not get relief. His body still ached with the need she'd wrought inside him.

He tensed as she reached over and stroked a hand across his chest. Instantly desire fired through him. Her fingers curled in his chest hair, then uncurled and moved down lower.

As she wrapped her fingers around him more intimately he hissed in a breath. She was trying to kill him with pleasure. "Janette," he said, the word more a plea than a protest as he'd intended.

"Just…just let me," she replied, her voice husky and deep.

Dalton had always been an active participant when he made love to a woman, but as she stroked him he remained on his back, not moving to touch her in any way.

She leaned forward and pressed her lips against his chest, and that coupled with her warm hand surrounding him nearly undid him. He hung on to control by a thread.

She moved her lips up his chest to capture his in a fiery kiss. Her breathing increased, and when she raised her head to look at him he saw the glaze of want in her eyes.

The most difficult thing he'd ever done was to remain passive. He wanted to reach up for her, take her into his arms. He wanted to taste her skin, feel the soft weight of her breasts, but he remained unmoving, allowing her to stay in total control.

Her naked body gleamed in the lamplight and her blond hair glistened as it fell forward, the tips trailing across his chest in added torment.

Her nipples were out and he fought the impulse to lean up and capture one in his mouth. Although he wanted to touch her, there was something unbelievably erotic in allowing her to make love to him on her own terms.

It wasn't until she moved to get on top of him that he finally spoke. "There's a condom in my wallet," he managed to gasp.

She left him just long enough to open his wallet and retrieve the foil packet inside. She opened the packet and rolled the protection into place. He moaned with pleasure as she eased onto him, her sleek legs on either side.

He closed his eyes, knowing that if he continued to look at her he'd lose control too quickly. Her warmth gripped him tight as she rocked against him.

Her breaths came in quick pants and when he looked at her again her eyes were tightly closed and an expression of intense bliss shone on her features.

She moved faster and then she gasped and cried out his name. That was all it took. Dalton's release came in an explosion that rocked him to his very core. It was only then that he touched her. He cupped her face with his hands and drew her down for a kiss.

She melted against him, her body warm against his,

her lips sweet and yielding. When they finished kissing she rolled off him and to her back.

"Thank you," she said softly.

A small burst of laughter escaped him. "Don't thank me. That was absolutely amazing." He rolled off the bed. "Don't move, I'll be right back."

He padded into the bathroom to clean up. Once alone, he thought about what had just happened and the fact that it shouldn't have.

She was getting to him. Oh, but she was getting into places inside him that he hadn't allowed anyone in for a very long time. And that scared him. That scared the hell out of him.

This situation…*she* was temporary. He'd sworn to himself that he would never again put himself in the position to help heal a woman so she could move on and fall in love with another man.

He'd sworn to himself he'd never again be a temporary hero for any woman, and yet wasn't that exactly his role in this case? If he were smart he'd go back into the bedroom, get dressed and get the hell away from her.

But the moment he reentered the bedroom, all thoughts of leaving fled his head. She gave him that smile of hers, the one bright enough to light up the room, and patted the empty side of the bed.

"I hope you aren't one of those men who fall immediately to sleep after sex," she said.

No, he was the type of man who felt the need to run for the door and escape. Not exactly the actions of a gentleman. He slid back beneath the sheets.

"Are you accustomed to men who fall asleep after sex?" he asked teasingly.

She plumped the pillows behind her head and sat

up, the sheet clutched modestly at her neck. "I've only had one real long-term relationship and, yes, he used to fall asleep."

He rolled over on his side to face her and propped himself up on his elbow. "Is that why you aren't with him anymore?"

She grinned, looking incredibly sexy with her hair tousled and her full lips still slightly swollen from his kisses. "No. He worked as a rehab nurse and I met him when Nana needed rehabilitation after her stroke. We dated for almost a year." She pulled her knees up to her chest and wrapped her arms around them, her features contemplative. "He got a job offer from a hospital in Indianapolis and moved there."

"He didn't ask you to go with him?"

"No. I think he knew I wouldn't go, that I couldn't leave Nana. It wasn't a great love affair. It was pleasant and nice while it lasted, but after he was gone I realized I wasn't deeply, madly in love with him."

"And that's important to you? To be deeply, madly in love?" he asked.

She flashed him that brilliant smile of hers. "Of course. I think it's what every woman wants, among other things."

"And what other things do you want?" He tried to tell himself that he really didn't care, that he was just trying to hold up his end of the conversation. But deep inside he knew that wasn't true. He wanted to know her desires, her wants, the very dreams that drove her.

"A home, security. I want a job that I love and to be able to provide Sammy with things and opportunities I didn't have. I want to be able to afford to order pizza whenever I want it. Oh, yeah, and world peace."

He laughed and she unclasped her hands from around her knees and stretched out on her side facing him. "Now tell me about the women in your past."

"There's nothing to tell. I've had a few relationships, but nothing too serious. I've told you before, I like living alone, being alone." He needed to remind himself as much as her of this fact.

At that moment Sammy began to cry from the living room. He watched as she slid from the bed, grabbed a robe from the nearby chair and pulled it on. "I'll be right back. Don't go away."

As she left the room Dalton rolled on his back and stared up at the ceiling. The feeling returned—the need to run, to escape. Not just from Janette, but from the whole situation. He'd talked her into agreeing to stick around, to help them bring Brandon Sinclair to justice.

The man was dangerous and until they could get the evidence they needed to put him behind bars, he was a threat to Janette's very life.

He felt fairly confident having her here at the cabin. Deep on West property, the cabin was known only by a few. The ranch hands would certainly notice a stranger wandering the property and would demand an explanation of his presence.

Still, if anything happened to her or to Sammy, Dalton would feel responsible for the rest of his life. He hoped he hadn't made a mistake in talking her into staying and fighting, because it could be a mistake with deadly consequences.

Janette stopped in the kitchen to fix Sammy a bottle and carried it into the living room. The minute he saw her he stopped fussing. He'd drink this bottle then would sleep through the night.

She changed his diaper, then carried him back into the bedroom and sat on the edge of the bed to give him the bottle. She was conscious of Dalton's gaze on her as she looked down at her son. "He makes me want to be better than I am," she said. She looked at Dalton. "That's what kids do for you." Sammy grinned at Dalton around the bottle nipple, as if punctuating her sentence.

For a few minutes they were silent, the only sound Sammy greedily drinking his formula. Janette's head was filled with myriad emotions. Love for her son tangled with an underlying fear of what lay ahead and, as she cast a surreptitious glance to Dalton, other less easily defined emotions rose up inside her.

Certainly gratitude filled her heart, not just for what he'd done in taking her in and keeping her safe, but also for allowing her to reclaim a piece of herself, a piece she'd thought forever broken.

"You gave me back my life tonight," she said to Dalton.

He raised a dark eyebrow. "Don't you think that's a little dramatic?"

"No, I don't," she countered. "I didn't think I'd ever be able to experience joy in lovemaking again. I thought my experience with Sinclair had destroyed that part of me. You showed me tonight that he didn't."

She frowned thoughtfully, remembering those moments of sudden panic when Dalton had moved on top of her. "I know it's going to take time before all the trauma of Sinclair is gone, but tonight definitely went a long way in my healing process."

"You'll be fine," he assured her. "Someday you'll

find the man who can give you all the things you want from life."

She smiled. "I don't need a man to give me all the things I want. I intend to go out and get them. But, it would be nice to have somebody to share it all with."

She looked back down at Sammy. She had the feeling Dalton had said what he had to remind her that he wasn't the man for her. He didn't have to bother.

Even though she realized her heart was getting hopelessly involved with him, she knew better than to expect a happy ending. He'd made his position perfectly clear and she didn't expect that to change.

"Once Sinclair is in jail, do you intend to return to Sandstone?" he asked.

"To be honest, I haven't had enough time to think about it." She glanced back down at Sammy. The trailer they'd called home was gone. "There's really nothing left for us there except bad memories. If you're putting Nana in a safe place in Kansas City, then maybe that's the place where we should start over."

Sammy had fallen back to sleep, his bottle empty and his belly full. "You want me to bring the cradle in here?" Dalton asked.

"Do you mind?"

He got up and pulled on his briefs, then left the room. As he exited, she couldn't help the flutter of heat that swept through her at the sight of his near-nakedness. He had a physique that most men would envy and most women would want. And she wanted him again.

It surprised her, the healthy burst of lust that filled her. She hadn't thought about sex in over a year, but one time with Dalton and suddenly her head was filled with lustful thoughts.

And there was nothing more sexy than a man in briefs carrying a cradle, she thought as he returned to the room. He set the cradle on the floor on her side of the bed, then got back beneath the sheets.

She got up and put Sammy back into the cradle, then got back into bed next to Dalton. He turned off the lamp and the room was plunged into darkness with just a faint cast of moonlight dancing shadows on the walls.

Closing her eyes, she tried not to think about what she'd agreed to do by staying here. Even if the bus pulled up in Cotter Creek tomorrow, she wouldn't get on it.

A sliver of fear iced through her, chilling her to her bones. What if the special prosecutor didn't believe her story? Right now Sinclair could be manufacturing all kinds of evidence against her. He could bully anyone in town to say anything he wanted about her.

She fought the impulse to lean over and take Sammy from the cradle and hold him in her arms. She wanted to hold him tight, kiss his cheeks and smell his baby sweetness, because she had no idea if a time would come in the future when he'd be lost to her forever.

Dalton awoke first and found his arms filled with a warm, sleeping Janette. They were spoon fashion, him curled around her slender back. He drew in the scent of her, that floral perfume that enticed him.

It was only now, in this moment with her body warm against his and his defenses not erected that he could admit to himself that he'd grown to care about her more than he'd ever thought he'd care about a woman again in his life.

It was late. He could tell by the cast of the sun shining through the window that he'd slept longer than he'd intended. Of course, he hadn't drifted off to sleep until the wee hours of the morning.

He'd spent much of the night listening to Janette breathing peacefully in sleep and worrying about the decision he'd encouraged her to make. He now contemplated what he needed to accomplish that day because it was easier to focus on that rather than the feelings he had for Janette.

He needed to call Trent Cummings, the special prosecutor, and see when he could get the man out here to meet with Janette. He also needed to make arrangements to get Nana out of Sandstone and to the safe house in Kansas City.

Hopefully they could connect with Trent in the next day or so and get things rolling. He closed his eyes and breathed in Janette's scent.

In many ways she amazed him. He'd expected her to fight him about staying and seeking justice, he'd expected her to demand he put her on the next bus out of town. The fact that she'd agreed to stand and fight against Brandon Sinclair instead of running showed him the immense inner strength she possessed.

He knew he wasn't only getting too close to her, but she was getting too close to him, as well. Their relationship, such as it was, was built on forced proximity and circumstances beyond their control.

It had nothing to do with reality. He was a temporary measure of safety in her life, just as he'd been in Mary's. He rolled away from Janette and off the bed, glad that he didn't awaken her in the process.

He grabbed his clothes from the floor and padded into the bathroom. Minutes later, standing beneath a hot shower, he tried not to think about how her long legs had felt when she'd straddled him, how hot her mouth had been against his skin.

Brandon Sinclair had left scars inside her that would take time to heal, but Dalton felt certain that eventually Janette would be able to have a loving, passionate relationship with a special man.

He frowned, irritated by the fact that he didn't like the idea of Janette making love with another man.

By the time he was out of the shower and dressed, Janette was up and making coffee in the kitchen. Clad in her pink robe, she looked soft and utterly feminine and a renewed burst of desire hit Dalton hard in the stomach.

"I've got to get back to town," he said gruffly.

"Surely you can stay long enough to have coffee and some breakfast," she replied. "I was just going to make some scrambled eggs and toast."

"Okay," he conceded. "I've got a lot to do today. And you need to call your nana and tell her what's going on." He sat at the table. "I'll call you later with details and we can set up getting her moved as soon as possible."

"Good, that will make me feel better." She poured him a cup of coffee, set it in front of him then returned to the counter where she put two slices of bread into the toaster, then began to crack eggs into an awaiting bowl. Sammy began to fuss from the bedroom.

"Want me to get him?" Dalton asked, figuring he needed to go back in the bedroom to get his wallet and gun, anyway.

"Thanks, I'd appreciate it."

The minute Dalton entered the room, Sammy stopped his fussing and began to coo, as if attempting to tell Dalton something very important.

Dalton grabbed his wallet and shoved it into his back pocket, then tucked the gun into the back of his waistband and picked up the little boy.

Sammy wiggled in his arms and flung out a hand that promptly latched on Dalton's nose. "Hey, little buddy," Dalton whispered. "That's my nose." Sammy smiled in delight and Dalton's heart moved. This little boy had no idea that he was in the center of a storm, a storm that had the potential to see his mother either in jail or dead.

I can't let that happen, Dalton told himself. He had to summon every skill he possessed as a bodyguard in order to keep Janette safe until this was all over and she could begin a new life in whatever city she chose.

He carried Sammy back into the kitchen where Janette had already fixed a bottle for the little guy. As Dalton sat once again at the table with Sammy in his lap, she held the bottle out to him. "Do you mind?"

Dalton took the bottle and gave it to Sammy, who sucked greedily on the nipple. His innocent little blue eyes stared up at Dalton with intense concentration.

Dalton was shocked to realize if he wasn't careful Sammy would steal his heart completely and make him remember all the old dreams that he'd once possessed.

He refused to entertain those dreams again, especially with Janette and her son in a starring role. That would only lead to a new heartache, and he wasn't interested.

By the time they finished breakfast it was after nine o'clock. With Sammy on a blanket in the living room, Dalton picked up the phone and dialed the number for the special prosecutor's office in Oklahoma City.

It took him nearly fifteen minutes, but he was finally

connected to his old friend Trent. He quickly explained the situation and was disappointed in Trent's reply.

"I definitely want to pursue this and talk to your friend, but there's no way I can get to Cotter Creek for at least a week. I'm in the middle of something here that I'm hoping to tie up in the next week to ten days."

Dalton frowned. He'd hoped to get Trent here a lot sooner…like the next day at the latest. "You'll call me if you get free sooner?"

"Definitely." The two men spoke for a few more minutes, then Dalton hung up.

"Is he coming?" Janette asked hopefully.

"Not for a week to ten days."

A look of panic swept over her features. "So long? What happens in the meantime?"

A new burst of tension twisted Dalton's guts. "In the meantime we can only hope that Brandon Sinclair doesn't discover where you are. You know how to shoot a gun?"

Her eyes widened. "No. Why?"

He pulled his gun from his waistband. "I'd feel better if I left this here with you."

"I wouldn't," she said flatly. She leaned back against the sofa, a troubled expression on her face. "As much as I hate him, as much as I fear him, I'm not sure I could shoot him." She looked from the gun to Dalton. "I don't know if I could really pull the trigger and kill somebody."

Dalton tucked the gun back into his waistband. He knew that a gun was only as effective as the person who held it. "Maybe I should have Tanner or one of my other brothers keep an eye on you."

"No, please. I feel safe here. There's no way Sinclair

can know about this cabin and I'd rather nobody else know I'm here. It's been my experience that the more people keeping a secret, the more difficult the secret is to keep."

Dalton nodded, his head whirling. "When I get back to town I'm going to rent a room at the motel and I'll have one of my brothers sit on it. Maybe we can catch Sinclair breaking the law and put him behind bars before Trent ever gets here. If nothing else the ruse of the empty room might keep Sinclair focused on the idea that you're there."

"I'm all for any plan that keeps him as far away from me as possible," she replied.

"I'd better get moving," he said.

She got up and walked with him to the door and he fought the impulse to lean down and capture her lips before he left. Minutes later, as he headed back toward town, he could only hope that he could keep Brandon Sinclair at bay until Trent arrived in town.

Chapter 10

It snowed again late that afternoon and Dalton called Janette to tell her not only would the weather make it impossible for anyone to get to Nana, but also he wouldn't be coming to the cabin that night.

She was bitterly disappointed with the length of time it would take before she could talk to Trent Cummings, with the damnable winter weather that complicated everything, but more important, with the fact that she wouldn't have Dalton's company for the evening.

Falling asleep the night before with him lying next to her had been heavenly. The very sound of his even breathing had made her feel safe and warm. Watching him give Sammy his morning bottle had stirred a wistful hope that she knew could only lead to disappointment.

For just a moment, as she'd scrambled eggs and Dalton had held Sammy in his arms, she'd wanted this life with him to last forever. With each moment she spent in Dalton's company it was getting easier and easier to imagine what life with him would be like.

And that was dangerous. Dozens of times he'd said in one way or another that he wasn't interested in a relationship. He had no desire to be a husband or a father. It was a shame, because she thought he would be wonderful at both.

She now stood at the living-room window and watched the snow falling in big fat flakes. She hoped it didn't snow too much. She didn't like the idea of being snowed in here all alone.

Sammy was taking a nap, the cabin was silent and she was restless, filled with an uneasy sense of impending doom. "It's just the snow," she said aloud, hoping the sound of her own voice would soothe her. It didn't.

But she knew what would make her feel better. She walked over to the sofa, curled up in one corner and picked up the telephone. She punched in Nancy's number, and the older woman answered on the second ring. "Nancy, it's me. May I speak to Nana?"

When Nana's voice came across the line Janette fought against a swell of emotion that momentarily clogged her throat. She hadn't spoken to her grandmother since the night Sinclair had shown up on Dalton's doorstep, and she realized now that she had so much to tell her.

"Are you still at Dalton West's apartment?" Nana asked.

"No, I'm in a little cabin on the West property." She explained about the sheriff showing up, about the fire and subsequent shooting.

"Nana, I'm not leaving. I've decided to stand and fight him."

There was a long moment of stunned silence. "You know I've always supported you in every decision you've made," Nana said. "And I'm proud of you for wanting to fight him, to bring him to justice. But, I'd be lying if I told you this is what I want for you. I'm scared for you, for Sammy. Are you sure you're making the right decision?"

Janette wanted to laugh. Was she sure? Definitely not. She was filled with trepidation and doubts. But despite her fear and doubts she was committed to doing what was right.

"Of course I'm nervous and afraid. But Dalton believes me. He believes my story and he knows a special prosecutor who handles cases like this. Nana, I don't want to spend the rest of my life looking over my shoulder, afraid that Sinclair will find me, will find us. I want him to pay for what he did to me."

A swell of anger tightened her chest. "Nana, I'm not sure I'll ever be whole if I don't do this."

"Baby, if this is what you need to do, then do it. You know I'll stand right beside you," Nana replied.

For the next few minutes Janette explained to her grandmother about moving to the safe house in Kansas City. "I'm not doing that," Nana argued with a touch of her legendary stubbornness. "I'm perfectly fine here with Nancy and I'm not going to go anywhere unless you're with me."

"But, Nana, I'd feel so much better if I knew for certain you were safe."

"Don't you worry about me none," she said. "I've

got so many friends in this trailer park, that man will never be able to find me."

Janette wasn't surprised by her grandmother's vehemence in remaining where she was. She'd had a feeling she'd never be able to talk her into going to Kansas City.

"Janette, honey. I'll leave Sandstone when this is all over and the three of us can go someplace new, if that's what you want. But, in the meantime I'm staying put right here where I'm at least close enough to you to get to you in a half an hour."

"Somehow I had a feeling you'd say something like that," Janette said dryly.

"Do you trust this man? This Dalton West?"

"With my very life," Janette responded without a second thought. "More important, I trust him with Sammy's life."

"Then that's good enough for me."

"He's a wonderful man, Nana. He's smart and kind. He can make me laugh and he makes me feel smart and pretty."

"Don't you go getting your heart all twisted up in this," Nana warned softly. "Dalton is helping you bring a bad man to justice, but that doesn't mean he's making a place for you in his life."

"I'm aware of that." Hadn't she spent most of the morning reminding herself of that very fact?

The two talked for a few more minutes then finally Janette said goodbye and hung up. *Don't you go getting your heart all twisted up in this.* Nana's words whirled around and around in Janette's head.

It was too late for the warning. She got up from the sofa and walked once again to the window to stare out at the falling snow. Her heart was already twisted up with Dalton.

She wasn't sure how it had happened, that in the space of so few days her heart could get so tangled up. But she knew she was precariously close to falling completely and irrevocably in love with Dalton West.

She drew a deep sigh. This cabin was so isolated. She'd never known such darkness as that which came with nightfall here. Last night there had been the faint illumination of the moon. But tonight, with the clouds, there would be no moonlight, no star shine, just deep, impenetrable darkness. If Sinclair somehow found her here, nobody would even hear her scream.

Releasing another tense sigh, she stepped away from the window and paced the length of the living room. The evening stretched out before her, empty and lonely.

The living room had a television but Janette had never been much of a TV watcher. She thought about waking up Sammy, but decided that was the height of selfishness, to wake up her infant son because she was lonely and bored.

Maybe it was time for her to get out her book bag and do a little studying. She didn't intend to work as a waitress for the rest of her life, and the best way to get ahead was to get that GED.

She went into the bedroom and opened her suitcase. For several long moments she simply stared at the red book bag. She remembered vividly the last time she'd carried it out of the building where she'd been taking the classes.

Proud. She'd been so proud of herself for taking her future in her hands, for making the effort to change her life for the better. Now as she stared at the book bag all she could think about was what had happened on her way home that night.

As she carried the bag to the kitchen table she realized Sheriff Sinclair hadn't just raped her body that night on the side of the road. He'd also raped her mind. He'd taken all her insecurities and thrown them in her face, telling her she was poor, stupid trailer trash.

Janette refused to allow Brandon Sinclair to define her. She'd been his victim for a brief period of time, but she wasn't a victim anymore.

With a new burst of determination she reached into the book bag and withdrew her notebook, a study guide and her mini–tape recorder.

She punched the rewind button on the tape recorder then opened the study guide to find the page she'd last worked on. She'd loved school and it didn't take her long to become totally absorbed in the work.

It was long after dark when she decided to fix herself a cup of tea. She punched on the tape recorder to hear the last lecture that she'd taped, then got up to heat some water for the tea.

"The United States constitution consists of a preamble, seven articles and twenty-six amendments." A pleasant female voice filled the room. Mrs. Rebecca Winstead had been the woman working to help adults achieve their GED. The last class Janette had attended had been going over the constitution.

"Over the next couple of nights we're going to be talking about the components that make up the document that is the supreme law of the land."

As Janette made her cup of tea, she listened to the tape, trying to absorb everything that might be important when she eventually took her test.

She carried her cup of tea to the table and at that moment Sammy awakened. She hurried into the bedroom. "Hey, little man." She picked up the smiling, wiggling boy and placed him on the bed to change his diaper. "Did you have a nice little nap?" she asked and efficiently took care of the wet diaper, replacing it with a clean one.

"Turn off your lights and get out of the car," the deep male voice boomed, and Janette froze.

Sinclair. His familiar voice shot a stabbing panic through her. He was here! He'd found her! Wildly she looked around the room, trying to remember where she'd put her knife.

"Well, well, don't we look all sexy in that little skirt?"

She frowned, picked up Sammy and stepped back into the kitchen. The hated voice came from the small recorder in the center of the table.

She stared at the tiny machine as it continued to play the sounds of that night…the sounds of her rape. Somehow when she had reached into her book bag that night to retrieve her driver's license, she must have hit the record button.

Tears streamed down her cheeks as she hugged Sammy close.

They were tears of sorrow for the innocent girl she'd been and tears of happiness because the tape was evidence, solid evidence that would put Brandon Sinclair behind bars for a very long time.

She started for the phone to call Dalton, to tell him the news, but halfway to the phone she changed her mind. She'd tell him tomorrow when he was here. It would be her surprise.

"We've got him, Sammy," she whispered, and for the first time since this all began, hope filled her up.

Dalton sat in the West Protective Services office and stared out the window. The snow that had fallen the day before hadn't been enough to create anything but minor problems and Main Street of Cotter Creek was back in business.

He'd called Janette first thing that morning to tell her he'd try to get to the cabin that evening. He'd come into the office in an attempt to keep his schedule as normal as possible. He didn't want anyone noticing that he was acting out of character until they had Brandon Sinclair in Trent Cummings' custody.

A room at the motel was now rented in his name and his brother Clay was sitting on it, watching for Sinclair to make a move. He'd told his brother only the minimum of information and that if he saw a man resembling the good sheriff trying to get into the room, he was to call Zack and Dalton.

He leaned back in his chair and frowned. He'd rather be at the cabin. He'd rather be with Janette and Sammy than sitting here wondering where Sinclair was now and what he might be doing.

Drumming his fingers against the desktop, he fought against a feeling of impending catastrophe. He had no idea why the disquiet roared so loudly in his head. He had a plan, he'd set it in motion and all they had to do was keep Janette hidden until Trent arrived in town.

Unless Sinclair knew the specific location of the cabin, Dalton couldn't imagine how he would find it, find her. Everything was under control, and yet he couldn't stop the worry that whispered through him.

He wished Janette would have agreed to keep his gun. He wished she would have told him she was a sharpshooter in another lifetime.

It was just after noon when the door opened and Zack walked in. Following at his heels was Brandon Sinclair. Dalton narrowed his eyes.

If he'd been a dog his hackles would have risen. As it was, every muscle in his body tensed. He nodded to his brother but didn't get up from behind the desk.

"Dalton, I understand you and Sheriff Sinclair have met," Zack said. Dalton merely nodded.

Sinclair cleared his throat and stepped closer, a flyer in his hand. "I've been passing out these photos of the woman I've been looking for. Maybe you've seen her around town."

Brandon Sinclair had the eyes of a predator, ice-cold, and as he looked at Dalton they were filled with a silent challenge.

Dalton took the flyer from him, gave it a cursory glance then tossed it on the desk in front of him. "Sorry, haven't seen her."

"She's a bad one, Mr. West. I told your brother here, Janette Black is a danger to anyone she gets close to. I want to get her into custody before she harms anyone."

Dalton raised an eyebrow. "I thought you told me the other night that she had already hurt somebody. Didn't you tell me she'd killed her grandmother?"

Red splotches appeared in Brandon's cheeks. "We don't know for certain what's happened to her grandmother. Initially we thought she was in the fire that destroyed the trailer where she and Janette lived, but our investigation turned up no bodies."

"Then what exactly is it she's wanted for?" Dalton held Sinclair's gaze intently.

"She's wanted on a number of charges. Theft and drug trafficking for starters. There's also been a number of home invasions recently and we think she was involved in those."

"She's just a regular one-woman crime spree," Dalton replied. Zack shot him a sharp glance. "Look, I told you the other night I hadn't seen her, and nothing has changed, so if you'll excuse me I've got work to do." He pointedly turned his chair to face the computer, effectively dismissing both his brother and Sinclair.

"I've got to get the rest of these flyers handed out," Sinclair said to Zack.

As the two men left the office Dalton picked up the flyer. The photo of Janette looked like a typical school photo. She looked younger and her hair was shorter. She'd said she'd had to quit high school her junior year. If he were to guess, this was probably the last school picture she'd had taken.

He still held the photo when the door opened and Zack came back in. He set the flyer aside. "I figured you'd be back."

Zack sat in the chair opposite the desk and studied his brother. "You want to tell me what's going on?"

"What makes you think anything is going on?" Dalton countered.

Zack's dark eyebrows pulled together in a frown and he leaned forward and thumped a finger in the center of the flyer. "You know something about this, about her. I know you do."

"What makes you think that?"

"Because I'm your brother, Dalton. I know when

you're lying. Look, you don't want to put yourself in the middle between a lawman and a criminal. If you know anything about the whereabouts of this woman you need to tell me now."

"I've got nothing to tell you." Dalton leaned back in his chair. He hated lying to Zack, but until they connected with Trent Cummings he wasn't willing to share anything with his brother. As much as he didn't want to be between a lawman and his criminal, he didn't want Zack to be in the middle of a lawman and his own brother.

Zack leaned back in his chair and expelled a deep sigh, his gaze still on Dalton. "What's up with you lately?"

Dalton frowned. "What are you talking about?"

"It seems like for the last six months or more you've withdrawn from all of us, withdrawn from life. You stay holed up either in here or at your apartment. You don't visit anyone, you don't date. You don't share anything of yourself with anyone."

"When did you get to be Dr. Phil?" Dalton asked with more than a touch of irritation.

"If I were Dr. Phil, I'd not only be able to point out the problem, but I'd also have an idea what had caused it."

"There's no problem," Dalton replied emphatically. "I like being alone. Why is that an issue?"

Zack raked a hand through his dark hair. "I guess it's not, if that's the life you choose." He stood and started for the door, but before he reached it he turned back to face Dalton. "Dad said he's seen your truck passing by the house a couple of times in the last couple of days."

"I've been staying off and on at the cabin. George is doing a little remodeling work."

Zack held his gaze for another long minute, then turned and left the office. The moment he was gone Dalton picked up the phone and called Emmett Treadwall, a local handyman and made arrangements for him to paint Dalton's apartment immediately. He then called George to let him know that the apartment was going to be painted. Covering tracks, covering his lies.

Maybe he should have confided in Zack, but without any real evidence to damn Sinclair, he just wasn't sure what his brother would be forced to do.

In just a matter of days it would all be over. Hopefully Trent would believe Janette enough to start a full-blown investigation that would lead to Sinclair's arrest. Then Janette and her grandmother and little Sammy would begin a new life someplace where there were no reminders of the horror she'd experienced.

Temporary. All of this was temporary. Another week or so and she'd be gone. Once again he picked up the flyer and stared at her picture.

He'd been irritated the night of the snowstorm, irritated that even for a single night he had to share his space, accommodate somebody else's needs. He'd told himself he was living a solitary life, but maybe it was in reality a selfish life.

He tossed the picture aside and frowned, not wanting to chase that thought any further. Just a couple more days, then he could get back to his own life.

What he didn't understand was why that particular thought didn't hold much appeal.

Chapter 11

She was waiting for him at the door when he pulled up in front of the cabin just after seven. Knowing that Sinclair was in town, he'd driven around for an hour before coming here, making sure that he wasn't being followed.

The sight of her with Sammy in her arms warmed his heart despite his need to remain emotionally distant. As he approached, Sammy wiggled with delight, arms flailing as if to reach for him.

There was no way to maintain any kind of distance from an almost six-month-old baby. Dalton took the little boy from her arms as he stepped through the door. "Hey, buddy," he said, then smiled at Janette. "I think you've got a heartbreaker on your hands."

She laughed. She looked brighter, happier than he'd ever seen her and a thrum of tension wound tight in his gut. He wanted her. God help him but he wanted her again. Even knowing that in a matter of days she'd be out of his life, even knowing that he could only be a temporary fixture in her life, he wanted her.

She grabbed him by the arm and pulled him toward the kitchen. "I hope you haven't eaten yet. I made a meatloaf and I've got a wonderful surprise."

"I haven't eaten, and what's the surprise?"

"Let's have dinner first, then I'll tell you."

"Sounds good. And I have some news, too," he said.

He stepped into the kitchen and looked around in surprise. The table was set and in the center were two tall candles and a bottle of wine. He shifted Sammy from one arm to the other. "Where did all this come from?" he asked.

"I called Savannah. She did me a favor and picked up some things from the store and brought them out this afternoon." She took Sammy from his arms. "Sit. I'm just going to put him down, then I'll be right back to serve the meal."

As she disappeared into the bedroom Dalton sat at the table. The candles gave off a pleasant glow and their vanilla fragrance mingled with the scent of the meatloaf. And beneath it all he could smell the scent of Janette, the honeysuckle that now reminded him of making love with her.

He could get used to this, coming home from work to her and Sammy. He steeled himself against the very thought, against the sense of homecoming that had filled him the moment he'd seen her and Sammy at the front door waiting for him.

She came back into the room a few minutes later,

the glow of happiness still lighting her features. "You look unusually happy tonight," he said.

"I am." She went directly to the oven and pulled out a meatloaf surrounded by potatoes. "First of all, I cooked Smiley's special meatloaf. Even people who profess to hate meatloaf love Smiley's recipe." She set the dish on the table. "Second, there's nothing better than candlelight to put a woman in a good mood. And third, I can't wait to tell you about my really big surprise. But first, we eat."

From the refrigerator she pulled out a salad, then joined him at the table. "And how was your day?"

He opened the bottle of wine and filled their glasses, then began to fill his plate. "Boring," he said, "except for the visit I got from Sinclair and Zack." One of her pale eyebrows danced upward. "Sinclair has been passing around flyers in town with your picture on it."

"Where did he get a picture of me?" She passed him the salad bowl.

"Looked like an old school photo. Did anyone else in town see you besides me?"

"The guy at the bus station was the only person I saw, and if Sinclair asks him any questions all he'll be able to say is that he saw me the night of the storm but didn't know where I went."

Dalton nodded. "I do have some good news."

"What's that?"

"I got a call from Trent today. He was able to wind things up sooner than he expected in Oklahoma City so he's planning on coming to Cotter Creek sometime late tomorrow afternoon. As soon as he arrives in town I'll drive him out here to hear your story."

Her blue eyes held his steadily. "So this could all be over by tomorrow night."

"That's right. If everything goes well, Sinclair could be in custody as early as tomorrow night." He looked at her curiously. "Why don't you look pleased with that news?"

"Oh, I am pleased," she quickly said, then frowned, a charming little wrinkle appearing between her brows. "I was just thinking that I need to figure out what happens next."

"When you get your GED, what are your plans then?"

She took a sip of the wine, the set her glass back on the table. "I'd like to get a job that pays well enough that I can help support Nana and Sammy and also pay for college night classes. Eventually I'd like to be a teacher."

"An admirable profession. Is that something you've always wanted to do?"

She grinned at him. "Only after I'd finally given up my desire to be a princess."

He laughed and for the next few minutes they ate and exchanged small talk. Again Dalton was struck not only by her beauty, but by her intelligence and sense of humor, as well. Whenever she finally got settled in someplace she would have no problems dating and would eventually find a man who didn't want to live without her.

After they'd eaten they cleared the table and cleaned up the kitchen. Despite his desire to the contrary, every bump of their shoulders, every brush of their hands as they worked side by side, sent sizzling electricity through him.

"Now are you going to tell me the secret that has you so excited?" he asked.

She poured them each another glass of wine, handed him his then pointed him toward the living room. "Go make yourself comfortable and I'll be right back." She disappeared into the bedroom.

Dalton carried both his wine and hers to the living room and sank down on the sofa, his curiosity piqued. A moment later she came into the living room carrying a red book bag.

"This is the bag I carried back and forth to the GED classes I was taking," she said as she set it on the coffee table. "I hadn't opened it since that night with Sinclair. Yesterday afternoon I decided maybe it was time to pull out the books and start studying again."

She sat next to him on the sofa and took out the books that were inside, then pulled out a small tape recorder. "I used to tape the classes so if I got confused about something or felt I missed something I could listen to the class as many times as I needed to."

He nodded, wondering where she was going with this. He reached out for his wineglass and took a sip, aware of a palpable tension radiating from her. He set his glass down and frowned. "Are you okay?" She was staring at the tape recorder as if it were a coiled rattlesnake getting ready to strike.

She looked up at him and smiled, a beatific smile that shot a new ripple of desire through him. "I'm better than okay. Anyway, that night I had the book bag next to me in the car when Sinclair pulled me over. The best way to explain all this is this." She leaned forward and pushed the play button on the recorder.

"Turn off your lights and get out of the car."

Dalton nearly fell off the sofa as Brandon Sinclair's deep voice boomed from the recorder.

"Well, well, don't we look all sexy in that little skirt."

As the tape played, a sickness welled up inside Dalton as he heard the sheriff bully Janette. It was only when he heard Janette whimper from the tape and say no that he leaned forward and shut off the recorder. He couldn't stand to hear the rest. He didn't want to hear the sounds of her being taken against her will.

For a long moment they were both silent. Dalton stared at the tape recorder with a vague nausea rolling around in his stomach.

"I didn't know I had it until yesterday," Janette said, her voice seeming to come from far away as it penetrated the veil of rage that had descended over him. "I must have accidentally hit the On button when I went into the book bag to get my license."

She reached out and took one of his hands between hers. "The whole thing is on tape. We've got him, Dalton. It's not just my word against his. There's no way he can dispute what's on that tape."

Dalton stared at her. Although intellectually he'd understood that she'd been raped, that whimper he'd heard coming from the tape, the terror-filled protest that she'd released, moved it from intelligent knowledge to emotional sickness.

He wanted to kill for her. He wanted to weep for her. Her strength awed him…humbled him. He squeezed her hand, fighting for words.

"Dalton?" Her soft voice pierced the haze that had fallen over him. "Are you all right?"

He let go of her hand and instead pulled her into an embrace. She laid her head on his shoulder and he stroked the silk of her hair. "I'm just sorry. So damned sorry." Tears burned at his eyes.

"It's okay. I'm okay, especially now that I know he is going to pay for what he did." She looked up at Dalton and he saw that there were no shadows in her eyes, no pain of any kind. Instead her eyes sparkled with hope, with a new kind of peace.

As he held her gaze her mouth opened slightly and she leaned forward. He intended a soft, gentle kiss of healing, but the moment his mouth claimed hers and her tongue swirled with his the kiss became something much different.

Her arms curled around his neck as her kiss grew hot and demanding. He knew they were going to make love again, tasted it in her kiss, felt it in the willing way she filled his arms.

He told himself he didn't want to, that it would do nothing but complicate his conflicting emotions where she was concerned. But as she snaked her hand beneath his shirt and caressed his chest, he was helpless against the onslaught of sensations her touch evoked.

In all probability she would be out of this cabin, out of his life within the next two days. But at the moment she was warm in his arms and he allowed good sense to be swallowed by desire, knowing that it would only make it more difficult when the time came to tell her goodbye.

A quiet desperation simmered inside Janette as she kissed Dalton. It was the desperation of a woman who had fallen in love with the wrong man.

She kissed him with all the heart, all the soul she possessed, needing to take the memory of this last chance to be in his arms with her when she left.

Her fingers danced across the warmth of his broad

chest as their kiss grew more frantic, more needy. She broke the kiss only long enough to pull her sweatshirt over her head, then to draw him down to the floor.

"I want you, Dalton," she said fervently.

"I want you, too." He ripped his shirt over his head and tossed it aside, then stood and took off his jeans. While he was doing that Janette finished undressing, then when they were both naked, she lay back on the rug and beckoned him back into her arms.

He lay beside her, his gaze as hot as his hands as he caressed the length of her. His lips followed the path of his hands, nipping lightly at the base of her throat then kissing the fullness of one breast. A moan escaped her lips as rivulets of pleasure swept over her.

She knew this would be the last time she'd make love with him and she wanted to capture his taste and his touch in her memory. She knew his strength and his belief in her would sustain her through whatever her future held.

When she reached down to wrap her hand around his hardness, he released a low deep moan that only increased her excitement.

She hadn't realized that as a woman she'd been dead until Dalton had brought her back to life. Gratitude mingled with love, intensifying this moment in time with him.

They caressed each other as if they'd been making love together for years, with easy, sure movements that evoked the most intense sensations.

As he touched her intimately the build began, a rising wave of pleasure so intense she thought she'd go mad with it. And when the peak came, she cried out his name, trembling as the release swept her away.

She knew he was waiting for her to take the lead as she had the last time they'd made love. But she didn't want the lead. She parted her legs and motioned for him to get on top.

He hesitated, his eyes glowing and the muscles in his neck strained. "Are you sure?"

"I'm sure."

He moved on top of her and she waited for the panic to strike. The scent of him surrounded her, clean and with that touch of sandalwood she found so attractive.

He didn't take her, but instead held himself above her, as if waiting to see if she'd freak out. She realized at that moment that she wasn't going to freak, that her trust in Dalton was so complete, all she wanted was to be surrounded by him.

She pulled him closer and as he eased into her, there was no thought of anything but him. His mouth sought hers as his hips moved against her. She clung to him, loving the feel of his broad back beneath her fingers, wanting to urge him deeper into her.

He moved faster, faster still, his lips leaving hers as their breaths mingled in quick pants. When he stiffened against her she wanted to cry, because she was free of the specter of Brandon Sinclair, because she loved Dalton West.

He moved his upper body off hers and stared at her in the waning light. "We didn't use protection."

"Don't worry, I'm on the Pill. After...what happened, I wanted to make sure that if I ever got pregnant again, it would be my decision." His statement was a jolt back to reality. He was worried because he didn't want a baby. He didn't want a wife. There was no happy ending here with him.

She scooted out from beneath him. "I'll be right back. I'm going to take a quick shower." She left the living room and went into the bathroom and a moment later stepped beneath a warm spray of water.

Although she'd been with Dalton less than a week, the love she felt for him was deeper and stronger than anything she'd ever felt for any man. And visualizing a future with him was just as silly as visualizing herself a princess or a ballerina.

The door to the shower opened and Dalton peeked in. "Mind some company? I'm great at washing backs."

She smiled at him and stepped aside to allow him entry into the small shower. Even knowing that loving him was a study in futility, there was no way to guard her heart against him.

Twenty minutes later he was dressed and she sat at the kitchen table in her robe. "The next time you see me I'll have Trent with me," he said as he pulled on his coat. "I'll call you tomorrow and let you know what time we'll be here. Meanwhile, I'll fill in Zack and play the tape for him."

She nodded and stood to walk him to the door. She was glad he wasn't spending the night. Sleeping in his arms would only make things more difficult.

When they reached the front door he turned, drew her into his arms and smiled down at her. "Just think, by tomorrow night this will all be over. You can move on with your life and not be afraid of Brandon Sinclair any longer."

"It's truly over, isn't it?"

He nodded, his eyes suddenly dark. "You and your nana and Sammy are going to have a wonderful life." He kissed her on her brow, then released her and walked out.

She stood at the door and watched as he got into his truck. It was over. Tomorrow night she would tell her story to a man who had the power to bring Sheriff Sinclair to justice. With the tape, it was no longer a question of she said, he said. There was enough evidence to put him behind bars.

She should be feeling euphoric, but instead an unexpected chill walked up her spine. Twenty-four hours, she told herself. That's all she had to get through. Another twenty-four hours and it would all be over.

He knew where she was, and it wasn't in the motel room that had been rented by Dalton West. Brandon lay in bed next to his sleeping wife, his mind whirling. He'd thought Janette might have been moved to the West property, then had dismissed the idea as being too obvious.

A headache that afternoon had given him the information he needed. He'd been standing in front of the pain relief medications in the grocery store when he'd heard a woman asking about baby formula in the next aisle.

A glance around the corner had let him know it was Savannah West. He'd done his research on the West clan and knew she didn't have a baby.

He'd paid for his medicine, taken two of the gel-coated tablets, then had gotten into his car and waited for Savannah to emerge from the store.

A few minutes later she'd come out with a basket of groceries, then had gotten into her car and driven off. Thank God he had driven his personal car that day instead of his official car. It had been easy to follow her as she headed north of town.

When she'd turned onto the West property, he'd known Janette was there. He'd returned to Sandstone to plot and plan.

Damn the bitch for leaving Sandstone, for thinking she could escape him. And damn Dalton West for sticking his nose where it didn't belong.

He didn't just want that kid, he wanted Janette Black dead, dead so she couldn't talk, dead so she couldn't cause him any more problems.

She'd probably already told Dalton a tale, but he could easily deny that he'd done anything wrong. Okay, he'd had sex with her, but that didn't make him a criminal. He'd tell Dalton that they'd had a brief affair, that the sex had been consensual.

He smiled in the darkness of the room. By this time tomorrow night his life would be back to normal. Janette would be dead and, eventually, after all the red tape was through, that boy would be his.

Chapter 12

It snowed again the next afternoon. Janette stood at the window and stared at the fat flakes falling from the sky. She hoped it didn't snow enough to postpone Trent Cummings' arrival in Cotter Creek.

She was ready to get it over with, needed to get on with her life away from Dalton. He'd crawled too deeply into her heart. He'd made her wish for things that would never come true.

It was time to go, while she still had her dignity. She had a life to build for her, for Sammy and for Nana. She moved from the window and to the kitchen table where a cup of tea was growing cold.

Sammy was napping and she had spent much of the time after lunch trying to decide if they should go back to Sandstone or move to a whole new city.

When Sinclair was arrested the whole story would

come out and Janette wasn't sure she wanted to be known around the small town as the woman the sheriff had raped. Still, Nana had a support system in Sandstone and she would miss her friends desperately if they chose to locate someplace else.

The trailer had been insured, so there would be some money from the insurance company that might be enough to buy another mobile home and place it on the lot where the old one had been.

Once again her gaze shot out the window where the snow seemed to have picked up in intensity. She couldn't wait for spring. She ached for budding flowers and greening grass and a sun of healing warmth.

Where would she be in the spring? At the moment Tucson sounded like a great idea.

She'd called Nana earlier to let her know that by the end of the evening, the nightmare should be over. She'd mentioned to the older woman that, if all went well, she hoped Nana could get a ride to Cotter Creek in the morning and meet Janette at the motel. They'd figure out what to do from there.

She took a sip of the lukewarm tea and frowned thoughtfully. Maybe she should turn on the television and see if they were under any sort of snow watch or warning.

That's just what she needed, another blizzard moving in that put her life on hold for another week or so. What worried her most with each day that passed was the fear that Sinclair would eventually figure out where she was.

Even if he thought she was on the West property, she was comforted by the fact that the cabin was so well hidden. And surely if a stranger were wandering the West land, somebody would notice, a ranch hand or one of the Wests themselves.

She finished her tea, then went into the living room and sat on the sofa trying to decide if she should call Nana or not. Before she'd made up her mind the phone rang.

It was Dalton, and at the sound of his deep, familiar voice she sank back against the cushions and squeezed the receiver closer to her ear.

"Hi," he said. "How are things there?"

"Okay. I've just been watching it snow. I used to love the snow, but lately it seems like all it does is complicate things. Did you meet with Zack, and have you heard from Trent? Is the snow going to postpone his arrival?"

"I tried to reach Zack, but he got called to an accident and didn't get back last night. I've left a message for him to get in touch ASAP. And I spoke to Trent just a few minutes ago," Dalton said. "He can't get away from Oklahoma City until about three this afternoon. That would put him here after six and he promised me that the weather wouldn't interfere except that it might take him longer to make the trip."

"Thank God, because I'm ready to get this over with," she said.

"Yeah, it's past time we both got on with our normal lives," he said.

She knew he didn't mean the words to hurt, but somehow they did. They reminded her that she was really nothing more than an inconvenience in his life. Oh, he might have enjoyed their lovemaking. After all, he was a man, but just because he'd liked having sex with her didn't mean he felt any kind of emotional attachment to her.

"That's what I've been doing all morning. Trying to figure out where I want to pick up the pieces of my life and start again."

"You aren't going back to Sandstone?" he asked.

She twisted the phone cord around her finger. "I don't know. I'm sure Nana would be pleased if I decided that we were going to stay there, but I'm not sure that's where I want to be. After tonight everyone in town will know that Brandon Sinclair raped me. I'm not sure I want to raise my son someplace where people know that information."

"What are you going to tell Sammy about his father?"

"Eventually the truth, but I want him to hear it from me, not from some kid down the block or some whispers in a store. I'll choose the right time and place to tell him about his father. Maybe by that time there will be a man in my life, a man in Sammy's who will fill any void he might feel."

There was a long moment of silence. "I hope so," he finally said.

"Any sign of Sinclair today?" she asked.

"Haven't seen or heard from him all day. I did hear from my brother Tanner. I'd had him working on a background check of Sinclair and unfortunately it turned up nothing."

"Did you expect it to turn up anything?" she asked.

"I figured it was worth a try, but no, I guess not. Savannah has tried to make contact with that waitress you spoke to her about, but so far she hasn't had any luck."

"None of that matters now," she replied. "We have Sammy and we have the tape and we have me. That's all we need to put him in prison. Do you have the tape in a safe place?" He'd taken the tape player with him the night before when he'd left.

"It's in the safe here in the office," he said.

She twisted the phone cord more tightly around her finger, vaguely wondering in the back of her head why nobody had replaced the phone with a newer cordless model. "What happens after tonight? Once I tell my story to Trent?"

"Hopefully Trent will be able to get a judge to issue an arrest warrant, then we'll have my brother Zack pick him up." He paused a moment, then continued, "Janette, I know you aren't sure what your next move might be, but I want you to know that you're free to stay in the cabin as long as you need to until you figure out where you're going to go."

"Thanks, but I'm planning on having Nana meet me at the motel here in town tomorrow afternoon so if you can just take me there tomorrow, I'll be fine." She couldn't stay here, not in the place where she'd realized her love for him.

"Have you checked with the motel to make sure they have a room?" he asked.

"I intend to do that as soon as we hang up."

"If they don't have any available rooms, I have one rented there in my name. You could stay in it as long as you want or need."

"I'll play it by ear," she said.

They spoke for a few more minutes then hung up. She got up from the sofa and walked back to the window where the snow was still falling in small flakes.

What she really wanted he couldn't give her. Two wishes filled her heart. The first was that Brandon Sinclair would pay for what he'd done to her, and that was going to happen. The second wish was that Dalton West would love her enough to want to leave behind his solitary life and spend his future with her and Sammy.

She supposed she should be happy with fifty percent of her wishes being fulfilled, but just as Brandon Sinclair had left an indelible mark on her soul, Dalton had left a very different, but equally powerful mark there.

Brandon Sinclair was a lucky man. Dalton shut off the tape player and got up from his desk, fighting a raw aching grief and a rage so great it threatened to consume him. Sinclair was lucky in that he wasn't around for Dalton to put his fist in his face. He wasn't around to be introduced to the explosive rage that Dalton barely managed to contain.

He'd decided to listen to the tape in its entirety before Trent Cummings arrived. He'd known Trent would want to hear it and Dalton hadn't wanted to be blindsided by unexpected emotion in front of the special prosecutor.

And he had been surprised by the depth of his emotion as he'd listened to Janette's rape at the hands of Brandon Sinclair.

She'd never screamed. Although the rape had been brutal and there had been moments when he'd wanted to scream for her, she'd never screamed. But she'd said no. Fourteen times, she'd said the word. Twelve times she'd pled with him to stop.

Dalton slammed his palm against the doorjamb, needing to vent some of the rage that clawed through him. He was sorry he'd heard the tape, but much more sorry that Janette had experienced the ordeal.

How strong she was, how utterly amazing. A survivor, not a victim. A woman who had decided not to run but rather to face her abuser even when she'd known the stakes were so high.

He would make certain her bravery counted. He

wouldn't rest until Sinclair was in jail, serving hell time for his crimes. It was the least he could do for Janette before he told her goodbye.

He stared out the window where the snow was once again falling. It had snowed off and on all day. Thank God Trent had called him a little while ago and told him he was half an hour outside Cotter Creek and should arrive within the next forty-five minutes. It would be after dark by the time they got to the cabin.

He had fallen in love with her. The thought came out of nowhere and hit him hard in the gut, taking his breath half away.

He'd made the same mistake he'd made with Mary. He'd gotten too close, allowed himself to get too involved. Only this time it was worse. The depth of his emotion for Janette was so much greater than anything he'd ever felt for Mary. He'd opened his heart not just to Janette, but to Sammy, as well, and when they left they'd take a huge piece of him with them.

And they would leave and he wouldn't try to stop them. He knew the drill. He'd been an important part of her life for a brief time, but he'd never been meant to have a permanent place there. She was in transition, had come to him in the middle of a storm, but the storm would pass and she'd move on.

He moved away from the window and returned to his desk where the small tape recorder awaited the arrival of Trent. Again his heart clenched as he thought of what Janette had endured.

She deserved happiness and he knew without a doubt she'd find it. She'd build a wonderful life for herself, her son and her grandmother. She was strong and beautiful and eventually she'd find a man who wanted to share his life with her.

He knew she'd grown close to him, but that was only because she'd had to be dependent on him for a brief time. Once she got back her independence and was no longer ruled by fear, she'd recognize what she thought was love for him was actually gratitude.

Apparently that was his place in life, to protect and serve, to help heal vulnerable women, then let them go to find happiness elsewhere. He'd thought he was happy alone, believed that his life was exactly the way he wanted it.

He realized he'd been fooling himself. He was a man meant for a family. The days that Janette and Sammy had shared his space had made him recognize that he didn't want to live a solitary life.

He wanted laughter. He wanted love. He wanted somebody to share his life with, somebody to kiss goodnight. Maybe eventually he'd find that special somebody. But in the meantime he just had to figure out how to tell Janette goodbye.

Brandon pulled the collar of the white parka closer around his neck and narrowed his gaze. A half an hour ago, when he'd parked his car, he'd cursed the falling snow, but now he welcomed it as he crept closer to the sprawling West house.

It had been a day of frustration. His presence had been required in Sandstone for a meeting with the mayor of the small town. During the meeting, which had seemed to last an eternity, all Brandon could think about was finding Janette and shutting her up for good.

Finally, at five that evening, he'd told his wife he would

be gone all night on a stakeout and had left the small town. He'd come prepared. Not only was he wearing white ski pants and the white parka that would allow him to blend in to the surroundings, but he also had another unregistered throwaway gun and a high-beam flashlight.

Now all he had to do was find her, and it was reasonable to assume that she was somewhere on the West property. He'd driven in earlier, holding his breath as he'd coasted past the main house with his lights off. He'd parked behind an old shed and now was headed toward the house where he knew the patriarch, Red West, had raised his family.

Before the night was over, he'd search every structure on the West land, scour every inch of the place in an effort to find her.

He approached the main house, where light danced out the windows. The illumination would make it easy for him to peer inside.

The wind howled like a banshee and sliced at any area of skin that was exposed. Snow crunched underfoot and he cursed beneath his breath, irritated with the weather, but more irritated by the very existence of Janette Black.

His heart beat fast as he eased up to one of the lit windows and looked inside. It was the kitchen of the house and there were two people there, an old man and woman. That would be Smokey Johnson and his new wife, Kathy.

Brandon had done his research. He knew that the old cowhand had married the retired FBI agent a month before and the two shared the house with Red West.

There was no sign of the bitch he sought in the kitchen, so he moved on to the next lighted window. In the living room an older man was in a recliner with a book open on his lap. He was asleep, and Brandon assumed the man was Red West.

So where was Janette?

He wasn't a stupid man. He knew that if the right people listened to her, she had the potential to screw up his life. He couldn't let that happen.

He moved from window to window, fighting a swell of frustration that nearly blinded him. Patience, he told himself. He needed patience. At any minute she might walk into the living room, or go into the kitchen to get something to eat or drink. Once she showed herself to him, it would all be over.

It didn't bother him that she might be in a house filled with others. Three old people were not going to stop him from getting what he wanted.

It took him twenty minutes or so before he decided to move on. He knew that Red's oldest son, Tanner, had a house somewhere on the property. Maybe Dalton had stashed Janette there.

The snow was coming down more heavily now. Already his footprints around the house were disappearing, covered by the new layer of snow. That was fine with him. Hopefully by the time the dead were found the weather would have destroyed any evidence the authorities might try to find.

He'd had chains put on his car tires, so hopefully when it was time to leave the snow wouldn't impede his escape. He got into the car and pulled forward, seeking the house where Tanner lived.

He continued to drive without headlights, using the pasture fences as guidelines to stay on the road, until he spied the next house. His deadly intent burned inside him, warming him despite the plunging temperatures and the icy wind that blew from the north.

A half an hour later his frustration was a gnawing beast inside him. As far as he could tell there was nobody home in Tanner's two-story house.

He returned to his car. Maybe she was in that motel room that Dalton had rented. Maybe he'd done the expected, thinking that Brandon would think it too obvious. He *had* thought it was too obvious and had made the decision to stay away from there.

Dammit. He'd been so certain she was here. In his mind there was no other logical place for her to be. He drove farther into the property and came to a house under construction. Brandon had heard that Clay West was in the process of building a home, and this was probably it. It had been framed, but the walls weren't up. Janette couldn't be hiding there.

He knew he should head back to Sandstone before the snow got so deep that even chains wouldn't allow forward movement. But he kept creeping forward, unwilling to give up the hunt.

He had just decided to head back to Sandstone when he saw it…a faint light glimmering among a grove of evergreen trees.

Where there was light, there was a source of that light. New energy filled him as he parked the car, got out and moved as quickly as a streak of moonlight over the snow.

He saw the cabin nestled among the trees and he knew she was there. He also knew there was no way Janette Black was going to survive this night.

Chapter 13

Janette paced the living-room floor as she waited to tell her story to Trent Cummings. Dalton had called a few minutes before and told her Trent had arrived in Cotter Creek and they would be leaving the West Protective Services office within the hour.

She had a feeling the hour would be spent discussing her case with Trent and listening to the tape that had captured Sinclair's crime against her.

She was glad Dalton was playing it for Trent in his office. She hoped to never hear it again unless it was at Brandon Sinclair's trial.

It was strange. She was at the end of this particular journey in her life, but she didn't feel the expected relief she'd thought tonight would bring. An uneasiness filled her.

She thought it was because tomorrow she'd have to

face the rest of her life—a life without Dalton. On impulse she went over to the sofa and picked up the phone. She punched in the number that would connect her to her grandmother.

Nancy answered on the second ring and immediately put Janette's grandmother on the phone. "Honey, how are you doing?" Nana asked. To Janette's surprise she began to cry. "Janette, what's wrong?" Nana asked urgently.

"Nothing…nothing's wrong," Janette managed to say. She swiped the tears from her cheeks and warbled an uneasy laugh. "I don't even know why I'm crying. Dalton is supposed to be here anytime with the prosecutor, and it looks like things are finally at an end."

"Then maybe those tears are ones of relief and hopefully a little bit of closure," Nana replied.

"Maybe," Janette agreed, but she knew where the tears were formed. They were created in her heart as she thought of never seeing Dalton again.

"Nancy's brother is driving me into town tomorrow afternoon," Nana continued. "I'll be at the motel by three or so."

"Good. I thought we'd stay a day or two and talk about where we go from here," Janette said.

"Janette, I want you to know that I don't want you making decisions with me in mind. I want you to build a life for you and that precious little boy of yours. Nancy has told me I can live here with her. I don't want you thinking you have to provide for me. I'm an old woman at the end of my life and you're a young woman, a new mother with your life ahead of you. Reach for all the happiness you can grab, honey. You deserve it."

They spoke for another few minutes then hung up.

Janette got up from the sofa and walked to the doorway of the bedroom to stare at Sammy sleeping in the beautiful cradle.

Once again she felt the burn of tears in her eyes. Maybe it was just the relief of knowing it was all finally over. She could let go of the fear that had been with her every day since the rape. She'd never again have to look over her shoulder and be afraid that Brandon Sinclair was just behind her, ready to wreak havoc in her life.

She turned away from the doorway and instead paced the kitchen, thinking about her conversation with Nana. Even though Nana had said she could live with Nancy, had insisted that Janette think only of herself and Sammy, Janette knew Nana would miss them desperately if Janette chose to leave her behind.

And to tell the truth, she didn't want to leave her behind. There was no question that Janette's life would be easier with Nana in it. While she worked and went back to school, somebody would have to watch Sammy, and Nana was the one person she trusted to take care of her little boy.

She didn't just need Nana in her life, she wanted the old woman to play a major role there. Wherever she went, she wanted Nana to go with her.

Maybe Kansas City was a good place to start again, she thought as she drifted into the living room. There would be plenty of job opportunities there and community colleges galore. She and Nana could make a decision tomorrow at the motel.

Reach for all the happiness you can grab, Nana had told her. If she were to reach for what she truly wanted, she'd grab Dalton West and never let him go.

She'd build a life with him that others would envy.

They'd share their lives during the days and share their passion for each other during the nights. He'd be the one who would teach Sammy how to be a man, and Sammy would grow up to be strong and morally decent and good.

It was a wonderful fantasy, but it had nothing to do with reality. She glanced at the clock on the top of the television. After seven. Where were Dalton and Trent? It had been well over an hour since Dalton had called.

She moved back to the front window and peered out. It was still snowing, more heavily than it had all day. She hoped the weather didn't hold up Dalton and Trent too long. She wanted tonight to be done and tomorrow to begin. She needed to get away from this cabin, away from thoughts of Dalton and what might have been.

She started to turn away from the window when, from the corner of her eye, she saw movement. It was just a flash, a blur of something, but fear spiked through her and she backed away from the window with a small gasp.

Although she hadn't gotten a real look at whatever was moving outside, the impression that burned in her head was that it had been far too big to be an animal. It had been big enough to be a man.

Dalton or Trent wouldn't be walking around outside, and if it was one of the Wests, surely they'd knock on the door to find out who was staying in the cabin.

It could only be one person.

Brandon Sinclair.

Somehow he'd found her. Her heart beat so fast she couldn't catch her breath for a long moment. The back of her throat closed up as panic took over.

He was here!

She couldn't think, couldn't move. It was as if the cold of the night had moved inside and frozen her in place. *Nobody will hear you scream.* The words pounded in her head. She was so isolated that when Sinclair got inside the cabin, as he killed her then stole her son, nobody would hear her cries.

"No." The word of protest broke her inertia. No, she wasn't going to allow that to happen, at least not without a fight.

She raced to the phone and picked it up. No dial tone greeted her. The line was dead. If she needed any further evidence that Sinclair was somewhere outside, the dead phone was it. He'd made certain she couldn't call for help.

As she left the living room and hurried into the bedroom, a fist slammed against the locked front door. "Janette, open the door. We need to talk." His deep voice held the authority and confidence of his position.

Inside the bedroom Janette fumbled beneath her pillow and pulled out the knife she'd carried since the night of her rape. The knock came again, this time harder against the wood of the door.

"Janette, open the door or I'll break it down. We have official business to discuss."

Frantically she looked around the small bedroom, seeking another weapon or an escape route. Her gaze landed on the window. She raced to it and threw it open. Frigid air blew in, chilling the last of any warmth that might have been left in her body. With trembling fingers she removed the screen.

Where were Dalton and Trent? She needed them here now. As she picked up the sleeping Sammy and wrapped him tightly in the towel she'd used as an extra blanket, she heard a crash at the front door and knew Sinclair was breaking it down.

She couldn't stand and fight him, knew that she'd never stand a chance against him. There was only one possible means of escape, and that was out into the snowstorm.

Holding Sammy tight against her, she went out the window, the icy cold and snow stinging every inch of her bare skin. Someplace in the back of her mind she knew it wouldn't take long for her to die of exposure. She wore no coat, no hat and no snow boots. She was clad in only a T-shirt, a pair of jeans and a pair of thin cotton slippers. But that couldn't be helped now.

As she began to run away from the cabin, away from Brandon Sinclair, the snow continued to fall like beautiful white death from the sky.

Behind her she heard the crash and a roar and knew that Sinclair had gotten inside. A sob ripped through her as she ran, knowing that she'd rather die in the snow than at the hands of the man who had raped her.

Dalton hung up the phone and tried to squash the worry that roared through him. "The phone's dead," he told Trent, who stood at the West Protective Services front door.

"Maybe the storm blew down a line," Trent offered.

"Maybe," Dalton said, but wasn't sure he believed it. A thrum of disquiet kicked up inside as he grabbed his truck keys off the desk. He hadn't talked to Zack yet, which didn't help his mood. "Let's get out of here. We need to get to the cabin."

Together the two men left the office and got into Dalton's truck. They had spent the past hour with Dalton filling in his old friend about the particulars of the case. Trent had heard the tape and had also listened to Dalton's suspicions that it had been Sinclair who had set the fire and fired the shots the night Dalton had moved her to the cabin.

Trent's expression had grown more grim with each word that Dalton spoke about Sinclair. Dalton knew there was nothing Trent loved more than putting away bad guys who masqueraded as good guys.

Dalton tried to ignore the uneasiness that coursed through him as he started the truck engine. She'd never not answered the phone before.

He attempted to tamp down the anxiety as he turned on the wipers to swipe at the snow that had gathered on the windshield.

"You're sure she'll testify?" Trent asked as Dalton backed out of his parking space.

"She'll do whatever she needs to do to make sure Sinclair goes to prison."

"The tape is good evidence, but could be easily disputed without her testimony," Trent said thoughtfully.

"She's solid," Dalton said. "She's come too far now to back down. She wants Sinclair behind bars far more than you or I do."

"I'm not sure that's possible," Trent said as he narrowed his eyes. "There's nothing I love more than putting a crooked lawman behind bars. Sinclair is a disgrace to the men and women who put their lives on the line every day for the good of their communities."

"I wish I would have seen him the night of the fire," Dalton said. "Then we could get him for attempted murder."

"We'll get him," Trent replied. "And I'll see to it that he's put away for as long as possible."

The street was slick and Dalton had to keep his speed at a minimum. As he drove he fumbled for his cell phone and punched in the number for the cabin. The phone rang and rang and rang. He clicked off, his apprehension exploding into full-blown fear.

"No answer?" Trent asked, his handsome features lit by the dashboard light.

Dalton shook his head. "I've got to admit, I'm worried." That was the understatement of the day.

He opened the cell phone again and quickly punched in a new number. "My brother Tanner lives close to the cabin where Janette is. He can get there quicker than we can." He sighed in frustration as Tanner's phone went directly to voice mail.

Tossing his cell phone to the seat between them, Dalton tightened his grip on the steering wheel and stepped on the gas.

Janette was in trouble and it was his fault. The knowledge thundered in his head. He should have insisted she keep a gun with her, he should have made other arrangements for her. Jesus, he should have done something different to ensure that Sinclair wouldn't find her.

Dammit, what had made him think that she'd be safe in the cabin all alone? He hadn't believed that Sinclair would be able to find her there, but apparently he'd underestimated the sheriff.

The snow made visibility difficult and Dalton felt the spin and slide of the tires on the slick road beneath them. The wind howled and buffeted the truck and he silently cursed the conditions that kept him from going as fast as he wanted to go.

Let her be okay. Don't let anything happen to her. Dalton's brain said the words over and over again, his heart pounding so loud in his ears he wondered if Trent could hear it.

Trent braced himself with a hand on the dash as the back of the truck spun out. Dalton quickly corrected the spin, the panic inside him nearly unbearable. But it wasn't the panic of nearly losing control of the vehicle, it was the sheer terror that had loosened itself inside him for Janette and Sammy.

"You going to kill us before we get there?" Trent finally said with a touch of dry humor.

"I'm trying not to." Dalton eased up on the gas, knowing that if they wrecked there was no way they could be any help at all.

His cell rang. He picked up the phone and checked the ID. Zack, finally. "Zack, I need you to meet me at the cabin immediately."

"What's going on?" Zack asked.

"You know that woman Sheriff Sinclair was looking for? Janette Black?"

"What about her?"

He didn't bother trying to fill in Zack on the tape and details. "I've got her at the cabin and I think she's in big trouble." As Dalton spoke those words aloud, his heart squeezed so tight in his chest he momentarily felt light-headed. "Hurry, Zack."

Zack hung up and Dalton tossed the phone aside again, hoping and praying that there was a logical explanation for Janette not answering his calls, hoping and praying that she and Sammy were just fine and Brandon Sinclair was nowhere in the area.

The snow was both a blessing and a curse. As Janette ran from the cabin, she was glad that the heavy snowfall would make it more difficult for Sinclair to see her.

The curse was that it hadn't taken long for her feet to become chunks of ice, causing her to stumble more than once as she ran blindly into the night.

Sammy had awakened and fussed against her, and she tried to soothe him as she ran, afraid that if he began to wail Sinclair would hear and would be able to pinpoint her exact location.

Her breaths came in painful pants, the cold air stabbing her lungs with each intake of air. Her bare hands ached, as did her face where the icy flakes of snow clung to her lashes, her lips and her cheeks.

Somehow in the space of a dozen footsteps she'd become disoriented. She was no longer sure she was going in the right direction to find help and with each step she took she grew more exhausted.

Eventually the cold disappeared and instead she became numb, feeling nothing but the screaming in her head. And that scream intensified when she turned and saw the beam of a high-powered flashlight just behind her.

He was coming! A sob ripped from her throat as she stumbled forward. The snow and the darkness of the night couldn't hide her if his high beam fell on her.

The flashlight swiped from side to side, and she knew at the moment he didn't see her, didn't know that she was so close.

Exhaustion pulled at her, but she forced herself to

move on. She wasn't so worried about her own safety, but for Sammy's. She had to keep him safe from the man who had fathered him.

She pushed herself forward, putting one numb foot in front of the other in an effort to escape. She could hear him now, the swish of his pant legs as his thighs rubbed together, and her heart pounded so hard, so fast, she wondered if she were having a heart attack.

At least if she died she knew Dalton would somehow, someway get Sammy. Even if Brandon Sinclair plucked Sammy from her dead arms, she was confident it would only be a temporary thing. Because she trusted Dalton. Because she knew he'd fight for her son if she couldn't fight for him herself.

Cold.

She was so cold. It was becoming more difficult to put one foot in front of the other. She just wanted to lie down and sleep and dream of Dalton and what might have been.

She knew that was the cold talking and so she pushed herself forward. Half-blinded by the snow, she nearly crashed into the small shed. All she could think about was getting out of the snow before her legs stopped moving altogether.

Sammy had become an unbearable weight in her arms and no matter how close she held him to her chest, she knew he must be feeling the sting of the cold.

Without conscious thought, she opened the shed door and went inside, then shoved the door shut behind her. Without the aid of a light she couldn't see what the shed contained. All she knew was the blessing of being out of the howling wind and the icy air. She'd take a minute and catch her breath, warm herself just a bit before leaving the structure and continuing to run.

It wasn't until she heard Sinclair roar her name from just outside the shed that she realized what she'd done. She'd run herself into a dead end, a blind alley. The only way out was back through the door she'd entered and on the other side of that door was death.

Chapter 14

The mind was a strange thing. In the flash of a moment it could process enough impressions and instincts to make a man sick. Dalton was definitely sick as his brain not only worked to wrap around the grim possibility that Sheriff Sinclair had found Janette, but also highlighted every mistake he'd made as her bodyguard.

And he'd made plenty.

"I shouldn't have left her out there all alone." He spoke one of his biggest mistakes aloud.

"You did what you thought was right at the moment," Trent replied, once again bracing himself as Dalton turned into the West property and nearly took out a wooden post as the truck spun out. "Don't second-guess yourself. That can make a man crazy."

Dalton's heart beat so fast it hurt. The snow had stopped falling and a sliver of moonlight sliced through the clouds, faintly illuminating the wintry landscape.

He flew past his dad's place, his brain screaming a litany of pleas. *Let her be okay. Please let her be safe.* Over and over the words played in his mind. It was as if, if he thought it often enough, that would make it so.

His hands ached from his fierce grip on the steering wheel, but that pain was nothing compared to the one that pierced his heart as he thought of Janette and little Sammy being in danger.

He raced by Tanner's house, skidded around Clay's half-built place and toward the grove of evergreen trees that surrounded the little cabin. He turned through the small lane and pulled up in front. Horror swept through him as he saw that the old wooden front door had been crashed in. He was out of the truck, gun drawn, in a frantic heartbeat.

Trent was right behind him and together the two men approached the silent cabin. Dalton stepped through the doorway and crouched with his gun held in both hands in front of him.

There was nobody in the living room. "Clear," he called out, and Trent stepped inside. As Dalton moved toward the kitchen his biggest fear was that he'd find only Janette's body somewhere in the cabin. The smashed front door seemed to cry that he and Trent were too late.

Emotion pressed thick in Dalton's chest and he drew a steadying breath as he entered the kitchen. Nothing. No body, no signs of any struggle, nothing. "Clear," he called to Trent, who followed at his heels.

Trent checked the bathroom, then stepped back into the kitchen and both men looked at the bedroom door. It was closed, and a fear like he'd never known clawed at his insides.

Dalton moved to the door. His hand trembled, dread

welling inside him as he reached for the knob. He flung open the door and the first thing he saw was the open window.

Relief shot through him as he easily realized the scenario. Sinclair had somehow found the cabin. He'd come in through the front door and Janette had escaped through the window. But the relief was short-lived as he realized it was possible he'd find her body in the snow.

"She's outside."

Together the two men hurried back to the front door. When they stepped outside the wind nearly stole Dalton's breath away. It cut sharp and deep, and frantic need welled up inside him. Even if Sinclair hadn't found her, the elements would be as deadly as the determined lawman.

They hurried around to the back of the cabin. Dalton stopped at his truck only long enough to retrieve a flashlight. Trent looked at Dalton. "Which way would she have run?"

Dalton stared out at the wide expanse of pasture that surrounded them. Janette was smart. She wouldn't have just taken off running without a plan of some kind.

She would have headed toward Tanner's house. Confirmation of his thoughts lay on the ground in faint footprints. However, it wasn't dainty small feet that had left the prints. It was big boot prints that filled his heart with a new sense of terror.

If he'd had any doubt of what had happened here tonight, those large footprints froze them away and also froze a part of his heart.

"Janette," he yelled, but the howl of the wind competed with his voice.

He and Trent trudged through the snow, following

the barely discernible footprints as Dalton swept the flashlight in front of them. Dalton felt as if they were moving in slow motion as they systematically searched the area looking for Janette…or her body.

As they walked, the mistakes Dalton had made roared through his head. He should have gotten his family involved, but he'd been so busy isolating himself, so worried about giving any part of himself away, that he'd made what he hoped wouldn't prove to be a fatal mistake.

"Dalton!"

Dalton turned at the sound of his name and saw Zack running toward them. "What's going on?" he asked when he caught up to Dalton and Trent.

"Brandon Sinclair is trying to kill Janette," Dalton said. "He raped her, and now he's trying to kill her. We have proof." He could see that Zack was confused, but he couldn't take the time to go through everything. "I'll explain later. Right now we need to find Janette."

Find Janette.

Find Janette.

The words pounded in Dalton's head as it began to snow once again. He was relatively certain she was out here without a coat and possibly without shoes. She wouldn't have taken time to bundle up before escaping out the window.

If they didn't find her soon the icy cold and snow would do the job for Sinclair. Unless the sheriff had already found her. Unless it was already too late.

The gunshot exploded the night and the sound ripped through Dalton's heart. *Too late,* his brain screamed. *You're too late to save her.*

"It came from over there." Zack pointed to the right and they all took off running.

The cold air sliced at his lungs as he raced toward the direction where they thought the shot had come from. The flashlight beam bobbed as he ran and fear made him feel as if he were dealing with an out-of-body experience.

As the flashlight beam fell on the old storage shed, Dalton's blood ran cold. Brandon Sinclair stood in front of the shed, and when he saw the beam of light he whirled around to face them. He had his gun drawn and wore a fierce look of determination.

"Sheriff West, I'm glad you're here," Sinclair said, ignoring both Dalton and Trent. "I have my suspect holed up in this shed. I need her out of there and placed in my custody."

Dalton started forward, but Zack grabbed his arm to hold him in check. "We heard a gunshot," Zack said.

"I fired a warning shot to let her know I meant business."

"Looks to me like you fired that warning shot right through the door," Zack observed.

"Look, I don't want any trouble here. I just want to get my prisoner into custody and get her back to Sandstone," Brandon said.

"You lying son of a bitch," Dalton exploded. This time it was Trent who grabbed hold of him as he tried to lunge forward. "If you've hurt them I'll kill you." He tried to escape Trent's firm grasp. He needed to get inside that shed.

Why didn't Janette come out? Was it possible that the single shot Brandon had fired through the door had found her and she was now lying bleeding—or worse—on the other side of the door?

"I suggest you get your brother under control, Sheriff," Sinclair said.

Zack narrowed his eyes. "I suggest you put your gun away and let me figure out just what the hell is going on here."

"I told you what's going on," Sinclair exclaimed, impatience obvious in his voice. "I just want to get my prisoner and go home." He must have seen something in Zack's eyes that made him holster his gun.

"I'm afraid that isn't going to be possible," Trent spoke for the first time. He looked at Zack. "I'm Trent Cummings, special prosecutor, and I want you to place Sheriff Brandon Sinclair under arrest."

"For what?" Brandon's hand moved down toward his gun.

"Don't do it," Zack warned as both he and Trent advanced on Sinclair.

"Rape. You're under arrest for the rape and attempted murder of Janette Black," Trent said as Zack plucked the gun from Sinclair's holster then cuffed him.

Dalton could stand it no longer. He raced for the shed door and tried to push it open, but it refused to budge. "Janette, it's me. Open the door."

The silence that greeted him was deafening. A sob ripped from him as he shoved and pushed against the door, hoping…praying that it wasn't her dead body blocking the way.

Trent helped, putting his shoulder against the door next to Dalton and together they managed to get the door open. "Janette!" Dalton cried, his flashlight frantically scanning the area.

He found her crouched behind an old love seat, her knife held tightly in one hand. "Is he gone?" she asked, her blue lips trembling uncontrollably.

The relief that crashed through Dalton nearly brought him to his knees. "It's over, honey. He can't ever hurt you again." Dalton helped her to her feet, noting that her eyes were huge in her deathly pale face. He hurriedly took off his coat and wrapped it around her slender shoulders as she cuddled Sammy tightly against her chest.

As they stepped out of the shed he gripped her closer to him as she saw Sinclair. "Whatever she's told you, it's a lie," he yelled and twisted his shoulders as if trying to escape from his handcuffs. "I'll admit we had sex, but she wanted it. She begged me for it."

Dalton tightened his arm around Janette's shoulders. "That's funny. The night you pulled Janette over for a speeding ticket, she had a tape recorder running. We've got that entire night's events on tape. You're going to prison."

Sinclair looked stunned.

Janette raised her trembling chin and smiled. "Gotcha," she said.

The night seemed to last forever. Dalton wanted Janette and Sammy to be taken to the hospital, but she refused, insisting that all she needed to recover from her ordeal was warmth.

They left the cabin and drove into town, where Sinclair was locked in the jail. The rest of them went to Dalton's apartment, where Janette was questioned by both Zack and Trent.

As the night progressed, she felt Dalton distancing

himself. He grew quiet, adding nothing to the conversation, and his green eyes seemed to stare at everything in the room except her.

Her worst fear had been realized. Brandon Sinclair had found her, but she'd survived. Sammy had survived. And now Janette's future stood directly in front of her.

It was almost four when the talk was finally finished. She promised Trent that no matter where she and Nana settled, she'd give him their address so he could let her know when Sinclair would go to trial.

She would be the prosecutor's star witness, and that fact held a certain poetic justice that sent a sense of peace through her.

After Trent and Zack left, she fell into Dalton's bed, exhausted by the trauma of the night. Sammy slept peacefully next to her and she fought the impulse to pull him close against her, to assure herself that they both truly had survived.

As she'd hidden in the shed, she'd believed she wouldn't leave it alive. She had thought she'd never see Sammy take his first step, say his first real word. She'd believed she would never hear Nana's voice or see Dalton's handsome face again.

Sleep, when it finally came, drifted over her like a soft, warm blanket and held no nightmares. She awakened to the sun shining through the window and a sense of peace she'd never known before.

The man who had forever changed her life would now face Lady Justice and have his freedom taken away for a very long time. She no longer had to be afraid. She would not live her life looking over her shoulder.

She frowned as she stared at the window. The cast of

the sun shining through the window made her realize it was late morning. Why hadn't Sammy awakened her?

She turned over and found the bed empty. Panic sliced through her for a split second, but it quickly ebbed. She wasn't sure exactly where Sammy was, but she knew he was safe, because they were in Dalton's apartment and Dalton wouldn't let anything happen to them.

Getting out of bed she tried to shove away the aching sadness that found her heart, the sadness of knowing that today she would tell Dalton a final goodbye.

After a quick stop in the bathroom to brush her teeth and wash her face, she belted her robe around her waist and went in search of the two men in her life.

She found them in the kitchen, and for a moment she stood just outside the door and peeked in. Dalton sat at the table with Sammy on his lap. He was trying to feed Sammy rice cereal, but it looked as if Dalton was wearing more than Sammy was eating.

A smile didn't make it to her lips, but it squeezed her heart as she watched the man she loved interact with her precious baby.

"Come on, buddy. We can do this," Dalton said. "Don't you want to grow up to be big and strong?" He held a spoonful of the cereal and Sammy laughed and waved his hand, striking the spoon and sending the cereal to the front of Dalton's shirt.

"Why don't I just lay you against my chest and let you graze off my clothes?" Dalton muttered.

"Problems?" Janette asked as she stepped into the room.

"If he makes this big of a mess with cereal I can't wait to see him with a bowl of spaghetti," he said.

Again an internal fist squeezed Janette's heart. They both knew he wouldn't be around to watch Sammy eat spaghetti. He wouldn't be around to see that Sammy grew big and strong.

"Coffee's made," he said, as if he sensed the awkward moment between them.

"Thanks." She moved to the counter and poured herself a cup. "Usually when he gets to the point that he's knocking it out of the spoon instead of eating it, I figure he's finished." She sat at the table.

"That works for me," he agreed easily. He stood with Sammy in his arms and carried the little boy over to the sink. "I'm not sure who needs to be hosed down first, you or me," he said to Sammy, who grinned and released a string of gibberish.

When he had Sammy clean she held out her hands and he placed the baby on her lap, then sat once again at the table across from her.

"You look well rested. I figured you could use a little extra sleep this morning, so when I heard Sammy start to fuss I got him."

"I appreciate it." She took a sip of her coffee as he stared at a point just over her head.

A new silence descended and she guessed it was the awkward silence of the end of a relationship when there was nothing more to say. She finished her coffee, then carried her cup to the sink. "I'm going to go take a shower and pack up my things."

"I'll hang out with Sammy so you can get showered," he offered.

As he took her son from her, she wanted to say something to break the somber mood between them, but she didn't. She simply went into the bedroom to take her shower and pack her belongings in preparation for going to the motel to meet Nana.

It was as she stood beneath the hot spray of the shower that she recognized that she couldn't leave here without telling Dalton how she felt about him. If she kept her feelings inside, she'd always wonder what might have been different if she'd spoken them aloud.

As she thought of baring her heart, a touch of fear fluttered inside her stomach, and that seemed ridiculous given what she'd just gone through the night before.

She'd faced a man whose sole desire was to see her dead, yet her heart beat just as wildly as she thought of facing Dalton and telling him how she felt.

As she packed her suitcase she found herself revisiting each and every moment of the time she had spent with Dalton. Who knew that when she'd walked out of that bus station so alone, so afraid, that she'd walk into the arms of a man whom she'd want to hold her for the rest of her life?

And he didn't want a wife. He had no desire for a family. She knew she could do nothing to change that, that her words of love would probably fall on deaf ears. But that didn't mean she didn't intend to speak them, because she refused to live the rest of her life with regrets.

When she pulled her suitcase into the living room, Sammy was propped up in the corner of the sofa and Dalton was playing peekaboo with him.

It amazed her that this big strong man had a soft center he displayed with Sammy. He was meant to be a father. He was meant to be *Sammy's* father. But, no matter how much she wanted it, no matter how much she needed it, she couldn't make him be something he didn't want to be.

He caught sight of her and stood. "It's still early," he said. "I thought maybe you'd like to go to the café in town and have lunch."

"Actually, I have something I'd like to say to you before you take me to the motel." She felt the swell of emotion in her chest as she gazed into his beautiful green eyes.

"Is something wrong?" He sank back to the sofa and patted the cushion next to him.

She remained standing, afraid that if she sat beside him, she'd fall to pieces. She searched her mind, struggling to find the right place to begin. "I don't know how I would have survived without you, Dalton."

He frowned and his eyes darkened. "You would have probably been just fine on your own. I spent most of the night kicking myself for all the mistakes I made."

"Mistakes? What are you talking about?"

"I almost got you killed last night because I didn't want to allow anyone else in my life. I should have had somebody at the cabin with you every minute that you were there."

"I have to accept part of the responsibility for the decision you made," she countered. "I made you swear that you wouldn't tell anyone I was there."

"But he could have killed you because I didn't do my job."

For the first time that day, she realized the deep torment he felt and hope blossomed in her heart. Surely a man who didn't care wouldn't be so tortured. Surely a man who didn't love her wouldn't care as deeply as what she saw shining from his eyes.

With a new courage she walked over to the sofa and sank down beside him. "You saved my life, Dalton.

Without you I would have been out in the snowstorm alone and afraid. Without you I would have never had the courage to face Brandon Sinclair."

He smiled then, a soft smile that pierced straight through to her heart. "I have a feeling you would have been just fine on your own. You're an amazing woman, Janette Black."

"You're an amazing man. In fact, you're so amazing I've fallen in love with you." Her breath caught in her throat as the words hung in the air between them.

He stared at her, and she wasn't sure if he was stunned or horrified by her words. He got up from the sofa as if goosed by an invisible hand and stepped back from where she sat.

"Janette, I appreciate the idea that you think you're in love with me, but I'm sure once you get away from here, once you get away from me, you'll realize it's not really love."

She would have been able to deal with him telling her he didn't love her. She would have accepted him explaining that he didn't feel the same way about her. But his attempt to negate her feelings altogether shot an edge of anger through her.

"Don't try to tell me what I feel and what I don't feel," she exclaimed as she got up from the sofa.

Dalton swiped a hand through his hair and frowned at her. "Look, you've just come off a roller coaster of traumatic events. We've been cooped up together, and emotions got out of control." He cast his gaze away from her but not before she saw something in his eyes that encouraged her.

She stepped closer to him. "Dalton, I don't know a lot of things, but I know that I'm in love with you, and there have been times in the last couple of days that I believed that you were falling in love with me and with my son."

He looked at her then, his expression dark and unfathomable. "I'm sorry if I gave you that impression. I thought I'd been clear about the fact that I'm not interested in any long-term relationship or in having a family."

Even though she'd suspected their relationship would end this way, it didn't stop the hot press of tears that burned at her eyes. How was it possible that his eyes told her one thing and his mouth said another?

It didn't matter. Now that she'd bared her soul, all she wanted to do was escape. She walked over to where Sammy was sitting on the sofa and picked him up, cradling him close to her breaking heart. "I'd like to go to the motel now."

There was no point in spending another minute with him. She needed to get away, to cry, to mourn, to once again find some way to heal herself and move on.

He didn't argue with her. Instead he got her coat and silently they prepared to leave. She felt numb. She hadn't realized how much she'd hoped that he would take her in his arms, confess that he loved her, too, until that hope had been stolen away.

She should have known better, she thought bitterly as she got into his truck. He was an educated man who enjoyed listening to jazz and reading thick tomes. Why would he want to bind himself to an uneducated woman with a baby?

She gasped when she saw the infant car seat in the backseat of his big cab. The fact that he'd thought of Sammy's safety only broke her heart again.

The drive to the motel was silent except for Sammy's cooing talk. She kept her gaze averted out the passenger window, afraid that if she looked at Dalton she'd cry.

She'd endured a rape and being chased out into the snow by a man who wanted to kill her, and she'd survived. And she would survive Dalton West's rejection, as well. But it was going to take time.

Dalton pulled up in front of the motel office and parked, then turned to look at her. His eyes radiated a deep pain. "You'll be all right?"

"Of course we will," she replied, her voice sounding clipped, brittle to her own ears. "Nana will be here around three and we'll figure out where we go from here."

"If you ever need anything…"

"We'll be fine," she quickly interjected. "You've done more than enough for us already." She opened the truck door and took Sammy out of the car seat as Dalton got out of the vehicle.

He grabbed her suitcase from the back and carried it to the front door of the motel office as she followed just behind him. She'd known telling him goodbye would be difficult, she just hadn't imagined it would be this difficult.

"I can get it from here," she said.

He nodded and set the suitcase down. "Here's the key to the room." He told her the number. "I guess this is goodbye."

"Before I tell you goodbye, I just want to say one more thing." She searched his stern features, remembering how they had softened into something beautiful as they'd made love, how they'd transformed with laughter as he'd interacted with Sammy.

She drew a deep breath and consciously willed away the tears that threatened. "Even though you don't love us, I hope you'll eventually open yourself up to loving some woman. You'd make a wonderful husband, Dalton, and you'd be an awesome father." The tears she'd tried to hold in now splashed onto her cheeks. "I don't know what made you decide to live your life alone, but you're cheating some woman from finding happiness with you, and you're cheating yourself, as well."

She didn't wait for him to answer. She grabbed the handle on the suitcase, turned and hurried away, eager to get into a room where she could cry in private.

Minutes later, she sat on the edge of one of the two double beds in the room and tried to keep the tears from flowing. She was afraid that if she started to cry she wouldn't be able to stop, and she didn't want Nana to arrive and see the depths of her despair.

Besides, she had a future to plan, a life to live. She knew eventually her heart wouldn't hurt so much, but at the moment it ached with unrelenting sadness.

One man had raped her and the other had thrown away her love. Both had left indelible scars on her soul, but it was Dalton's kindness, his passion and laughter that would linger in her thoughts for a very long time to come.

She stretched out across the bed, grabbed one of the pillows and cried into it, not wanting her sobs to disturb her sleeping son.

Later she would figure out where her life went from here, but for now she'd give herself time to mourn what might have been.

Chapter 15

Dalton opened his apartment door, stepped inside and drew in a deep, weary breath. She was gone. All trace of her and Sammy were gone except the faint scent of honeysuckle that lingered in the air.

The silence felt odd, but he knew eventually it would feel familiar and safe. He shrugged out of his coat and hung it in the closet, then eased down in his chair and stared around the room.

The painter he'd hired hadn't even begun the job yet. The walls didn't really need to be painted, but Dalton wouldn't cancel the job. Maybe the smell of fresh paint would remove the last trace of her scent from the apartment.

He leaned back in the chair and closed his eyes, fighting against the emotion that pressed tight in his chest. He'd done the right thing. He knew how these things worked. He'd learned the hard way by his experience with Mary. He didn't believe in repeating past mistakes.

Janette would move on, build a life and realize that what she'd really felt for him was nothing more than gratitude. However, he wasn't confused about his feelings for her. He loved her. His feelings for Janette were far deeper, far more profound than anything he'd felt for Mary.

A solitary life. That's what he'd believed he wanted, but now he realized how selfish he'd become. He'd guarded himself from not only women and dating, but also from his family and life.

For the first time he thought about all the reasons he'd distanced himself from his family, and for the first time he realized the answer.

His brothers had all found love. They'd found the special women with whom they would spend the rest of their lives and build happy families. He'd been glad for their happiness, but their happiness had pointed out the utter emptiness of his own life.

He needed to go into the office. He needed to do something, anything to get away from his own thoughts. He'd have one more cup of coffee then head to the West Protective Services office and spend the rest of the day there taking care of boring paperwork.

As he entered the kitchen and headed for the coffeepot his gaze fell on the bowl in the sink. It was half-full of rice cereal, and the sight of it convulsed his heart so hard, so unexpectedly, it brought tears to his eyes.

Janette wasn't the only one he'd fallen in love with. Sammy had stolen his heart the first time he'd grinned at Dalton and cooed.

"I did the right thing," Dalton said aloud, but his

voice lacked conviction. He just didn't understand how doing the right thing could feel so terribly wrong.

"You look peaked." Nana stared at Janette closely as she stepped into the motel room. "You aren't getting sick, are you?"

"No, I'm not getting sick," Janette replied. Definitely heartsick, but that didn't count. She gave her grandmother a fierce hug. Nana dropped her small overnight bag on the floor and beelined to Sammy, who had awakened and had somehow found his own toes with his hands.

"Look at you!" Nana picked him up and nuzzled his neck. "You look like you've grown a foot." She settled on the bed with Sammy in her arms. "So, where are we going from here?"

Janette sat on the opposite bed and frowned thoughtfully. "I don't know. It's a decision I didn't want to make without your input."

"I'll be honest, if I had my way we'd go back to Sandstone and get a new trailer. I've got my friends there, but I know that isn't what you want, so whatever you decide is fine with me." Nana's smile was filled with love and her expression was soft as she gazed first at Janette, then at Sammy. "I just want you and this little boy to be happy. That's all I really care about."

At the moment happiness seemed a distant state that no bus ride could ever take her to, but she didn't tell that to Nana.

"We don't have to make a decision right this minute," Nana said. "What I want to hear right now is how you and this Dalton of yours got Brandon Sinclair arrested."

This Dalton of yours. How she wished it were so.

For the next thirty minutes she related all that had happened to Nana.

She'd just finished her story when a knock sounded. Janette jumped off the bed and opened the door to see Dalton. She'd left something behind, that was the first thought that jumped into her head at the sight of him. He was here to deliver whatever item she'd forgotten to pack.

"We need to talk," he said without preamble. He started to step inside but she held the door to keep him out.

"I'm all talked out," she replied.

"Janette, please. It's important." His body vibrated with tension and a fierce intensity radiated from his eyes.

Janette looked over her shoulder at Nana seated on the bed holding Sammy, then back at Dalton. "We can't talk in here."

"In my truck, then."

She hesitated, wondering if she could handle any more from him. "Okay, I'll be out in just a minute." She closed the door and turned to face her grandmother. "It's Dalton. He says he needs to talk to me. It's probably about the case." She grabbed her coat and pulled it on. "I should be back in just a few minutes."

Nana stared at her for a long moment. "Follow your heart, honey," she said as if she knew everything that had happened between Janette and Dalton.

Janette slipped out of the door and headed for his truck, all the while telling herself that she'd followed her heart and it had led her into pain.

She opened the passenger truck door and slid inside. "What's up?" she asked.

For what seemed like an eternity he stared directly ahead, as if she wasn't seated next to him and waiting for him to speak.

What was he thinking? Why was he here?

"A year ago I was on assignment in Tulsa guarding a woman who'd been the victim of domestic abuse." He didn't look at her but continued to stare out the front window. "We both got caught up in each other, started making plans for our future together. When the assignment was over I came back here to Cotter Creek, certain that within a short period of time Mary and I would begin to build a life together. But before that happened, she realized that she'd mistaken gratitude for love, had gotten caught up in the fantasy we'd spun. It was a fantasy that had nothing to do with reality."

His words stunned her, and her heart swelled with grief for him, for the dreams of happiness he'd obviously had for himself, dreams that had never come to fruition.

He turned and looked at her then, and his eyes were as dark, as mysterious as a primal forest. "My feelings for you have made me realize Mary was right. Not only did she not love me, but I wasn't really in love with her. I'm in love with you, Janette, but I can't go through it again. I don't want to bind myself to you heart and soul only to find out a month or two from now that what you feel for me really isn't love after all."

"Dalton, there are many things in my life at the moment that I'm uncertain about, but my love for you isn't one of them." She reached out and placed her hand on his forearm, needing to touch him.

"I don't love you because you gave me shelter from a snowstorm, and I don't love you because you saved me from Brandon Sinclair. I love you because when you look at me, I feel strong and beautiful. I love the sound of your laughter and that little wrinkle you get in your forehead when you frown."

Tears filled her eyes as she continued. "I love your strength but I also love your weaknesses. Oh, Dalton, don't you see? I'm a woman who has been able to separate my feelings about Sinclair and what he did to me and love the result of that horrible act. I'm certainly able to know the difference between my gratefulness to you and my love for you."

His eyes began to sparkle with a light that warmed her heart. "What weaknesses?"

She laughed, because she saw her future shining from his eyes. "Hopefully we'll have many years together for me to point out each and every one of them."

He leaned toward her and traced his finger down the side of her face, all trace of humor gone. "Stay, Janette. Stay in Cotter Creek with me. Let me be more than just a temporary bodyguard in your life. Let me be the man who stands beside you and Sammy for the rest of your life."

"Yes," she whispered. "I want that."

"And I want it, too." He dropped his hand from her face. "And now we need to get out of this truck so I can really hold you in my arms and kiss you hard enough, love you enough that you never doubt how much I love you."

"Dalton West, you take my breath away," she said as she opened the truck door. They met in front of the truck and he grabbed her in an embrace that left no room for doubts, no question that her future would be one filled with laughter and love.

Epilogue

"How soon can we get out of here?" Dalton leaned over and whispered in Janette's ear.

Here was a tent on the West property where Meredith West and Chase McCall had just exchanged their wedding vows. It had been a beautiful ceremony and the late-March weather had cooperated with a day of sunshine and blue skies.

The band was playing and people not only danced on the wooden dance floor, but also helped themselves to the banquet that had been prepared for the big event.

"Why are you in such a big hurry, Mr. West?" she asked lightly. "It's a beautiful day and Nana is babysitting."

"That's exactly my point, Mrs. West." His eyes glittered. "We could be spending this entire afternoon in bed."

Mrs. West. She and Dalton had married in a quiet ceremony at city hall two weeks ago, and she still thrilled at the words that identified her as his wife.

"Nana is keeping Sammy overnight so there's plenty of time for us," she replied with a grin.

At that moment Red West stepped up in front of them. "I make it a habit despite my arthritis to dance with every one of my daughters-in-law, and I haven't had the pleasure of dancing with you yet." He held out a hand to her.

Janette smiled warmly. "I'd be delighted." She took his hand in hers and together they walked toward the dance floor.

"I understand congratulations are in order," Red said as they began to move to the slow music.

A burst of pride filled Janette. "Yes. It was a long time coming, but I finally got my GED."

"And Dalton tells me you've already signed up for college classes for this summer."

"I have. I'm really excited about it. I hope to get a teaching degree and I'd love to teach first or second grade."

"You'll do well." Red smiled down at her and Janette felt his affection radiating from his pale blue eyes.

Over the past two months, Dalton's family had embraced her with warmth. Nana had gotten settled in a brand-new trailer on the lot where her old one had burned down, and Janette and Dalton were house-hunting, as the apartment was too small for a family.

The biggest news over the past two months had been the eight women who had contacted Trent to tell him that they, too, had been raped by Brandon Sinclair. Much to Janette's surprise, she had found herself something of a local hero.

"I'm a happy man today," Red said, and she followed his gaze to the area where the family was congregated together. "Tanner has his Anna and their new little baby. Zack is happy with Katie. Clay and Libby and little Gracie are building a wonderful life together. Savannah was the best thing that ever happened to Joshua, and Meredith has finally married the man who makes her happy.

"Then there's you." Once again he smiled. "You and that little boy put a smile on my son's face and a lightness to his step. All my kids have found love, and I expect their mama is smiling down from heaven."

Janette looked up at the old man. "And she must be proud of you for raising her children to be wonderful adults."

"I expect she is," he agreed as the music ended.

As he led her off the dance floor Dalton stood, his eyes gleaming with wicked delight. "She's a keeper, son," Red said as they reached him.

"I know, Dad. Believe me, I know." As Red left, Dalton leaned down to Janette. "Now can we get out of here? All this wedding stuff has made me want to spend alone time with my wife."

"I'll race you to the truck," she said and whirled around and began to run.

She heard his burst of laughter just behind her and she slowed to let him catch her as love swelled inside her. The storm had passed and spring had come, and it had brought with it all her heart desired.

* * * * *

We hope you enjoyed reading

GLORY, GLORY

by *New York Times* bestselling author

LINDA LAEL MILLER and

SNOWBOUND WITH THE BODYGUARD

by reader-favorite author

CARLA CASSIDY.

Both were originally Harlequin® series stories!

Discover more compelling tales of heart-racing romance and high-stakes suspense from the Harlequin® Romantic Suspense series. Featuring strong, adventurous women and brave men, Harlequin Romantic Suspense stories are filled with powerful relationships and life-and-death situations that deliver a strong emotional punch and a guaranteed happily-ever-after.

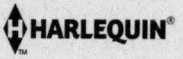

ROMANTIC suspense

Look for four new romances every month from Harlequin® Romantic Suspense!

Available wherever books are sold.

www.Harlequin.com

NYTHRS1013

SPECIAL EXCERPT FROM

HARLEQUIN™

ROMANTIC suspense

When Arabian princess Laila agrees to help stop a terrorist group within her country's borders, she never expects to find love with the distrusting FBI agent who will do anything to keep her safe.

Read on for a sneak peek of

PROTECTING HIS PRINCESS

by C.J. Miller, available November 2013 from Harlequin® Romantic Suspense.

"What are you doing?" Laila asked, taking his arm.

Harris stared at her. "Why didn't you go with your family?"

"And leave you here alone?" Laila asked.

He didn't want Laila in the thick of this. An attempt had been made on her life in America and he didn't know if she had been one of the targets of the bombing here. "You need to be somewhere safe."

She gripped his arm harder. "I am safest with you."

Another explosion boomed through the air. Harris grabbed Laila and shielded her with his body, pulling them to the ground. Was the sound a building collapsing from the damage or another bomb? Harris guessed another bomb. Laila was shaking in his arms. Harris waited for the noise around him to quiet and concentrated on listening for the rat-tat-tat of gun shots or another bomb.

His protective instincts roared louder. He wouldn't let anything happen to Laila. "I'm going to help where I can."

Her eyes widened with fear. "What if there is another bomb—"

He had some basic first-aid training and he'd been a marine. Dealing with difficult situations had been part of his training. "There might be another one. There's no time to wait for help."

"I can help, too," Laila said, lifting her chin.

"You aren't trained for this," he said.

"No, but I'm capable and smart. I will be useful. Don't treat me like a crystal vase."

Laila wouldn't back down. She wouldn't leave the scene, not when her countrymen needed help. Arguing wouldn't get him anywhere. He'd seen her strength many times before. She might act like a shrinking violet in front of her brother or other males, but she had an iron core. "You're stubborn when you want something."

"So are you," Laila said, giving him a small smile.

Don't miss
PROTECTING HIS PRINCESS
by C.J. Miller,
available November 2013 from
Harlequin® Romantic Suspense.

Copyright © 2013 by Cynthia Miller

HRSEXP1013

HARLEQUIN®

ROMANTIC suspense

Heart-racing romance, high-stakes suspense.

Save $1.00 on the purchase of

PROTECTING HIS PRINCESS

by C.J. Miller,

available November 5, 2013,

or on any other Harlequin® Romantic Suspense book.

Available wherever books are sold, including most bookstores, supermarkets, drugstores and discount stores.

Save $1.00

on the purchase of
PROTECTING HIS PRINCESS
by C.J. Miller,
available November 5, 2013, or on any other Harlequin® Romantic Suspense book.

Coupon valid until January 21, 2014. Redeemable at participating retail outlets in the U.S. and Canada only. Limit one coupon per customer.

52611142

Canadian Retailers: Harlequin Enterprises Limited will pay the face value of this coupon plus 10.25¢ if submitted by customer for this product only. Any other use constitutes fraud. Coupon is nonassignable. Void if taxed, prohibited or restricted by law. Consumer must pay any government taxes. Void if copied. Nielsen Clearing House ("NCH") customers submit coupons and proof of sales to Harlequin Enterprises Limited, P.O. Box 3000, Saint John, NB E2L 4L3, Canada. Non-NCH retailer—for reimbursement submit coupons and proof of sales directly to Harlequin Enterprises Limited, Retail Marketing Department, 225 Duncan Mill Rd., Don Mills, ON M3B 3K9, Canada.

5 65373 00076 2 (8100)0 11883

U.S. Retailers: Harlequin Enterprises Limited will pay the face value of this coupon plus 8¢ if submitted by customer for this product only. Any other use constitutes fraud. Coupon is nonassignable. Void if taxed, prohibited or restricted by law. Consumer must pay any government taxes. Void if copied. For reimbursement submit coupons and proof of sales directly to Harlequin Enterprises Limited, P.O. Box 880478, El Paso, TX 88588-0478, U.S.A. Cash value 1/100 cents.

® and TM are trademarks owned and used by the trademark owner and/or its licensee.
© 2013 Harlequin Enterprises Limited

NYTCOUP1013

Celebrate the holidays with this remarkable McKettrick tale by beloved #1 *New York Times* bestselling author

LINDA LAEL MILLER

With his wild heart, Sawyer McKettrick isn't ready to settle down on the Triple M family ranch in Arizona. So he heads to Blue River, Texas, to seek a job as marshal. But in a blinding snowstorm he's injured—and collapses into the arms of a prim and proper lady in calico.

The shirtless, bandaged stranger recuperating in teacher Piper St. James's room behind the schoolhouse says he's a McKettrick, but he looks like an outlaw to her. As they wait out the storm, the handsome loner has Piper remembering long-ago dreams of marriage and motherhood. But for how long is Sawyer willing to call Blue River home?

Available October 29, wherever books are sold!

Be sure to connect with us at:

Harlequin.com/Newsletters
Facebook.com/HarlequinBooks
Twitter.com/HarlequinBooks

PHLLM785